THE BRIDEGROOM

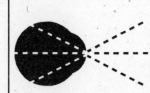

This Large Print Book carries the
Seal of Approval of N.A.V.H.

THE BRIDEGROOM

LINDA LAEL MILLER

THORNDIKE PRESS
A part of Gale, Cengage Learning

GALE
CENGAGE Learning

Detroit • New York • San Francisco • New Haven, Conn • Waterville, Maine • London

GALE
CENGAGE Learning

Copyright © 2009 by Linda Lael Miller.
Thorndike Press, a part of Gale, Cengage Learning.

Thorndike Press® Large Print Romance.
The text of this Large Print edition is unabridged.
Other aspects of the book may vary from the original edition.
Set in 16 pt. Plantin.

LIBRARY OF CONGRESS CATALOGING-IN-PUBLICATION DATA

Miller, Linda Lael.
   The bridegroom : a Stone Creek novel / by Linda Lael Miller.
      p. cm. — (Thorndike Press large print romance)
   ISBN-13: 978-1-4104-2828-8 (large print : hardcover)
   ISBN-10: 1-4104-2828-1 (large print : hardcover)
   1. Single women—Fiction. 2. Domestic fiction. 3. Large type
books. I. Title.
PS3563.I41373B745 2010
813'.54—dc22   2010013707

Published in 2010 by arrangement with Harlequin Books S.A.

For my Rebel cousins,
Doris Parker Brooks and Jim and
Gladys Lael.
Thank you from the bottom of this ole
Yankee heart.

CHAPTER ONE

Phoenix, Arizona, summer 1915

Except for the old codger huddled on the stool at the far end of the bar and the barkeep, who looked vaguely familiar, Gideon Yarbro had the Golden Horseshoe Saloon to himself, and he liked it that way. Just wanted to drink his beer in peace, wash some of the inevitable sooty grit from the long train ride from Chicago to Phoenix out of his gullet, and gear himself up to travel on to Stone Creek come morning.

His brothers, Rowdy and Wyatt, would be after him to stay on once he got home, settle down, pin on a badge like Rowdy had, or start a ranch, like Wyatt. Get himself married, too, probably, and sire a pack of kids. Both considerably older than Gideon, who was the baby of the family, the former outlaws had left the urge to wander far behind them, long ago. They were happy in their new lives, and for them the lure of the

7

trail was a distant memory.

Not so for Gideon.

One of the things he loved best about his work was that it took him to places he'd never been before. This time, though, it was taking him home.

He sighed, reminded himself that Wyatt and Rowdy meant well. It was just that, being Yarbros, they tended to come on strong with their opinions, and they treated him like a kid brother — emphasis on "kid."

He was twenty-six, damn it. A man, not a boy.

Gideon reined his musings back in, corralled them in the right-now. Distractions could be lethal for someone in his line of work, and of course trouble tended to strike when a person was thinking about something other than the immediate situation.

Against the far wall, up to its clawed crystal feet in dirty sawdust and peanut shells, the piano gave a ghostly twang, as if one of the wires had snapped. Gideon spared enough of a grin for one corner of his mouth to quirk up, but the face he saw reflected in the streaked and dusty mirror behind the long bar barely registered the change. His dark blond hair was in need of barbering, he noticed, and he'd need a shave, too, if he didn't want a lot of hectoring from his sisters-in-law, Lark and Sarah, when he showed up in Stone Creek tomorrow.

Again, the piano sounded just the echo of a note, a sort of woeful vibration that trembled in the air for a few moments, along with the tinge of stale cigar smoke and sour beer.

"Damn place is haunted," the barkeep said, either to everybody in general or nobody in particular. He was a bulky type, balding, with a belly that strained at the buttons of his stained shirt and a marked tendency to sweat, and watching him wipe down glasses with a rag made Gideon wish beer came in bottles. "I swear it's that piano player that got himself shot in the back last year. Never had no trouble until ole Bill Jessup bit the dust."

Gideon didn't acknowledge the remark — he placed little or no stock in tales of spooks and specters — but he recalled the shooting well enough. Rowdy followed such things, being a lawman, and he'd mentioned the incident, in passing, in one of his letters. Mail from home — Stone Creek being the only place Gideon ever thought of in that particular context, and then not with any great degree of sentimentality — was infrequent, and since he moved around a lot in

9

his profession, it generally took some time to catch up to him.

"You want another whiskey there, Horace?" the barkeep asked the old man. He sounded nervous, like he didn't want to offer, but feared dire consequences if he failed to make the gesture. Not that the leprechaun represented any threat to the bartender; Gideon would bet the shriveled-up little old man wouldn't have weighed in at more than a hundred pounds if he'd been sopping wet and wearing granite shitkickers.

And from the looks — and smell — of Horace, he'd gone past "enough" a long time ago, but he grunted, without looking up, and shoved his glass out to be filled again.

The barkeep poured the whiskey, standing back farther than seemed sensible and sweating harder. Gideon took all this in, not because he was interested, but because it was what he did. Working for the Pinkerton Agency after college, and then for Wells Fargo, he'd learned to pay attention to everything going on around him, even in the most ordinary circumstances.

Especially then.

He'd have bet that barkeep hadn't washed his hands in weeks, let alone taken a bath.

Gideon frowned and studied his beer mug more closely, but except for a few smudges and a thumbprint or two, it looked passably clean. He wasn't back East anymore, he reminded himself, with another slight contortion of his face that might have been accepted as a smile in some quarters. Best get over being so fastidious.

He felt the slight shift in the air even before the doors to the street swung open, a sort of quiver, similar to the throb of the piano strings, but soundless.

Setting his beer mug down, he watched in the mirror as two men came in from the street, single file, both of them the size of grizzly bears raised up on their hind feet.

No, Gideon corrected himself silently, these yahoos would *dwarf* the average grizzly. Despite the heat — he'd left his own suit coat at the train station, with his bags — they wore the long canvas coats common to gunslingers as well as ordinary ranchers, and both of them carried sidearms, the butts of long-barreled pistols jutting out of the waistbands of their dark woolen pants. Their gazes tracked and found the old man, sliced over to Gideon, sharp as honed knives, then swung back and bored into their target again.

"Monty," one of them ground out, presumably greeting the barkeep. They'd paused just inside the doors, which were still swinging on their rusted hinges.

Monty gulped audibly, set down the bottle he'd poured the old coot's drink out of, and took a couple of steps backward. Came up hard against the shelf behind him, with its rows of bottles and glasses. The front of his shirt, damp before, was nearly saturated now, he was perspiring so heavily.

"I only give ole Horace more whiskey 'cause he asked me to," Monty spouted, as if he'd been challenged on the matter, working up a grimace of a smile that wouldn't stay put on his face.

Entertained, Gideon suppressed a smile, along with the sigh that came along behind it. When he got to Stone Creek and started his new job — the one he'd lied to Rowdy and Wyatt about in his last letter — such amusements as this one would be few and far between.

He was in the Golden Horseshoe Saloon, he reminded himself, to have a beer, not watch a melodrama — or to participate in one. Still, the fine hairs were standing up on the nape of his neck, and the sixth sense he'd developed working as a detective was in fine form.

"You'd better go on back to the storeroom

or the office and check on whatever needs checking on," the taller of the two men told the barkeep. His voice had a thick, stuffy sound, as if at some point he'd had his head held under water for too long, or hadn't gotten enough air in the first few minutes after he was born.

It was hard to imagine him as a baby, Gideon thought, amused.

His mama must have been a big woman — or else she'd have split wide-open giving birth to the likes of him.

Monty was only too glad to check on whatever needed checking on — he gave Gideon a look, part warning and part pity, and skedaddled.

Gideon felt no need to reach for the Colt .45 riding low on his left hip, but he did take some comfort in its presence. Straightening, he rolled his shirtsleeves down and fastened the cuffs; and though he knew he appeared to be mainly concerned with emptying his mug, he had a full mirror-reflected view of the room through his eyelashes.

One of the men cleared his throat, though the pair still hadn't moved from their post just over the threshold. "Ma says supper's gonna be ready early tonight," he announced, not exactly cautious in relaying this news, but definitely tentative. "She wants to be at the church on time for the pie social."

So she *had* survived childbirth, Gideon thought. Either that or the woman in question was a stepmother. Out West, a lot of men ran through a whole slew of wives, wearing them out with hard work and childbearing and all the rest of it.

Gideon's own mother had perished giving birth to him.

The old man grunted once more, that being his primary means of communication, apparently, but didn't turn around or speak an intelligible word. He just drained his glass, made a satisfied sound as the firewater went down and reached for the bottle poor old Monty had left behind on the bar when he fled.

At last, the giants moved again, as one, like Siamese twins with no visible attachment. Strange for sure, that was Gideon's involuntary assessment.

There were times when he'd rather just ignore goings-on, and this was one of them, but it wasn't in his nature. He pondered everything, weighed and considered and sorted.

The taller fellow snagged Gideon's gaze in the saloon mirror. "We don't want no trouble now, friend," he said. "We've come to take Dad home for supper, that's all, so we'd be obliged if you didn't mix in."

Gideon gave a disinterested nod, waited to see if the old whiskey-swiller would raise an objection to what he'd no doubt regard as a premature departure.

There wasn't much to him, for all that his sons were big as trees.

Like as not, he'd go along peaceable. Then Gideon would finish his beer, leave payment on the bar, and go on about his business — checking in to the hotel across the street, having some of his gear brought over from the train depot, getting himself shaved and sheared and bathed. He'd stop by the post office, too, in case some mail had straggled in since the last time he'd passed through Phoenix.

The brothers positioned themselves on either side of the bar stool, set their feet as if they meant to put down roots right through the sawdust and the plank floor beneath, exchanged wary glances, and simultaneously cleared their throats.

"Get on home," the old man croaked, thereby proving he possessed a vocabulary after all, however limited, though he didn't look at either one of them. All his attention seemed to be fixed on the bottom of that whiskey glass, Gideon observed, as if there was some kind of scene being played out there. "Tell your ma I'll be along when I'm damn good and ready, and not before."

"She said we'd better not come home without you if we know what's good for us," the smaller brother said gravely. "And you know we've got to mind, lest Ma lose her temper."

With that, and another glance at each other, the brothers closed in and took hold of the old man's arms.

And that was when all hell broke loose.

Dear old Dad turned into a human buzz saw, all jagged edges, ripping into the air itself, and practically throwing off blue sparks. He kicked and twisted and punched, spitting out oaths and cusswords that even Gideon, raised in the back of a saloon in Flagstaff, had never heard.

The brothers had all they could do to contain their pa, and the three of them tangled all the way across the saloon floor to the doors, a blur of fists and flying coat-tails and swearwords that sizzled like water flung onto a hot griddle.

Gideon pushed back from the bar, walked to the swinging doors, stopped their wild swaying with both hands. Watched over the top as old Horace's sons flung him into the

16

back of a buckboard by his suspenders, like a bale of hay by the twine. One of them scrambled up to take the reins, while the other climbed into the wagon-bed to hold the old man down with both hands.

And that took some doing, all by itself.

"Are they gone?" Monty asked tentatively, from somewhere behind Gideon.

Gideon turned, saw the bartender back at his post, but poised to hit the floor or make another dash for safety if Dad and the boys chanced to return.

"On their way home to supper," Gideon said. "Looks like Ma will be right on time for the pie social."

With that, he plucked a coin from the pocket of his tailored vest, walked over to the bar and laid it down.

"I don't believe I caught your name," Monty said, after swiping the coin off the bar with one paw.

"I don't believe I gave it," Gideon replied.

Monty narrowed his eyes, and recognition dawned, though Gideon had hoped it wouldn't. His kinfolk were well-known in Phoenix, since it was only about a day's ride from Stone Creek, and Rowdy, along with his best friend, Sam O'Ballivan, often had business there. As a boy, Gideon had accompanied them once or twice.

17

"You're that Yarbro kid, aren't you? The marshal's little brother. I used to work in one of the saloons up there in Stone Creek, and I recollect that you took a bullet at a dance one night, trying to catch hold of some fool that rode a horse right into the Cattlemen's Meeting Hall."

As always, the word *kid* made Gideon bristle, way down deep where it didn't show, and being over six feet tall, he didn't consider himself anybody's "little" *anything,* but he was feeling charitable after the beer, and somewhat resigned, so he let the comment pass.

"Yep," he said simply, turning to leave.

"That Chink sawbones fixed you up," Monty prattled on. Maybe it was nerves, considering the scuffle just past, but he'd sure turned talkative. "Wouldn't have given spit for your chances, but he pulled you through with his needles and poultices."

That Chink. The term stuck under Gideon's hide like a cactus needle.

"He saved my life," Gideon said stiffly, "and the life of somebody I cared about." Lydia Fairmont had been the other patient, he recalled, eight years old and one of Lark's students. Rowdy's wife had been the schoolmarm up at Stone Creek back then, and had taken the neglected child under her wing. Where was Lydia now? Maybe Lark would know. "And his *name* was Hon Sing."

Monty hastened after him, came all the way to the sidewalk. "I didn't mean no disrespect, Mr. Yarbro," he prattled. "I truly did not set out to offend."

Hon Sing, along with his wife, Mai Lei, had gone back to China, after inheriting the old Porter house and eventually selling it at a high profit, once copper was discovered in the foothills rimming the still-small town.

And that copper mine was the reason Gideon had been sent to Stone Creek. There was a strike brewing, and his job was to see that it didn't happen.

He made no response to the bartender's apology, beyond a cursory nod. Turning his mind to other things, he crossed the street, wending his way between horses and buggies and slow-moving wagons headed in opposite directions. The Desert Oasis Hotel offered some attractive amenities, including hot and cold running water, a decent restaurant and its own barbershop.

The lobby was opulent by Western standards, with carpets on the floors, leather sofas and copious potted palms.

Gideon registered for a room on the second floor and sent the hotel's sweep-up man — a boy, really — back to the depot for his suitcase. Climbing the broad staircase, intending to put the tub in his room to immediate use, he wondered again, now that she'd staked out a place in his thoughts, how little Lydia Fairmont was faring. She'd be an adult now, since ten years had passed, and maybe not so little anymore, either, he reflected with a smile. She was probably married — even at eight, with her silvery-fair hair and violet-blue eyes, she'd shown the promise of growing into a very fetching woman one day.

Gideon's smile slipped a little as he took out his key and let himself into the room. Lydia, grown up, with a husband and children? For some reason, the idea didn't set well with him.

It was because she was delicate, he told himself. Too fragile, surely, to be bearing some man's babies, or chopping wood, or any of the thousand other hard tasks a wife was called upon to do.

He pushed the recollection of Lydia Fairmont to the back of his mind.

In Stone Creek, he'd have plenty to occupy his thoughts, between Rowdy and Wyatt and their families and the work he'd be doing at the Copper Crown Mine. He'd told plenty of lies as it was, and he'd have to tell more before it was over. Keeping track of them, so his story stayed straight and his brothers didn't figure out his real reason for coming back home, would be as much as he could manage.

Anyhow, there was no place in his plans for a woman — at least, not the kind Lydia had surely turned out to be.

Lydia's two great-aunts, Mittie and Millie, spinsters the pair of them and both in their late sixties, twittered like schoolgirls as they peered through the tall, narrow windows on either side of the front door.

A loud chugging sound came from the street, along with an ominous bang that caused Lydia, lurking unnoticed in the doorway to the main parlor, to start slightly.

"Here he comes now," Mittie enthused, under her breath.

"Too bad he's so fat and old and homely," Millie lamented. "Our Lydia requires a *handsome* husband, one who'll give her lots of children."

"Hush," Mittie scolded, in a whisper. "Lydia will hear you! And for the life of me, I can't think why she would turn up her nose at a man like Jacob Fitch. He might be portly and of a certain age, and I'll even concede that he's not much to look at. But he's rich and he owns an *automobile*."

Lydia, carefully trained, since she'd been brought to this imposing house as an eight-year-old orphan, in many things, not the least of which was the wholesale impropriety of eavesdropping, cleared her throat delicately in order to make her presence known.

Both aunts blushed prettily when they turned to face her.

"Mr. Fitch has arrived," Millie announced, recovering first. Like Mittie, she was small, almost doll-like, with the near-purple eyes that were the pride of the Fairmont line. As young women, the sisters had been breathtakingly beautiful, as their portraits attested. According to Helga, the housekeeper, Millie had loved a Confederate major, Mittie, a Union captain. Both men had been killed in the line of duty.

Word of the deaths had arrived on the same day, the legend went, and the aunts had worn mourning gowns ever since. Now, they contented themselves with the ups and downs of other people's romances, especially their only niece's.

If indeed the arrangement between Lydia and Mr. Fitch could be *called* a romance. It certainly didn't feel like one to her.

"Let's go and make tea," Mittie said, snatching Millie by the puffed sleeve of her sad black dress and dragging her past Lydia, in the direction of the kitchen.

Lydia suppressed an urge to flee, or beg her aunts to tell Mr. Fitch she was indisposed — *anything* to avoid receiving the man and passing an interminable hour of "courting" in the parlor.

But, like eavesdropping, lying to evade one's social obligations was not considered proper — and Lydia placed a great deal of importance on propriety.

As always, Fitch pounded at the front door, foregoing the bell, with its pleasant, jingly little ring.

Lydia smoothed her lavender dress, laid out for her that morning by Helga, because it matched her eyes. That, of course, had been before Mr. Fitch had sent his calling card ahead to announce an impending visit.

She dredged up another smile — it took considerably more effort this time — and went to open the door.

The man Lydia was to marry the following afternoon stood impatiently on the verandah, his motoring goggles pushed up onto his forehead in a way that was probably meant to appear jaunty, but instead gave him the look of a very plump bullfrog. He was covered in road dust — Mr. Fitch did love his automobile and was constantly racing along the dry and rutted roads of Phoenix at speeds of up to twenty miles an hour.

Often, he insisted that Lydia accompany him.

Now, he clutched a bouquet of wilting flowers, probably purloined from some neighbor's water-starved garden, in his left hand. "Good afternoon, Lydia," he said.

"Mr. Fitch," Lydia acknowledged, with a coolness she couldn't quite hide.

His small, too-watchful eyes swept over her. "You're not dressed for the road," he pointed out, his tone mildly critical. "Any wife of mine will always be prepared to go driving."

Any wife of mine . . .

Lydia managed not to shudder, though the smile she'd put on — if it *was* a smile and not the death grimace it felt like — wobbled on her mouth. "It's such a hot day," she said. "I was hoping we could stay inside." *And I'm* not *your wife, Jacob Fitch. Not yet, anyway. Not until tomorrow.*

Mr. Fitch trundled past her, into the house, nearly stomping on her toes. "Honestly, Lydia, this *delicacy* of yours is bothersome. Any wife —"

Lydia closed the door smartly behind him, cutting off the rest of his sentence. She was

24

not delicate, had not been seriously ill since she was a child, though admittedly her appearance made her seem fragile. Like her great-aunts, she was small-boned, though at five feet two inches, she was taller than Mittie and Millie, and she *did* have a nice bosom.

Protesting that she was as healthy as anyone, however much she wanted to do just that, would serve no purpose. Jacob Fitch did not *listen* to anything she said, unless, of course, it was precisely what he wanted to hear.

He fairly shoved the flowers at her.

Lydia took them, and her heart turned over at their thirsty state. "I'll just put these in water," she said brightly. "Do sit down in the parlor, Mr. Fitch, and make yourself at home. I'll only be a minute."

Fitch tilted his head back, admired the high, frescoed ceilings, fading now, but still finely crafted. The huge crystal chandelier glittered, though unlit — at night, powered by gas, it glowed, and even after all these years, it seemed magical to Lydia.

A faint smile touched Mr. Fitch's narrow lips. "The old place could use a man's touch," he said huskily, letting his gaze drift slowly to Lydia, then over her, like a spill of something viscous. No doubt he was anticipating their wedding night. "And so could you."

Again, Lydia managed not to shudder, but just barely.

The thought of Jacob Fitch putting his hands to that lovely old house, much less to her naked body, made the pit of her stomach drop, as if from a great height.

Overcome with a flash of pure dread, she turned on one heel, biting her lower lip, and fled to the kitchen. Oh, to go right on through, out the back door, down the alley to —

To where?

She had no place to go.

No one to turn to.

Months ago, in a fit of panic, she'd sent off the letter, the one Gideon Yarbro had written to himself in case she ever needed to send it — *Please come and get me right away,* was all it said — when she was a little girl, recovering from pneumonia and the loss of her father. But there had been no reply, of course.

There wouldn't have been, though, would there? Gideon, a mere boy at the time, anxious to reassure her, had scratched out that single line in penciled letters, sealed the envelope, addressed it to: *Gideon Rhodes, Deputy Marshal, General Delivery,*

Stone Creek, Arizona Territory. Heaven knew where he was now, after a decade — he'd been bound for college that year, so it was unlikely that he was still the deputy marshal up at Stone Creek. And Arizona wasn't even a territory anymore, it was the forty-eighth state.

These and other equally hopeless thoughts tumbled in Lydia's mind as she ignored Helga's penetrating gaze and filled a vase with cool water for the fading flowers. Now, she simply felt foolish for adding postage to that very old letter and dropping it through the slot down at the post office. She blushed to imagine it actually reaching Gideon — especially at this late date — and silently prayed that it had gone astray.

And yet it was her one hope, that letter.

"Why don't you just tell Jacob Fitch to get back into that smoke-belching horseless carriage of his," Helga, never one to withhold advice, asked intractably, "and drive himself straight off the nearest mesa?"

Helga's disapproval of Mr. Fitch was of long standing, and so was her opinion of the automobile. One of the first such machines to appear in Phoenix, a point of pride with Jacob, the vehicle, with its constant sputtering and backfiring, frightened old Mrs. Riley's chickens so badly they wouldn't

27

lay. Helga had laid the fault for more than one skimpy breakfast at Mr. Fitch's door.

"You know I can't," Lydia said softly, taking longer than necessary to attend to the flowers.

Helga had been running the household for years — only Mr. Evans, the late butler and sometime carriage driver, had worked for the family longer — and she felt free to express herself on any and all matters concerning the Fairmonts. "Miss Nell," the sturdy middle-aged woman said implacably, "must be rolling over in her grave. You, the last hope of the family, marrying that old —"

Tears stung Lydia's eyes, and she sniffled once, raised her chin, the way she always did when a weeping spell threatened. Nell Baker, her father's only sister, had come to fetch her up at Stone Creek after Papa's death in a blizzard, thereby saving her from two equally frightening alternatives: being sent to an orphanage, or left in the care of her selfish, slatternly stepmother, Mabel. Nell had raised Lydia, with help from Helga, Evans and the great-aunts, hired private tutors because the local schools did not meet her standards, clothed and fed Lydia, allowed her to keep stray cats, bought her watercolor paints and fine brushes at the first indication of talent.

Most of all, Nell, a childless widow herself, had *loved* her.

Aunt Nell had passed on suddenly, the previous year, and Lydia still felt the loss like a nerve laid bare to a winter chill.

"I'll tell him *for* you," Helga said, in an almost desperate whisper, when Lydia didn't reply to her suggestion. "I'll send him packing, once and for all, and good riddance!"

Lydia, having forced herself to start toward the parlor, where Mr. Fitch was waiting, closed her eyes. They'd had this discussion before — Helga knew full well that most of the Fairmont money was gone. The house would soon follow, since it was heavily mortgaged. And while both Lydia and Helga would be fine if that occurred — eventually, anyway — what would happen to the great-aunts?

Phoenix had been a mere crossroads when Mittie and Millie had come to the Arizona Territory with their widowed father, Judge William Fairmont, after Union troops had burned their Virginia plantation, fields, house and outbuildings, during the war. This house, originally only three rooms, but enlarged as the Judge prospered and then grew even richer than he'd been in Virginia, was their haven, a sanctuary in a world that had already proved itself violent and harsh. Every corner, every nook, held some precious memory.

Except for church services on Sundays, the aunts never ventured farther than the garden out back.

"You must stay out of this, Helga," Lydia said, after swallowing and without turning around.

"You could marry any man in this town!" Helga argued.

There was some truth in that assertion, Lydia supposed, but none of the men who'd offered for her had Jacob Fitch's money, or his power. None of them could save the big stone house and its cherished furnishings, each one with a story attached. And none of them would be willing to provide house-room to two very old ladies who still suffered from fiery nightmares and woke up screaming that the Yankees had come.

Mr. Fitch, the only son of an elderly mother, had already promised that Lydia, the aunts and Helga could all stay right here under this roof. On their wedding day — dear God, *tomorrow* — he would pay off any outstanding debts and declare the mortgage, held by his bank, paid in full — he had given Lydia his word on that. Even had documents prepared, so stating.

All Lydia had to do was marry him.

When she could sign "Lydia Fairmont Fitch" on the appropriate lines of the papers Jacob's lawyers had drawn up, the aunts and their memories would be safe.

Again, Lydia thought of the letter she'd mailed off to Gideon in a fit of panic, and something rose into her throat and fluttered there, like a trapped bird.

Even supposing Gideon would be *willing* to help her, what could he possibly do?

Nothing, that was what.

She had to stop this incessant spinning back and forth between hope and despair.

Gideon wasn't coming to her rescue, like some prince in a storybook.

No one was.

Tomorrow afternoon at two o'clock, wearing Aunt Nell's altered wedding gown, she would stand up beside Jacob Fitch in front of the cold fireplace in the formal parlor in that burden of a house and vow to love, honor and obey the husband she didn't want.

"Lydia?" Helga whispered miserably. "Please. You mustn't be hasty —"

"The decision," Lydia said, for Helga's benefit and for her own, "has been made,

Helga, and there will be no further discussion."

With that, Lydia left the kitchen, the vase containing Jacob's flowers shaking in her hands, fit to slip and shatter into a million fragments.

Because Gideon passed through Phoenix at least once a year, he kept a postal box there, as he did in several cities around the country. That afternoon, shaven and barbered and bathed, he stuck the appropriate key in the lock and opened the heavy brass door, stooped a little to peer inside. Straightened as he removed the usual printed sales fliers and outdated periodicals.

Throwing these things away in a small barrel provided for the purpose, he nearly missed the thin, time-tattered envelope tucked in among them.

The letter had been forwarded numerous times, but beneath the cross-outs and travel stains, Gideon saw his own youthful handwriting, nearly faded to invisibility.

Gideon Rhodes, Deputy Marshal
General Delivery
Stone Creek, Arizona Territory

For a few moments, Gideon's surroundings faded away, and he was back in Mrs. Porter's kitchen up in Stone Creek, handing the letter to a wide-eyed, frightened child.

He heard his own voice, as if he'd just spoken the words of the promise he'd made that long-ago winter day.

". . . *if you ever have any trouble with anybody, all you'll have to do is mail the letter. Soon as I get it, I'll be coming for you. . . .*"

CHAPTER TWO

Having come down with a sick headache five minutes after joining Mr. Fitch in the parlor, Lydia had nonetheless soldiered through the ordeal. The instant her future husband had departed, however, she'd retreated to her room upstairs and collapsed onto the bed without even removing her shoes.

She was still lying there, staring up at the shifting ceiling-shadows cast by the branches of the white oak outside her window, when a light rap sounded at the door, and Mittie poked her head in without waiting for a "Come in."

This in itself was highly unusual; although they were window-peekers, the aunts never entered Lydia's "bedchamber," as they called it, without permission. Given their old-fashioned sensibilities, they were probably terrified of accidentally catching her in a state of undress.

But here was Mittie, with her aureole of snow-white hair gleaming fit to hurt Lydia's eyes in the dazzle of late-afternoon sunshine, and her faced glowed with something very like wonder. She looked downright . . . *transfigured.*

An aftereffect of the headache, Lydia thought, sitting up. They often affected her vision. Now, however, the worst of her malady had passed, and Aunt Nell's kindly but firm voice echoed in her mind. *Mustn't shirk our duties, Lydia. After all, we are Fairmonts.*

Was it already time to help Helga set the table for supper?

Mittie, fairly bursting with news, continued to shine as brightly as if she'd climbed a ladder into a night sky and gobbled the moon down whole, like one of the small, sweet biscuits she enjoyed every afternoon with her tea.

Finally, breathless with excitement, the old woman could not contain the announcement any longer. "You have a *caller!*" she bubbled. "A *gentleman* caller."

Lydia frowned as the faint pounding beneath her temples began again. "Mr. Fitch is back?"

"No," Millie blurted, appearing just behind Mittie, popping her head up over her

35

taller sister's right shoulder, then her left. "This man is *handsome!*"

"He doesn't have an automobile, however," Mittie pointed out, sobering a little. "And while his clothes are certainly well fitted, I doubt he's at all rich."

"Who on earth — ?" Lydia muttered, stooping to glance into the mirror on her vanity table and assess the state of her hair.

A few pats of her hands set it right.

And neither Mittie nor Millie said a word.

They simply stood there, in the doorway, gaping at her as though she'd changed somehow, since they'd seen her last.

"Is there a calling card?" Lydia prodded, staring back.

Neither answered.

Lydia tried again. "Did he at least give his name, then?"

"He did," Millie said, her nearly translucent cheeks blushing pink, "but I'm afraid I was so taken aback by his resemblance to dear Major Bentley Alexander Willmington the Third that it has completely escaped me."

At this, Mittie bristled. "He *does not* resemble the major, sister. He is the *image* of my own Captain Phillip Stanhope."

Millie straightened her narrow shoulders. "You refer, of course," she replied stiffly,

36

"to that *traitor* to the Southern cause?"

"Captain Stanhope was *not* a traitor, Millicent Fairmont! He was a man of principle who could not abide the Peculiar Institution —"

"Ladies," Lydia interceded, hoping to head off another of the sisters' rare but spirited battles. The term *Peculiar Institution* referred to slavery, and with her marriage to Mr. Fitch fast approaching, Lydia found the subject even more abhorrent than usual. "Whoever this man is, I'm sure he looks exactly like himself and no one else."

As she swept toward the door, forcing her aunts to part for her like small waves on a sea of time-faded ebony bombazine, Lydia's response echoed uncomfortably in her fogged brain.

She was only eighteen, and already she was starting to sound just like Mittie and Millie.

If the mysterious caller turned out to be a bill collector, as she suspected he would, she would simply inform him that, as of tomorrow, all claims should be referred to her husband, founder and president of the First Territorial Bank. There were, after all, a *few* consolations attached to her forthcoming marriage.

The aunts crept along behind Lydia as

37

she descended the stairs, calling upon all the dignity she possessed. After today, she would not have to deal with visits like this one.

"He's in the parlor!" Mittie piped, in a voice sure to carry far and wide. Like Millie, she was midway down the stairs, clinging to the rail, as eager-faced as a child about to open gifts on Christmas morning.

Lydia put a finger to her lips and tried to look just stern enough to silence them, but not so stern as to make them cry.

She could not bear it when the aunts cried.

Reaching the entryway, Lydia drew a deep breath. Then, after straightening her skirts and squaring her shoulders, she marched through the wide doorway and into the parlor — and nearly fainted dead away.

Gideon rose out of the Judge's leather chair — no one, not even Jacob, sat in that chair — and regarded her with a pensive smile, his handsome head cocked slightly to one side.

"You look all right to me," he said.

Lydia was so stunned, she could not manage a single word.

Gideon pulled an all-too-familiar envelope from the pocket of his shirt, held it up. Her letter.

"It finally reached me," he told her quietly. "I don't go by 'Rhodes' anymore — that was my brother Rowdy's alias, and I borrowed it for a while. But my last name is 'Yarbro.'"

He seemed to be waiting for some reaction to that.

Flustered, Lydia croaked out, "Do sit down, Gid— Mr. Yarbro."

He grinned. She remembered that grin, slanted and spare. It had made her eight-year-old heart flitter, and that hadn't changed, except that now the reaction was stronger, and ventured beyond her chest.

"Not until you do," Gideon said, his green eyes twinkling a little for all their serious regard.

Lydia crossed the room and sank into her aunt Nell's reading chair, grateful that her wobbly knees had carried her even that far.

Once she was seated, Gideon sat, too.

"The letter?" Gideon prompted, when Lydia didn't speak right away.

Lydia felt her neck heat, and then her face. If only the floor would open and Aunt Nell's chair would drop right through, and her with it. "It must have been sent by accident, Mr. Yarbro, and you must pay it no heed," she said, in a rush of words. "No heed at all —"

Lydia stopped herself from prattling with a determined gulp. What was the *matter* with her? First, she hadn't been able to utter a syllable, she'd been so thunderstruck, and now she was inclined to chatter senselessly.

"Gideon," he said, very solemnly, his eyes still watchful.

"I beg your pardon?" It took all the force of will Lydia possessed not to squirm in her chair.

"Call me Gideon, not Mr. Yarbro." He leaned forward, easy in the imposing chair, easy in his skin. Rested his elbows on his thighs and looked deep inside Lydia, or so it seemed. His probing gaze made her feel uncomfortable, intrigued, and almost naked, all of a piece. "You sent the letter, Lydia," he reminded her, "and I don't believe it was an accident."

"She's getting married tomorrow," Helga proclaimed loudly from the parlor doorway, a herald in a plain dress, apron and mobcap. All she lacked, in Lydia's fitfully distracted opinion, was a long brass horn with a banner hanging from it and velvet shoes with curled toes. "To a man she *hates.*"

Lydia's face throbbed with mortification. "Helga," she said firmly, "I *do not* hate Jacob Fitch, and you are overstepping — *again.* Kindly return to the kitchen and attend to your own affairs."

Helga didn't obey — she never did — and the aunts stayed, too, hovering behind the housekeeper, all aflutter.

"All right," Helga conceded, "perhaps you don't actually *hate* Fitch, but you certainly aren't in love with him, either!"

Lydia's humiliation was now complete.

Gideon rose from his chair, crossed the room, and spoke so quietly to the women clustered in the doorway that Lydia couldn't make out his words. Miraculously, the avid trio subsided, and Gideon closed the great doors in their faces.

Lydia sat rigid, and squeezed her eyes shut.

She didn't hear Gideon approaching her, and when his hand came to rest on her shoulder, she started, gave a little gasp. It wasn't so much surprise that had made her jump, she realized, horrified, but the strange, sultry charge Gideon's touch sent coursing through her entire system.

"Open your eyes, Lydia," he said. "Look at me."

He was crouched beside her chair now, his green gaze searching her face, missing nothing, uncovering secrets she'd kept even from herself.

Or so it seemed.

"It's really a misunderstanding," she whispered, trying to smile.

Gideon took her hand. Squeezed it gently. "Stop lying to me," he said, his voice husky and very quiet. "Who is this Jacob Fitch yahoo, and why are you getting married to him if you don't love the man?"

Lydia swallowed, made herself look directly at Gideon. She forced out her answer. "I have my reasons."

"And those reasons are . . . ?"

Tears blurred Lydia's vision; she tried to blink them away. "What does it matter, Gideon? I have no choice — that's all the explanation I can give you."

He straightened, reluctantly let go of her hand, went to stand facing the marble fireplace, his back turned to her. Looked up at the life-size portrait of the Judge looming above the mantel, dominating the entire room, big as it was.

At least, Lydia's great-grandfather's painted countenance *had* dominated the room, seeming so real that she'd swear she'd seen it breathing — until Gideon Yarbro's arrival.

"There are always choices, Lydia," Gideon said gruffly. *"Always."*

He turned around, leaned back against the intricately chiseled face of the fireplace, folded his arms. His shoulders were broad, under his fresh white shirt, and his butternut-colored hair, though still slightly too long, had been cut recently . . .

She gave herself a little shake. Why was she noticing these things?

Lydia sat up a little straighter in her chair. Maybe there *were* "always choices," as Gideon maintained, but in her case, all the alternatives were even worse than the prospect of becoming Mrs. Jacob Fitch.

The aunts, fashionably impoverished now, would become charity cases. Their cherished belongings would be sold at auction, pawed through and carried away by strangers.

And she herself, with no means of earning a living, might be reduced to serving drinks in one of Phoenix's overabundance of saloons — or worse.

No, she would marry Mr. Fitch.

The following afternoon, at two o'clock, she'd be standing, swathed in silk and antique lace, almost where Gideon was standing now, with Jacob beside her and his termagant of a mother looking on from nearby, while a justice of the peace mumbled the words that would bind Lydia like ropes, for the rest of her life.

"Lydia," Gideon said firmly, sending her thoughts scattering like chickens suddenly overshadowed by the wingspan of a diving hawk. "Talk to me."

"I'll lose this house if I don't marry Mr. Fitch," Lydia heard herself say. "The aunts — you saw them, they're *ancient* — will be displaced — no, *destitute*. It doesn't — it doesn't bear thinking about."

Gideon tilted his head back, scanning the high ceiling, with its hand-carved moldings and thousands of tiny inlaid seashells imported from some faraway ocean.

Lydia wished she could magically transport herself to that ocean. Jump in and sink beneath its waves and never be seen again.

But, alas, there she remained, in that august parlor, in the middle of dry and dusty Phoenix, with no handy place to drown.

"It's a fine house," Gideon allowed. "But it's *only* a house. And your aunts would adapt to new surroundings. People do, you know — adapt, I mean."

Lydia stood up abruptly, found that her knees were still quite unreliable, and dropped back into her chair again. "You don't understand," she protested weakly.

Gideon's handsome face hardened a little. "I'm afraid I do," he answered. "You're willing to sell yourself, Lydia. And the price is a *house*. It's a bad bargain — you're worth so much more."

His statement stung its way through Lydia, a dose of harsh medicine.

But then a strange, twittering little laugh escaped her, as she remembered just how hopeless her situation truly was.

Would the embarrassment *never* end? Again, she found that she could not look at Gideon, could not expose herself to the expression she'd surely catch on his face if she did. "Just forget the letter, Gideon," she said. "I'm sorry if I inconvenienced you, made you go out of your way, but, really, *truly,* I —"

"I can't," Gideon broke in. "I can't 'just forget the letter,' Lydia. Our agreement was that you'd send it if you were in trouble, and I know you are. In trouble, that is." He paused. "And I just accused you of *selling yourself.* Did you miss that? Most women would have slapped my face, but you didn't even get out of your chair."

Lydia didn't trust herself to answer.

Gideon strode across the room again, bent over her, his hands gripping the arms of her chair, effectively trapping her between his arms.

"There's nothing you can do to help," Lydia nearly whispered. She simply couldn't lie anymore. Nor could she meet his eyes, though the sunlight-and-shaving-cream scent of him filled her nose, and invaded all her other senses, too, and made her dizzy. "Please, Gideon — just go."

He didn't move. His voice was a rumble, low and rough, like thunder on the distant horizon. "I'm not going anywhere — except maybe to find your bridegroom and tell him the wedding is off."

Lydia flinched, her gaze rising to collide with Gideon's now. "You mustn't do that!" she cried, aghast at the prospect. "Gideon, you *mustn't!* This house, my aunts —"

"*Damn* this house," Gideon growled, backing up now, but just far enough to take hold of Lydia's shoulders and pull her to her feet. "You are *not* marrying a man you don't love!"

At last, Lydia dredged up some pride. Lies hadn't worked. Neither had the truth. Bravado was all that was left to her. "You can't stop me," she said fiercely.

She saw his eyes narrow, and his jawline harden.

"Yes, I can," he ground out.

"How?" Lydia challenged.

And that was when he did the unthinkable.

He *kissed* her, and not gently, the way a friend might do. No, Gideon Yarbro kissed

46

her hard, as a lover would, slamming his mouth down on hers — and instinctively, she parted her lips. Felt the kiss deepen in ways she'd only been able to imagine before that moment.

That dreadful, wonderful, life-altering moment.

Gideon drew back too soon, and Lydia stood there trembling, as shaken as if he'd taken her, actually made her his own, right there in the parlor, both of them standing up and fully clothed.

"It won't be like that when he kisses you," Gideon said, after a very long time. Then he let go of her shoulders, he turned, and he walked away. He opened the parlor doors and strode through to the foyer, then banged out of the house.

Lydia couldn't move, not to follow, not to sit down, not even to collapse. She simply *could not move.*

Damn Gideon Yarbro, she thought. Damn him to the depths of perdition. He'd ruined everything — by being right.

Jacob Fitch would never kiss her the way Gideon had, never send thrills of terrible, spectacular need jolting through her like stray shards of lightning. No, never again would she feel what she had before, during and after Gideon's mouth landed on hers.

47

In some inexplicable way, it was as though he'd *claimed* her, conquered her so completely and so thoroughly that she could never belong to Jacob, or any other man, as long as she lived.

Gideon had aroused a consuming desire within Lydia, simply by kissing her, and simultaneously *satisfied* that desire. But — and this was the cruelest part of all — that sweet, brief, soul-drenching satisfaction had shown her what a man's attentions — one *certain* man's attentions — could be like.

He'd left her wanting more of what she could never have — and for that, she very nearly hated him.

The aunts and Helga rushed into the room, like a talcum-scented wind, pressing in around Lydia, so close she nearly flailed her arms at them, the way she would at a flock of frenzied, pecking crows.

"You look *ghastly!*" one of the aunts cried, sounding delighted.

"Do sit down," begged the other.

"Glory be," Helga exalted, throwing up her hands like someone who'd just found religion. "That man kissed you like a woman *ought* to be kissed!"

Lydia recovered enough to sweep all three women up in one scathing glance. "Were you peeking through the keyhole?" she demanded. It was as if another, stronger self had surged to the fore, pushed aside the old, beleaguered Lydia, taken over.

That self was a wanton hussy, mad enough to spit fire.

And not *about* to sit down, whether she looked "ghastly" or not.

"Helga was," Mittie said righteously. "Millie and I would *never* do any such thing. It wouldn't be genteel."

"To hell with 'genteel,'" Helga said joyously. "He might as well have laid you down and had you good and proper as to kiss you like that!"

Mittie and Millie gasped and put their hands to their mouths.

Even the wanton hussy was a little shocked.

"Helga!" Lydia erupted, her face on fire.

"Such talk," Mittie clucked, shaking her head.

"Major Bentley Alexander Willmington the Third used to whisper naughty things in my ear," Millie confessed, succumbing to a dreamy reverie, "while we were rocking on the porch swing of an evening. Papa would have had him horsewhipped if he'd known."

"Millicent!" Mittie scolded.

Helga laughed out loud. "Glory be," she

repeated, turning to leave the room. "Glory be!"

"You don't understand," Lydia said, for the second time that afternoon. The wanton hussy had suddenly vanished, leaving the fearful, reluctant bride in her place, virginal and wobbly lipped and tearful. "Gideon accused me of — he left here in a rage —" She began to cry. "He's never coming back."

"You're a damn fool if you think that," Helga answered, from the doorway. "He'll be back here, all right, and in plenty of time to put a stop to this wedding foolishness, too."

"You didn't see — he was furious —"

"I saw him," Helga countered, more circumspectly now that the *glory be*s had subsided. "He nearly knocked me down, storming through this doorway like he did. No denying that he's fighting mad, either. But he'll be back just the same. You mark my words, Lydia Fairmont. *He'll be back.*"

The prospect made Lydia feel both hope and fear, as hopelessly tangled as the mess of embroidery floss in the bottom of her sewing basket.

Mittie, now solicitous, patted her arm. "Has your headache returned, dear?" she asked. "You really do look *dreadful*. Perhaps you should lie down, and Helga will bring

50

you your supper in bed —"

"I will *not* serve Miss Lydia's supper in bed!" Helga shouted, already halfway to the kitchen, from the sound of her voice. "She's not an invalid — so just forget that nonsense, all of you!"

Mittie, Millie and Lydia all looked at each other.

"I think Helga has grown a mite obstinate," Mittie confided, wide-eyed.

"Papa would never have tolerated such insolence," Millie observed, but her expression was fond as she gazed toward the space Helga had occupied in the parlor doorway.

"Oh, for heaven's sake," Lydia snapped. "Have neither of you noticed, in all these years, that Helga not only manages the household, she manages *us?*"

"Perhaps we should send her packing," Mittie said, tears forming in her eyes at the very idea.

"Show her the road," Millie agreed, crying, too.

"She's not going anywhere," Lydia told her aunts, softening at their obvious dismay. "You're not, either, and neither am I."

Mittie sniffled. "We're not?"

"No," Lydia assured her, slipping an arm around each of her aunts' shoulders.

No, echoed a voice deep within her heart,

51

with sorrow and certainty. *Because Gideon Yarbro or no Gideon Yarbro, tomorrow afternoon, at two o'clock sharp, you're going to do your duty as a Fairmont and marry Jacob Fitch.*

Lydia lifted her eyes to the Judge's portrait, glaring down at her from above the fireplace.

Sure as sunrise, he was breathing.

The first thing Gideon had to do was talk himself out of going back to the Golden Horseshoe Saloon and swilling whiskey — forget beer — until he stopped thinking about Lydia Fairmont.

The second thing was track down Jacob Fitch.

That was easier. He asked about Fitch on the street, and was directed to the First Territorial Bank, right on Main Street.

Still full of that strange fury Lydia had stirred in him, Gideon strode into that bank as though he meant to hold it up at gunpoint, and the few customers inside actually fled as he approached the counter.

The clerk, apparently alone in the place, looked as though he might drop right to the floor and cover his head with both hands.

Gideon slapped his palms down on the counter top. "I want to see Jacob Fitch," he said. *"Now."*

The clerk, a small man with a twitch under his right eye and a nose that wriggled like a rabbit's, blinked behind his thick spectacles. "Well," he said tremulously, "you can't."

"Why not?" Gideon demanded, not to be put off.

"Because he's not here," the clerk retorted, getting braver. "He's at the tailor's, being fitted for his wedding suit."

"And which tailor would Mr. Jacob Fitch be patronizing?" Gideon asked.

"I don't have to tell you that," the clerk said.

Gideon reached over the counter, got the little man by his shirt front, and pulled him clear off his no doubt tiny feet. He didn't normally *handle* people, at least not ones that were smaller than he was, but he was in a state and nothing would do him but finding Jacob Fitch. *"Which tailor?"* he repeated. Then, realizing the man couldn't answer because he was being choked, Gideon slackened his grip just enough to allow the fellow to suck in some wind.

"Feinstein's," the clerk sputtered. "On Third Street."

Gideon allowed the man to slide back to his feet. "Thank you," he said moderately, and left the bank.

He found the tailoring establishment right where the clerk had said it would be. Mindful of the stir he'd caused in the bank — and regretting it a little — Gideon paused on the sidewalk out front to draw a deep, slow breath. He read and reread the golden script printed on the pristine display window — *Arthur Feinstein, Purveyor of Fine Men's Wear* — even examined the three-piece suit gracing a faceless mannequin, as though he might be in the market for new duds.

When he thought he could behave himself, Gideon pushed open the door and went into the shop.

A little bell jingled overhead.

The place seemed deserted, a development that threatened Gideon's carefully cultivated equanimity.

"Anybody home?" he called. You could take the boy out of Stone Creek, he reflected, but you couldn't take Stone Creek out of the boy.

A bald head appeared between two curtains at the back of the store. "I'll be with you right away, sir," the man said, speaking clearly despite the row of pins glimmering between his lips.

Mr. Feinstein, no doubt. Purveyor of fine

men's wear.

"I'm looking for Jacob Fitch," Gideon said, raising his voice a little.

Another head appeared beside Feinstein's, also balding. The face beneath the pate was sin-ugly, and none too pleased at having the fitting interrupted.

"I'm Fitch," the second man said. "Who are you and what do you want?"

Lydia, Gideon answered silently. *I want Lydia.*

"My name is Gideon Yarbro," he said aloud, nodding to the tailor. "And I think you'd prefer it if we had this discussion in private."

"Feinstein has been my tailor for years," Fitch said. "I've got no secrets from him."

Gideon did not remark on the oddness of that statement. "All right, then," he said. "I want to talk to you about Lydia Fairmont."

Fitch's face broke into a broad and somewhat lecherous smile, which did nothing to improve Gideon's mood. "My little bride," he said. "The wedding is tomorrow."

"The wedding," Gideon said, amazed at his own audacity even as he spoke, "is postponed. Maybe even cancelled."

Fitch stared at him, finally came out from behind the curtains. He was wearing a fancy suit, with the cuffs of the trousers pinned up, but no shirt. Whorls of thick hair covered his chest. "Is Lydia sick?" he asked.

"No," Gideon said. "She just needs a little time to think."

What was he *doing?* Had he gone crazy?

Lydia had *told* him, straight-out, that she meant to go ahead with the marriage. He had no earthly right, interfering this way.

And yet, she'd sent that letter.

Kept it all those years, and then mailed it.

That, he couldn't ignore.

Fitch reddened, clearly displeased. Mr. Feinstein ducked back behind the curtains, looking as though he might swallow the pins in the process.

"Time to think?" Fitch thundered. "What is there to *think* about?"

"Well, sir," Gideon said diplomatically, "she's not sure she loves you."

"What?"

"Things like this happen. Women get the jitters. What with the wedding night and all —"

"Who the *hell* are you?" Fitch shouted, knotting his banker's fists at his sides, but not advancing.

A prudent choice, Gideon thought.

"I told you. My name is Gideon Yarbro."

Fitch, still seething, drew both eyebrows together into one long, bushy streak of hair.

"And what have *you* to do with Lydia?"

"I'm an old friend," Gideon said.

Fitch glowered. "Before Almighty God, if you've *tampered* with her —"

" 'Tampered' with her?" Gideon asked.

"You know damn well what I mean!"

Gideon was prepared to go to almost any length to prevent this wedding, but not quite so far as besmirching Lydia's reputation. "No," he said. "But I did kiss her this afternoon."

"You *kissed* my fiancée? And she *allowed that?*" Now, Fitch looked as though he might blow a vessel, which would be an unfortunate solution to the whole problem.

"I can't say as I gave her much opportunity to decide whether to allow it or not," Gideon admitted affably. He'd said too much already, he knew that. Adding that Lydia had responded to his kiss, nearly melted under it, would be over the line. "She needs time, that's all I'm saying. A week. A month. A year?"

Fitch practically spat his answer. "Until two o'clock tomorrow afternoon," he said. "*That's* how much *time* I'll give her."

With that, Lydia's unlikely intended disappeared behind the curtains again. Short of going back there and hauling the man out by the scruff — and then doing what?

— Gideon was out of ideas.

Except one, that is.

And the contingency plan had to do with Lydia herself, not Jacob Fitch.

CHAPTER THREE

Lydia did not sleep a wink that night, and little wonder, with her wedding scheduled for the very next day and the memory of Gideon's unexpected visit to plague her thoughts.

At the first crow of the neighbor's rooster, Lydia arose from her bed, washed and dressed and replaited her hair, pinning the braid into a heavy knot at her nape.

Just the way Jacob liked it. She was to wear it just so once they were married, he'd declared on more than one occasion. Modesty befitted a banker's wife.

Lydia stared miserably at her own reflection, pale in the mirror above her vanity table. Her eyes were hollow, the color of bruises, not violets, and her mouth pinched.

Gideon, she thought, knowing she was torturing herself and unable to stop, would prefer her hair *down,* tumbling in curls to her waist.

Behind her, the bedroom door opened.

Helga, who never knocked, appeared in the gap, looking troubled. She'd been so sure Gideon would return — now, it seemed, reality was setting in. "Will you be coming down for breakfast?" she asked, keeping her voice low so she wouldn't wake the aunts, who shared a room across the hall from Lydia's.

Lydia shook her head. If she tried to swallow so much as a morsel, she would surely gag.

Helga hesitated, then stepped into the room. Crossed to stand behind Lydia and lay a hand on her shoulder. Her gaze strayed to Nell's wedding dress, hanging like a burial shroud from a hook on the inside of the wardrobe door, came back to Lydia's wan face, reflected in the vanity mirror. "You don't have to do this," the housekeeper said awkwardly. "You *mustn't* do this. Lydia, *please* don't sacrifice yourself to save a lot of musty old keepsakes and dented silver —"

"Are the *aunts* 'musty old keepsakes,' Helga?" Lydia retorted quietly. "They won't survive without the roof and walls of this house to shelter them. It's their entire world."

Helga gave a disgusted little snort, but her

eyes were sad, and her mouth drooped at the corners. "They *survived* a *war,* Lydia," she insisted. "They survived seeing their *first* home ransacked and then burned to the ground, losing the men they loved, traveling all the way out here to Arizona with the Judge and starting over from scratch. Their father pampered them, treated them like a pair of china figurines that would break if anyone breathed on them. Then Nell did the same, God rest her generous soul, and now you're carrying on the tradition. Don't you see, Lydia? No one ever gave Miss Mittie and Miss Millie a *chance* to show how strong they really are."

"They were young when all those things happened," Lydia countered, very softly. "The war and the rest of it, I mean." She'd tried to imagine what the raid on the plantation back in Virginia must have been like — flames everywhere, consuming all but a few portraits, some jewelry, a small sterling vase that had been a gift from George and Martha Washington, presented to a Fairmont ancestor in appreciation for flour and dried beans sent to Valley Forge during that desperate winter — but she knew such trauma was *beyond* imagining. Mittie had suffered severe burns, saving the letters Captain Stanhope had written her after accepting a commission in the Army of the Potomac, and Millie had nearly been raped by one of the raiders. A former slave called Old Billy had intervened, according to Nell's rare and whispered accounts — shared with Helga, not Lydia — and died for his chivalry, shot through the throat.

"Give them a chance," Helga pleaded. "You'll see what those old aunts of yours are made of, if you'll just *ask them* how they'd truly feel about leaving here."

Lydia considered the idea, and then shook her head. Mittie and Millie were old now, too old to change. For her sake, they might try to make the best of things, but it was simply too much to ask of them, so late in life.

Swallowing, she made herself meet Helga's gaze, there in the mirror glass. "There's been no word from Gideon, then?" she asked, tentatively and at considerable cost to her pride.

"Not yet," Helga answered solemnly, but there was a faint glint of hope in her pale blue eyes. "Not just *yet*."

"He won't come," Lydia said, almost whispering.

But he *had* come when he'd received the letter, hadn't he?

And he'd kissed her.

"I think you're wrong about that," Helga replied, turning, starting for the door. "I'll bring you some coffee and a roll. You have to eat something, Lydia — whatever happens today, you'll need your strength."

There was no point in arguing. Helga would do what Helga would do.

And *Lydia* would do what Lydia would do: pour the coffee out the window, and leave the roll on the sill for the birds. Because unless a miracle happened, and Lydia had never personally encountered one of those, she would be Jacob's wife in a few hours — with all the attendant responsibilities, including the conjugal ones.

With *that* prospect ahead of her, food was out of the question.

"Thank you," she murmured. "But I'd rather come down to the kitchen to eat, like everyone else."

Helga nodded, resigned, and remained her usual salty self. "Just don't go getting the idea I'm going to be waiting on you hand and foot like some servant," the other woman warned, "because I'm not."

Lydia laughed, in spite of all she would have to endure in the coming hours, days, months and years. Helga kept that huge house clean, and prepared three meals a day, but she didn't wait on anybody unless they were about to be buried — or *married.*

When Helga had gone, Lydia forced some starch into her spine, sat up straight, and regarded her image directly.

"You have got to marry Jacob Fitch," she told herself, "whether you want to or not. So stop whining about it and carry on."

The short lecture strengthened Lydia; she rose from her seat in front of the vanity table, made up her bed as neatly as she would have done on any ordinary day, and approached Aunt Nell's wedding dress, where it hung on her wardrobe door. Although yellowed in places, with brownish crinkles where it had been folded for so many years — said crinkles had thwarted even Helga's efforts to press them away with an iron heated on the kitchen stove — the gown was still a confection of silk, hand-knotted German lace, seed pearls mellowed by age, and faded but intricately woven ivory ribbon in the bodice.

Regarding that remarkable dress, Lydia couldn't help thinking about how different things had been the *last* time a bride donned it. Nell Fairmont had been even younger than Lydia was now — only sixteen — when she'd married Mr. Baker, a newspaper man twice her age, in a church ceremony with all the trimmings — flowers, a cake, an emerald-studded band for her finger. And on that sunlit day, so long ago, Nell had walked down the aisle on the Judge's arm, wearing this very dress.

Nell had been a mere babe-in-arms, her one sibling, Lydia's father, barely a year old, when the Judge had fled Virginia with his daughters and two orphaned grandchildren. Nell and Herbert's mother, Louisa, had died only a few months after the war began; it was said she simply hadn't been able to bear being separated from her husband, Andrew Fairmont, gone for a soldier. Andrew, Mittie and Millie's younger brother, had been wounded early on, spent months in a Union hospital, and finally, after an exchange of prisoners, made his slow and painful way home, only to be told that Louisa had perished. He'd stood over her grave for hours, as Nell told the story, and then gone into an outbuilding and hanged himself from one of the rafters.

Nell had been raised in Phoenix, along with her brother, and she'd grown up strong and single-minded, a true child of the frontier. Herbert — nicknamed Johnny by his grandfather, aunts and sister — would one day become a doctor, marry, and sire Lydia. Johnny Fairmont, as the only male member of the family, other than the Judge of course, had been, in Helga's readily offered opinion, "overindulged."

Lydia did not recall her mother, who had died when she was very small.

Thinking of her aunt, missing her with an intensity that was almost physically painful, Lydia laid the fingertips of her right hand to the fragile lace of the skirt. "I'm doing the right thing, aren't I, Aunt Nell?" she asked, very softly. "Making sure the aunts always have a home?"

There was, of course, no answer.

Nell Fairmont Baker had been a spirited woman, widowed young and childless, and bearing up admirably under her private disappointments. When she'd learned of Lydia's father's death, she'd traveled to Stone Creek immediately, and taken charge.

She'd always done whatever needed doing, Nell had. She'd prided herself on that. In the same circumstances, wouldn't she have done her duty for the sake of the family and married Mr. Fitch, just as Lydia was about to do?

Or would she have cut her losses and run — loaded the aunts and Helga into a stagecoach or onto a train and found a place, found a *way,* to start over?

Lydia had been over this same ground so many times, she was weary of it. She turned

66

from the dress and left her room, set on pretending to eat the roll and drink the coffee Helga was preparing, then gathering flowers from the garden. She would fill the parlor with colorful, fragrant blossoms, she decided, and wear Aunt Nell's lovely dress, and play the part of a happy bride.

Even if it killed her.

Gideon had prowled the streets and alleys and saloons of that lively desert town for most of the night, asking questions about Jacob Fitch. And he liked what he'd heard in response even less than he'd liked the man himself.

Fitch was wealthy in the extreme — no surprise there — though his only evident extravagance was the automobile he'd special-ordered from Henry Ford's factory. He lived in rooms above the bank with his elderly mother and had never, to anyone's knowledge, been married or even kept public company with a woman, before Lydia.

Back in his room, watching the sun rise, Gideon went over the plan — the only one he'd been able to come up with — for the hundredth time. It was drastic, it was desperate, and if the rumors he'd gathered the night before had any validity at all, it was dangerous, too. Now that he knew Gideon intended to stop the ceremony any way he could, Fitch was allegedly trying to hire thugs to guard the doors at the Fairmont house.

Gideon had considered wiring Rowdy and Wyatt, asking for their help; he knew they'd ride hard for Phoenix if he did, without requiring an explanation beforehand. But they couldn't possibly get there on time, not on horseback anyhow, and the train didn't head south until 3:10 in the afternoon. The stagecoach routes had been cut to almost nothing, now that everybody traveled by rail, and it would be too slow anyhow.

Besides, Gideon doubted his brothers would be willing to break up somebody else's wedding just on his say-so. No, they'd go straight to Lydia and ask her what she wanted to do, and she'd answer that she wanted to go through with the ceremony, because that was what she'd made up her mind to do. Rowdy and Wyatt would take her at her word.

Gideon couldn't do that, because of the letter.

Resigned, he changed his shirt, brushed his hair, and left his room, taking his satchel with him. He checked out of the hotel, walked down the street, and bought a buckboard and a team at the first livery stable he came to. Then he headed for Lydia's place on foot.

The day before, he'd strode right up onto the front porch and rung the bell.

Today, he went around back. If Fitch had managed to put those thugs on his payroll, none of them were in evidence.

The housekeeper answered his knock, a hefty woman with salt-and-pepper hair and blue eyes that seemed somehow faded, as though they'd been worn down by seeing too many hard things.

Her face lit up when she recognized him, though.

"I *knew* you'd come back," she said, putting a hand to her ample bosom.

Gideon put a finger to his lips. "Where is Lydia?" he asked quietly.

The woman stepped back, gestured for him to come inside. "In the parlor," she said, "arranging flowers. The poor thing is *determined* to make this stupid plan work — she's stubborn, our Lydia."

Gideon grinned at that, but not with much spirit. "The aunts — are they around?"

"Miss Mittie and Miss Millie are in their room," the housekeeper told him. "This is their time for correspondence, though heaven only knows who's left for them to write to."

"Would you mind getting them for me, please?" Gideon asked. Then, with another grin, he added, "And keeping Lydia busy for a few minutes?"

The housekeeper beamed. "Best you wait in the library. Lydia won't go near it today — with all that's on her mind, she won't be doing any reading."

Gideon nodded. "Thank you, Miss — ?"

"Helga," the woman insisted. "Call me Helga."

Gideon shoved his left hand into his pants pocket, so he wouldn't shove it through his hair and show how nervous he was. "I'm much obliged, Helga," he said.

She showed him to the library, a long room jammed with volumes, and he paced after she left, too agitated to thumb through some of the books, the way he would have done on any other day of his life.

He could see why leaving this house would be a wrench for the old ladies, and for Lydia herself. There probably wasn't another one like it in all of Arizona, though he'd seen grander ones back East. Not many, though.

Presently, Helga returned, shooing Lydia's aunts before her and hushing them every step of the way. Gideon was struck, once again, by their diminutive size — they reminded him of little birds perched on a ridgepole in a high wind and about to be blown away.

Still, he saw intelligence in their eyes, dignity in the way they held their snow-capped heads. They stuck close to Helga, though, and watched him with frank and wary curiosity.

Gideon kept his distance, lest he frighten them away.

At his urging, they sat down, side by side on a small settee, shoulders touching, gazes intent. They folded their hands in their laps, after smoothing the skirts of their worn black dresses.

"Have you come to kiss Lydia again?" one of them asked.

Although Helga had introduced them to him by name, Gideon could not have said which was which. The sisters were so alike that they might have been two versions of the same person. Or, of course, twins.

"No," Gideon answered solemnly, after forcing back a grin.

Both ladies looked genuinely disappointed by his reply.

"Miss Mittie, Miss Millie," he went on, bowing slightly and hoping he'd addressed them in the correct order, "I'm here to ruin Lydia's wedding, and I'll need your help to do it."

Their eyes widened. Helga, standing watch at the library doors, smiled to herself.

"You'd better explain yourself, Mr. Yarbro," said Millie. Or Mittie. "Ruining a wedding is serious business."

Gideon suppressed another smile. "Indeed it is," he agreed. And then he proceeded to outline his plan.

"What do you *mean* you can't find the aunts?" Lydia demanded, at one-fifty-five that afternoon, again seated at her vanity table. Helga had helped her into the gown, and was now tucking tiny rosebuds into her hair, since there was no veil. "Where could they possibly have gone?"

Helga tried to look innocent as she shrugged. "Today was correspondence day," she said, avoiding Lydia's mirrored gaze. "Perhaps they went to the post office."

Lydia whirled and stood in one fluid motion, causing the skirts of the dress to rustle around her. "Today is *my wedding day,*" she said. "Guests have been arriving for the last hour, Mr. Fitch and his mother are waiting downstairs, with the justice of the peace, and the aunts — who never leave this house except to go to church — have gone to the *post office?*"

"I'm sure they'll be back in plenty of time for the ceremony," Helga said, backing up a step or two.

Lydia set her hands on her hips and advanced. "*What* is going on here?" she demanded.

"A wedding," Helga answered, with just the faintest snip in her tone. "More's the pity."

"You've spirited them off somewhere," Lydia accused, almost beside herself now. The aunts were virtually recluses — that was why she'd insisted that the ceremony be held in the parlor, over Jacob's mother's objections, instead of in the church. "Helga Riley, you'd *better* tell me where they are — this instant!"

"They left with Gideon," Helga admitted, though her eyes snapped with a sort of smug defiance. "Packed up their old love letters and their best jewelry and walked right out of this house without even looking back."

"*What?*" A thrill of anger went through Lydia — anger and something else that wasn't so easy to define. "They *wouldn't* have gone willingly — he must have — have *abducted* them!"

"Oh, they were quite willing," Helga insisted, stiffly triumphant. "And it's *you* Gideon Yarbro means to abduct. Assuming he can get past the toughs Jacob Fitch has stationed at both the doors, that is."

"I'll have the law on him!" Lydia raged. "This is *outrageous!*"

Helga arched one eyebrow, and a smile tugged at the corner of her mouth. "Don't be a ninny — it's wonderful and you know it. Get out of that dress and into something fit to travel in, and climb down the oak tree outside that window, like you used to do when you were a little girl. Fitch's men will be too shocked to try and stop you and —"

"Helga," Lydia broke in, still barely able to credit that her aunts, of all people, had lit out with Gideon. "Have you *gone mad?* Has *everyone* gone mad?"

Helga ignored the question of sanity and marched over to the wardrobe, rifled through it until she found the divided riding skirt Lydia hadn't worn since she used to range over the desert on horseback with Nell.

"Put this on," Helga commanded, thrusting the garment at Lydia, along with the matching jacket and a long-sleeved white shirtwaist with a ruffled collar. "Hurry! If you won't climb out the window, then I'll see what I can do to keep that criminal watching the back door busy for a few minutes —"

"Helga, *listen to me*," Lydia blurted. "I don't know what's come over the aunts, but they're bound to come to their senses by nightfall, if not before, and when they do, they're going to be inconsolable —"

"*You'll* be the one who's inconsolable by nightfall if you go through with this wedding, Lydia Fairmont," Helga said, thrusting the garments into Lydia's hands.

Downstairs, the enormous longcase clock tripped through a ponderous sequence of chimes, then bonged loudly, once. Twice. Before Lydia had fully accepted that the hour of her doom had arrived, she heard shouting, some sort of scuffle below, on the ground floor.

Alarmed, she rushed out of her room and down the corridor to the top of the stairs, and looked down to see Gideon standing halfway up. His hair was mussed, and his lower lip was bleeding. Seeing Lydia, he blinked once, shook his head, and then extended a hand to her, a broad grin spreading across his face.

Lydia could barely tear her gaze from him, she was so stricken by the mere fact of his presence, but when Jacob stumbled out of

75

the parlor, even more mussed and bloody than Gideon, she gasped.

"You will lose everything," Jacob vowed, very slowly and precisely, glaring at her. The look of fury in his eyes was terrifying. *"Everything."*

Lydia looked back at Gideon again. He was still holding his hand out to her.

She took a step toward him, and then another.

"Everything!" Jacob roared. "This house, your good name, everything!"

By then, she was only a step or two above Gideon. "You're hurt," she said, dazed, reaching out to touch his lip.

"Not as hurt as I'm going to be if we don't get out of here before the guards come to," Gideon said easily, still grinning. With that, he suddenly hoisted Lydia off her feet, flung her over his right shoulder and bolted down the stairs.

Lydia was too stunned to protest; in truth, she was certain she must be dreaming; such a thing simply could not be happening.

But it was.

Jacob's mother appeared behind her son in the parlor doorway, her long, narrow face pinched with disapproval. Even lying over Gideon's shoulder like a sack of chicken feed, Lydia caught a glimpse of something

76

else in the woman's eyes as they passed.

It was a sort of triumphant relief.

Jacob shouted invective and started forward, surely intending to block Gideon's way, but Mrs. Fitch restrained him simply by laying a hand on his arm.

"Let her go, Jacob," she said. "Let the trollop go."

The *trollop?* Suddenly furious, Lydia began to kick and struggle, not because she didn't want, with all her heart and soul, to escape this curse of a marriage, but because she *did* want to tear into that vicious old woman like a she-cat with its claws out.

Gideon, swinging around in an arch toward the kitchen, gave Lydia a swat on her upended, lace-covered bottom, not hard enough to hurt, but no light tap, either.

If Lydia had been furious before, she was *enraged* now. "Put — me — *down!*" she sputtered.

Gideon didn't even slow his pace, much less do as he'd been told. "If I do," he said, sounding slightly breathless now, "we're both going to be in a lot more trouble than we are now." They'd reached the kitchen, and Lydia tried in vain to grab at the doorframe as they went out.

A man lay sprawled on the back porch, raising himself to his hands and knees as they passed, shaking his head as if befogged. Helga, carrying a handbag and a small reticule and wearing a hat, waited at the bottom of the steps.

Looking down at the man on the porch, Helga put a foot to the middle of his back and flattened him again.

Gideon's strides lengthened, increasing Lydia's discomfort *and* her ire. Helga, keeping pace, gave her a look of reprimand.

"I can't *believe* you're doing this!" Lydia cried.

Gideon all but flung her into the back of a buckboard. "Believe it," he said, helping Helga up into the wagon with considerably more courtesy and then scrambling up in the box to take the reins.

Lydia heard the brakes squeak as Gideon released the lever, probably with a hard thrust of his foot, and the rig lurched forward as he yelled to the horses.

The ride through that alley was so rough that Lydia had to make three attempts before she managed to sit up.

The man from the porch was running behind them; he caught hold of the tailgate with hands the size of Easter hams and started to climb inside.

Helga fell back onto her elbows and kicked with both feet, as hard as she could, and the man screamed and let go, falling to the ground, bellowing curses after the rapidly departing wagon.

The buckboard careened around a corner, onto a side street, throwing Lydia hard against the side. She tried several times to climb up into the box beside Gideon, but each time there was another corner, and she fell back again, bruising herself.

If this *was* a dream, it was entirely too realistic for Lydia's tastes.

Hauling herself onto her knees, grasping the side of the wagon to keep from being hurled down again, Lydia watched in disbelief as they came abreast of the train depot. Steam belched from the stack of the huge engine, and the whistle blew, shrill enough to make her let go and cover her ears with both hands.

Through a haze of shock and utter confusion, she thought she caught a glimpse of her aunts, smiling down at her from one of the passenger car windows. They were both wearing enormous hats, bedecked in flowers and feathers.

Surely, Lydia thought distractedly, she was mistaken. Seeing things. Millie and Mittie hadn't ridden a train, let alone bought new hats, since Lincoln was president.

But she had no time to consider the matter further, because Gideon brought the wagon to a lurching stop, jumped from the box, raced around to wrench open the tailgate, and hauled Lydia out, flinging her over his shoulder again.

This time, she was too exhausted to fight back.

"Hurry!" Helga yelled to him, over the whistle and the rising chug of the train engine. "They're coming!"

The next thing Lydia knew, she and Gideon and Helga were onboard the afternoon train, Gideon carrying her down the aisle between the rows of seats as easily as if she weighed no more than his saddlebags.

Passengers observed the scene with amused interest, to Lydia's everlasting mortification.

The train was already moving, quickly picking up speed, when he finally plopped her into a seat, then stood there glaring down at her, his breath coming hard.

Across the aisle, Mittie and Millie, clad in bright blue silk dresses to match their hats, smiled winningly.

"This is so romantic," Mittie said. "Don't you think so, sister?"

Millie nodded. "It's almost as if Major Bentley Alexander Willmington the Third had come back to life," she replied. Then, with a wistful sigh, she added, "Major Will-mington was so very dashing, you know."

Lydia returned Gideon's glare. "I will *never* forgive you for — for —"

Gideon leaned until his nose was almost touching hers. His lip, she noticed, had stopped bleeding. "For what?" he demanded, through his teeth.

"For *striking* me!" Lydia whispered, well aware that she and Gideon were the center of attention and so embarrassed that she thought she might actually die of it.

Gideon straightened.

His eyes widened slightly.

And then he threw back his head and shouted with laughter.

CHAPTER FOUR

Rowdy boarded the train the moment it pulled into the depot at Stone Creek, his face chiseled into angry lines as he stormed along the aisle toward Gideon, paying no mind at all to greetings from other passengers as he passed.

"Have you completely lost your mind?" he rasped, reaching Gideon's seat and looming over him.

Gideon, who had been dozing for the past couple of hours, exhausted from a sleepless night and the rigors of stealing a bride over the considerable objections of the groom and his hired henchmen, grinned up at his older brother, just to piss him off further.

"I guess the law down in Phoenix must have sent you a telegram," he said cheerfully. "Reckon it said you ought to be on the lookout for a kidnapper."

Rowdy's ice-blue eyes sliced to Lydia, sound asleep in her rumpled wedding dress, her head resting on Helga's shoulder. A faint smile touched the marshal's mouth. "Is that who I think it is?"

Gideon nodded, stretched. "Lydia Fairmont," he confirmed. "All grown up."

"I'll be damned," Rowdy said. A decade before, as the new town marshal, he'd been the one to go out looking for Lydia's father, in the middle of a blizzard. He'd found Dr. Fairmont sitting frozen in his buggy, along a lonely road, and brought the body back to Stone Creek after spending a long night standing between two horses to keep his own blood from turning to ice.

"Are we under arrest?" one of Lydia's aunts piped up, from the row of seats just behind Gideon's, having spotted Rowdy's badge, most likely. He'd be damned if he could say whether she was Millie or Mittie — the two swore they weren't identical twins, but as far as he was concerned, they might as well have been, because he sure as hell couldn't tell them apart.

Rowdy, ever the gentleman, at least in the presence of a lady, whatever age she might be, smiled winningly and swept off his hat. "No, ma'am," he said. "You are most definitely *not* under arrest." But when that sharp blue gaze swung Gideon's way again, another chill had set in. "*You,* on the other

83

hand —"

By then, the other passengers had disembarked, some heading to one end of the car and some to the other, but none trying to get past Rowdy, blocking the aisle like an oak tree sprung up through the floorboards. Lydia was sitting up, blinking away sleep, yawning prettily, looking confused and warm and so delectable she made Gideon's mouth water.

"Rowdy?" she asked, looking pleased to see Gideon's brother again. Doubtless, she remembered him as some kind of hero, which was galling to Gideon. "Is that you?"

Rowdy inclined his head in the cowboy version of a bow. "Miss Lydia," he said, acknowledging that she'd remembered correctly, "you have grown up to be a beauty."

She blushed and lowered her eyes.

"How's Lark these days?" Gideon asked his brother pointedly, annoyed that Rowdy could charm Lydia so easily when *he'd* been the one to save her from Jacob Fitch and her own pigheaded sense of familial duty.

Rowdy chuckled. "My wife," he said, "is as lovely as ever."

Now that they were well away from Phoenix, and effectively out of Fitch's reach, Gideon wondered what he was going to do with all these women. It had been one thing

84

giving the aunts money, after he'd talked them into leaving home that morning, and turning them loose in the ready-made section of the biggest mercantile in town. Feeding and sheltering them on an ongoing basis would be quite another, and there was Lydia, besides. And Helga.

He surely hoped Stone Creek still had a hotel, with rooms enough to house ladies who were used to genteel surroundings — but with the mine bringing in all sorts of people from all parts of the country, it most likely had several. He'd been planning on staying with Rowdy and Lark himself, since they had plenty of room, until he could find a boardinghouse.

Rising from the train seat, Gideon chuckled. From the look on his brother the marshal's face, lodgings might not be a problem, for him, at least. Maybe he could talk Rowdy into putting the ladies up in adjoining cells.

"I guess we'd best get off this train," Rowdy joked, for the benefit of the women, "before we find ourselves rolling on toward Flagstaff."

Lydia smiled and stood, studiously ignoring Gideon.

Helga and the aunts rose, too.

Since nobody had any baggage, including

Gideon, who had left his suitcase behind in the rush to leave Phoenix, there was nothing much to gather. Both the aunts had a small valise, containing what they'd referred to as their "necessities," and Helga had packed a carpetbag with a few things of her own and Lydia's. Taking the bag and one of the valises and shoving the second satchel into Gideon's hands with unnecessary force, Rowdy assured the women that it was a short walk to his place, and his wife, Lark, would be pleased to serve them tea and refreshments and provide whatever else they might need. At this last, his gaze lingered a moment or two on Lydia's wedding gown.

"Maybe you'd like to wait for me in my office," he told Gideon, and while his tone was cordial, the expression in his eyes was razor-sharp. "While I get the ladies settled and all."

Since there would be a yelling match at best, and an arrest at worst, and Gideon figured the Fairmont women and their housekeeper had been through enough for one day, he didn't argue. He just carried the valise as far as the end of Main Street, and didn't protest when Helga took it out of his grasp.

Rowdy's office and the jail were housed in a rambling brick structure, on the site of the original one-cell hole in the wall. Wyatt had gotten the first jail blown up during his brief tenure as deputy marshal, and Gideon felt a little nostalgic for the old place. As a boy, he'd slept in that lone cell often, not because he'd been locked up, but because Rowdy and Lark, newlyweds back then, still living in the tiny house provided for the marshal, hadn't had an extra bed.

Pardner, the old yellow dog, was long gone, a fact that made something catch in Gideon's throat as he wandered over the threshold into Rowdy's spacious office. He was pleasantly surprised to find another dog curled up on the rug in front of the wood-stove, just the way Pardner used to do, way back when. The mutt was the same color as his predecessor, and Gideon's eyes smarted a little as he crouched to say howdy.

Pardner's double licked his hand and looked up into his face with a doleful little whimper of sympathy.

"Yep," Gideon told him. "I'm in trouble."

"His name's Pardner, too," a familiar voice said. "Guess Rowdy just couldn't bring himself to call a dog anything else."

Gideon stood, turned to see his other brother, Wyatt, towering in the doorway leading outside. Taller than Rowdy and leaner than Gideon, Wyatt was the eldest of the Yarbro brood, and his hair was dark, rather than fair like theirs. His eyes were an intense blue, and they could penetrate a man's hide, just the way Rowdy's lighter ones did.

"You back to working as a deputy?" Gideon asked. In his day, Wyatt had been an outlaw, like Rowdy, rustling cattle and robbing trains. All that had changed, though, when he met up with Sarah Tamlin, the banker's daughter.

Wyatt stepped inside, shut the office door against the noise and dust of the street. "I'm still ranching," he answered. "I help out once in a while when Rowdy's shorthanded — since that copper mine started up, Stone Creek's been right lively. I just came by today because Rowdy rode out and told me about that wire he got from the U.S. Marshal down in Phoenix. What you just told that dog, boy, was truer than you probably know. You *are* in trouble."

To show he wasn't intimidated, and he wasn't the little brother Wyatt and Rowdy remembered him as, either, Gideon took a seat behind the biggest desk — there were two others in the room, accommodating Rowdy's regular deputies, probably — leaned back and kicked his feet up. "I did what I had to do," he said easily.

Wyatt went to the stove, picked up the blue enamel coffeepot, gave it a shake and frowned. "You might be a big Wells Fargo agent now," he drawled, carrying the pot to a nearby sink and pumping water into it to brew up another batch, "but you're not above the law. And the law says you can't carry a woman out of her own home against her will and haul her away on a train."

"Lydia didn't want to marry Jacob Fitch anyhow," Gideon said, trying not to sound defensive. "She as much as said so — yesterday."

" 'As much as'?" Wyatt repeated skeptically. "And just because a woman says something, that's no guarantee she means it." He paused a moment to reflect on some private thought, shook his head. "No, sir, that is no guarantee."

"Got on the wrong side of your Sarah, did you?" Gideon teased.

"Sarah doesn't *have* a wrong side," Wyatt replied. "And don't try to change the subject. There's a warrant out for your arrest, Gideon, and it's federal."

Gideon considered his outlaw blood and wondered if it had gotten the best of him after all. "Soon as she's had time to calm down a little," he said, with a confidence he didn't really feel, "Lydia will put an end to

89

that. Like I told you, she didn't want to go through with that wedding."

Wyatt did not look convinced. "According to the bridegroom's report to the marshal down in Phoenix, she was kicking and clawing to get away from you."

"She was just mad because I whacked her one on the backside," Gideon said. "She'll be fine as soon as Lark lends her a dress so she can get out of that wedding gown. I think it was that, more than anything — traveling in a bride's dress and everybody looking at her — that got under Lydia's hide."

Although Wyatt was in profile, Gideon saw the twitch of amusement flicker across his mouth before sobriety set in again. "If Miss Lydia Fairmont presses charges," Wyatt said, concentrating on brewing that new pot of coffee, "you could go to prison. Kidnapping is a federal offense, in case they didn't teach you that in detective school."

"She won't," Gideon said, but he wasn't as sure as he sounded, and Wyatt probably knew that. Lydia *had* been plenty mad when he swatted her on the bustle to get her to stop wriggling so he could carry her out of that house before the hired muscle was on them.

"Even if she doesn't throw the book at

you," Wyatt replied, "Jacob Fitch probably will. If he hasn't already."

"He can't do that."

"Maybe back East, he couldn't. But this is Arizona, little brother. It's still the Wild West. The man was as good as married to Lydia, and that will carry some weight."

Gideon had no time to waste lolling around in one of Rowdy's cells. He had a job to start, at the Copper Crown Mine, bright and early the next morning, and Wyatt knew that as well as Rowdy did. What Gideon's brothers *didn't* know was that his taking up a shovel was a ruse to get inside, win the miners' trust, and do whatever he had to to subvert any plans they might be making to go out on strike.

The mine's owners stood to lose a fortune if that happened, and Gideon was being paid — *well* paid — to prevent that from happening.

With the coffee started, Wyatt left the stove, walked over to the chair facing Rowdy's desk, and sat himself down.

"If I were you," he said, "I'd have my feet on the floor when the marshal comes back. Rowdy's mad enough to horsewhip you from one end of Main Street to the other as it is — and his temper is shorter than usual, what with all the trouble coming out of the mining camp."

"I'm not afraid of Rowdy," Gideon replied, and that was true — so far as it went. He'd never had any *reason* to be afraid of his brother, and therefore had never tested the theory.

"That's the curse of the Yarbros," Wyatt said, mock-somber. "None of us has the sense to be scared when we ought to be."

"Once I explain —" Gideon began, and then stopped himself, because he didn't want to sound like he was apologizing for what he'd done. If he hadn't wooed the aunts away and then taken Lydia out of that house, she'd be Mrs. Jacob Fitch by now.

And this would be her wedding night.

The thought of Fitch or anybody else stripping Lydia to the skin and having his way with her made Gideon shudder. God knew, she'd grown into the kind of woman a man would want to handle, but another part of Gideon, a *big* part, still saw that lost, terrified little girl he'd known a decade before, whenever he looked at Lydia.

"I'm not sorry," he avowed, lest there be any misunderstanding on that score.

"No," Wyatt agreed easily, "I don't imagine you are."

Bristling, Gideon decided it would be best to change the subject. "How are Sarah and the kids?" he asked.

Wyatt gave one of those spare Yarbro grins, as if they were in short supply and thus hard to part with. They'd gotten that trait from their famous train-robbing father, Payton Yarbro. There were three other brothers, too — Ethan, Levi and Nick — but Gideon had never made their acquaintance, so he didn't know if they had the same way of hoarding a smile.

"Sarah's fine," Wyatt said. "The kids are fine. The *ranch* is fine, since you were probably going to ask about that next. And we're not through talking about that stunt you pulled down in Phoenix today, Gideon. If it hadn't been for Rowdy, that train would have been stopped and you'd have been dragged off and handcuffed. That's how powerful this Jacob Fitch yahoo is."

The crimson heat of indignation throbbed in Gideon's neck, and the backs of his ears burned. "Will you stop talking to me like I'm some kid about to be hauled off to the woodshed for a whipping? I'm twenty-six years old, I went to college, and I've worked for the Pinkerton Agency *and* Wells Fargo."

Wyatt gave a low whistle, causing the dog to perk up its ears and pricking at Gideon's already flaring temper. *"Twenty-six,"* he marveled. "You have attained a venerable age, little brother. At the rate you're going, though, you might not get much older."

Wyatt, Gideon figured irritably, was around forty-three. Evidently, he thought that made him a wise old man, with the right to preach and pontificate. "Stop calling me 'little brother,' " he bit out.

Wyatt merely grinned.

And right about then, Rowdy walked in, slammed the door shut behind him. "Get your feet off my desk," he growled, after raking his gaze from one end of Gideon's frame to the other.

Gideon took his time, but he did comply, and that nettled him further.

"Lark's feeding the women supper, and we'll put them up for the night," Rowdy said, heading for the coffeepot. He frowned when he realized the stuff was just beginning to perk — both Rowdy and Wyatt liked their coffee, Gideon remembered distractedly. Drank the stuff like tomorrow had been cancelled. "By morning," he added, "Fitch will probably be here to get them."

"What?" Gideon shot out of Rowdy's chair, which might have been exactly what his brother had *intended* to happen, though by the time that idea came to mind, it was already too late to spite him by staying put.

Wyatt and Rowdy exchanged grim glances.

"There's only one way out of this one," Rowdy mused, after a few moments.

"Afraid so," Wyatt agreed.

Gideon waited, too cussed to ask what that way might be, as badly as he wanted to know. He'd been a sort of lawman himself, until he'd taken a leave of absence from Wells Fargo to work for the mine owners, and yet he hadn't considered any of the ramifications of his actions, legal or otherwise.

All he'd wanted to do was get Lydia out of Jacob Fitch's reach.

"You'll have to marry the girl," Rowdy said slowly, like he was explaining something that should have been obvious even to an idiot. "Tonight."

"Of course, there are other choices," Wyatt allowed thoughtfully.

"Like what?" Gideon snapped.

"Well, you could go to prison for kidnapping," Wyatt said.

"Or hand Lydia over to Jacob Fitch when he gets here," Rowdy speculated.

"I'll be damned if I'll do either one of those things!"

"Then you'd better get yourself hitched to her," Wyatt said.

"If she'll have you," Rowdy added. "After today, that seems pretty unlikely to me."

Rowdy and Wyatt were, for all practical intents and purposes, the only blood relatives Gideon had left, not counting his many nieces and nephews. His father had perished in a shoot-out, years before, and his mother had died before he was a day old, so he had no memory at all of her — not even a tone of voice or a scent. He wouldn't have recognized Ethan, Levi or Nick if he'd met them on the street, and the sibling he'd truly loved — his half sister, Rose, born to his father and a madam who called herself Ruby — had been killed in an accident when she was just four years old, and he was six.

Gideon had witnessed that tragedy — seen Rose run into the street in front of Ruby's Saloon over in Flagstaff, pursuing a scampering kitten, seen her fall under the hooves of a team of horses and the wheels of the wagon they'd been pulling. He'd grieved so long and so hard for Rose that he'd sworn never to care as much about anyone or anything again.

And he never had.

Still, what his two older brothers thought mattered to him, with or without the sentiment plain folks and poets called *love*.

They'd been outlaws, Wyatt and Rowdy, desperate men with nothing but a hangman's noose in their future, and yet, somehow, they'd turned their lives around. Married good women, fathered children, earned fine reputations and accumulated property.

It was because of them, and the examples they'd set, both good and bad, that Gideon had gone to college when he would have preferred to stay in Stone Creek, playing at being a lawman. He'd worked hard at his studies, kept his nose clean even though the Yarbro blood ran as hot in his veins as it had in theirs.

For that reason, and a few others he couldn't have put a name to, he stayed in that office, on the night of the day he'd stolen another man's bride, and did his best to keep a civil tongue in his head while his brothers basically called him a fool.

"Fitch could take Lydia back to Phoenix and marry her? Even if she didn't want to go?" Gideon asked, the fight pretty much gone out of him now.

"He couldn't legally force her to leave with him if she didn't want to," Rowdy reasoned quietly. "But there's no telling if he'd give her a choice in the matter — any more than you did."

For the first time since he'd carried Lydia

out of that mansion, tossed her into the back of the wagon, and forced her onto a departing train, Gideon squared what he'd done with the excuses he'd made for doing it.

"Damn," he muttered.

"Yeah," Wyatt said. "Damn."

"You can still make this right, Gideon," Rowdy said. "I ought to throw you straight into one of those cells back there, keep you in custody until the marshal in Phoenix either gives me leave to release you or sends a deputy to fetch you back to give an accounting to some federal judge. But you're my lit— you're my brother, and I don't want to see you head down the wrong road, especially after you buckled down and got through college and worked a man's job after that. So I'm giving you a chance, Gideon. You go and talk to Lydia. If she's willing to throw in with the likes of you — and again, I've got my doubts about that, since she seems like the sensible sort — the two of you could be married tonight. That would prevent Fitch from taking her anywhere." He paused — for Rowdy, this was a lot of talking to do at one time — and huffed out a weary breath before finishing up. "There's one other thing, Gideon. After what happened today, and never mind that it was through no fault of her own, Lydia will be the subject of some gossip down in Phoenix, thanks to the scandal you started by stealing her that way."

Since he wasn't overly concerned with propriety himself, Gideon hadn't thought about that any more than he'd thought about the possibility of being charged with a crime. But he'd created a scandal even by the standards of a scrappy, boisterous cowtown like Phoenix — which made him wonder if Jacob Fitch still wanted Lydia for a wife, or if he just wanted to punish her for making him look the fool.

Gideon sat down in one of the other chairs, braced his elbows on his thighs, and put his face in his hands. He'd had the best of intentions, and look what had come of it. Still, what could he have done differently? He'd approached Fitch at the tailor's shop, after talking to Lydia, and asked the man to give her more time.

Fitch had refused adamantly, and without a second thought.

Gideon felt a hand rest briefly on his shoulder, knew it was Rowdy standing by his chair even before he heard his brother's voice.

"If it's any consolation, Gideon," Rowdy said gruffly, "I'd have done the same thing in your place, most likely."

"Me, too," Wyatt admitted.

Rowdy spoke again. "I'd tell you to forget this mining job you've signed on for — I don't know why you'd want it anyway, with your education and experience working for Pinkerton Agency and then Wells Fargo — and light out of here, pronto. But I think you did what you did because you have strong feelings for Lydia Fairmont, and that's something a man should never run away from."

"Amen," Wyatt said. "I'd be dead by now, if it hadn't been for Sarah."

Gideon raised his head, squared his shoulders. Whatever he felt for Lydia — a desire to protect her, mostly, he supposed — it wasn't like what Rowdy had with Lark, or what Wyatt had with Sarah.

"I'll talk to her," he said, after a long time, getting to his feet.

Rowdy glanced at the clock — it was a little after eight. "Don't wait too long," he advised. "Lydia's had herself quite a day, and she'll likely want to turn in soon."

Gideon nodded glumly, started for the door.

Wyatt was fixing to leave, too, while Rowdy banked the fire in the potbellied stove. Neither of them had drunk so much as a drop of that coffee they'd set such store by, Gideon noticed.

"Sarah will be watching the road for me," Wyatt said. Then he grinned. "If there's about to be a wedding, though, maybe I ought to stay around and see what happens *this* time."

Although nothing was funny to Gideon at that moment, most especially weddings, he still gave a raspy chuckle as he stepped out onto the sidewalk.

Rowdy whistled for the dog and caught up to him in a few strides. Wyatt had a horse waiting, so he swung into the saddle and reined toward home.

As much as he'd jabbered inside the jailhouse, Rowdy didn't say a thing as he and Gideon and the dog named Pardner headed for the big stone house at the end of a treelined lane behind the marshal's office. Lights glowed in all the windows, and the sight made Gideon yearn to belong in such a place, like Rowdy, to have a wife watching the road for him, the way Sarah watched for Wyatt. Maybe even a few kids and a dog of his own.

Instead, he was about to face a woman who had every reason to want him lynched.

The Yarbro house was big, though not

101

nearly as big as Lydia's home in Phoenix —
her *former* home, that is. The furnishings
were simple, the ornaments few and sturdy,
and little wonder with four high-spirited
children chasing each other through the
spacious, uncluttered rooms — and another
little Yarbro on the way, by the looks of
Lark's burgeoning middle.

When Lydia had first known Lark, as her
teacher, Lark's hair had been dark, but now
it was almost the color of honey. Even as an
eight-year-old, with problems aplenty of her
own, Lydia had sensed that "Miss Morgan"
was unhappy, and running away from something — or someone. Evidently, Lark had
been trying to disguise herself back then —
changing the color of her hair had been a
drastic measure, one no respectable woman
would undertake without good reason.

The dilemma, whatever it was, had apparently been resolved — Lydia wouldn't have
presumed to ask any personal questions in
order to find out, though she burned to
know — with Lark's marriage to Rowdy.
Lydia had never seen such serenity in a
woman's face and bearing as she did in Lark
Yarbro's, even with a houseful of unexpected
company.

Lark had immediately lent Lydia a dress,
as well as a nightgown for later, since Helga

102

had packed only her most prized personal mementos. Lark had served them all supper, keeping plates warm in the oven for Rowdy and Gideon, and graciously settled the aunts, both mute with exhaustion and residual excitement, in a guest room on the main floor.

Lydia and Helga would be sharing the double bed in a small chamber behind the kitchen — Helga, like the aunts, had retired immediately after supper, utterly worn out and still defiantly pleased with her part in the disasters of the day.

"You're so grown up, Lydia," Lark sighed, as they sat at the kitchen table, having after-supper cups of tea. "It's wonderful to see you again."

Lydia blushed. "The circumstances leave something to be desired, you must admit."

Lark smiled at that, shook her head. Lydia had told her the story of her interrupted wedding — she'd *had* to, arriving at the woman's door in a bridal gown the way she had. And what details she'd left out, Helga and the aunts had hurried to provide.

They seemed to think this was all some grandly romantic adventure.

Lydia, apparently the only one still in possession of her senses, knew it for the calamity it was.

"These Yarbro men," Lark said. "A woman never knows what to expect next."

"I certainly didn't expect to be abducted on my wedding day," Lydia said, but now that some of the panic had subsided, along with the shock, she'd admitted the truth, at least to herself. She was *glad* Gideon had kept her from marrying Jacob; she'd hoped all along that he would come for her, that was why she'd sent the letter in the first place.

It was purely selfish to be so relieved, given the bleak future she and the aunts and Helga would have to face, but she *was* relieved. If it hadn't been for Gideon, Jacob Fitch would be doing unspeakable things to her in his bed by now, with the blessing of God and man. Instead, she was sitting quietly at a kitchen table, in a lovely house at the end of a quiet country lane, sipping tea with her former teacher.

Except for her aunt Nell, Lydia had never admired another woman as much as she did Lark.

She was just about to excuse herself and retire when the screened door opened, and Rowdy came in, with a dog trailing behind him and Gideon following somewhat forlornly behind the dog.

Rowdy approached his wife's chair, bent

to kiss the top of her head. Lark glowed, smiling up at him.

"I've kept your supper warm," she told him.

"I'll eat later," Rowdy answered, with a twinkle in his eyes. "Right now, you and me and Pardner are going to make ourselves scarce for a little while."

Lydia felt a jolt of something very complicated as her gaze skirted Lark and Rowdy and connected with Gideon's face. What she felt was partly alarm, partly annoyance, and mostly a complete mystery to her.

Gideon, meanwhile, hovered just over the threshold, as if struck dumb, long after Lark and Rowdy had left the kitchen.

"I didn't know what else to do," he finally said. "But if you want to go back to Jacob Fitch — if that's really what you want — I'll take you to him myself."

It was too late to go back now, though Gideon probably didn't realize that. Even if Jacob was willing to take the chance that Lydia hadn't been "compromised," as he would undoubtedly have put it, his mother *wouldn't* be. The look Lydia had seen on the woman's face before leaving the house with Gideon was burned into her memory — Malverna Fitch was not the sort to forgive such a disgrace.

Furthermore, without Mr. Fitch to guarantee payment of the family's many debts, the creditors would close in, possibly as soon as tomorrow morning, since word of the aborted wedding had surely spread from one end of Phoenix to the other within a matter of minutes, like the wildfires that plagued the desert.

"I haven't the first idea what I'm going to do, Gideon Yarbro," Lydia said presently, with what sternness she could muster. "But I most certainly *won't* be returning to Phoenix."

Gideon, standing so still for so long, finally moved. He crossed to Lydia, crouched beside her chair, the way he'd done in the parlor at home the day before, took her hand, and looked up into her face. "I'm not a rich man," he told her solemnly, "but I work hard, and I've got a little money put by. I can look after you, Lydia, and your aunts, too. Even Helga, if she doesn't mind earning her keep."

Lydia stared at him, dumbfounded — again. She could not think of a single other person who had Gideon's capacity for surprising her. "Are you proposing to me?" she asked bluntly, because she was simply too spent to arrange her words in any other way.

"I guess I *am* proposing," Gideon said, after swallowing visibly. "Rowdy said it was the least I could do, after today."

If Lydia hadn't wanted so badly to cry, she would have laughed. No wonder Rowdy had squired Lark out of the kitchen so quickly, leaving the two of them alone. He'd probably *ordered* Gideon to make things right. "That's why you're offering for me, Gideon? Because your *brother* thinks you ought to?"

Gideon made an obvious attempt to smile, and failed utterly. His expression was one of resignation, not ardor. "He's right, Lydia," he said. "It's the least I can do."

"The least you can do," Lydia echoed. She found herself possessed of an almost incomprehensible urge to touch his face, tell him everything would be all right. At the same time, if she'd had the strength to slap Gideon Yarbro silly, she probably would have done it.

"I'm getting this all wrong," Gideon said, and this time he did smile, though sadly. "It won't be a real marriage, Lydia. I won't expect you to share my bed, that is. You'll have a home, and so will the aunts, and Fitch won't be able to cause you any trouble because you'll be my wife. That's not such a bad bargain, is it?"

107

It was, in Lydia's view, a *terrible* bargain, especially the part about not sharing a bed. Gideon had awakened a formidable hunger in her when he'd kissed her, and now he expected to *marry* her and still leave that hunger unexplored, unsatisfied?

On the other hand, he made a good case.

The aunts would be safe, with food to eat and a roof over their heads, and they obviously trusted Gideon or they wouldn't have left the house with him, let alone bought new hats and dresses and traveled all the way to Stone Creek onboard a train at his behest.

As for herself, once she'd exchanged vows with Gideon, she would be part of the Yarbro clan. Lonely all her life, she would have sisters, Lark and Sarah, and a brother, as well, in Rowdy. She would have nieces and nephews and, in time, perhaps even friends, people who liked her for herself and not because she was a Fairmont.

"But what about you, Gideon?" Lydia asked softly, after mulling over all these things. "What could you possibly gain from such an arrangement?" A dreadful thought struck her then. "Suppose you meet another woman someday, and fall in love with her and —"

And I won't be able to bear it if you do.

A muscle in Gideon's strong, square jaw bunched, then relaxed again. "I'll never fall in love with another woman, Lydia," he said. "I can promise you that."

"How can you, Gideon?" Lydia asked. "How can you promise such a thing?"

Gideon rose to his full height then, but he still held her hand. "A long time ago," he answered, looking directly, unflinchingly, into her eyes, "I made up my mind never to love anybody. And so far, I've stood by that. That's not likely to change."

Looking back at him, Lydia knew Gideon meant what he said.

And even as she made a firm decision of her own — she *would* accept his proposal, if only to protect herself, the aunts and Helga from the wrath of Jacob Fitch — she felt her heart crumble into dry little fragments, like a very old love letter found in the bottom of a dusty box and handled too roughly.

CHAPTER FIVE

Once the decision was made, Rowdy went to fetch the preacher, and the aunts and Helga were awakened to stand witness to the ceremony in their nightgowns, sleeping caps and wrappers.

Lydia put on her aunt Nell's wedding gown, for the second time in one day, and Gideon allowed Lark to drape him in Rowdy's best Sunday coat and knot a string tie at his throat.

It might as well have been a noose, considering his expression, Lydia thought, finding herself in a strange state of happy despair.

"We'll have to hold a reception as soon as we can," Lark fretted happily. "Sarah and Maddie will never forgive us if we don't."

Lydia knew that Sarah was Wyatt's wife, though she had yet to meet her second prospective sister-in-law, and vaguely recalled Maddie as Mrs. Sam O'Ballivan. A prosperous rancher and a former Arizona

Ranger, Mr. O'Ballivan had been Stone Creek's leading citizen when Lydia had lived there as a child.

"There'll be no fuss," Gideon said to his sister-in-law, sternly alarmed at the prospect of a party to celebrate the marriage. "I mean it, Lark."

Lark smiled. "I'm sure you do, Gideon, dear," she replied lightly. "But this time, you're not going to get your way. *Fuss* isn't the word for what's going to happen when this town finds out you've come home and gotten married, all in the same day and without a howdy-do to anybody."

"I haven't had *time* for a howdy-do," Gideon snapped. "And I've got to be at the mine, ready to work, at seven o'clock sharp tomorrow morning. When I'm through there — after a little matter of, oh, *ten or twelve hours* — I'll be turning the town upside-down looking for a place to put all these women —"

A place to put all these women.

The phrase echoed in Lydia's mind, brought a sting of humiliation to her cheeks. Gideon made it sound as though she and the aunts and Helga were a band of unwanted horses in need of stabling.

If she'd had anywhere else to turn, any honorable way to earn a living, she would have told her clearly reluctant bridegroom to go and — well — do something else beside marry her.

The minister arrived, a plump, middle-aged man, looking sleepy and surprised, the fringe of hair around his bald pate still shining with the water he'd used to slick it down in his haste to answer Rowdy's summons.

A license had been hastily prepared, and Gideon signed it with a bold, harsh flourish. Lydia's own hand trembled as she penned her much less spectacular signature beneath his.

Probably anxious to get the whole thing over with, so he could return to his bed, the man of God took up his post with his back to the fireplace, and impatiently pointed to where the groom ought to stand. Lydia stood frozen for so long that Helga finally put her hands on her shoulders from behind and pushed her to Gideon's side.

For an event of such momentous significance — neither Lydia's life nor Gideon's would ever be the same, after all — the ceremony went very quickly. In fact, Lydia noted, stealing glances at the mantel clock behind the minister's right shoulder, the whole thing was finished in under ten minutes.

Lydia responded when she was supposed

112

to — with prompting from Helga, who kept nudging her in the ribs. Gideon, she saw out of the corner of her eye, had to unclamp his jaw before every utterance he made.

Finally, the clergyman, after a nervous glance at Rowdy, who was standing at Gideon's right side, announced loudly, "I now pronounce you man and wife. Mr. Yarbro, you may kiss your bride."

Lydia, concentrating on getting through the wedding without fainting or bursting into tears, had not thought about the traditional kiss. She'd barely had a moment to steel herself for it when Gideon turned her to face him and gave her a brief, almost brotherly, peck on the mouth.

"Well, then," the minister said, all but dusting his hands together. "That's done."

The aunts giggled like little girls and clapped their hands together, and Helga muttered, "Thank heaven!"

Lark gave Gideon a scathing look as he left Lydia's side, without so much as a backward glance, to pay the minister for his services and escort him to the door. Then she hugged Lydia, whispering close to her ear, "Everything will be all right — I promise."

Rowdy, clearly as annoyed with Gideon as Lark was, smiled and kissed Lydia on the forehead, welcoming her to the Yarbro family.

His words brought tears to her eyes and, seeing them, Rowdy wrapped his strong arms around her and drew her close against his chest for a long moment. "You've got brothers now," he told her. "Wyatt and me. And we'll look after you, even if that young fool yonder doesn't."

Lydia let her forehead rest against Rowdy's shoulder. She nodded, too overcome to say thank-you.

The celebration, alas, was as short as the ceremony.

The aunts each kissed Lydia on the cheek, and then turned to go back to their room. Helga actually shook her hand, as though they'd completed some business arrangement, and returned to the nook behind the kitchen, yawning as she went.

Rowdy and Lark each skewered Gideon with a look and then vanished, like the others. Rowdy's supper, evidently, had been delayed long enough.

And so Lydia found herself alone in the parlor with Gideon.

Her husband.

What was she supposed to do now?

Gideon looked as uncertain as she felt.

"I guess that wasn't the wedding you

probably dreamed about, growing up," he said, smiling for the first time since they'd all assembled in the Yarbros' front room a mere fifteen minutes before.

He was wrong about that, at least in part, though Lydia would never have told him so. She *had* dreamed of marrying Gideon many, many times, as a child, as a young girl, as a woman. But in her fancies, he'd always been eager to make her his bride, and there had been church bells, and flowers, and pews full of well-wishers. And a romantic honeymoon afterward.

Speechless, Lydia simply shook her head.

Gideon shoved a hand through his hair, glanced toward the stairs. "I know I said I wouldn't make you share my bed," he began, "but —"

Lydia found her voice. She even came up with a shaky little smile, then finished the sentence for him. "But they'll expect us to sleep in the same room, since it's our wedding night."

Gideon nodded. He looked so glum, so tired, that Lydia's foolish heart went out to him.

She walked over to him, took his hand. "It's all right, Gideon," she teased in a mischievous whisper, once again taken over by a bolder, stronger version of herself. "I

115

promise I won't compromise your virtue."

He laughed, and the sound heartened Lydia. "Come along, then, Mrs. Yarbro," he said, squeezing her fingers lightly. "Let's turn in for the night, like the respectable married couple we are."

Lydia's heart sprouted wings and flew up into her throat, fairly choking her, but she allowed Gideon to lead her up the stairs, in that ancient, thrice-worn wedding dress.

Putting a finger to his lips as they passed the rooms where his nieces and nephews were sleeping, he led her into a chamber at the end of the hall, under the slant of the roof. A beautiful china lamp glowed softly on the nightstand, and the window was open to the night breeze.

Lydia forced her gaze to the bed, drew in her breath when she saw how narrow it was, and again when Gideon immediately began shedding his clothes. The coat went first, then the tie, then the shirt.

"You're not sleeping in that gown, are you?" he asked, down to his trousers and boots by then. He sat down on the edge of the mattress, and Lydia knew he was watching her, but the angle of the lamp left his face in shadow, so she couldn't make out his expression.

She did see the scar on his shoulder,

116

though. She wondered what had happened to him, but couldn't bring herself to ask.

Almost saucy before they ascended the staircase, Lydia was once again her normal shy and reticent self. "Lark lent me a nightdress," she heard herself say, "but it's in Helga's room, where I was supposed to sleep tonight."

Gideon didn't speak. His face was still unreadable, but she saw his throat move as he swallowed.

"I'll go and fetch it," Lydia said.

Gideon stood, crossed to her, turned her around and started undoing the many buttons at the back of her dress. "No need," he said, his voice strange and hoarse. "You can wear one of my shirts."

Lydia supposed that was better than sleeping in her drawers and camisole and corset, all of which were uncomfortable, but in a way it seemed even more daring than lying down next to Gideon with nothing at all on. She yearned for one of her own nightgowns, with their long, full sleeves, high necklines, and ruffled hems brushing the floor, but they had all been left behind in Phoenix.

If she went downstairs to claim the one Lark had offered, she would have to face Helga and, anyway, she didn't think she had enough starch left in her knees to make it that far.

"All right," she said.

Gideon went to the large mahogany wardrobe on the far wall, took out a shirt. Brought it to her.

"You keep clothing here?" she asked, knowing the question was inane but unable to bear the silence. Accepting the garment, she averted her eyes.

"I've been known to visit occasionally," Gideon answered, oddly affable after the way he'd acted downstairs, before, during and after their wedding ceremony. "Lark and Rowdy set this room aside for me when they built the place."

With that, he turned his back, allowing Lydia time to step out of the gown she'd been clutching to her, shed her corset and underthings, and scramble into the shirt. The tails reached past her knees, and the cotton fabric smelled pleasantly of Gideon — soap, aftershave and, oddly, since she hadn't seen him on or near a horse, saddle leather.

"W-what will you sleep in?" she asked. She still hadn't moved from the center of the room, and Aunt Nell's cherished gown lay in a pool at her feet. Hastily, Lydia stepped out of the billow of yellowing lace and silk and gathered it up, clutched it to her.

Gideon laughed, low and quiet, surely mindful, as Lydia was, of the children slumbering in nearby rooms. "Normally, Mrs. Yarbro," he replied, still keeping his back to her, his arms folded, "I don't sleep in anything at all. Can I turn around now?"

Lydia bit her lower lip, nodded, realized that he couldn't possibly have seen that gesture, and said, "If you must."

He approached the bed, threw back the lovely faded quilt and top sheet beneath. "Which side do you want?" he asked, before yawning expansively.

Lydia managed to move far enough to lay the folded wedding dress down carefully on top of an old steamer trunk in one corner of the room. From what she could see of that bed, it was barely big enough for Gideon, let alone the both of them. And he expected her to choose a *side?*

"Maybe I should sleep on the floor," Lydia said.

"You're not sleeping on the floor," Gideon countered immediately, and with a touch of impatience. A pause followed. "And neither am I."

Lydia realized she had to make a decision and act upon it. "You sleep next to the wall, then, and I'll have the outside."

Gideon, still wearing his trousers and nothing else, executed a sweeping bow, and when he straightened, the lamplight splashed across his face and Lydia saw that he was grinning. "A wise choice, Mrs. Yarbro," he said. "That way, if I decide to ravish you in the middle of the night, you have at least a fighting chance to escape."

"I wish you'd stop calling me 'Mrs. Yarbro,'" Lydia said, embarrassed because Gideon had guessed *exactly* why she'd chosen to sleep on the outside. Thank heaven he couldn't suspect how strenuously another part of her had argued for the *inside*. "It sounds so — formal."

"Formal or not, you are legally my wife. That makes you Mrs. Yarbro." Gideon unfastened the top button of his trousers as he spoke, causing Lydia to turn around again, this time with a whirling motion. And making Gideon *laugh* again, a throaty rumble that struck a corresponding note deep inside her. "Some husbands would wonder if they'd married a virgin or not. I'd say there's no doubt about that where you're concerned."

Lydia heard the creak of bedsprings and knew Gideon had finally reclined, leaving her with nothing else to do but climb in beside him or curl up on the hooked rug

120

like a dog settling down for the night.

When she could make herself meet Gideon's gaze, she found that his face was in shadow once more — except for the flash of his white teeth. He was grinning again, apparently amused by her discomfiture.

"For God's sake, Lydia," he said, "get into bed before I change my mind, break my word, and have you right and proper."

"That," Lydia responded pettishly, "is hardly reassuring." But she drew nearer, reached for the ornate key that would turn the wick and extinguish the china lamp.

"Leave that," Gideon said gruffly.

Although she had neatly skipped over the word *obey* in the vows she and Gideon had so recently exchanged, Lydia found herself doing as she was told, leaving the lamp to spill light over them both, squeezing into bed next to him.

The warmth and steely hardness of Gideon's body were hard to ignore, pressed against her like that, but Lydia was determined to notice as little about her husband's anatomy as she could. She shifted onto her back, thinking it was a good thing neither of them were any bigger than they were.

She'd almost convinced herself that she could close her eyes and sleep lying next to a naked man, when Gideon stretched across

121

her, his arm brushing her suddenly sensitive nipples as he reached to turn the lamp key.

Lydia felt like a patch of tinder-dry sagebrush in the path of a wildfire.

Gideon was almost on top of her, and if he so much as kissed her or stroked her hair, she knew she would ignite and be consumed. The wanton hussy, barely under control even now, would surely assert herself.

But Gideon did not kiss her.

After passing over her again, having plunged the room into darkness by turning the lamp, he lay down, and within a few moments, Lydia knew by his breathing that he'd gone to sleep.

She felt both relief and disappointment — she'd expected him to at least *try* to seduce her. After all, agreement or no agreement, it was their *wedding night,* and given the incendiary nature of the kiss they'd shared the day before — had it really been only yesterday? — she'd thought he might succumb to temptation.

Not that she'd *tried* to tempt him in any way, of course.

She'd been the very soul of modesty.

Maybe she should have, though, she reflected fitfully, feeling hot and achy and oddly moist in the private place between her legs. As sheltered as she'd been, she knew that men were by nature lusty creatures and could not be expected to control their impulses in certain situations — the aunts had warned her about this on numerous occasions, usually after they'd had too much sherry.

Lydia knew Gideon wanted her — they were in such close proximity in that narrow bed that no amount of naïveté would have allowed her to delude herself in the matter — but it seemed he was *quite* able to control his masculine appetites, because he was most certainly asleep.

A deep and sudden stab of loneliness struck Lydia then, and that was indeed strange, given that Gideon was lying not just beside her but *against* her.

Tears stung her eyes; she blinked them back.

Although she'd dreaded having relations with Jacob Fitch, she imagined the worst would have been over by now if she'd gone through with the *first* wedding of the day. Having sated himself, Mr. Fitch would probably have lapsed into near-unconsciousness long since, leaving Lydia free to creep out of bed, wash herself thoroughly, and find a private place to cry.

As much as she abhorred the idea of

submitting her body to Mr. Fitch night after night, she knew she would have gotten used to it eventually, learned to endure what happened in the marriage bed by thinking of other things until it was over. Millions of women did just that, didn't they? According to Helga — who had been unhappily married at one time, before her husband had had the good grace to run off with a dance-hall girl, never to be seen again — the first experience was painful, the next few merely uncomfortable. After that, though, it was something one simply waited out, and invariably quick to end.

Yes, it was true that Mr. Fitch had made her feel revulsion and not much else, and Gideon inspired desire instead. But at least if she'd stayed and married Mr. Fitch, she and the aunts and Helga would still have their home and their own things around them — the books in the library, the garden full of hardy flowers they'd worked so hard to coax from the earth, the dour but blessedly familiar portraits dominating virtually every wall.

What would happen to the flowers now, with no one to carry water to them? The thought of them waiting in vain and then wilting deepened Lydia's sorrow, made it nearly unbearable.

Now, suddenly, she was a guest in another woman's house, sleeping in a man's shirt because she didn't own a nightgown and didn't want to traipse through dark rooms to recover the one she'd borrowed. She had a husband who did not want to be married to her.

The tears came again, and this time, Lydia couldn't hold them back.

Some inner sense must have alerted Gideon; he shifted behind her, rested his arm across her waist, though not heavily.

Lydia bit her lip to keep from sobbing aloud.

She felt the backs of Gideon's fingers brush her wet cheek.

He drew her closer, if that was possible, so they lay tucked together like spoons in a drawer, and that comforted her a little. At the same time, it made her want him more.

"Don't be afraid, Lydia," Gideon murmured. "Don't be afraid."

"I'm n-not," Lydia lied.

Gideon drew her around to face him, wrapped her in a loose embrace. He was hard *everywhere*, his chest, his shoulders, his arms and thighs — and, of course, *there*.

"We'll find a house of our own tomorrow," he said. "Then you can have a room all to yourself."

A room to herself.

That was what he thought she wanted.

And she didn't know how to tell him how wrong he was, because she wasn't at all sure what she *did* want, beyond release from the physical need he'd aroused in her.

What such a release would be like she couldn't say precisely, but she knew instinctively that it was part of the reason Lark glowed the way she did, especially when Rowdy was around.

Lydia cried all the harder.

Gideon sighed. He'd told her he had to work in the morning; he was growing impatient because she was keeping him awake. "What is it?" he asked, very quietly.

She hadn't meant to say what she did next, it simply came out. "The way Lark is —"

"Pregnant?" Gideon prompted, with a tinge of amusement in his voice.

In for a penny, Lydia thought, in for a pound. The darkness gave her courage — or just made her reckless. "The way she is with Rowdy —"

"Ah," Gideon said. "That."

"That?"

"If I show you what makes Lark shine like she swallowed every streetlight in town, will you go to sleep?"

A thrill of sweet terror went through Lydia. "That depends," she said, suddenly breathless.

Gideon rested his hand on her lower belly, began easing the shirt upward, baring her thighs and then more of her, and still more. With a low, sleepy groan, he nibbled at her earlobe, sending fire racing under every inch of her skin, making her quiver.

"Depends on what?" he asked lazily.

"I'm — I'm not sure," Lydia admitted.

He chuckled at that. "I'm going to hate myself for this," he said.

Lydia squirmed as the unnamed need intensified with every featherlight pass of his fingers over her bare skin. Gave a little gasp when Gideon suddenly parted the nest of curls between her legs and began to caress her in earnest, though very slowly.

"Oh," she whimpered, stunned by the delicious sensations launching themselves from that tiny nubbin of flesh to race skyward like Chinese rockets. *"Oh."*

"Umm-hmm," Gideon affirmed, his fingers making circles, going around and around. Moist before, Lydia was wet now, and the slickness of her skin increased the rising, panicked pleasure with every movement of his hand, however slight.

"Ooooh," Lydia gasped.

"Shh," Gideon said, teasing her now, plucking at her, drawing a strange, silent music from the very core of her body, leading her, note by note, toward some shattering crescendo.

Lydia's hips began to move, with no prompting from her mind, causing the bedsprings to squeak slightly.

Gideon chuckled into her hair and worked her harder, and yet with a tenderness that opened new places inside Lydia, revealed a world of fierce desire she'd never dreamed was there. "Easy," he mumbled. "You don't want to get there too soon."

Lydia had no idea where "there" was — all she knew was that she wanted more of what Gideon was doing to her — much more. That she would surely die if he stopped caressing her.

"Oh — Gideon —" she pleaded "— *Gideon* —"

He slowed his fingers, nibbled at her neck and the edges of her ear, sighed again.

"Faster — *oh* — Gideon, *faster* —"

"Shh," he said again.

She tried to part her legs farther, but there was no way to do that, in such a confined space, and Gideon seemed to find the dilemma amusing, because another hoarse chuckle escaped him. Finally, he left off

128

stroking her toward madness to run his hand along the quivering flesh of her thigh to her knee. He grasped it, though gently, and lifted and, again by instinct alone, Lydia caught her foot behind Gideon's calf.

When he went back to plying her with his fingers, she couldn't keep quiet anymore. She turned her face into the pillow, to muffle the ragged, involuntary cries of ecstatic desperation.

Gideon continued to pleasure her with his hand, groaned again as he brushed his lips across her nape.

Lydia was feverish by then, mad with need — and with curiosity. "What is — oh, dear God — what is happening to me — ?"

"You're about to find out," Gideon drawled, increasing the pace.

Lydia's hips wanted to fly now, but Gideon had somehow pinned her against him, making it impossible to move. When a low, steady moan poured from her, one even the pillow couldn't stifle, he shifted her to lie flat beside him and covered her mouth with his.

When his tongue passed her lips, all of Creation splintered into a blinding light, full of color and fire.

Lydia bucked wildly under Gideon's hand, and he contained her cries by deepening the kiss. And even as she came apart in his arms, he didn't stop making those slow, fiery circles with his fingers.

That first release was so calamitous in scale that it nearly consumed Lydia and yet, as she descended from the heights, Gideon continued his leisurely pleasuring. Every few seconds, she'd catch on another, softer peak, and then soar helplessly, and then fall again.

When he'd coaxed her body through the last spasm of surrender, never letting the devastating kiss end, he somehow knew she was finished, and slid his hand to her lower belly, let it rest there.

"That," he said, "is why Lark lights up when she's around Rowdy."

Lydia's face burned in the darkness. It was a long time before she could breathe well enough to answer. "But there's more — isn't there?"

"Yes," Gideon answered. "There's more. But that isn't going to happen — not tonight — so go to sleep."

"But what — what about you?"

"I'll survive," Gideon ground out in response. "I think."

"Gideon?"

"What?"

"It was — wonderful. I never — I never

guessed —"

"Neither did I," Gideon said. "Neither did I."

CHAPTER SIX

It was a dreary relief to Gideon when the first pinkish-gold light of dawn finally crawled over the eastern hills to seep into the darkness and slowly diffuse it. Ahead of him lay a ten-hour shift spent sweating and straining in the belly of the earth, loading copper ore into carts on iron rails, keeping his eyes and ears open the whole time. By comparison to the night just past, it would be easy.

After he'd introduced Lydia to that most innocent of pleasures, she'd sunk into a blissful sleep, just the whisper of a contented little smile resting on her mouth. *He,* on the other hand, still ached with the need of her.

Resigned, he eased out of bed without waking Lydia — no small feat, given that he had to span her to do it, using complicated motions of his elbows and knees — pulled plain trousers and a shirt from the wardrobe where he kept a minimal supply of clothing for visits to Stone Creek, dressed himself.

Down the hall, in the fancy bathing room, he splashed his face a few times at the sink, scrubbed his teeth with baking soda and a brush, ran his fingers through his rumpled hair. There was no time for a bath — he could have used a very cold one — nor did he take time to shave. He needed to look like a miner, not a dandy, and he'd lingered too long in his bed, wanting Lydia and silently reciting all the reasons why he shouldn't take her.

It was crazy, but in the daylight he thought of her as a child — the ailing little girl whose father had frozen to death in a buggy, on a lonely winter-buried road. Lydia had certainly been all woman the previous night, though, responding to his every touch with soft moans, small, rippling quivers he felt through the silken warmth of her flesh. That first lusty climax that would have roused the household if he hadn't covered her mouth with his, but there hadn't been much he could do about the complaining bed-springs.

Carrying his boots in one hand, Gideon descended the back stairway, found Rowdy in the gaslit kitchen, with coffee brewing on the stove.

"Mornin'," Rowdy said, and when he

turned to nod at Gideon, there was a little smirk quirking the corner of his mouth and his blue eyes were dancing.

So his brother had heard enough to guess that something had happened, Gideon concluded glumly, despite his efforts to keep Lydia quiet. Lark probably had, too — and that possibility added significantly to his embarrassment.

"Mornin'," Gideon responded, without smiling.

Rowdy poured a second mug of coffee, set it on the table in front of Gideon when he sat down to pull on his boots. "Lark fixed you a lunch," Rowdy said. "It's over there on the sideboard, in that lard bucket." With a glance at the clock, ticking loudly on a shelf, he added, "Reckon you didn't leave yourself enough time for breakfast, though."

"I'll be all right," Gideon said, wondering if he would. He supposed it was a good thing that the house was full of people, because if it hadn't been, he'd probably have said to hell with his lucrative assignment at the Copper Crown, gone back up those stairs and shown Lydia Fairmont Yarbro every trick he knew, and a few he'd only heard about.

"You want to tell me what you're really up to?" Rowdy asked easily, after pulling

134

back a chair of his own and sitting down. Pardner came over and rested his muzzle on Rowdy's thigh, for an ear-ruffling.

For a moment, the question didn't fully register with Gideon, given the distractions going through his mind. He shook off the mental seduction of his nubile wife, reminded himself that he couldn't afford to let his thoughts wander, not if he wanted to live into old age.

He looked at Rowdy over the rim of his coffee mug, took a sip, savored it and swallowed before replying — and even then, he hedged. "Up to?" he echoed, raising one eyebrow in feigned puzzlement.

Rowdy thrust out an irritated sigh. "Spare me the theatrics, Gideon. You were a Pinkerton agent before you signed on with Wells Fargo, and before that, you plied your trade with one of the biggest railroad companies in the country. Now, suddenly, you've decided you want to be a miner instead. Half the pay, if that, and ten times the work. So I'll ask you again — what are you up to?"

Gideon wished he could tell Rowdy the truth — there wasn't a man on earth he trusted more — but he'd given his word to the mine owners when he'd accepted the job and a sizable initial payment for his services, and that was that.

So he managed a shrug as he stood to leave, and he lied. An irony, he knew, given the lengths he'd go to keep his promise to his new employers. "Maybe I just want to know I can do a day's labor," he said, finding the lard tin, picking it up by the handle, and silently blessing Lark for her generous foresight. "Like any other man."

"And maybe you're full of shit," Rowdy countered, and though he was grinning a little, his eyes had turned solemn and a mite too watchful for Gideon's comfort. Most men were easy enough to fool — but Rowdy wasn't most men, and neither was Wyatt. "There's been a lot of rumbling in the camps about a strike," he went on, after a long pause. "Especially since the cartel keeps cutting wages and increasing hours — they're down to one shift these days, but they expect the output of three. Does your new job have anything to do with that, *Agent Yarbro?*"

Gideon did not dare meet Rowdy's gaze; his brother had struck way too close to the bone, and he'd know it for sure if he got so much as a glimpse of Gideon's face. "No," he said, heading for the door. The mine was less than a mile outside of town — he'd walk there instead of borrowing a horse.

It was a rare thing for a miner to own a horse.

"Gideon?"

Something in Rowdy's tone stopped him on the threshold, with the cool of a northern Arizona dawn easing him a little. Lying next to Lydia all night had left his flesh feeling as though it had been seared raw.

"Watch yourself," Rowdy told him, after a brief silence. "Folks around Stone Creek know you've been to college and worn white shirts and ties to work. They're going to wonder why you'd suddenly give all that up to break your back down in some hole in the ground, with a shovel and a pickax."

Gideon closed his eyes for a moment. Lying was a way of life for him, vital in his profession, but this was Rowdy, and he looked up to him, same as he looked up to Wyatt. So the story he'd rehearsed so many times snagged in his throat, tearing like rusty wire when he forced it out. "There was a — problem," he said, without turning around. "On the job, I mean." *Careful,* he thought. *Parcel it out in small doses.* "Wells Fargo showed me the road and put out the word that I wasn't to be trusted, so you might say I'm running a little short on employment opportunities these days."

Rowdy didn't reply to that — maybe he

believed the yarn, maybe he was just sifting and weighing and measuring, the way he did most everything — and Gideon used that delay to make his escape.

Rowdy was a lawman, Gideon reminded himself, as he strode through still-quiet streets in the direction of the mine, and he might go so far as to wire Wells Fargo to inquire about the "problem" that had allegedly caused his younger brother's dismissal.

What he was told would depend on who was on the receiving end of the telegram. Gideon hadn't been fired from Wells Fargo, nor had he resigned — he was on voluntary leave — and he'd asked his friend, Christian Hardy, the company's head telegrapher, to field any inquiries concerning his departure from the ranks and say only what he'd been told to say. Everything would be fine if Hardy was the one Rowdy got hold of, but if it was one of the men who worked under him, the whole ruse might go up in smoke in short order.

Rowdy wasn't one to spread tales; insofar as keeping the secret went, there was no danger in his finding out the truth. But he'd worry the subject like an old hound dog worries a soup bone, and if Gideon admitted his real reason for being in Stone Creek, Rowdy would be furious and raise every kind of hell.

Clearly, Rowdy's sympathies lay with the miners, not the rich cigar-smoking men who held the claim to one of the biggest copper deposits ever discovered west of the Mississippi.

Striding through the first faint glimmers of morning, the shadows of oak and cotton-wood leaves flickering in his path as he passed through a copse of trees along the western bank of the creek for which the town was named, Gideon told himself what he always did when he started a new assignment: *Nothing is too small to be important, so listen and watch. And don't let your mind go woolgathering, because that'll be when they get you. Pay attention, or next thing you know, you'll be laid out on the undertaker's table with pennies on your eyes.*

The speech usually worked.

That day, though, with every cell in his body aching for the release only Lydia could give him, he knew he'd have to be twice as vigilant as ever before.

"It's bigger than I remember," Lydia said, sitting in the buggy beside Lark, who was at the reins, and gazing up the house she'd last visited as a frightened little girl. With Helga around to keep an eye on the aunts and the Yarbro children, Lark had suggested a ride and hitched up the horse herself.

Now, she smiled, nodded. "Everyone still calls it the Porter house," she answered, tucking a lock of pale honey hair behind her right ear when the breeze set it dancing on her cheek. "Even though I bought it from Hon Sing and Mai Lei when they decided to go back to China. Folks are a little superstitious, and I guess they figure poor murdered Mr. Porter might rise up out of the cellar some dark night and scare them right into the Beyond."

Lydia had left for Phoenix with her aunt Nell by the time Mr. Porter's remains had been discovered, and she'd been too young to follow the no-doubt sensational story in the newspapers, but she recalled Hon Sing and Mai Lei well enough. The doctor and his wife, along with Lark, had tended to her when she came down with pneumonia. Without Hon Sing and the strange collection of thin, gleaming needles he'd pierced her with, she would surely have perished.

That morning, after Lydia, waking alone in her marriage bed, had finally worked up the courage to put on the calico dress the Yarbros' eight-year-old daughter, Julia, had brought to the door of Gideon's room, and march herself downstairs to breakfast, Lark

140

had related most of the tale. Since the children had already eaten, and raced outside to play, and the aunts were still sleeping, only Helga had been privy to the exchange.

Lydia wondered about a great many things, sitting there in that buggy with her former teacher, not the least of which was why Lark would buy the Porter house and then leave it standing empty. If propriety had allowed, she would have asked straight-out how the Yarbros could afford it, on top of the huge place they lived in, and all this on a town marshal's salary. But propriety did *not* allow, so Lydia held her tongue, and waited for Lark to say why she'd brought her here.

Memories clouded Lark's eyes for a moment as she regarded the former boarding-house where she'd lived when she taught at Stone Creek's one-room schoolhouse. Then, with a sigh and a resolute smile, she set the brake lever, wrapped the reins around it and climbed carefully down.

"It's fully furnished, and Sarah and Maddie will help us with the cleaning," she said, putting both hands to the small of her back and stretching, making her baby-swollen midriff jut forward for a moment.

Lydia just sat there on the buggy seat, still

confused.

"You and Gideon will need a place to live," Lark pointed out, smiling. "There's room for Helga and the aunts, too. Don't you want to go inside and have a look around?"

"We'll find a house of our own tomorrow," Lydia heard Gideon saying, the night before. *"Then you can have a room all to yourself."*

Lydia hesitated, biting her lower lip. At least at Rowdy and Lark's, she got to share Gideon's bed, and could hope he would — well, *touch* her again, the way he had the night before. Here, she would be sleeping alone.

"I know it isn't as grand as the house in Phoenix," Lark said gently, watching her from the wooden sidewalk, one hand resting on the gate latch, her brow creased with concern.

Lydia blushed and hastened to get down out of the buggy to stand facing Lark. "It isn't that," she rushed to say. "It's — it's just that you've already been so generous, and now —"

"You're part of our family, Lydia," Lark said, with affection shining in her eyes, "and this house — well — it's Rowdy's and my wedding gift to you and Gideon."

Lydia's mouth nearly dropped open; she caught it just in time. "It's too much," she protested.

Lark laughed and opened the gate. "Frankly," she answered, starting up the walk, "I'll be glad to have this place off my hands. I only bought it because Hon Sing and Mai Lei were so eager to go home."

The yard looked well kept, and there were flowers blooming in beds on either side of the wide porch steps. A huge lilac bush nodded nearby, attended by several bees, its scent dizzyingly pungent.

"Surely you could have sold such a lovely house," Lydia ventured, following Lark up onto the porch, waiting while the other woman thrust a brass key into the lock.

"Like I told you, practically everyone in Stone Creek believes it's haunted," Lark answered, with another smile and a shake of her head. Then, in a teasing tone, she asked, "You're not afraid of ghosts, are you, Lydia?"

Lydia was nervous, but it had nothing to do with spirits. Gideon's lovemaking — if *lovemaking* was the term for it — had set her all a-jangle inside and, even now, hours later, she felt an occasional, twitching echo of the pleasure he'd given her. She was at once sated, and in dire need of more intimate attention.

"Oh, no," she said, with a little laugh. "I don't believe in ghosts."

Indeed, for all that had happened there, much of it truly tragic, the Porter house seemed to embrace Lydia when she stepped inside, just behind Lark. She felt as though it had been waiting to welcome her back, to enfold her and offer her solace.

"Good," Lark said, sort of waddling over to the longcase clock standing silent against the foyer wall. Gently, she opened the glass door on its front, reached inside to pull up the heavy brass weights, shaped like pinecones, and, after consulting the tiny watch pinned to her bodice, move the hands to their proper places. "Empty houses make me sad. They should be full, don't you think? Full of laughter and life and —" she paused, her eyes twinkling as she looked into Lydia's face "— children. Lots of noisy Yarbro children."

Lydia's cheeks heated. She'd found it impossible to lie still while Gideon was working her up into a frenzy in their narrow bed, after the wedding — had Lark and Rowdy heard some revealing noise? Or was it just that, Gideon and Lydia being newly-weds, everyone simply assumed the marriage had been promptly consummated, like any other?

"That would be . . . nice," she answered, somewhat forlornly.

Lark stopped, there in the large, blessedly cool entryway, and regarded Lydia seriously. "I know the wedding was a little — hurried," she said, her voice quiet, though the two of them were alone in that spacious old house. "But — well — when I saw the way you looked at Gideon, I thought — was I wrong?" She chuckled, shook her head again. "That was certainly jumbled. I'm just going to ask you straight-out, Lydia — do you love Gideon?"

Tears sprang suddenly to Lydia's eyes, giving her no opportunity to weave a deceptive answer. Even if she'd been willing to lie to Lark, which she wasn't, it would have been impossible. "Yes," she said miserably. "I think I fell in love with him years ago, when he brought me here, to this house, from the school, in the middle of that terrible snowstorm. And if it wasn't then, it must have been when he gave me that letter —"

Lydia very nearly broke down then, bit her lower lip and looked away, her shoulders trembling with the effort to contain the choking sob that flew into the back of her throat, like some trapped and frantic creature, flapping dry and boney wings.

Tenderly, Lark took Lydia by the shoulders. "If you love Gideon," she asked gently, "then why are you crying?"

Because he doesn't love me.

Lydia might not have been able to get those words out, her fondness for her sister-in-law notwithstanding, even if she hadn't been stricken to silence. For Lydia's besetting sin was pride, and Gideon's disinterest chafed her there, and sorely.

"Oh," Lark murmured, saddening a little. "Even after the way Gideon behaved last night — well, I thought everything was all right, because you were glowing when you came downstairs this morning —"

Mortification swept through Lydia. She put her hands to her face, wanting everything to disappear when she pulled them away again — Lark, the wonderful, lonely old house, Stone Creek.

And Gideon.

Lark embraced Lydia, offering sisterly comfort. When she took hold of Lydia's shoulders and held her away to look into her face, Lark's eyes fairly twinkled with warmth and fond sympathy — but not pity. Thank heaven, not pity — Lydia could not have borne that from a stranger, let alone a person she admired so much.

"When Gideon got the letter," she reminded Lydia, "he rushed to save you from Mr. Fitch. From what the U.S. Marshal said in the wire he sent to Rowdy, he turned half the town upside-down to do it. That *means* something, Lydia. My guess is Gideon just hasn't figured out what that something is yet."

"Rowdy and Wyatt *forced* him to marry me," Lydia finally managed to say. "I *know* they did!"

Lark chuckled at that. "Lydia," she said firmly, "no one *forces* a Yarbro to do *anything,* especially not another Yarbro." She smiled more broadly then. She tilted back her head, took in their surroundings. "You and Gideon will have a fine home here," she went on presently, and in a tone of happy resolution. "Together."

Lydia could not hold back her confession; it burst from her, partial and broken, the thing with boney wings escaping to fly free. "He didn't — he hasn't —"

Lark frowned, quickly discerning Lydia's meaning. "But this morning — the way you looked —"

Lydia said nothing. What *could* she have said?

"Oh," Lark said, as realization dawned. *"Oh."*

Lydia clutched at Lark's hands. "You

147

won't tell anyone, will you? Not even Rowdy? I'd *die* if anyone knew!"

"It's natural for a man to please a woman, Lydia," Lark answered. "There's no shame in that."

Recalling the things she'd felt when Gideon kissed her, when he touched her in such intimate ways, *reliving* those things so intensely that her very core seemed to be ablaze, Lydia shook her head. "What he did to me was — it was *wonderful,* Lark. But for anyone to know he didn't — he didn't want me —"

"Oh, he wants you all right," Lark broke in. "He's a man, and a *Yarbro* man, in the bargain. Whatever his reasons for not making love to you, Lydia — and I'd guess it's some foolish idea that it would be dishonorable — he won't be able to withstand the temptation forever." A light went on in Lark's lovely, serene face. "What you have to do is *seduce* him!" she cried. "A challenge with the aunts and Helga around, I know, but still — a glimpse of an ankle here, a soft touch to the back of his neck there —"

"How can I seduce him?" Lydia blurted. "He told me last night that as soon as we found a place of our own, we'd have separate rooms —"

Lark laughed. "Oh, he *is* deluded," she said. "Unless he locks his door, or shoves a bureau in front of it, he won't be able to keep you out of his bed."

Lydia stared at her former teacher, shocked. "Lark Yarbro," she whispered. "Are you suggesting that I *barge in where I'm not wanted?*"

Lark laughed again, harder this time. "Of *course* that's what I'm suggesting," she said. Then she lumbered toward the staircase. Her time, Lydia thought distractedly, must be near. "Come with me, Mrs. Yarbro. If there are keys for any of the doors upstairs, we're going to make sure they go missing."

Lydia snatched up the skirt of her borrowed dress with one hand, so she wouldn't trip on the stairs, and dashed after Lark. "I couldn't *possibly* —"

Lark turned, one hand on the banister, and her eyes sparkled as she looked back at Lydia. "Get into bed with your own husband?" she finished. "Sure you can. And I'm going to tell you just what to do when you get there."

There were several bedrooms upstairs, all fully furnished, though everything was draped in old sheets. Only the largest chamber had a key, hanging from the knob by a faded loop of ribbon, and Lark quickly pocketed that.

She went straight to the windows, threw the dusty curtains aside, and raised the sashes to let in the fresh summer breeze. The lush scent of the lilac bush by the porch rose to perfume the dusty air.

"This," Lark said, mischievously decisive, "is going to be *fun*."

Lydia could not seem to help fussing. "Gideon would be furious if he knew —"

Lark dismissed the partial statement with a wave of one hand and a *phoof* sound. "Who cares if Gideon is furious?" she countered. "It's not as though he's Henry VIII, and could have you beheaded or locked away in some tower." She smiled, pulled the covering off an old rocking chair. "Sit down, Lydia."

Lydia sat, overwhelmed. And strangely hopeful.

Lark took a seat on the edge of the bed, bounced once, and looked pleased when the springs protested with a rusty whine.

"Now," she said, smoothing her skirts and settling her very pregnant self for a chat. "Here's what you do first —"

Gideon hadn't expected the job to be easy. Mining, after all, was treacherous work done in the dank and the dark, brutally hard, with

150

only a few kerosene lanterns to illuminate the hole. The lamps, of course, represented a danger in their own right, partly because the flames consumed oxygen, but mostly because they could ignite invisible gases at any time, and blow every miner caught below ground to the proverbial smithereens.

He kept mostly to himself that first day, shoveling ore into a seemingly endless line of carts, knowing he'd arouse the other men's suspicions if he seemed too eager to join whatever circles they'd formed among themselves.

At noon, when the whistle blew, he sat down with the lard pail Lark had filled for him, ravenously hungry since he'd missed breakfast, dirty as the devil himself, and aching in every joint and sinew. His clothes had soaked through with sweat, dried to a clammy chill, and then soaked through again. The calluses on his fingers — the same fingers he'd used to bring Lydia to several howling climaxes in the sweet privacy of the night — stung as intensely as if he'd already worn the hide away.

There were twenty other men underground with him, give or take a few, but they kept their distance, working in twos and threes, muscular brutes, mostly Irish, accustomed to punishing labor. They talked

151

and joked in grunts and undertones, but they were careful not to let the new man hear — and hearing was almost impossible, anyhow, with the shovels and the picks pinging off stony walls of dirt and the wheels of the carts screeching fit to make Gideon's back teeth quiver as they rattled in and out of the mine.

God bless her, Lark had packed three pieces of fried chicken, two slices of dried apple pie, and a heel of generously buttered bread into that lard tin, and Gideon consumed every bite. He craved coffee — something he could usually take or leave — and smiled to himself, thinking he might turn out to love the stuff, the way Wyatt and Rowdy did.

Wyatt and Rowdy.

Right about now, Wyatt was probably riding a fence line in the open air, or flinging hay out of the back of a wagon for his herd of cattle, or sitting across the kitchen table from his beautiful wife, Sarah.

Maybe, if the kids were away from the house — they were a bunch of happy hellions, like Rowdy's brood, and ranged far and wide on foot and on horseback — Wyatt and Sarah were making love.

Gideon decided not to go down that road. He'd been waiting all morning for his own need to bed Lydia to ease up, and so far, it hadn't.

He turned his thoughts to Rowdy, with force, the way he'd rein a green-broke mule off a path it was determined to follow.

As marshal, Rowdy was probably making rounds — counting horses in front of saloons. That was his time-honored way of gauging the prospects for shoot-outs and hell-raising in general, day or night — if there were too many horses in front of any given drinking establishment, the chances of somebody disturbing the peace of Stone Creek went way up.

A lot of people might have considered that technique simplistic, but Gideon had seen it work time and time again. Perhaps because he'd been an outlaw himself, Rowdy knew what to look for, how to scent trouble in the wind.

Or maybe, since it was noon, Rowdy was home, having his midday meal. Or having Lark — there was a reason those two had so many kids, and another due at any minute. Like Wyatt and Sarah, they could barely keep their hands off each other.

There he went again. Right down a road that led straight to Lydia.

Warm, sweet Lydia, who'd so enjoyed the ministrations of his hand, and shyly asserted her belief, after that last bout of complete abandon, that there was more to lovemaking than what she'd experienced.

Thinking about that *more* made Gideon ache in ways swinging a shovel could never do. He turned his thoughts again, but it wasn't quite so easy as it had been the first time.

"Have some of this?"

The voice startled Gideon; he'd been so caught up in the struggle to govern his imagination that he hadn't heard or seen the other man's approach. Now, a big Irishman, his hair and eyes as black as the soot covering his skin and clothes, sat beside Gideon on the ledge of rock where he'd perched to eat his lunch, holding out a cup.

Coffee.

"Thanks," Gideon said, taking the cup. It was a blue enamel mug, and though the coffee inside had long since grown too cold to send off steam, it was delicious nonetheless, laced with sugar and a dollop of whiskey.

"Mike O'Hanlon," the big man said, putting out his free hand, for he had a mug of his own in the other, and sipped from it with obvious appreciation.

"Gideon Yarbro," Gideon answered, extending his own hand.

O'Hanlon's grip was calculated to make

Gideon wince.

He didn't.

"We'll all be headin' over to the Blue Garter Saloon after the whistle blows," O'Hanlon said. "Just to toss back a few and wash the copper dust out of our throats. Care to join us?"

Gideon debated — or pretended to. "Not tonight," he finally replied, with what he'd calculated to be just the right note of regret. "My wife will be waiting for me."

O'Hanlon chuckled, finished off his coffee, made a satisfied sound that put Gideon in mind of old Horace, down in Phoenix, draining his whiskey glass, either not knowing his sons were about to haul him out, or resigned to it and determined to enjoy every last drop of the cure-for-what-ailed-him. "Tied to some colleen's apron strings, are you?"

Gideon grinned. "I just married her last night," he said easily. "It's not her apron strings I'm thinking about."

All of which was true — though not something he would normally confide in a stranger. Nor, as much as Gideon wanted Lydia, did he intend to do anything about it.

"Well, then," O'Hanlon allowed, in a good-natured way Gideon knew was at least partly put on, "that's different, then. You've got honeymoonin' to do. Another time, maybe?"

"Another time," Gideon confirmed, handing back the empty coffee mug.

O'Hanlon stood, like a man meaning to go his way, but instead he lingered, towering over Gideon, letting him know he ran at the head of this particular herd. "You done this kind of work before?" he asked, and though the question sounded like an afterthought, Gideon knew it was the whole reason the Irishman had approached him in the first place.

"No," Gideon said, because there were times when the truth was more effective than any lie. "Does it show?"

"Just a bit," O'Hanlon allowed, flashing a grin in the semidarkness. Then, still casually he continued, "Where'd you draw your wages from last, if you don't mind my askin'?"

Gideon sighed, but not too heavily. "I was a bank clerk," he said. "Out in San Francisco. Couldn't take another day of wearing a coat and tie."

O'Hanlon weighed that. "You related to the marshal?"

"He's my brother," Gideon said.

"Rowdy's a good man," O'Hanlon allowed. "If you're like him, you'll do fine down here." An unspoken *if-not* hung at the end of the Irishman's sentence. Did the crew already suspect he was a ringer, or were they just naturally careful around a stranger?

Gideon was betting on the latter.

And he sure as hell hoped he was betting right.

If these miners ever found out he'd be reporting everything he saw and heard to the owners, smuggling dispatches out of Stone Creek on the stagecoach to avoid using the telegraph, he might meet with some kind of melancholy misfortune — and never get out of the hole.

O'Hanlon walked away.

The whistle blew again, signaling the end of the twenty minutes allotted for a midday meal.

And Gideon went back to work — wishing to God he could go home that night and take real solace in Lydia's arms. Instead, he'd use Lark and Rowdy's elegant porcelain bathtub, gulp down what supper he could manage, and collapse into bed, exhausted.

He'd get Lydia's nightgown — if she'd remembered to recover it from Helga's room — up around her waist. He'd pleasure her again, a little more boldly this time, and that would be the next best thing to taking his own satisfaction.

He might lie awake the whole night, once he'd banked the fire in Lydia.

Or he might fall asleep with his head between her legs.

Time would tell.

CHAPTER SEVEN

"They're all over at the Porter place," Rowdy informed Gideon, as soon as he dragged himself through the kitchen door that night, after his shift at the mine had straggled to its merciful end, and he looked around the softly lit room with an expression that must have revealed a lot more than he'd intended. "Lark, Lydia, Wyatt's Sarah and Sam's Maddie, the old ladies and the kids — the whole lot of them."

"Oh," Gideon said. It hurt to bend and stroke Pardner's head in greeting, but he did it, just the same. Seemed like the dog was the only one glad to see him.

Rowdy, who had been reading at the table — no sign or scent of supper — watched as Gideon kicked off his boots and placed them on the back step. "Aren't you going to ask what they're doing over there?" he wanted to know.

"I figure you'll get around to telling me

sooner or later," Gideon replied wearily, heading for the coffeepot. He poured a mugful, added a dash of whiskey from the bottle Rowdy kept on a high shelf, took a gulp and waited for the fire to surge through his tired muscles. "I guess Jacob Fitch didn't show up, looking to reclaim his bride?"

Throughout the long day, when he hadn't been thinking about mining strikes and deflowering his virgin wife, Gideon had fretted over Fitch, tallying up all the ways the bastard might be plotting to avenge his honor.

"Not so far," Rowdy admitted, closing his book, taking off the wire-rimmed spectacles he wore when he read for any length of time. "I did get another telegram from the U.S. Marshal down in Phoenix, though. He's sending a couple of men up here to speak to Lydia — make sure the marriage is valid and she didn't enter into it under duress."

Ravenous, Gideon cast a glance toward the stove, even though he knew it was cold. Nothing waiting in the oven, then.

"All right," he said, leaning back against the spotless counter under Lark's cupboards and folding his arms, "what are the women doing over at the Porter house?"

Rowdy grinned, rose at last from his chair, and approached the ice box. Drew out a plate of cold chicken and brought it to the table. Took his sweet time answering.

"They're getting it ready for you and Lydia to live in," he finally said. Mischief flickered in his eyes, indicating that he'd had a much easier day than Gideon had. "You might want to oil the bedsprings before you turn in for the night, though."

Focused on the platter of cold chicken — the hungry hordes had already picked through it, evidently, because what was left was mostly wings and necks and scrawny backs — Gideon pumped water at the sink, washed his hands, and sat down at the table. For all that his stomach was rumbling, the comment about the bedsprings had made his neck heat up.

"I won't be oiling anything tonight," he said, avoiding Rowdy's gaze and tucking into the food. If his brother planned to eat, he'd have to fend for himself. "All I want is a bath and eight hours of oblivion."

Rowdy laughed. Sat down again and folded his hands on top of the closed book — for a moment, he put Gideon in mind of a preacher with a Bible. "You might get the bath, if you hurry," he allowed. "But I'm not sure about the oblivion. When those women get back here — that'll be anytime now, since it's almost the kids' bedtime — they'll be full of chatter about curtains and rugs and flowerbeds. And our lot, brother, is but to listen."

Gideon barely suppressed a groan. He'd forgotten how respectable women loved to talk, especially if they had taken up some cause; when it came to females, he'd mostly limited himself to the *un*respectable variety. That kind didn't talk much — just did what needed doing and went on about their business. "I can't afford the Porter house," he said, remembering how big it was, and how grand — at least, by Stone Creek standards.

"Lark signed it over to you this afternoon," Rowdy said. "It's a wedding present."

Gideon nearly choked on the last bite of chicken he'd taken. *"What?"*

"Lark thinks you and Lydia ought to have a house," Rowdy told him, as though it were an ordinary thing to do. "So she gave you one."

Lark, Gideon knew, had inherited her first husband's railroad and a fortune to go with it when the son of a bitch had done the world a favor by getting himself killed. That was why she and Rowdy had been able to build a house like this one, but except for having more space than most folks did, they lived modestly — so modestly that it was easy to forget they had money.

"Damn it," Gideon growled, "I can't accept a *house*. Whatever happened to *reasonable* wedding presents, like tablecloths and teapots?"

Rowdy chuckled at that. "There's nothing 'reasonable' about my wife, once she takes a notion into that beautiful head of hers," he said. "If you've forgotten that, little brother, you've been away from home too long."

By then, Gideon had gobbled up all the chicken there was, and pushed back from the table to set the platter in the sink. He was bound and determined to get to that bathtub before the women got back and he lost his chance.

He wanted to tell Rowdy that he couldn't take the house for another reason, besides its being too costly a gift. Once he'd ruined any plans O'Hanlon and the others had to go out on strike, he'd be dangerously unpopular around Stone Creek, which meant he'd be leaving in a few months, probably sneaking out of town like a thief in the night, and staying gone for a good long while.

Possibly forever.

Of course, he couldn't say anything, given his agreement with the members of the mining cartel. Besides, when he'd laid his initial plans, Lydia, the pair of elderly aunts and Helga the housekeeper hadn't figured into them. He meant to travel light — that would be a necessity — and the harem he'd acquired would need a place to live after he was gone.

Gone.

The thought of leaving Lydia behind made the pit of his stomach drop, like a trap door swinging open over an abyss with the fires of hell itself waiting at the end of a long fall.

But leave her he would.

Wrenching himself back to the right here, right now, he concentrated on matters at hand. He'd gulp down his pride, the way he had his coffee a few minutes before, and the fried chicken, and thank Lark kindly for the house.

"The men at the mine think highly of you," he told Rowdy in parting as he headed for the back staircase. It was a concession of some kind, though he couldn't have said why he felt the need to make one.

"They have it hard, Gideon," Rowdy replied quietly. "The miners, I mean. So do their wives and children." He patted the dog's head, resting on his thigh again. "Pardner here eats better than they do.

When you get a chance, pay a visit to the shanties behind the mine and see for yourself."

Rowdy's words pierced Gideon's conscience, so far untroubled, at least as far as the men and their families were concerned, in some tender places.

Pretending he hadn't heard, he headed upstairs.

The aunts had chosen the spacious room behind the kitchen for their quarters — it had a fireplace and a writing desk, and they were charmed to know Lark had coveted that chamber herself when she first came to Stone Creek, as the new schoolmarm, and boarded with Mrs. Porter.

Maddie O'Ballivan, Sam's brown-haired, bright-eyed, spirited wife, expressed misgivings, having discerned that the spinster sisters had been gently raised, despite the industry they'd displayed throughout the day, dusting and sweeping.

"But there's only one bed," Maddie said, concerned.

"We've shared since cradle-days," Mittie responded. Then, with an impish little smile, she added, "And it's a good distance from the master bedroom, isn't it?"

Lydia, busy washing out cupboards, while

Sarah, the sister-in-law she'd met just that day, dried the last of the dishes, blushed at her aunt's inference, despite all the careful plans she and Lark had laid for Gideon's seduction.

Helga was taking the tiny room under the stairs — swearing up and down it would do just fine and she liked the idea of being near the kitchen so she could keep the fire properly stoked on cold winter nights — and that meant Lydia and Gideon would have the entire second floor to themselves.

At least until the babies started arriving, anyway.

"Look at the time," Lark said, peering down at the watch on her bodice. She'd had supper sent over from the hotel dining room, and now that the children, her own tribe, as well as Sarah's and Maddie's, had eaten, they were starting to run down. A few were irritable, and small skirmishes had broken out here and there. "We'd better go, and leave Lydia to welcome her husband home from a hard day's work."

Lydia had known all along that she would be staying behind, while the aunts and Helga returned to Lark and Rowdy's house for the night, but now that the first stage of the plan was at hand, she felt a little shy.

"Surely there's no hurry," she said awkwardly, wiping her hands on her apron.

But the work was done. The house was livable, and the women were already removing their own aprons, pulling the kerchiefs from their heads, gathering handbags and baskets, herding fractious, exhausted children toward the door.

Helga planned to walk back to the Yarbro house, as did Hank, Julia, Marietta and Joseph, Lark and Rowdy's brood. So the whole lot of them set out suddenly, and in a cluster, without so much as a goodbye to Lydia.

The aunts would squeeze into the buggy with Lark, and they, too, seemed at haste to leave. After placing simultaneous kisses on Lydia's flushed cheeks, they departed.

Maddie and Sarah shepherded their lively offspring out next, Sarah calling back a reminder that Lydia mustn't forget about the reception on Sunday afternoon. All the women had promised to return and help with the preparations for the delayed celebration of Lydia and Gideon's marriage.

Soon, Lydia was alone with Lark, her fellow conspirator, in the kitchen that would now be her own.

"I'll give you time to bath and change," Lark said, squeezing Lydia's hands in parting. "Then I'll send Gideon over. Remember what we talked about."

Lydia swallowed hard, nodded. Laughed a little, albeit nervously. Coming from anyone but Lark Yarbro, the advice she'd given Lydia in that upstairs bedroom soon after they'd arrived at the house that morning, would have seemed downright scandalous. "How could I forget?"

Lark smiled. "The pantry is stocked," she reminded Lydia practically. She'd sent Hank and Julia to the mercantile with a list, soon after they'd turned up at the Porter house, and the food and sundries had been promptly delivered. "Make Gideon a big breakfast, and pack him something hearty to take along to the mine in the morning, too." She paused, frowned prettily, stretched again, as she'd been doing all day, to ease her overburdened back. "You *can* cook, can't you?"

Helga had always prepared the meals, and what little Lydia knew of the kitchen arts, she'd learned by observation, not actual doing — but how difficult could it be, she asked herself, buoyed with the confidence she'd gained by a day of competent house-keeping, to fry eggs and slice meat and bread for sandwiches?

"I can cook," she said.

Lark started for the door.

Lydia trailed after her. "Lark?"

The other woman turned, looking tired and pleased by a good day's work. "Yes?"

"Thank you," Lydia said.

Lark smiled. "What are sisters for?" she countered.

And then she was gone, and Lydia was truly alone.

For a long time, she simply stood there, in the middle of that freshly scrubbed kitchen, with its full larder and ice box, paralyzed with hope.

Then, resolved, she made for the rear stairway.

There was a modern bathroom on the second floor, and Sarah had shown her how to light a fire under the small copper boiler, so there would be plenty of hot water.

Her husband would be home soon.

And Lydia Fairmont Yarbro still had preparations to make.

So she started pouring water into the huge claw-foot tub and began stripping off her clothes.

While the bath, hot and deep, didn't resurrect Gideon — he still felt half-dead — it did revive him a little. He soaked for a while, then soaped himself from head to foot, and soaked again.

169

A delicate knock at the door brought the odyssey to an end.

"Uncle Gideon?" a small voice called, from the other side.

Julia, Gideon thought. Or little Marietta, the shy one. "Yo," he answered.

"I need to get in there, really, *really* bad!"

"I'll hurry," Gideon replied. If he'd had a little longer, he'd have shaved, but he didn't want to keep his niece — whichever one it might be — waiting.

"Hurry *fast!*"

Gideon chuckled, pulled the plug, rose out of the water, toweled off quickly, dragged on the clean trousers and cotton shirt he'd brought with him from his room.

When he opened the door, Julia shot past him, making straight for the commode and already hiking up her skirts.

He stepped out into the corridor, only to run into his eldest nephew, Hank. Blond and blue-eyed, Hank was Rowdy in miniature, though he had some of his mother's grace, too. Thank God.

"Mama sent me up here," the boy announced staunchly, "to tell you you're to get over to the Porter house right away because Lydia is there alone and that won't do."

Gideon blinked. "Lydia's still at the Porter

170

house?" he asked. He'd expected his wife to return, with the others, and he said as much.

Hank shrugged. "I reckon she's planning to spend the night. When we left, she was scrubbing down the kitchen cupboards, but that was a while ago."

"If I give you a nickel," Gideon ventured, bending a little and lowering his voice, "will you go over there and fetch her back here?"

Hank looked tempted, but in the end, he shook his head, Rowdy-stubborn. "I'd better not do that," he decided. "Mama said tell *you* to go."

"Hell," Gideon muttered.

Behind the bathroom door, the commode flushed.

Julia appeared, a female version of her older brother, though smaller of course, and with a higher voice. "Uncle Gideon, you said a swearword!" she accused.

"Nothing wrong with your hearing," Gideon replied, resigned.

"You'd best be getting on over to the other house," Hank advised solemnly. "If you don't, you'll have Mama to deal with."

"Perish the thought," Gideon said.

He was tired.

His joints were starting to ache again as the effects of the bath began to wear off.

And now he was expected to traipse all

171

the way to the other side of town because his bride was waiting.

A weary smile broke across his face.

His bride was waiting.

Why was he still standing there, in the upstairs hallway of his brother's house? He started toward his room, meaning to fetch work clothes for the morning, along with his toothbrush and some other things, and stuff them into a satchel, but Julia stopped him with a tug at his shirtsleeve.

"You'll *catch it,*" she informed him, looking up at him with those huge, cornflower-blue eyes of hers, "if you leave the bathroom looking like it does right now."

Stifling another swearword, Gideon went back into the room in question, rinsed the tub thoroughly, and picked up his dirty clothes and the towels he'd used.

"Are you happy now?" he asked his niece, who was still waiting in the hall, along with Hank. They resembled a pair of small sentinels, standing there.

Julia beamed up at him, nodding pertly, and Gideon noticed for the first time that she was missing her two front teeth.

Right about then, Rowdy, wearing his spectacles again, appeared at the top of the stairs, a storybook under one arm.

"Why aren't you in bed?" he asked his two

eldest children. "Like Joe and Marietta?"

"Mama sent me up here to tell Uncle Gideon to skedaddle, and I just got done doing that." Hank eyed the book. "And I'm too old for bedtime stories."

"I'm not," Julia said, sidling up to her papa.

Rowdy's gaze connected with Gideon's, after he'd given one of Julia's pigtails an affectionate tug, and the contentment Gideon saw in his brother's eyes made him smile. The famous outlaw, the erstwhile train robber, a man once wanted in practically every state that side of Kansas, was about to read to a pack of towheaded hellions who all looked just like him.

Gideon nodded a good-night, took his laundry and dumped it on his bedroom floor, and gathered up the things he'd need in the morning.

When he reached the hallway again, it was empty, but he could hear Rowdy's voice, low and full of dramatic inflection, coming from behind one of the closed doors.

Gideon paused to listen for a moment.

Some princess, to hear Rowdy tell it, was in big trouble.

Gideon smiled again as he walked away, but this time, he felt something more than amusement, a sort of lonely longing, with threads of pure envy woven through it.

What would it be like, he wondered, to have what Rowdy had — kids, a wife, a real home?

Taking the rear stairway, Gideon reminded himself that *he* had a wife, too. And she was waiting for him at the Porter house, all alone.

The old ladies were in the kitchen, seated primly at the table, when he passed through, the pair of them wearing ruffled nightcaps, gowns and wrappers, and sipping tea. They watched him intently as he crossed to the back door, opened it, and then paused, turned to face them, realizing it would be rude to leave without acknowledging them in some way.

"Good night, ladies," he said.

"You be gentle with our Lydia, Mr. Yarbro," one of them told him, her voice a twittery chirp. He still had no idea which one was which.

"Don't be rough," counseled the second sister.

Gideon colored up. How was he supposed to respond? If he promised to "be gentle" with Lydia, they'd figure he meant to deflower her — assuming they didn't consider that water under the bridge. If he *didn't* promise, they might decide he was a brute,

174

and fret over their great-niece the whole night long.

He hadn't had much experience with little old ladies, but he knew they tended to worry.

"Lydia," he finally replied, "is safe with me."

He ducked out before either of them could speak again, his clothes and shaving gear under one arm.

Lydia *was* safe with him, he thought, as he made his way across the darkened yard, through the back gate, and onto the long driveway leading out to the main street.

The knowledge should have been a comfort to him — but it wasn't.

Lydia had finished her leisurely bath and donned the ruffled nightgown Lark had provided. She'd let her hair down, and brushed it until it crackled, and dabbed perfume — from a tiny bottle some previous resident had left behind in the bathroom cabinet — in back of her ears and on the insides of her wrists.

She went into the bedroom she hoped to share with Gideon, her heart beating wildly, and sat down on the edge of the bed to wait.

Lark had assured Lydia that Gideon would join her at the Porter house — she'd see to it — but suppose he'd balked? Suppose, feeling, as the aunts would have put it, *commandeered,* Gideon chose to remain at Lark and Rowdy's?

There was only one possibility more alarming than that one, as far as Lydia was concerned — that he would simply do as he was told and show up. There were lots of beds in this house — he might well choose to sleep in a different one.

Or he might decide to set aside his confusing reticence and ravish her.

A little thrill, partly fear and partly anticipation, rushed through Lydia as she considered *that* prospect.

Last night's episode had been pleasurable, to put it mildly.

But being *ravished* might be quite another thing.

What if it hurt terribly?

Downstairs, and far in the distance, a door opened and closed.

Lydia's fluttering heart shinnied right up into her throat.

"Lydia?" It was Gideon's voice, of course.

Lark had kept her promise.

Lydia swallowed.

"Let him come looking for you," Lark had told her, in this very room, that morning. Eons ago, it seemed to Lydia.

How much persuading had Gideon needed? Had he resisted, or agreed readily?

She heard his footsteps, brisk on the stairs.

Again, he called her name.

She had to bite down on her lower lip to keep from responding. The old-fashioned kerosene lamp on the bedside table was turned down low, but she reached out and turned the knob, so the wick lengthened and the light grew bright again.

"It's good for a man to wait," Lark had said. *"And wonder a little, too."*

The bedroom door swung open then, startling Lydia so that she jumped.

Gideon stood in the gap, like a living portrait in a frame, the glow from the gas lamps lining the hallway walls catching in his damp, butternut hair.

The sight of him, broad-shouldered, with golden bristles on his cheeks because he needed a shave, literally took Lydia's breath away. Left her reeling a little, at least on the inside, where she prayed it didn't show.

He started to say something, then stopped as he took in her hair, tumbling free to her waist, the thin but not sheer nightgown, the covers turned back on the bed.

Completely stricken, Lydia found she could not speak.

Gideon shook his head, as though he

thought he might be seeing things that weren't really there, but did not move from the doorway. "Didn't you hear me calling you?" he asked, at some length and very quietly. He looked utterly confounded — so much so that Lydia wanted to laugh, and would have, if she hadn't been so deliciously frightened.

"I heard you," she confirmed.

"Then why didn't you answer?" Gideon sounded curious, but not impatient.

"Because," Lydia said, drawing now on her own relatively limited personal resources and not the things Lark had told her, "a lady does not yell."

Gideon absorbed that. Then, to Lydia's utter surprise, he threw back his head and gave a single and wholly masculine shout of laughter. When he met her now-widened gaze again, he countered very gruffly, "Doesn't she?"

Lydia blinked. No suitable answer came to mind.

Gideon finally entered the room, though just far enough to close the door behind him. "Last night," he said, "if I hadn't kissed you at exactly the right time, you would have yelled fit to raise the roof."

Lydia opened her mouth, then closed it again.

"But, then," Gideon continued easily, "you weren't exactly behaving like a *lady*, now, were you?"

Lydia blushed, watched in stubborn, flummoxed silence as Gideon walked across the room, not toward her, but to take a seat in an old rocking chair. As calmly as if he'd strolled into this bedroom every night of his life, he pulled off his boots, first one, then the other, and tossed them aside.

"Lady or not," he said, raising his head to take her in with a slow, sweeping glance that left her feeling as though he'd removed every stitch she was wearing, "you *are* beautiful."

What did one say, in such circumstances? "Thank you" didn't seem quite proper. And where was the wanton hussy, now that Lydia needed her?

Gideon stood, unbuttoned his shirt, shrugged out of it.

His chest, though scarred, looked Grecian to Lydia, perfectly chiseled, dusted in hair the color of his beard.

Lydia searched her mind for some tidbit of conversation, uncomfortable with the silence, wanting to turn the topic in another direction, but once again came up dry.

She squirmed a little, perching there on the edge of the mattress.

"I like your hair down," Gideon said. He was very near by then, turning down the lamp until the wick sputtered and the flame went out. Moonlight spilled through the nearby window.

Gideon stood silently for a long time, just looking at her.

Then, still without a word, he went back to the door, opened it and stepped out. The gas lamps in the hallway went dark.

A little shiver of — of *something* scurried through Lydia on millions of tiny, silvery feet.

Gideon returned. "Shall we test your theory, Mrs. Yarbro?" he asked.

Lydia finally found her voice. "W-what theory would that be, Mr. Yarbro?" she countered.

He didn't reply right away.

But he came to stand directly in front of Lydia, so close that his legs brushed her knees, and cupped a hand under her chin, raised her face to make her look at him.

"I promised two old ladies I would be gentle with you," he told her, "and I will."

Lydia swallowed, full of joyous terror.

His hands shifted to her shoulders, and he eased her gently onto her back. Leaned to taste her mouth, nibble at her lower lip, trace the length of her neck with a single, unbearably light pass of his lips.

"I won't hurt you, Lydia," he said, once he'd set her trembling in earnest. "But I do intend to prove you wrong about one thing."

Staring up at him, brimming with crazy hopes and frenzied trepidations, Lydia managed to murmur, "What?"

Her legs were still dangling over the side of the high bed.

Gideon knelt between them, took her ankles gently into his hands, and set her heels on the mattress. Not in a hurried way, but firmly, he pushed her nightgown up, inch by inch, until she was bared to him, from her shoulders to her toes.

"A lady *does* yell," he murmured, parting her most intimate place, putting his mouth where his fingers had been the night before.

And feasting upon her.

Like something wild, seized with the instinct to mate, Lydia arched her back and cried out as Gideon alternately suckled and teased.

She felt his chuckle move through her, a vibration riding bolts of purest fire. And then he devoured her, the way a hungry man might devour a ripe and juicy peach, with relish and no little greed.

And one heretofore prim and proper lady — yelled.

CHAPTER EIGHT

Lydia soared to peak after peak, each one higher than the last, as Gideon enjoyed her, over and over again. Presently, he rose from his knees and joined her on the bed, held her while she recovered, but except for his boots and shirt, he remained fully dressed. He ran his fingers through her hair, seemingly fascinated by it, kissed her eyelids and murmured senseless words as she made her slow descent, once again reaching small, soft climaxes as she floated down from beyond the clouds.

"More?" he asked, his voice husky, when she'd finally settled back into herself.

That ordinary word sounded foreign to her; she could not divine its meaning. She made a small, crooning sound, hoping it would suffice as an answer to whatever Gideon's question had been.

Gideon didn't inquire again. He took Lydia by the hips, rolled onto his back, and set her down squarely on his mouth.

Lydia was startled by the instant, consuming need his swift action — and his open mouth — ignited within her. She flung back her head and shouted his name, raspy-voiced, desperate, and groped with her hands for the railings in the headboard, sure she'd rocket right through the ceiling if she didn't hold on for dear life.

Once again, Gideon drove Lydia to a shattering, cataclysmic release, and then another. When he knew she'd been thoroughly, mercilessly satisfied, he laid her down beside him, stroked her hair, murmured tender words that did not string together in sentences, caressed her breasts and her thighs and her belly, as though he couldn't touch her enough.

She was certain he would take her then. Part her legs and mount her, make her truly his wife.

But he did not.

Lydia was too spent to cry, or even to speak. Joy and sorrow tangled within her, in knots that might never be untied. The day, and Gideon's assiduous lovemaking, had left her exhausted, and sleep began to pull at her, dragging her down into dark, enfolding arms.

As she drifted off, though, she thought

she heard Gideon mutter, "God help me."
Oh, but that might have been part of the
dreams that immediately swamped her.

When Lydia awakened, many hours later,
she instantly realized that she was alone in
bed, and bolted upright in a sudden, uncom-
prehending panic. The room was dark, but
gradually swelling with the faintest traces of
light.

It was morning — or *almost* morning.

But where was Gideon? Had he left her,
gone to sleep in another bed, in another
room?

Like a mermaid struggling free of entwin-
ing seaweed, Lydia unwound herself from
her hair and the bedclothes, got up, and
hastily donned the calico dress she'd worn
the day before. She might have worn the
nightgown instead, since it had no buttons
to contend with and she was in a significant
hurry, but it would be hours until she found
it, so far under the bed that she had to fetch
the broom to retrieve it.

She brushed her hair quickly, was plaiting
it as she rushed out into the hallway.

"Gideon?" Lydia whispered the name; he
could not possibly have heard her. She was
about to start opening doors when she
noticed a billow of soft light at the top of

the back stairway, the one leading down into the kitchen.

Holding the tip of her braid so it wouldn't come undone, she drew a deep breath and headed for the stairs.

Gideon was there, and since his back was to her and she was barefoot, making no sound on the plank steps, she had a moment to blink back smarting tears of frustration and relief. To gather her scattered composure, calm her floundering heart, slow her breath.

Dear God, he was so beautiful — if such a term could be aptly applied to a man — even in his rough workingman's clothes.

Why didn't he want her?

How could he teach her ecstasy — every touch of his hands and his mouth at once masterful and infinitely tender, nearly to the point of reverence — and still turn away without taking his own pleasure?

Was she repulsive to him in some way?

That couldn't be so, not when he'd made her cry out in lust and need and finally triumph, not once but many times, attended her with such stunning intimacy.

Lydia's cheeks were hot as she remembered, as she let her body remember. She'd *ridden* Gideon, ridden his tongue and his lips and his unabashed hunger for her, as though finding herself astride some mythical, runaway horse, winged and formed of fire.

She took another step, meaning to find a piece of string and tie the end of her braid, and Gideon heard her then, or sensed her presence somehow.

He turned, and she saw bleakness in his eyes, even though he was smiling, ever so slightly.

"I was just — I was just meaning to bind my hair —" Lydia stammered, flustered.

"No," Gideon said gravely, with a shake of his head. He'd brewed coffee, the aroma filled the cool, unstirred air of the kitchen, tantalizing and comfortingly normal, and now he set aside the cup he'd been drinking from. "Don't do that."

Lydia stood utterly still on the third stair from the bottom — odd, she thought, that she'd counted, given her state of mind — a very improper question struggling at the back of her throat, barely held in check.

Why, Gideon? Why don't you want me?

Slowly, he crossed to her, took her free hand, led her down one step, and then another, until they were face-to-face. Gently, he freed her braid from her fingertips, watched as the plait began to come undone.

"Gideon?"

He met her eyes, but with some difficulty, as though he did not want to look away from her hair, ever. "What?"

"Am I — am I ugly?"

His eyes widened. *"Ugly?"*

Lydia blushed furiously, full of misery. "Un-unattractive in some way?"

His gaze had returned to her hair again. Gently, he eased the strands apart, undoing the braid slowly, running splayed fingers through the unbound locks. "God, no," he replied, after a very long time.

"Then why?" Lydia asked, unable to restrain herself any longer. "Why don't you — why won't you — ?"

Gideon continued to comb his fingers through her hair, but he met her eyes. No answer he could have given would have stunned her, or broken her, more cruelly than what he said then.

"Because I'll be leaving you, one of these days." He thrust out a sigh, and Lydia, bludgeoned by a sorrow so deep, so consuming that she could barely stand up under it, thought she'd surely swoon. "I'll be leaving you, Lydia. And it will be all too soon."

Lydia's knees would no longer support her. She sank, aware of Gideon's hands taking firm hold on her upper arms, onto the steps. Sat there, trembling, wanting to scream, wanting to sob, but painfully unable to make even the smallest sound.

Gideon crouched, holding her hands now, looking up into her face. "You'll meet someone else," he promised, his voice still hoarse even after he'd cleared his throat once, "and you'll feel no shame in sharing a proper husband's bed."

Lydia longed, suddenly and ferociously, to bury her fists in Gideon Yarbro's thick, taffy-colored hair and snatch it out of his scalp in bloody-ended hanks. At the same time, she thought if she loved this man even a smidgeon more than she did at that moment, she'd shatter into tiny, brittle pieces and never be able to pull herself together again.

She dared not speak, dared not move.

"I should have left you alone," Gideon said, half to himself. "Just gotten you away from Fitch and *left you alone.*"

With no bidding from her, Lydia's hands rose to cup his cheeks — quite the opposite of what she'd wanted to do earlier. He'd shaved since leaving their bed, for his skin was smooth now. "Oh, Gideon," she managed. *"Gideon."*

Gently, and with a reluctance Lydia hoped she hadn't merely imagined, Gideon took hold of her wrists. Pulled her hands from

188

his face.

"I've got to go," he said.

Fresh alarm seized Lydia. "You're l-leaving *now?*"

Gideon's smile was sad as he straightened, stepped back. "I'm due at the mine, Lydia," he said, very quietly. "There's work to be done."

"But I was going to make hotcakes," Lydia burst out, marveling at the inanity of her protest even as the words tumbled off her tongue, helter-skelter. "And sandwiches for your midday meal —"

He picked up a bundle from the table, something wrapped in a blue-and-white checkered napkin. Raised it a little for Lydia to see. "I've got a little grub in here," he said. "And I had some bread and cheese for breakfast. I'll be all right."

With that, he nodded once, in farewell, turned and made for the door, a man in a hurry to be gone.

Lydia managed — heaven only knew how — not to cry until after the door had closed soundly behind him.

When Lydia was certain he wouldn't turn around and come back for some reason, she bent double, still sitting on the third step, until her forehead touched her knees.

She did not sniffle.

She did not sob.

She wailed.

Gideon's second morning at the mine was pretty much like his first, except harder. The soreness in his arms, legs and shoulders was exquisite torment — and yet it did not begin to match what was going on in his heart.

Lydia.

He hadn't meant to hurt her — only to get her safely away from Jacob Fitch. That had been what she wanted, hadn't it? She'd sent the letter, after all.

Instead of saving her, he thought dismally, he might have destroyed her instead.

As he worked, his body went numb, which was a blessing, but the bruises on the inside continued to pulse with every beat of his heart.

By the time the noon whistle sounded, and Gideon laid aside his shovel and sat down on the same ledge he'd occupied the day before, with his napkin-wrapped lunch lying untouched beside him, Mike O'Hanlon joined him, once again.

"You'll pardon my sayin' so," the big man remarked, in his rolling brogue, "but you don't look like a man who's been beddin' a willin' bride, young Yarbro."

A hufflike snort escaped Gideon, but he

didn't speak. He forced himself to open the bundle he'd brought along; his body was weak with hunger, even though he was sure his stomach would rebel if he tried to swallow a bite of the canned ham he'd found in the pantry that morning, along with an apple and a slice of bread.

O'Hanlon's blue gaze caught on the ham, and he gave a low whistle of exclamation. " 'Tis a feast, that," he said.

Shit, Gideon thought. He'd been a fool to bring an expensive tidbit like this one to the mine, let the other men see him eating like a king while they dined on lesser things; what had he been thinking?

He'd been thinking, he reflected grimly, about Lydia.

About the way she'd given up her whole self to him, flesh and spirit, the night before. About how badly he wanted her, and how much he hated himself for making a plaything of that responsive, delectably female body of hers.

He thrust the ham, still in its colorful tin, with the turn key on top, into O'Hanlon's hands.

"You have it," he said.

O'Hanlon accepted the ham, although Gideon knew it injured the other man's pride to do so. Just one more mistake, in a long line of them.

Out of the corner of his eye, he saw the Irishman stash the tin in his lunch pail, unopened.

"They'll be sendin' us home in a little while," O'Hanlon said, a few moments later. "With half a day's pay on the books and no knowin' what tomorrow'll bring."

Gideon frowned. It was barely twelve o'clock — the day shift wouldn't be over for nearly six hours. "What?"

"Foreman just came down and told me," O'Hanlon explained, splaying his huge hands on his thighs and heaving a sigh. "For all their millions, they'll squeeze a nickel clean through till their fingertips touch, the owners will, if they think there's a strain on the budget."

How, Gideon wondered, could there be a "strain on the budget"? Copper prices were high; the government and the big industrialists back east were buying ore by the freight-car load. The men he'd met with in Chicago had handed him a sizable bank draft, with more to come when the job was finished, without so much as a blink at the amount.

"I guess we're lucky they haven't brought in a bunch of Chinamen to take our places," O'Hanlon went on, but he didn't sound like a man who considered himself lucky.

And why wasn't he eating the ham? Gideon had caught a glimpse of the other man's lunch as he wolfed it down earlier — a heel of bread, probably stale, one hard-boiled egg and a sliver of cheese. Surely, big as he was, and as hard as he worked, O'Hanlon was hungry.

Looking around at the other men, gathered in little groups, mere shadows just outside the dim reach of the lanterns, Gideon figured O'Hanlon couldn't bring himself to partake of a "feast," as he'd put it, in front of them.

"The railroad's keeping most of them busy," Gideon said, referring to the Chinamen most laborers both hated and feared.

O'Hanlon, though dismal of aspect, gave a rueful chuckle. "There's that," he said. "There's that."

The quitting-whistle blew then — two long, shrill bleats echoing down the hole from high overhead. Some of the support timbers groaned, as if in answer.

O'Hanlon heaved another sigh, got to his feet. "Half day," he said, "half pay."

"Damn," Gideon replied, not because he'd miss the pittance, *or* the backbreaking work, but because the mine owners hadn't said anything to him about money being tight enough to cut the men's hours any further than they already had. And there was a good reason for that: it wasn't.

This was some kind of gambit to keep the miners needy, keep them in line.

Something soured in Gideon's empty stomach, roiled there.

In his mind, he heard the echo of something Rowdy had said to him the night before.

"They have it hard, Gideon. The miners, I mean. So do their wives and children — Pardner here eats better than they do."

Christ, Gideon thought. O'Hanlon hadn't eaten the ham because he meant to take it home to his family.

O'Hanlon had moved away, but he stopped, looked back at Gideon, who was still sitting on that ledge like a lump, listening to echoes.

"Come along," the Irishman said. "Paddy might let us have a dram, on the cuff, if we're charmin' enough."

It was the gesture Gideon had been waiting for, or one of them, anyway. He'd be inside the men's circle, if only for a little while, and "a dram," as O'Hanlon had put it, would almost certainly loosen their tongues. So why didn't he feel better about it?

O'Hanlon was waiting.

"Sounds good," Gideon said.

"And if Paddy won't give us credit," O'Hanlon went on, as if there'd been no break in the discussion, "maybe you'd spring for a round. Since you can afford ham that comes in a tin with a key on top."

Gideon saw the bait, and handily avoided it. "I stole that ham from my sister-in-law's pantry," he said. The relative truth of that statement eased his conscience a little. Lark *had* owned that house before she'd signed it over to him and Lydia, and she'd surely paid for the plentiful supply of canned goods and sundries on the shelves, since he hadn't and his wife was penniless. "But if we drink slow, I might be able to cover a round or two."

Pleased, O'Hanlon slapped him hard on the shoulder. "She owns her own railroad, that sister-in-law of yours. Seems she'd be able to come up with a job for you, if she had a mind to help out."

O'Hanlon, Gideon thought, was even smarter than he'd given him credit for. And still suspicious.

"Pinching a ham from the lady's cupboard is one thing," Gideon replied easily, "and going to her with my hat out is another."

The other men slowly gathered around them, grumbling about the short day. No doubt, like O'Hanlon, they had wives and children to support — but no fancy tinned ham to present for their supper.

"Yarbro here," O'Hanlon announced to the throng, "is buyin' a round at Paddy's."

The foreman, a man Gideon had never met, and whom the owners had assured him wouldn't be in on the plan, watched with folded arms and a hard look in his eyes as the miners trailed upward, toward the sunlight and the fresh air.

And Rowdy's voice came back to Gideon as he climbed, in their midst, secretly, selfishly pleased that the shift was over early.

"When you get a chance, pay a visit to the shanties behind the mine and see for yourself."

Reaching level ground, Gideon raised his eyes, saw the small raw-timber-and-canvas houses clustered close together on the barren hillside above. They had a precarious look, those shanties, as though they weren't sound enough to hold to their footings, and even from that distance, he could see that the thin-limbed children scurrying among them probably weren't accustomed to *supper,* let alone canned ham.

Helga and the aunts arrived at midmorning, riding in a wagon driven by Rowdy, their few belongings in tow.

By then, Lydia had recovered from her crying bout. She'd pressed a cold cloth to her eyes until the swelling and redness went away, and taken refuge in the room Lark referred to as "the study." Mr. Porter's books still lined the shelves, and she'd dusted them carefully, consoled by their presence, and chosen a volume of epic poetry to read later, after Gideon came home.

If Gideon came home.

After what he'd said that morning, he might not.

And now that Lydia had pulled herself together a little, she'd decided, with admitted bravado, that it would be just fine with her if he didn't. She'd lived a long time without Gideon Yarbro, and she had no intention of folding up when he'd gone.

Helga and the aunts were inside, chattering among themselves as they went about settling in, before Lydia noticed the worried expression on Rowdy's face.

Setting down the various valises, he nodded to Lydia and would have left without a word, if she hadn't pursued him out into the yard. Caught up with him as he started to climb back into the wagon.

"Rowdy, wait," Lydia said.

He shifted on the seat and took up the

reins, but didn't release the brake lever. Saying nothing, he simply waited to hear what she had to say.

"Is Lark all right?" Lydia asked.

"She's a little poorly today," Rowdy admitted. "I sent for Sarah to come and sit with her, in case her time is nigh."

Lydia waited out a rush of alarm. If Lark needed Sarah or anyone else to sit with her, she truly wasn't well. She'd worn herself out helping to get the house ready to occupy the day before, and if any harm came to Lark because of that, Lydia knew she'd never forgive herself.

"I'm coming with you," she told Rowdy. "I'll stay till Sarah comes."

"There's no need of that," Rowdy said. "That's what Lark would tell you, anyhow. Helga offered to look after her, or at least ride herd on the kids, but Lark wouldn't hear of it."

Lydia was already taking off her apron, smoothing her hair. "Please, wait for me," she said quietly. "I'm just going to tell the aunts I'll be out for a little while."

In spite of his earlier protest, Rowdy looked relieved. "I'll wait," he said gruffly. "And I'm obliged, Lydia."

Lydia dashed into the house, told Helga and the aunts she was going home with

Rowdy and could not say when she'd be back, and returned, scrambling ably up into the wagon box before he could get down to help her.

"Lark may need a doctor," she ventured, once they were under way.

"Doc Venable retired a couple of years ago," Rowdy said, looking straight out over the backs of the two-horse team, but seeing, it seemed to Lydia, something she couldn't, and slapping down the reins to hurry the animals up a little. "He still knows his business, but his eyesight isn't what it used to be and he doesn't make many house calls these days."

Lydia thought of her own father. He'd been a doctor, too, and a good one, though mostly ineffectual in every other area of his life. Although she hadn't missed him in a very long time, she did then.

"I see," she said. "And there isn't another physician in Stone Creek?"

Rowdy shook his head. "Sam O'Ballivan's been beating the brush for one, from here to San Francisco, but so far, no luck."

They reached the house quickly.

The Yarbro children were sitting on the porch, in a solemn, tight little row, their shoulders touching.

Lydia glanced at Rowdy, saw her own

deepening concern reflected in his face.

He'd barely brought the wagon to a stop when a long, shrill scream came from inside the house.

The children flinched.

"Christ!" Rowdy said, under his breath, bolting from the buckboard without setting the brake and running toward the house.

The children didn't move, except to break ranks momentarily so their father could dash between them. Their eyes were huge, and their faces were so pale, every freckle stood out.

Lydia, following quickly behind Rowdy, paused to speak to them.

"Hank," she said, to the eldest boy, "do you know where Dr. Venable lives?"

A tear streaked a crooked path down Hank's cheek. "Yes, ma'am," he said, stiffening when Lark screamed again.

"You go and fetch him right now," Lydia said.

Hank launched himself off the step and ran hard for town.

Lydia turned to Julia, who was shaking visibly, the two smaller children huddled against her sides.

"Can you take Marietta and Joe and go to my — to Mrs. Porter's house, Julia? Where we were yesterday?"

The little girl nodded, dashed at her face with the back of one hand. "I know right where it is," she said. "I've been there lots of times, with Mama."

"I want you to go straight there, then," Lydia instructed, with a calmness she didn't feel, especially after a third long, plaintive cry from Lark. "Helga and the aunts will look after you and Joe and Marietta until someone comes to bring you home."

Julia stood, taking her sister and brother by the hand. "Will you help my mama?" she asked. "She's been carrying on like that since right after Papa left the house with the ladies and their things."

Lydia's throat thickened, but she straightened her shoulders and raised her chin. "I'll do everything I can to make your mama feel better, Julia," she promised. "And I know it will ease her mind when I tell her you've been such a big, brave girl, and tended your brother and sister."

Mimicking Lydia's actions, Julia squared *her* shoulders, and raised *her* chin. "You tell Mama that Joe and Marietta will be fine, because I mean to see to it."

Lydia managed a smile. Nodded. She was too choked up to speak again.

She watched as Julia half dragged, half shooed the smaller children across the yard and onto the lane, where the puffs of dust Hank's feet had raised as he ran were still settling.

Neither Joe nor Marietta wanted to leave, which made Julia's task that much harder.

Joe shrieked for his mother, and Marietta was wailing at the top of her lungs, but Julia wouldn't let them turn back.

Lydia kept the three small children in sight until they'd rounded the bend and disappeared, then turned and hurried inside the house, up the front staircase, along the hallway.

Finding Rowdy and Lark's room wasn't hard; a door stood open at the end of the corridor and, through that door, Lydia could see Lark writhing on a bed soaked red with blood.

Lark's skin glistened with perspiration, and she was deathly pale, due to the blood loss, no doubt, and the pain. Rowdy sat beside her, holding tightly to her hand, his face stony with fear.

Seeing Lydia, Lark struggled to focus on her face. "The children?" she whispered raggedly. "Lydia — the children —"

Lydia was already rolling up her sleeves, marveling at the strange and sudden strength rising within her. "They're being looked after, Lark," she said. "And Dr. Venable will be here soon — Hank's gone to find him."

Lark sighed, closed her eyes, stiffening under another wave of pain.

Lydia turned her attention to Rowdy. "I'll need hot water," she said. "And plenty of clean cloth."

Rowdy hesitated, torn between doing what he knew had to be done and staying at Lark's side. Finally, after placing a kiss on Lark's grayish, sweat-slickened forehead, he rose, gave Lydia one glance of mingled pleading and gratitude, and went to fetch the things she had asked for.

Lark groped for Lydia's hand, and Lydia gave it.

"I can't leave them," Lark croaked, fairly crushing the bones in Lydia's fingers. "The children — Rowdy —"

"You're not going to die, Lark," Lydia said, again drawing on some heretofore unknown source of fortitude and certainty. "I won't permit it." She bent over Lark, so their faces were close together. "Do you hear me, Lark Yarbro? *I will not permit you to die.*"

CHAPTER NINE

The Blue Garter Saloon, Gideon soon discovered, was at the tail end of Main Street, standing at a little distance from its larger competitors. It had never seen a lick of paint, nor did it boast the usual swinging doors. There weren't any horse troughs and hitching rails out front, either.

No need for Rowdy to count cayuses here, obviously.

The shabby establishment was, in fact, hardly larger than the average woodshed, and surrounded on all sides by knee-high grass littered with old broken things of all types, empty bottles, weathered boards with rusty nails sticking out of them, the skeleton of a wheelbarrow.

Searching his memory as he and O'Hanlon and the others approached the Blue Garter in a crowd — he doubted they'd all fit inside unless the place was empty except for the bartender, and *he'd* better be pretty small — Gideon finally recalled the saloon from his early days in Stone Creek.

It had been a house back then, inhabited by a harried widow with a lot of kids.

He and Rowdy had dropped by, on occasion, with a fifty-pound bag of dried beans, a mess of trout or the odd basket of eggs.

He wondered, assessing the place, where that woman and her band of unkempt, perpetually hungry children had wound up.

O'Hanlon jarred him loose from his reflections — this habit of letting his thoughts scatter every which way was getting out of hand — by slapping him on the back so hard that he nearly stumbled over the threshold of the Blue Garter Saloon.

The fattest man Gideon had ever seen stood squeezed between the bar and the shelves of bottles and glasses, though there was no clientele in evidence. No piano player, either, since there was no piano.

As the men straggled in, the bartender dunked an enormous hand into a crock amid a row of half-filled whiskey bottles and brought out three or four pickled eggs, shoved them into his mouth, and worked his jaw.

The expression on his plate-size face was one of resignation, as he chewed and surveyed the new arrivals, rather than welcome.

"Another half day, Paddy," O'Hanlon announced. "And it's thirsty we are."

Paddy chewed, swallowed, shoved his hand into the crock again, for another serving of pickled eggs.

Gideon fought an urge to look away; watching the man eat took character.

"No more credit, Mike," Paddy said, after swallowing. His eyes were probably normal-size, but they looked small in the broad, copiously fleshy expanse of his face, and they tracked Gideon, marking him for a stranger. "And don't give me any of your blarney about all of us being brothers and sons of the Old Sod, either. I'm not running this place for my health, you know."

From what Gideon could see, Paddy wasn't doing much of *anything* for his health.

"Our young friend, Yarbro, here," O'Hanlon boomed, practically knocking Gideon over the bar with another slap on the back, "will stand good for a glass."

The fat man raised his eyebrows, strangely delicate in that face, feathery and smooth, like a woman's. "Yarbro," he repeated. "Any relation — ?"

"Rowdy and Wyatt are my brothers," Gideon said, to get it out of the way. Other assignments, in other towns, had been easier in at least one way — he'd been able to use an alias, and no need to explain relationships.

"Don't see much of the marshal around here," Paddy answered, replacing the lid of the crock and wiping his massive hand on the stained front of his shirt. "And before I pour a drop of whiskey, I'll have to see your money."

Were it not for his long-standing habit of carrying a twenty-dollar gold piece in his right boot — one of the few bits of advice his pa had ever given him that he'd actually followed — Gideon would have been on the spot, since his pockets were empty.

Grinning, he kicked off that boot, upended it over the bar, and watched the bartender's face as the gold piece clunked solidly onto the scarred wooden surface, along with some dirt and a few pebbles.

Paddy put out a paw and made the coin disappear, paying no mind to the red Arizona soil and the tiny rocks.

"Belly up, then," he said to the company in general, though his eyes lingered curiously on Gideon, who gazed steadily back at him. "Whiskey all around."

This brought a cheer from the assembly, and everybody shoved their way forward to hoist a glass.

Mike O'Hanlon stood so close to Gideon, of necessity in that throng, that their shoulders were wedged together. It was like leaning against a stone wall. "Twenty dollars, then," the Irishman remarked, attempting subtlety and going wide of the mark. "Quite a sum to walk around on."

Gideon sighed, eyed his portion of whiskey and wished he didn't have to drink it. Between Paddy's penchant for pickled eggs and the rank smell of so many sweating and seldom-bathed bodies in such close quarters, he felt a little on the queasy side.

He leveled a sidelong glance at O'Hanlon, mostly so he wouldn't have to look at Paddy, whose belly spilled over the top of that bar like a mud slide covering half a road.

"Maybe you'd like to know where I got that money, O'Hanlon," Gideon said. He'd explained the ham. He'd taken some guff about his sister-in-law owning a railroad. And that was all he meant to put up with.

"Call me Mike," O'Hanlon said, moving as if to slap Gideon on the back again, then apparently thinking better of it. His whiskey glass disappeared completely between his big hands. "Call me Mike, young Yarbro."

"My name," Gideon said in response, "is

Gideon."

"Good Bible name, Gideon," Mike allowed, before taking a lusty gulp from his glass.

Figuring the alcohol would kill most of the germs on his own glass, Gideon braced himself inwardly and took a slug himself. Managed not to wince as the rotgut burned its way to his belly and then did its damnedest to come right back up.

"They do this often?" he asked, when he was fairly sure he could speak in a normal, offhand tone of voice. Paddy, busy pouring whiskey all the while, was still watching him. "The mine owners, I mean? Cut a shift in half?"

Mike had emptied his glass, and shoved it forward for Paddy to refill.

Twenty dollars would buy a lot of whiskey, but Gideon wasn't expecting to get any change back.

"Every once in a while," Mike said, after a blissful shudder of appreciation. "It's how they repay us for our hard work, isn't it? We put them far enough ahead, they shove us backward a stride or two."

One of the other men spoke — the first time any member of the crew, besides Mike, had addressed Gideon with anything more than a glare or a grunt. "My youngest —

Molly — she's down with the croup. Half-starved on the wages I do bring home, and now I'll be short half a day's pay."

"If not more than that," another man said glumly. "I say we give them back some of their own. Shut the place down. See how they like that."

Mike leaned around Gideon to glare. "O'Brien," he growled, "mind your tongue."

A wave of grumbling moved through the group, but the men were all too busy bending their elbows, and trying to get into Paddy's pickled-egg crock, to comment.

Gideon forced himself to swallow the rest of his whiskey, and when Paddy passed over his glass on the next round, he felt appreciation, as well as an uneasy wondering.

The whiskey fest lasted almost an hour, before they got to the end of Gideon's twenty-dollar gold piece, but no more was said about a strike. Mike O'Hanlon made sure of that.

And when there was no more whiskey — and no more pickled eggs, to Paddy's visible irritation — there was no reason to stay, either. The men wandered out, by twos and threes, until only Mike and Gideon and the mountainous bartender remained.

"O'Brien was just flappin' his jaws," Mike said casually, and at some length, sighing as he shoved his glass away knowing it wouldn't be refilled this time. "About shutting down the mine, I mean."

Gideon shrugged. "Makes no difference to me," he said, pushing away from the bar.

Mike watched him with the usual intensity, and for a long time. "It *ought* to make a difference to you, young Yarbro," he said. "You've got a new wife to look after, now, don't you? Or are there a lot more gold pieces where that one came from?"

Gideon set his jaw, refused to answer.

"Show the man some gratitude, Mike," Paddy scolded, surprising Gideon — until he noticed that the watchful glint was still there, in the big man's pinhole eyes. "And a few *more* gold pieces wouldn't go amiss, as far as I'm concerned. You and the boys, for all your pissing and moaning about what the wives and kids will be doing without, must have close to a hundred dollars on my books, owing for whiskey."

Paddy didn't seem the sort to be concerned for the womenfolk and the wee-ones, not to Gideon, anyway. No, he was concerned about the money he had coming, and would probably never see.

Still, his words brought a crimson flush rushing up Mike's neck to pound bright in his face. For a moment, Gideon thought sure he was about to reach across that bar, take Paddy by the throat, and crush his windpipe.

Instead, Mike ground out, "A man's got to take his comfort somewhere, now, doesn't he?"

Gideon watched Paddy's reaction through his eyelashes, pretending to lament that his own glass was empty, and was interested to see a look of fear cross the man's face.

"I've got a wife and two babes of my own, Mike," he said. "We're barely holding on, just like you."

Mike, still standing closer to Gideon than he would have liked, had gone stiff with anger. Now, he let out a long breath, relaxed a little. "And your own dear wife would be my sister, wouldn't she?" he sighed, and the sound carried all the suffering of all the Irish, from time immemorial. "How is Maureen? According to my Mary, saint that she is, Maureen hasn't been around our place for a while."

Gideon might have made some excuse and gone home then, were it not for two things. One was his reluctance to face Lydia after what he'd told her that morning, about how he'd be leaving soon, and the other was the look he'd seen in Paddy's eyes when Mike stood up to him.

"Maureen's gone to stay with that cousin of yours for a while," Paddy said, fetching a filthy rag and beginning to wipe down the bar with it. "Took the kids with her, didn't she?"

Mike straightened, worked his broad shoulders as though they pained him. And maybe they did, because he'd probably been doing the work that, in a day and a half, had nearly killed Gideon, since he was younger than Rowdy's Hank.

"Ah, yes, Cousin Bridie," Mike drawled, in a tone that sounded idle and clearly wasn't. "Thinks highly of herself, our Bridie, with her easy life."

"She can put food in Maureen's and the babes' mouths," Paddy replied, his courage at least partly restored, it seemed. "That's more than I can do, Mike."

"Aye," Mike agreed wearily. "Or me, either."

O'Hanlon was drunk — or at least, he wanted Gideon to think so. Sure, he'd had a few, but not enough to show on a man his size. It could be, of course, that Mike wasn't so accustomed to swilling whiskey as he'd seemed, but with what he owed Paddy, that didn't seem likely.

"I'd send me own Mary to Bridie," Mike went on, readying himself to leave, though he hadn't moved far from the bar. "The little ones, too, if it weren't for this damnable pride of mine."

The inference might have been that Paddy, by contrast to his brother-in-law, was not troubled by a pesky little thing like masculine pride — the bartender certainly looked as if he'd taken the remark that way. Again, Gideon noted that Paddy seemed more afraid than angry.

"She's got a houseful," Paddy said, after a few moments of uncomfortable silence. "Bridie, I mean. And her just a maid, for all her haughty ways, with a couple of rooms to herself and the gall to snitch leftovers from a lady's kitchen."

"These are hard times, Paddy," Mike lamented, swaying a little now, as he reeled away from the bar. "Hard times indeed."

"Aye," Paddy agreed, getting more Irish with every tick of the clock. "And here I am, speaking ill of our own kin, I'm that ungrateful. Why, if it weren't for Bridie —"

"If it weren't for Bridie," Mike slurred, slamming a hand down onto the bar and making Paddy start, "you'd have to share them pickled eggs, now wouldn't you, *brother,* and everything else you stuff down that gullet of yours in the space of a day?"

Paddy had no answer for that. His bulk

told the story; this was his comeuppance, evidently, for remarking on the sum Mike and the others owed for whiskey.

Having said his piece, Mike staggered out into the daylight.

Following, Gideon wondered why Mike had decided to play the drunkard.

At the road, Mike said, "If you hear the whistle in the morning — three long blasts before the rooster crows — you'll know the mine is open and you ought to come."

Gideon nodded. Watched as Mike leaned — ably for a man supposed to be so far into his cups — and retrieved his lunch pail, a lard tin like the one Lark had packed for Gideon the day before, from the high grass, where he'd stashed it on the way in.

He pried off the lid, peered inside to make sure the tinned ham was still there, saw that it was.

"A good day to you, young Yarbro," he said.

And then he turned, without waiting for a response, and headed back toward the mine and the shanties beyond, weaving as he went.

Watching, Gideon was reminded of the way a wolf or coyote will pretend to be wounded, in order to draw its prey into the midst of the waiting pack.

Dr. Venable, Lydia soon learned, was a very old man, with a thin white film of cataracts covering both his eyes. His wife, Kitty, brought him to the house, sitting ably at the reins of a one-horse buggy, and when they came in through the back door, she carried his medical kit.

By then, with help from Sarah, who had arrived soon after Lydia had sent the children away, she had changed the bedclothes and Lark's nightgown, and it seemed the worst of the bleeding was over. Lark had stopped screaming, but whether that was because the pain had subsided or because she was simply too exhausted to cry out, there was no way to know.

Although awake, Lark was mostly unresponsive.

She found enough strength to speak when the doctor entered, though. "My baby," she whispered, when the old man bent over her, murmuring gruff *there nows* and pressing a stethoscope to her distended belly. "Doc, my baby —"

"Shush, now," he replied hoarsely. "I hear somebody in there, raising hell, like any Yarbro might be expected to do."

Lydia and Sarah, standing at the foot of the bed, exchanged hopeful glances. The baby was still alive, then.

This was something Rowdy would want to know. Wyatt had brought Sarah to the house, and persuaded his brother to come downstairs to keep his vigil.

Rowdy hadn't wanted to leave Lark's side, Lydia remembered, her throat tight. But Wyatt had spoken quietly, insistently, said they'd only be in the way if they stayed, a couple of outlaws like them. At a time like this, Wyatt's reasoning went, a woman wanted other females for company, and nobody else — except for a doctor.

"Turn back those covers," "Doc," as Lark had addressed him, told his wife. "Have a look and tell me what you see."

Sarah took Lydia's hands, squeezed it hard.

And by tacit agreement, the two of them slipped out of the room.

In all the excitement, Lydia and Sarah had not spoken much, but they'd worked in concert to make Lark more comfortable, and several times, Lark had managed a grateful if frighteningly absent smile that took them both in.

Rowdy and Wyatt were at the kitchen table, when the two women descended the rear stairway.

Sarah went, not to her husband, but to her brother-in-law. Laid a gentle hand on his shoulder. "Doc heard the baby's heart beating," she said quietly. "There's reason to hope, Rowdy."

He didn't move, or speak, just stared down into the full and obviously cold cup of coffee sitting in front of him.

"I've known Doc all my life," Sarah went on gently, probably thinking, as Lydia was, that while knowing his unborn child was alive was a great relief to Rowdy, he was still crazy with worry over Lark. "He was Papa's dearest friend. He'll take good care of them *both*."

Rowdy made a sound, but didn't lift his head. "He's blind," he muttered, a few seconds later.

"Kitty sees for him," Sarah replied. "You know that."

"I wish Hon Sing was here," Rowdy said.

Wyatt said something in response, but Lydia didn't hear what it was.

Needing something to do, so she wouldn't break down, Lydia set about brewing a pot of tea. She and Sarah could use the lift it would give them, and maybe Lark would even manage a few sips, though that probably wouldn't happen.

She hadn't thought of Gideon, except fleetingly, since she'd arrived at this house and heard Lark's terrible screams. Therefore, when, looking out the window above the sink as she pumped water into the copper teakettle, she saw him vault over the back fence, not bothering with the gate, and sprint toward the house, she was startled.

The door flew open, and Gideon spared her one brief glance, as though she were a mere acquaintance, someone he'd met once or twice, and her name escaped him.

Maybe it had.

It was plain from the pallor in Gideon's face that he'd learned that Lark was in a desperate way — most likely, he'd gone by the Porter house, earlier, and found Julia and the other children there. Julia, who adored her younger uncle, though he didn't seem to notice that, would have told him what few terrifying facts she knew.

"Lark — ?" he said to Rowdy.

"It's the baby," Rowdy said distractedly. "Something's wrong."

Wyatt looked up at Gideon, looming over the table, and ordered quietly, "Sit down. Doc's with her now, and there's not much any of us can do but wait."

Sarah had moved to stand behind Wyatt now, her hands resting on her husband's shoulders. But she looked at Gideon with such sisterly tenderness that Lydia's heart squeezed.

She wished she had the courage to stand behind her own husband, the way Sarah was standing behind Wyatt, and lay her hands on his shoulders, but she knew, after this morning, that Gideon wouldn't welcome such a familiar gesture.

Upstairs, Lark cried out again.

All three of the Yarbro men got to their feet at the same time.

"No," Sarah said, moving swiftly to block them from rushing up the stairs. "Let Doc do what he needs to do. I'll go up and see what's happening — and Lydia will make tea."

"Tea?" Wyatt croaked.

But he sat down again, and so did Gideon and finally, Rowdy, too, returned to his chair.

Lydia busied herself finishing up that batch of tea, shaking all over, Lark's latest anguished cry echoing in her ears. With her back to the men, she felt free to weep, and allowed her tears to flow.

Sarah went briskly up the stairs, a small, trim figure, all business.

Lydia continued to go through the motions, finding a spouted pot, and then

220

searching out the pretty enameled box where Lark kept tea leaves. She set a kettle on the stove to heat, barely glancing at Gideon as she passed because she wanted so badly to stop and touch him, reassure him somehow.

Gideon adored Lark, just as she did. Even when he was a boy of sixteen, and Lydia herself only eight, he'd looked up to the new schoolmarm. He'd even gone to class, Lydia recalled with a pang, though that had probably been because Rowdy had forced him.

She felt his gaze resting on her before she turned away from the stove, and when she did, their eyes connected, locked.

The despair Lydia saw in Gideon's face rocked her; left no room for hurt feelings. Looking at him, she felt only love, only a desire to hold him and tell him everything would be all right.

But that wasn't to be.

Sarah came back downstairs, hurrying, a little breathless, before Lydia could say a single word to Gideon.

"The baby's come!" Sarah cried, smiling and weeping both at once. "Rowdy, the baby's here, and she's — she's breathing —"

Rowdy scraped back his chair and headed for the stairs, and this time, no one tried to stop him. No one could have.

"Lark?" Wyatt asked hoarsely, when Rowdy had gone.

"She's — alive," Sarah whispered, dashing at her face with the back of one hand. "The baby is small, and she'll need extra care, but Doc says she's sound."

The newborn squalled just then, a puny sound, but a determined one.

Wyatt rose, went to his wife, took her into his arms. Held her while she wept, murmuring to her.

Lydia was so caught up in watching them, feeling both exultation over the baby's arrival and envy because of the tender way Wyatt and Sarah comforted each other, that she was caught unawares when Gideon stepped up behind her, pulled her back against him, and kissed the top of her head.

It was all she could do not to turn into his arms — but she knew she mustn't. Gideon meant to leave her — he'd told her so that morning, straight-out — and she had to stop loving him.

Had to stop needing him.

Somehow.

After a few moments, she stiffened, and, with a sigh, Gideon released her. Stepped away.

She went back to making tea.

Wyatt said he'd better go out to the ranch, see to the kids and feed the livestock, promised Sarah he'd come back as soon as he could, and left. After some private words between Wyatt and Gideon, too low to be heard but obviously heated, both men left the house.

The teakettle boiled.

Sarah fetched two cups and two saucers from the breakfront, and Lydia poured hot water into the teapot.

All this transpired without a word passing between the two women.

They sat companionably at the table, across from each other, and sipped from their teacups.

Some time had gone by when Doc Venable came carefully down the back stairs, Kitty holding his arm and carrying his kit.

Sarah and Lydia both rose immediately. Lydia's heart was pounding in her throat, and she suspected it was the same for Sarah.

"Lark?" both women asked, at the very same moment.

Kitty, not only the doctor's wife, it seemed, but his eyes, as well, smiled, though a little sadly. "She'll pull through, I think," she said. "But there won't be any more babies."

Doc made a harrumph sound. "Five ought

to be enough for anybody," he blustered.

Dizzy with relief, Lydia literally fell back into her chair.

"Lark will need some tending," Kitty went on, after giving her husband an affectionate elbow to the ribs in response to his crusty remark. "And since men aren't much good in these situations —" Doc harrumphed again at that "— one of you will have to sit with her until she's stronger."

"I will," Lydia and Sarah chorused.

A moment later, Sarah went to Doc, kissed his grizzled old cheek. "Lydia and I will take turns," she said. *Thank you.*

"Seems like I'm still good for something after all," Doc said heartily.

"I don't know what we'd have done without you," Sarah answered, and Lydia knew her sister-in-law had addressed the remark to Kitty, as much as the doctor.

"Send word," Kitty said, already steering her nearly sightless husband toward the rear door, "if Lark starts bleeding again, or shows any signs of a fever. Day or night — no matter the time."

Lydia and Sarah both nodded.

When they'd gone, Sarah turned to Lydia. Smiled gently. "You've been here for a long time," she said. "Go home, Lydia. Get some rest. I'll stay with Lark until morning, and you can come back then."

Lydia hesitated, then saw the wisdom in Sarah's words. There was no point in both of them staying.

"What about your children?" Lydia asked, worried.

"Wyatt will look after them, and our oldest boy, Owen, too — Owen and his wife, Shannie, will see to things — they live just over the hill from us. All the little ones will be fine, Lydia. And so, thank heaven, will Lark."

Lydia nodded, swallowed. She'd been so brave all day, but now that the crisis was past, at least for the moment, she felt as though the floor had turned spongy under her feet.

But Rowdy and Lark's four children would be waiting for word, and so would the aunts. They were old ladies, not used to such upheavals as they'd endured lately, and while Helga could be trusted to keep them calm, she'd probably had a hard day, too.

"What about Hank and Julia and the little ones?" Lydia asked.

Sarah smiled, though her eyes were bright with tears. "Send them on home. They'll want to see their mother, and their baby sister, too, and they need to be where Rowdy is, even though he probably won't pay them much mind for a while."

Again, Lydia nodded. She glanced once at the ceiling, offering a silent prayer for Lark and the new baby, for all of them, and started for the door.

Sarah stopped her with a few softly spoken words of concern. "You'll be all right? Walking home by yourself?"

"I'll be fine," Lydia said. For she'd learned something important about herself that day — that she was stronger than she'd ever dreamed of being. Even when Gideon was gone, she would go on, find ways to get through the days and, worse, the nights. "I'll be just fine."

The old Porter house was dark when Gideon let himself in through the kitchen door that night. No sign of the aunts or Helga — or Lydia.

They were probably sound asleep, all of them, even though it was relatively early. After all, it had been one hell of a day.

Gideon fumbled until he found one of the light fixtures, bolted to the wall next to the door, and turned up the gas until the room took on a soft glow.

He'd tried to be quiet, but without success evidently, because a door opened and closed somewhere nearby, and then Helga appeared, looking formidable in her night-cap and wrapper.

"There's a plate for you in the warming oven," she said, none too hospitably.

Gideon nodded, wondering if Lydia had confided in the housekeeper about his leaving, and decided she probably hadn't had the chance, given the events of the day. Lydia had spent the bulk of it tending Lark and, according to Wyatt, she'd done a fine job of it.

Gideon took pride in that, took pride in *Lydia.*

He went to the stove, took his somewhat shriveled supper — some sort of meat, boiled cabbage and a baked potato — from the warming oven. If he hadn't been in the presence of a lady, he wouldn't even have bothered to get silverware and sit down at the table to eat.

"Is something wrong?" he asked moderately, when Helga kept staring at him with undisguised irritation.

"Lydia is unhappy," Helga said, keeping her distance but showing no signs of retreating to her bedroom under the stairs and leaving him to eat in peace. "And that's your doing, unless I miss my guess."

"She's worried about Lark," Gideon said, sitting down, jabbing a fork into the potato.

That was true, wasn't it? Lydia looked up to Lark, took every word the woman said as gospel.

"Lydia had been crying when Miss Mittie and Miss Millie and I got here this morning," Helga insisted, grave and suspicious. "And that was before she knew there was anything the matter with Mrs. Yarbro."

Gideon didn't answer, and even though his appetite had gone, he kept eating because his hungry body wouldn't let him stop.

"I helped you steal Lydia because I knew she'd wither away and die if she married Jacob Fitch," Helga went on. "And I figured you must have cared about her plenty, if you'd go to all the trouble of carrying her out of that wedding and bringing her here."

"I care," Gideon said.

Helga studied him for a long time, her eyes narrowed. "You'd damn well better, *Mr.* Yarbro," she finally said. *"You'd damn well better."*

With that, she turned, practically on one heel, and left Gideon alone in that empty kitchen with his stewed beef, his cabbage, his potato — and his badly bruised conscience.

CHAPTER TEN

Lydia lay alone in her marriage bed, listened to Gideon's footsteps as he climbed the nearby staircase, paused outside her door, and then went on to the next room.

Her eyes smarted fiercely as she huddled there in the darkness, curled into a stiff little ball of abject sorrow. So the leaving had already begun, then; even while they still lived under the same roof, Gideon was moving away from her — one closed door at a time.

Crying would have been a relief, but Lydia had spent all her tears that morning, when Gideon had first told her he planned to go away and leave her behind, and through the long ordeal with Lark. She was dry-eyed now, scraped to a hollow rawness inside.

Had Lark been there to advise Lydia, she probably would have sent her marching right out into the hallway and then straight on into the room where Gideon clearly meant to pass the night. But Lark *wasn't* there, or in any condition to give counsel, even if she had been, and Lydia couldn't make herself go to her husband.

It wasn't pride that kept her where she was — she didn't have much of that left, thanks to Gideon. And it certainly wasn't a lack of desire — even now, her body, like the strings of an exquisitely tuned harp, yearned for the play of Gideon's fingers, his lips, his tongue. Everything Lydia was — flesh and spirit, substance and space — ached with the effort to contain that soundless music and the need to set it free.

No, what bound Lydia — *Mrs. Gideon Yarbro,* she thought bitterly — to that bed was simple common sense. The parting would be difficult enough, whether it took place tomorrow or months from now, and giving herself up to Gideon's attentions, and the inevitable, deeper craving to follow, would render it nigh onto impossible. Even if he stayed longer than expected, the waiting would be unbearable.

So Lydia didn't move.

And she didn't sleep until far, far into the night, when weariness at last overcame her and pulled her under.

Gideon awakened, after a fitful sleep,

fraught with nightmares and more wearying than restful, with the three blasts of the mine whistle Mike had told him would come if the mine was to be open that day.

Hastily, he rolled out of the bed he'd slept in — alas, a bed without Lydia in it, and narrow and hard in the bargain — grabbed up the clothes he'd discarded the night before, and pulled them on. Given that he'd only worked half a day in these duds, they were passably clean.

Passing Lydia's door, Gideon paused outside it, as he had the previous night, wanting to knock, go in, say something that might soothe her, or even make her smile.

But what was there to say?

He hadn't meant to speak so bluntly, down there in the kitchen yesterday morning, but nevertheless, he had. And he'd only told the truth — when his job in Stone Creek was finished, he'd be hitting the road, going back to Wells Fargo, working all of the country the way he had since he'd taken up his transient profession.

Most of the other detectives he knew were unmarried — they had to be ready to board a train for parts unknown at any time, with little or no advance warning, and that was no life for a woman. Especially a woman like Lydia, whose yearning for a home and a family showed plain in her face, at least to Gideon, every time she saw Lark and Rowdy or Wyatt and Sarah together.

A few — a very few — of the company wives did travel with their husbands, but the strain soon showed. City to city, hotel to hotel, boardinghouse to boardinghouse, always another train to catch, it wore on the women, and on the men, too.

No, Lydia would not be happy with such an existence, and she'd never leave the elderly aunts on their own anyway, not even with Helga around to look out for them.

So Gideon wrenched himself away from Lydia's door, went on down the corridor to the bathroom. There, he washed up, brushed his teeth, ran a dampened comb quickly through his hair.

He descended the back stairs carrying his boots, not wanting to awaken the household, and was unsettled when he found Helga already up and dressed, and one of the aunts — Mittie or Millie? — seated at the table.

The older woman was polishing an ornate silver vase, surely rescued from the house in Phoenix before the exodus, and when she saw Gideon, she smiled wistfully and said, "The Washingtons gave this to the Fairmont family many years ago."

Gideon said nothing.

"George and Martha Washington," Mittie-or-Millie elaborated.

He probably looked impressed then, since he was.

"I've fried up a few sausages and baked biscuits for your breakfast," Helga said, jamming herself into the conversation like a wedge, and her tone and manner were as patently unfriendly as they had been last night. "Put together a dinner pail, too."

The smell of the sausage and biscuits made Gideon almost light-headed; since starting work at the mine, he'd been perennially hungry. "Thanks," he said. On another morning, in another mood, he would have tried to coax a smile from Helga, just on general principle, but he had enough hard labor ahead of him at the mine without trying to ingratiate himself to a sphinx.

"We had a platter that Mrs. Robert E. Lee presented to us, too," Millie-or-Mittie prattled on dreamily. "But I imagine that's gone to auction by now, since it surely wouldn't have fit in Sister's or my reticule."

Gideon felt a pang, hearing that. Like Lydia, the aunts had given up so many things — because of him.

He took the sausages and the biscuits Helga thrust at him, bundled into a dish towel and tucked into the lard pail and, on impulse, returned to the table side to lean down and kiss the top of Mittie-or-Millie's shimmering-white head. "That," he said, meaning it, "is a story I'd like to hear."

The tiny woman beamed up at him. "They're only things, you know. Platters and books and the like. It's the *stories* that matter. My, but Mrs. Lee was a fine lady, though sickly."

"Let the man go, Miss Mittie," Helga said, solving one mystery, anyway, and holding out the lard tin with Gideon's lunch inside. "He's got a job to get to, and you'd keep him all day, prattling on about the Washingtons and the Lees."

"They were Virginians, you know," Miss Mittie confided, twinkling, "just like the Fairmonts."

Gideon grinned. "Soon as I get home, Miss Mittie," he said, with a quelling glance at Helga, "you can tell me as much as you want to — Lees, Washingtons, Joneses."

Miss Mittie twittered at that, pleased.

Gideon crossed to Helga, accepted the lard tin with a nod of thanks, and hurried out the back door into the predawn light.

As he strode in the direction of the mine, he consumed the sausages and biscuits almost as gracelessly as Paddy had stuffed down his pickled eggs the day before. Mike would ask more questions if he got a look at the food — would anyway, when and if he learned what a fine house Gideon lived in — and Gideon wanted to *ask* questions, not answer them.

Moreover, he was famished.

Mike was waiting with the others, when Gideon got to the mine, all of them lined up to take orders from the mean-eyed foreman.

"My wee-ones," Mike said quietly, when Gideon took the open place beside him, "surely relished their supper last night, young Yarbro. Can't recall when there was ham on my table before this."

Gideon merely nodded in acknowledgment.

The foreman was pacing in front of them now, a telegram in one hand, and he cleared his throat to stop the early-morning chatter.

"Here it comes," Mike whispered. "And the lot of us, standing here like fools, with our mouths open so he can spoon us shit."

"O'Hanlon," the foreman said, "shut up."

Mike saluted. Some of the other men, including Gideon, snickered.

The foreman scowled and then held the telegram up, like a paper flag. "This here's come from the bosses, all the way back in

Chicago," he said. "There'll be no more half days."

A murmur of relief rippled through the crowd, but there were a few skeptical grunts, too. One of them came from Mike O'Hanlon.

"Steady work, right on through the winter," the foreman went on. "That's their promise."

"But," Mike muttered, in angry anticipation.

"But," the foreman continued, "there will be a cut in wages."

This announcement met with loud groans and a few curses, and O'Brien, the man who'd spoken up in the bar the day before, only to be quickly shushed by Mike, growled, "I say we throw down our picks and shovels and be done with it!"

More than one man agreed, though Mike turned and sent a glare down the line that silenced all of them.

The foreman, red faced, the telegram no longer flapping at the end of his arm like a flag on a pole, but crumpled in his right fist, looked as though the top of his head might fly off on a geyser of steam. "Go ahead," he thundered, "walk out! They'll have a trainload of coolies here to replace you by nightfall, and then what will you do?"

"No need to call in the Chinamen, Wilson," Mike said to the foreman. His tone was deceptively mild; Gideon felt his rage, like heat emanating from an overstoked furnace. "We'll do the work, and we'll take the cut in pay, because we don't have a choice, do we? We've got babes at home, every one of them hungry."

Wilson stormed over to Mike, stood nose to nose with him. "Don't you yammer on about hungry babies, O'Hanlon," he snarled. "Do you think I don't know how much money you spend at Paddy's, and here's your wife taking in laundry to take up the slack?"

No one saw it coming, least of all, Wilson.

One moment, he was standing, the next he was flat on his back, bleeding from the nose and groaning in pain, and O'Hanlon was flexing the fingers of his right hand, as though he feared he'd broken them.

No one moved.

No one spoke.

Wilson hauled himself to a sitting position, the wadded telegraph forgotten on the ground beside him. He glared up at Mike, his hatred almost palpable in the soft coolness of the morning.

"I ought to fire you," he said. "Send you packing, right here, and right now."

"But you won't, will you, *Mr.* Wilson?" Mike asked, lethally affable. "Because if you do, why, I won't have nothin' left to lose, will I? And with nothin' left to lose, I might just stomp you into a pulp your own sainted mama wouldn't recognize, mightn't I?"

"Mike," someone muttered, but the tone wasn't one of protest. It was a warning.

"To work, then," Mike said, to the whole company. "A full day's sweat for half a day's pay." He looked down at Wilson, actually extended a hand to help the man rise, a hand that was pointedly ignored. "Is that about right, Mr. Wilson?" he asked. "Half what we were getting before?"

"It's right," Wilson allowed, holding his forearm to his face in a vain attempt to staunch the flow of blood.

"And what about you? Is it half wages for you, as well?"

"That's none of your damn business," Wilson answered, on his feet now, but swaying enough that Gideon had to restrain himself from reaching out a steadying hand.

The other men were heading into the mine by then, and Gideon trailed after them, but slowly, because Mike was still standing in the same place, leaning into Wilson a little, and that meant there might be more he needed to see and hear.

"You think that's a lot of blood, Mr. Wilson?" Mike asked, his voice as friendly as if they were two friends deciding whether to while away an afternoon playing checkers or horseshoes. "It's a trickle compared to what will flow through the streets of this town if they send coolies in here to take our jobs. Put *that* in your telegram, when you go tattling to the owners about how the big Mick knocked you on your scrawny ass."

Then, all but dusting his hands together, Mike turned, bent to pick up his lunch pail, and headed toward the mine entrance.

"To work, young Yarbro," he said, as he passed Gideon. "Time's wastin' and we have our half wages to earn."

"You mustn't overdo, dear," Mittie counseled, as Lydia finished the breakfast Helga had forced her to sit down and eat before she'd allow her to leave for Lark and Rowdy's place.

"You're delicate," Millie observed. "Just like your father was."

"Nonsense," Lydia protested, though keeping her tone moderate. "I am not the least bit delicate."

"Nursing is hard work," Mittie insisted. She'd been polishing the Washingtons' vase when Lydia stepped into the kitchen, fit to wear the silver surface away, and now it gleamed so brightly that it dazzled the eyes. "Sister and I have reason to know — we helped look after wounded soldiers during the War of Northern Aggression."

"I'm quite capable of hard work," Lydia said firmly. She'd eaten all she could, and pushed her plate away, still nearly full, ignoring the look of disapproval the gesture brought from Helga. She stood, gathered her handbag, and a shawl and the thick volume of poetry she'd selected from Mr. Porter's collection the day before. "Lark Yarbro looked after me when I was sick, and I will do the same for her."

"But you have shadows under your eyes," Millie said.

The aunts were dressed, and they'd pinned up their hair, but both of them were clearly worn out. Doubtless, they would pass the day polishing things and worrying.

"We've all been through a great deal," Lydia said. She appreciated the aunts' concern; they loved her, after all, looked to her to head the family, now that Nell was gone. "I'll be right as rain in no time at all."

With that, Lydia headed for the door, made it off the back porch and partway to the side gate before Helga caught up to her.

"Those shadows under your eyes," the

housekeeper said, "have nothing to do with Mrs. Rowdy Yarbro and *everything* to do with Gideon. That's what I'm thinking."

Lydia sighed. There was no telling how much Helga knew; she was a master spy. Having no intention of discussing her marriage with Helga *or* the aunts, but not wanting to speak sharply to someone who had always been kind to her, Lydia said, "Helga, you *must* stop fretting and fussing over me. When you worry, the *aunts* worry — you know that."

"I can't help it," Helga said unhappily, looking as though she might actually break down and cry. And since this was a phenomenon Lydia had never witnessed, the possibility distressed her. "I shouldn't have helped that young rascal steal you. Sure, you'd be married to Jacob Fitch, if he hadn't stepped in, but that's something you could have gotten used to, given time. You'd still have your own house, your belongings, if I hadn't interfered, and so would Miss Mittie and Miss Millie."

Lydia smiled, touched Helga's plump shoulder. "I don't miss my belongings, Helga, and as much as it surprises me, neither do the aunts, apparently. They have the Washingtons' vase, and their letters, and that seems to be enough."

"There *was* Mrs. Lee's china platter," Helga mourned.

"It was broken years ago," Lydia said. "As you are well aware. They just pretend it's still tucked away in the dining-room cabinet because that's what they're comfortable believing."

Helga gave a sniffly little laugh, nodded. "I want you to be happy, that's all. I want that so much, sometimes I think I can't bear it. When Gideon came along, I was so sure —"

Lydia silenced her friend with a kiss on the cheek. "We can't be sure of anything in this world," she said. "Except for good friends and the love of God. Haven't you told me that yourself, a hundred times?"

Helga sniffled again, nodded again. "I suppose I have."

Lydia held Helga's shoulders a moment longer, anxious to reassure her. "I must go to Lark and the baby," she said. "Sarah probably sat up all night, and she'll need to rest."

Helga swallowed. "Yes," she agreed with resignation.

That settled, Lydia set out for the other side of town.

She walked briskly, and with purpose, and found the fresh morning air a tonic after a difficult night, reaching the Yarbro's back door within a few minutes.

Sarah was in the kitchen, washing dishes, when Lydia entered.

"How are they?" Lydia asked, in an anxious whisper. Then, noting Sarah's weary eyes asked, "How are *you?*"

"Never mind about me," Sarah said. "A few hours of sleep, and I'll be fit for anything the devil throws in my direction. Lark is still weak, but she's able to nurse little Miranda. At the moment, it's *Rowdy* I'm concerned about. Once Wyatt gets here, I'm going to ask him to take charge of his brother."

Relieved at the news about Lark and the baby, Lydia smiled at the image of anyone, other than Lark, "taking charge" of Rowdy Yarbro. "Miranda," she said. "What a lovely name."

"It was their mother's — Rowdy's and Wyatt's and Gideon's, I mean. I never knew her, unfortunately — she died when Gideon was born."

Lydia, setting aside her shawl and handbag, keeping only the book, stopped to look at Sarah. "Gideon never told me that. That his mother died in childbirth."

Sadness overtook Lydia as the knowledge sank in, though it shouldn't have. After all,

243

it had happened a long time ago, and there were a *lot* of things Gideon hadn't told her.

And never would, probably.

Sarah seemed to be looking deep into Lydia, the way Lark had always done. "Lydia," she began, and then stopped, and then began again. "Lydia, are things — *all right,* between you and Gideon?"

Lydia blinked quickly, so she wouldn't cry. "It — it was a marriage of expediency," she finally said, with as much dignity as she could muster. "An arrangement. As such —"

"Rowdy told Wyatt what happened down in Phoenix," Sarah broke in, "and Wyatt told me. He said you were going to marry some man against your will and Gideon put a stop to it, and there had to be a wedding or he'd have gone to jail —"

Lydia's eyes widened. This was the first she'd heard about anyone going to jail.

Seeing her expression, Sarah groaned. "You didn't know."

"I didn't know," Lydia confirmed.

"Oh, Lydia," Sarah said, coming to her, taking both her hands.

Had Lark not needed her, and baby Miranda, too, Lydia would have stormed out of that house, gone straight to the mine, climbed down the shaft if she had to, and demanded an immediate explanation from Gideon.

"Tell me why Gideon would have been arrested, Sarah," she said evenly. "If he hadn't married me."

Before Sarah could answer, however, Rowdy appeared on the kitchen stairs, carrying little Marietta piggyback.

"Sarah," he said, sounding more like his old self, but still wan, "go and lie down somewhere, try to get some shut-eye. I'll do my best to keep the kids quiet."

Sarah hesitated, gave Lydia an apologetic glance, nodded to Rowdy, and left the kitchen through an arched doorway.

Rowdy came the rest of the way down the stairs, set Marietta gently on the floor to play.

"Sit down," he told Lydia gruffly. "Please."

"Lark —"

"She's fine for now," Rowdy said.

"I'm three," Marietta interjected cheerfully. "And I have *two* sisters now."

"Indeed you do." Lydia smiled, taking a seat at the table.

Rowdy joined her. "I thought Gideon would have told you by now," he said. "The U.S. Marshal down in Phoenix was prepared to file kidnapping charges against him. In fact, there will be a pair of deputies on the doorstep anytime now wanting to know if you came to Stone Creek and married Gideon willingly."

"Jacob went to the *U.S. Marshal?*" Lydia whispered, her head spinning.

"Yes."

"And if I told these — deputies — that Gideon forced me to leave Phoenix and marry him, they would arrest him?"

"That's about the size of it," Rowdy said solemnly, watching her very closely. "And the marriage would be annulled, if that's what you wanted."

Sending Gideon to prison was unthinkable, of course.

And yet, for one moment of vengeful temptation, Lydia considered doing just that.

In the next, she dismissed the idea.

Clasping her hands together in her lap, she lowered her head, too mortified to meet Rowdy's gaze because she was afraid, if he looked into her eyes, he'd see that for the merest fraction of a heartbeat —

She started slightly, but did not pull away, when Rowdy reached across the table and clasped her hand, squeezed it briefly before letting go. "Do you love my brother, Lydia?" he asked, very quietly.

Lydia bit down hard on her lower lip. She

wanted a life like Lark's, even after what she'd seen the woman endure, a life like Sarah's — a loving husband, babies of her own, a real, true home.

Could she have those things with Gideon?

Surely not. He'd already told her he didn't mean to stay in Stone Creek.

Still, she could not deny Rowdy an answer, because he'd asked so gently, as though he really cared.

Wretchedly, she nodded. "Yes," she said. "I love Gideon."

"But?" Rowdy prompted, still gentle. It touched Lydia deeply that, after all he'd seen Lark go through, all the suffering that had caused him, he genuinely wanted to help.

"He doesn't love me in return," Lydia managed, in such a small voice that Rowdy leaned forward a little to hear.

Playing on the floor, Marietta recited, "He doesn't love me in return."

"Hush," Rowdy told his daughter, without looking in her direction. "I'm sorry, Lydia — she's like a little parrot. Repeats everything."

"She's a darling," Lydia said, and began to cry. "I wish I had ten like her."

Rowdy chuckled at that. "Be careful what you wish for, Lydia Yarbro. Because you might just get it."

Hearing someone address her like that, by her married name, affected Lydia in an oddly profound way. "Lydia Yarbro," she repeated brokenly.

"That's who you are, isn't it?" Rowdy asked, his voice husky. "And why do you think Gideon doesn't love you?"

"Because — because he's leaving town," Lydia said, and immediately wished she hadn't.

"What?" Rowdy asked, not only surprised, but angry.

"He told me so yesterday morning," Lydia admitted, because she was in too deep now to go back.

Rowdy muttered a swearword, shoved splayed fingers through his already-mussed hair.

Marietta repeated the curse, beaming.

Lydia laughed, through tears, and got to her feet. "I've said too much," she told her brother-in-law. "If you'll excuse me, I'd like to go up and see Lark now, and — and the baby."

Rowdy nodded. "I suppose he's at the mine?"

"Yes," Lydia said on her way to the staircase, stooping to pat Marietta's golden head as she passed. Pausing on the first step, gripping the newel post, she added, "Please don't say anything to Gideon, Rowdy. Promise me you won't."

Rowdy pushed back his chair, rose. "I can't do that, Lydia. I can't make a promise I know I won't keep."

Lydia closed her eyes, once again wishing that she'd held her tongue.

When she opened them again, Rowdy was bending down, scooping Marietta up into his arms. Without a word, he left the room, probably taking his little girl to join her sister and brothers, in some other part of the house.

After a moment spent recovering her composure, Lydia climbed the stairs and walked along the hallway, let herself into Rowdy and Lark's bedroom.

Lark was sitting up, with pillows at her back, holding an impossibly small bundle in her arms. Although she was still very pale, when she smiled she looked almost radiant. "Come see your new little niece, Lydia," she said. "Miranda Jane Yarbro, this is your aunt Lydia."

Lydia's throat tightened with a fresh rush of emotion. She'd never been anyone's "Aunt Lydia" — until she married Gideon. Like someone in a daze, she approached the bed, sat down carefully, so she wouldn't jostle Lark, and accepted the tiny bundle.

Miranda was perfect, though hardly larger than a doll. As small as that bundle was, Lydia realized, it consisted more of blankets than baby.

Holding that child, Lydia felt such a terrible and hurtful yearning that she could not catch her breath.

Downstairs, someone turned the doorbell, loudly, insistently.

Lark frowned at the sound.

Lydia barely paid it any mind — she was absorbed in little Miranda, noting her every feature — unbelievably small fingers, complete with nails, a pert little nose, blue eyes with gossamer lashes. She had a shock of dark hair that would probably turn fair, and her ears — her *ears.* They were like tiny pink seashells, thin enough to see through.

The clamor on the front stairs finally distracted her from the baby, but barely. Carefully, and with a nearly overpowering reluctance, she handed the child back to Lark just as Hank burst through the doorway.

"Aunt Lydia," he said. "Papa says come quick!"

For the briefest moment, Lydia thought someone had come bearing word that Gideon had been hurt — or worse — at the mine. Hank immediately disabused her of that notion.

"Well," he said, his gaze connecting briefly with his mother's, "maybe he didn't say 'quick.' But there are men downstairs, and they have badges and round hats, like Sam O'Ballivan wears, and they want to see you."

Lydia cast a glance at Lark, who was frowning in concern. Rowdy probably hadn't told her that the deputies were on their way, given all they'd both had to cope with over the past twenty-four hours.

Standing, Lydia smoothed her hair and her skirts. She would tell the men that she'd left her home and Phoenix willingly, married Gideon Yarbro without coercion of any kind. And they would go away.

It was really quite simple.

But when she followed Hank down the stairs and into the front parlor, she nearly fainted on the threshold.

Jacob Fitch rose from a wingback chair and turned, smiling, to face her. "Enough of this foolishness, Lydia darling," he said. "All is forgiven, and I've come to take you home."

CHAPTER ELEVEN

Lydia stared at Jacob, stunned, though after a few moments of reflection, she decided she shouldn't have been at all surprised by the encounter. On some level, she'd known all along that she hadn't seen the last of her spurned bridegroom.

"Mr. Fitch," she said, in stiff greeting, flustered and quite unable to hide the fact from him *or* the imposing deputies, one standing with his back to the fireplace, the other perched on the edge of a chair seat, as though prepared to leap up and give chase if she fled.

Thank heaven Rowdy was there, and clearly had no intention of leaving her alone with two strangers and the last man on the face of the earth she wanted to see.

Fitch approached her, stood so close that she could feel his breath on her face, fetid and hot. " 'Mr. Fitch'?" he countered, speaking gently for Rowdy's benefit, and that of the deputy marshals. But *she* could see the dangerous fury in his eyes, the passion, not for her, but for revenge. "Come now, Lydia dear. You've never addressed me so formally before." This was untrue; she'd never addressed him by his Christian name, but she did not refute the statement.

He lowered his voice then, to a whisper, a bare breath of air. "Are you — are you *untouched?*"

Color surged into Lydia's face, but the source of it was indignation, not shame. Her first impulse was to lash out, to say that she had been *thoroughly* touched, but common sense warned her against it. In any case, it was none of Jacob Fitch's affair, what had and hadn't gone on between her and Gideon, nor was it something she would air in front of Rowdy and the deputies.

She remained stubbornly silent.

And something more frightening than fury moved in Mr. Fitch's eyes then — a coldness that sent icy chills through Lydia. Of course he had interpreted her silence as an acknowledgment that she was no longer the virgin he'd reserved for himself.

In the next instant, he'd changed again. Become the magnanimous gentleman, willing to overlook an indiscretion. "Either way," Jacob Fitch said, his voice swelling to fill the room again, "this silly little escapade is over." He drew his watch from the pocket of his brocade vest, flicked open the case with a quick motion of his thumb. "If we hurry, my dear, we can gather the aunts and that *housekeeper* you seem to hold in such high regard, and catch the afternoon train back to Phoenix — where we belong."

"I'm not going anywhere," Lydia said, knowing she might not have been brave enough to utter those words if Rowdy hadn't been there, but equally certain that she would fight to the death if Jacob Fitch tried to remove her from that house by force.

"Don't be stubborn," Fitch crooned, taking Lydia's chin between his fingers. Although the gesture probably *looked* like one of affectionate tolerance to the deputies and possibly even to Rowdy, it was, instead, a subtle show of power — only a shade more pressure, and he would have left bruises. "I haven't sold your things, or your aunts'. Mother and I have moved in, and all we lack for a happy household is *you,* darling."

Lydia finally found the strength to pull free of Mr. Fitch's grasp, step around him, and approach the nearest deputy, the taller one, standing silently in front of the fireplace.

The man's long face seemed wooden, and his deep-socketed gray eyes showed no expression at all. Overall, he reminded Lydia of Abraham Lincoln, with his melancholy countenance and homely features.

"I left Phoenix willingly," Lydia told him clearly. "And I married Gideon Yarbro because I wanted to be his wife."

The deputy's thoughtful stare was unnerving. "Mr. Fitch here," he finally said, his voice a deep and resonant base, "claims he and Mr. Yarbro exchanged blows, and then Mr. Yarbro carried you out of that house, kicking and struggling all the way. We've spoken to the justice of the peace and the other witnesses, Miss Fairmont, and they all confirmed Mr. Fitch's account of the incident."

"I am no longer 'Miss Fairmont,'" Lydia said evenly. "Please address me as Mrs. Yarbro, if you don't mind."

The deputy's smile came as a surprise, given his dour manner and plain features. "If you're afraid to tell us the truth," he said, quite kindly, but with an undercurrent of iron in his voice, "you needn't be. Mr. Sullivan and I are duly sworn officers of the law. We will protect you and escort you safely back to Phoenix, I assure you."

Rowdy gave a little snort at this, earning

himself a scalding glance from the tall deputy. Out of the corner of her eye, Lydia saw that her brother-in-law was undaunted by the look, and silently blessed him for standing by her.

"I'm not afraid to tell you the truth," Lydia said, holding her head high. "I have just *done* that. I am married to Gideon Yarbro in the eyes of God and man and I wish to remain so, and if you would please leave and take Mr. Fitch with you, I would be most grateful."

The deputy took her left hand, briefly, ran a calloused thumb across the knuckles. "You're not wearing a wedding band, Mrs. Yarbro."

"We haven't had an opportunity to purchase one," Lydia replied.

Mr. Sullivan, the second deputy, rose from his chair and spoke for the first time. He was shorter than his cohort, and stocky, with bristly black eyebrows and jowls. "Mr. Fitch," he said, swiveling his gaze to Jacob, "it appears the lady would prefer to remain in Stone Creek, with her husband. There is no more we can do here."

Fitch seethed visibly, nearly shimmered with the heat of anger, and even from a distance of several yards, Lydia felt the impact of his fury as surely as if he'd drawn back his hand and struck her.

"This is outrageous!" he ranted, spittle flying from his mouth as he spoke. So much for the generous gentleman, swift to forgive. "Can't you see — can't either of you see — what's happening here? Lydia is being held prisoner! And why has no one asked to see the marriage certificate?"

"I'll thank you to keep your voice down, Mr. Fitch," Rowdy said, in an ominously quiet tone. "My wife is not well, and I will not have my children frightened." Then, going to a desk and opening a drawer, he brought out the ornate sheet of paper Gideon, Lydia and the minister had all signed. "As for the legal evidence that a wedding did take place, here it is."

The Lincoln-like deputy took the certificate, examined it, handed it back. He hadn't needed to see it, Lydia knew; he believed her assertion that she wanted to stay in Stone Creek, with Gideon.

The front door opened, in the near distance, though Lydia could not see into the entryway from where she stood, and she raised a silent prayer that Gideon hadn't gotten word that Mr. Fitch and the deputies had arrived. He would either hand her over to Fitch with apologies for spoiling the first wedding, or get himself arrested on the spot for taking his fists to the man.

For all this, Lydia was disappointed, as well as relieved, when Wyatt stepped into the parlor, accompanied by a young man who resembled Sarah, though his hair was light, instead of dark like Sarah's and Wyatt's.

This would be Owen, she thought, calmer now that she knew the matter at hand had been settled, at least for the moment. To herself, she observed that Sarah hardly seemed old enough to have a broad-shouldered son, nearly as tall as Wyatt.

"I will not tolerate this, Lydia," Fitch raged, ignoring the new arrivals. All his attention was focused on her, and it burned like sunlight narrowed to a pinpoint through a powerful magnifying glass. "Do you hear me? I will not be played for a fool like this!"

"Seems a little late to avoid that," Rowdy drawled. "And I won't tell you to lower your voice again."

"I'll burn that stupid house to the ground!" Fitch answered, ignoring Rowdy, but he rasped the threat, instead of shouting like before. "Those precious paintings, the books and papers and bric-a-brac — all of it!"

The deputies closed in on either side of him, each taking an arm. "Arson is a crime,

258

Mr. Fitch," the tall one told him quietly. "Get hold of yourself."

With that, the two men propelled a still-sputtering Jacob out of the parlor, into the foyer, and then through the front door.

Lydia hurried to the window to watch the trio struggle down the front walk to the gate, Jacob Fitch resisting all the way.

"Are you all right, Lydia?" Rowdy asked quietly, standing at her side now, taking a firm but gentle hold on her elbow.

She nodded, swallowed, straightened her spine.

"I'd best get back to Lark," she said.

But her head swam suddenly, as she turned too quickly from the window, and she might have lost her balance, even fainted, if Rowdy hadn't been so quick to take a second, and much firmer, hold on her arm.

"I'm taking you home," he said.

She shook her head. "I'm quite all right, really —"

Wyatt spoke then. "Any fool could see you're not," he argued. "Owen, go and hitch up Rowdy's buggy and see your aunt Lydia home to the Porter house."

Owen nodded, and without a word, left the house to do Wyatt's bidding. Lydia had learned, during the cleaning party at her place, that Wyatt was actually Owen's stepfather, though Wyatt had adopted him soon after he and Sarah were married, and Owen had taken the Yarbro name.

"I don't want to go," Lydia protested. She had promised to spell Sarah, take over Lark's care for the day, but that wasn't the whole reason she resisted the idea. She was terrified that Jacob Fitch would somehow escape the deputies before they'd boarded the train and come in search of her.

The thought of Fitch confronting her at some unexpected moment sent a jolt of fear through her. He might lie in wait for her somewhere, awaiting his chance to catch her alone. And practically anyone on the street could tell him where Gideon Yarbro and his bride had taken up residence, seeing no reason to withhold the information. Suppose he came there while Gideon was working? She and the aunts and Helga would be alone, with no way to defend themselves.

She soon noticed that Rowdy was watching her closely; he'd clearly guessed what she was thinking — or simply allowed common sense to lead him to the same conclusions. "Wyatt, I'd be obliged if you'd see Lydia home yourself, and stay with her until Owen fetches Gideon from the mine to look after his wife."

The slight emphasis he'd put on the last two words reminded Lydia that Rowdy was still annoyed with Gideon, and it was her fault. She'd told him that Gideon planned to leave Stone Creek, after all.

Again, and sorely, she wished she hadn't.

"Please," she said, "this is all unnecessary—"

"I don't think so," Rowdy said flatly.

"Neither do I," Wyatt agreed.

And so it was settled.

Owen set out for the mine.

Wyatt went out to the large barn behind the house to hitch up the horse and buggy.

Barely a quarter of an hour later, Lydia was home, sitting glumly at her own kitchen table, while the aunts polished things and Wyatt sipped coffee and chatted idly with Helga. He seemed relaxed, but Lydia couldn't help noticing that he'd remained standing, and glanced out the side window every few minutes.

Perhaps half an hour had elapsed in this fashion when the back door slammed open and Gideon burst through the opening, wild-eyed and breathless. His gaze sought Lydia, moving from person to person, and landed on her with an actual impact.

"Holy Christ," he rasped, sagging against

261

the doorjamb.

"Mr. *Yarbro*," one of the aunts scolded, though kindly. "Taking the Lord's name in vain is hardly becoming."

Gideon did not respond, did not look away from Lydia's face, did not move even when Owen appeared behind him, and was blocked from entering the house because his uncle was still standing on the threshold.

"Guess Owen and I will be going now," Wyatt said, with a grin in his voice.

"And that's enough polishing for one day," Helga interjected, directing her words to the aunts. She'd been peeling potatoes for a stew, but now she dried her hands quickly on her apron, then removed it. "Miss Mittie, Miss Millie, get your shawls and parasols. We're going out for a constitutional."

The aunts seldom left home, let alone took constitutionals, but they fetched the specified items from their room and promptly vanished just the same, as did Wyatt and Owen.

Gideon, who had been forced to leave the doorway so they could all get out, closed the door with slightly more force than Lydia deemed necessary.

"Are you all right?" he asked, after a very long and very uncomfortable silence.

"Yes," Lydia said, without moving from her chair. "And you may rest easy, Mr. Yarbro. You will not be arrested for kidnapping me." She straightened a little. "Even though it would have been just what you deserved."

That familiar, maddening grin crooked up one side of his mouth. He hauled back a chair, turned it and Lydia's chair, as well, with her still in it, so they were face-to-face, with their knees touching.

"You started this," he reminded her easily, even lightly. "You sent the letter."

"Well, I *shouldn't* have."

"But you did." Wisely, Gideon did not touch Lydia, except where their knees met, because if he had, she would surely have slapped his face with enough force to turn his head. "I wrote that letter at this table," he said, thumping the surface once with the knuckles of his right hand. "Do you remember?"

Lydia closed her eyes, all of it coming back to her. She'd been small and sick and afraid, grieving for her dead father. Granted, John Fairmont had not been *much* of a father, but he'd been all she had, until Lark, until Nell.

Until Gideon.

"Of course I remember."

263

"I kept my word," Gideon went on. "I will *always* keep my word, Lydia."

By sheer force of will, Lydia did not give way to the tears scalding the backs of her eyes. Refraining from slapping him with all the strength she had proved still more difficult than before. "You promised to love, honor and cherish me, till death do us part," she reminded him. "But you *don't* love me. And — and you're leaving. Do you plan to 'honor and cherish' from a distance?"

"I won't be going away for a while," Gideon said, almost tenderly.

"Do you think that makes this easier to bear?" Lydia retorted hotly. "Any of it?"

"You could have left with Fitch and the deputies," he said reasonably. "Since we haven't consummated the marriage, an annulment would be easy to get."

"It would be simpler for you if I *had* gone back to Phoenix, wouldn't it, Gideon?" Lydia challenged, flushed and trembling a little. "You could have gone right on with your life as if nothing had happened, without troubling yourself over me, or the aunts or Helga."

"No, Lydia," Gideon answered patiently, "it *wouldn't* have been simpler for me. Fitch will hurt you, if he gets the chance, and I can't let that happen."

"How do you intend to prevent it?" Lydia asked, sounding far more reasonable than she felt. "When you're off to — wherever it is you mean to go when you leave here?"

"My brothers will keep you safe if the need arises, Lydia. Owen, too." He paused, chuckled, though without amusement. "All three of them will want to peel my hide off in strips, it's true. But you're a Yarbro and a woman into the bargain, and that matters to them."

"Does it matter to *you*, Gideon?"

He flinched slightly at the question. "Believe it or not, yes."

"Well, I *don't* believe it."

Gideon shrugged one shoulder. He was dirty from working in the mine, Lydia finally noticed, and his beard was coming in. "That's your prerogative, I guess," he said, with such exasperating equanimity that Lydia couldn't bear it.

She *did* strike him then, hard, with the flat of her palm.

She was instantly horrified at what she'd done, and yet not one bit sorry.

Gideon didn't move. He just sat there, with the mark of her hand flaring red on his cheek, and said nothing at all.

She pushed back her chair so rapidly, so suddenly, that it toppled over with a loud crash. As she stood and turned to flee, though, Gideon caught hold of her arm and pulled her onto his lap. Encircled her with steel-strong arms when she struggled to get free again.

Anger would have been far easier to endure than the way he held her, but even after she'd struck him, Gideon hadn't lost his temper. He propped his chin on the top of her head and murmured to her as though *she'd* been the one slapped.

She began to cry then.

"Shh," Gideon said, and pressed her head to his shoulder as gently as if she were again the child he'd brought safely through a snowstorm, on the back of a horse, ten years before. "Shh."

It was late when the knock sounded at the back door.

Gideon had been half expecting a visitor all evening — that was why he'd waited up. Lydia, the aunts and Helga had long since retired, vanishing to their various quarters as soon as the supper dishes had been washed and put away.

The meal would have been unbearable, he supposed, if the aunts hadn't regaled him with the promised stories about Mrs. Robert E. Lee, whom they'd been personally acquainted with, and the Washingtons, known through family lore.

Looking out the window before he unlatched the door, Gideon was surprised to see a boy standing on the porch. He'd expected Rowdy, come to lecture him on the duties of a husband, or maybe Wilson, bent on firing him from the mine crew for leaving in the middle of the morning and never going back.

He opened the door.

The boy, no older than ten or eleven, barefoot and wearing short pants, his face in shadow because of the brim of his ragged hat, shoved a slip of paper into Gideon's hand. "A feller paid me to bring this," he said. And as quickly as that, he was gone.

Gideon saw no use in pursuing the messenger to ask who the "feller" was — it was stone-dark out, with the moon gone behind the clouds, and the kid would have outrun him easily. He'd had the furtive look of somebody who ran from a lot of things.

So Gideon stepped back, shut the door, and opened the folded sheet of paper. The handwriting wasn't familiar, but the cryptic message included the code phrase he'd been told to watch for when he accepted the assignment.

Sorry to hear of your sister's passing. Services at noon on Sunday.

Gideon crumpled the note into a wad, found a match and struck it on the sole of his boot, and lit the thing on fire. Watched as it fell into the sink in a blazing ball, and was consumed.

He'd been expecting a summons like this one, of course, but not so soon.

Either his employers were expecting miracles, or there had been a change in plans.

Taking the train to Flagstaff would attract attention. He'd have to borrow a horse from Rowdy or Wyatt — hiring one at the livery stable would arouse comment, too, though not so much as *buying* one — and either or both of his brothers would have questions when he made the request.

He wouldn't have to lie, though — that was the only comfort. He *would* be visiting Rose's grave, a place he'd haunted like a ghost until he'd come to Stone Creek to stay with Rowdy, the year he turned sixteen. Even while he was away at college in Philadelphia, and then working, he'd sent money to Rose's mother, Ruby, on a regular basis, with the tacit understanding that she'd buy some trinket and snug it next to Rose's

268

headstone.

Under normal circumstances, Rowdy, already suspicious, might have insisted on coming along, but with Lark recovering from a birth that had nearly put her in a grave of her own, that wouldn't be a concern.

Wyatt would be honor-bound to stay in Stone Creek and make sure Lydia was in no danger from Fitch. As for Owen, well, he had a pretty young wife of his own to look after, plus his younger brothers and sisters and a ranch to run on top of that, with Wyatt and Sarah spending so much time in town. No, Owen would have neither the time nor the inclination to bird-dog Gideon to Flagstaff.

If there was a blessing to be found in Lark's recent ordeal, besides the baby, of course, it was that the wedding reception she'd planned to throw for him and Lydia, scheduled for Sunday afternoon, had surely gone by the wayside.

Explaining to Lydia shouldn't be difficult — she probably wouldn't be speaking to him anyhow. Helga and the aunts were another matter, but he'd get by them, too — somehow.

Thrusting a hand through his hair, Gideon tilted his head back to look up at the ceiling.

Was Lydia sleeping, or lying awake?

If he dared to set foot in that bedroom, would he be welcome, or would she greet him with a shotgun?

He smiled at the thought of Lydia armed and dangerous.

Oh, she was dangerous, all right. And shooting him might be a mercy, compared to what she was putting him through now.

He turned down the one gaslight he'd kept burning after the women went to bed, made his way to the back stairs, sat down on the bottom step to pull off his boots, and then climbed.

Again, he hesitated outside Lydia's door.

There was a rim of light beneath it — she was awake then, probably reading.

The temptation to go in there and do what came naturally was as formidable as any Gideon had ever experienced, but the grim truth was, he'd let things go too far already. Technically, Lydia was still a virgin, and she could seek an annulment with a clear conscience, but she wasn't the innocent young woman he'd carried out of that mansion in Phoenix, either.

He'd robbed her of that. Shown her things that should have waited until a *real* husband

270

came along, some fine day in the future. A man who could love Lydia the way she deserved to be loved.

Standing in front of the door to that room, Gideon braced his hands on the frame and lowered his head. Thinking of her sharing a bed with another man, giving birth to someone else's children, had struck him like a fist to the midsection. He needed to catch his breath.

When that door suddenly swung open, and Lydia was standing there in that nightgown he'd pushed up to her neck, with her hair neatly plaited and a book tucked under one arm, he couldn't think of a single reason for being where he was.

She simply stared up at him for a long time, her brow slightly furrowed. Then, sure enough, she found her tongue. "Why are you *skulking* outside my bedroom door, Gideon Yarbro?" she demanded, without the faintest trace of charity in her voice or her bristly countenance.

"Just making sure you're all right," Gideon said, priding himself on his quick thinking.

"I'm perfectly fine," Lydia replied pointedly.

The braid made her look like a schoolmarm, and Gideon wanted to undo it, but that would get him whacked again for sure, and his face was still smarting a little from the last time Lydia had let him have it.

"Well," he said, awkward now, "good night."

"Good night," Lydia answered tersely.

Right after that, she shut the door in his face.

He supposed it was better than another slap, but not by much.

By God, not by much.

With a sigh, he thrust himself away from the door casing, turned, and went on to his own room.

He was late for work the next morning because he wasn't about to leave Lydia, the aunts and Helga home alone until he had it on good authority that Jacob Fitch hadn't gotten away from those deputies somehow, that he was back in Phoenix. Which meant he had to herd all the females over to Rowdy's place, with the lot of them fussing, because Lydia was the only one who actually wanted to go.

Helga and the matched set of old ladies gave him guff the whole way. The aunts wanted to stay home and polish things — they'd hit the mother lode of tarnished silver, to hear them tell it, snooping through an old trunk they'd found in one of the closets, and Helga kept insisting that they'd be fine at home, since she'd take the stove poker to anybody who was up to no good, including Fitch.

Lydia, for her part, walked well ahead of the group and pretended she hadn't made their acquaintance — especially Gideon's.

"You two are the dangedest pair of newly-weds *I've* ever seen," Helga commented, noting the ample distance between Gideon and Lydia, as they walked. "What has gotten into her, anyhow?"

"How should I know?" Gideon grumbled. "I'm only her *husband.*"

"Then why don't you act like one?" Helga immediately retorted.

"What is that supposed to mean?" He instantly regretted the question, which had been uttered out of frustration and not as an inquiry, because there was a very real danger that Helga would haul off and answer.

The housekeeper moved a little closer to him, while the aunts did their best to catch up with Lydia. They must have made quite a spectacle, Gideon thought ruefully, straggling through the streets of Stone Creek like four hens and a rooster.

"I do the tidying up, remember," Helga

informed him, in a scalding whisper, "and there were *two* beds to make upstairs this morning, instead of one, like there ought to be. And it was the same yesterday, too."

Gideon set his jaw. Damned if he'd explain something that personal to Helga or anybody else. Hell, he couldn't even explain it to *himself.*

Rowdy's place was in sight now, at the end of the tree-lined lane. Gideon stopped and folded his arms, prepared to wait until he'd seen all four women go inside. When he had, he'd head for the mine on the double.

Wilson, the foreman, was bound to be in a foul mood after the humiliation he'd suffered at Mike O'Hanlon's hands the morning before, and he'd be looking for somebody to take it out on. As it was, Gideon had walked off the job yesterday, when Owen came to tell him Fitch and the U.S. Marshal's deputies had been at Rowdy's place questioning Lydia, and now he'd be showing up when everybody else was already down in the hole.

His assignment in Stone Creek would quickly become irrelevant if he got fired from the mining crew before he'd found out if there was a strike in the works or not, and taken the necessary steps to avert it.

Helga glared at him in parting — that was

more attention than *Lydia* had spared him — and trundled along that lane like an overloaded hay wagon on a downhill slope, turning once to call back to Gideon, "Stubborn! That's what you are, Mr. Yarbro — *stubborn!*"

He kept his arms folded, tapped one foot. He'd been called worse things than stubborn in his time.

After what seemed like the passing of a season, instead of just a few minutes, the females were all inside Rowdy's house.

Gideon didn't exactly *run* to the mine, but his strides were long.

" 'Tis lucky you are, young Yarbro," Mike informed him, when he set aside his lunch pail and grabbed a shovel. "Wilson's ailin' today — somethin' about his nose — and kept to his bunk this mornin'. If he was around, you'd be headin' right back down the road, with what little pay you have comin' and all the free time a man could want."

Gideon began shoveling ore into a waiting cart. "You know, O'Hanlon," he said, "I don't *feel* all that lucky."

Mike gave a snort at that. "Wife trouble," he diagnosed. "I'd know that look anywhere."

"What look?" Gideon snapped.

"Peckish," Mike said, leaning on the handle of his own shovel. "Tight around the mouth, and hollow-eyed, too. The little woman has turned you out of the marriage bed, hasn't she?"

Gideon heaved a double-load of ore into the cart. "O'Hanlon?"

"Aye?"

"Shut up."

Mike laughed at that, a great, booming shout of a laugh, loud enough to bring the support beams down on all their heads. When he'd regained his composure, he proceeded to dispense advice. "What you do, young Yarbro, is you show the little lady who's boss, and lose no time doing it, or she'll henpeck you till you bleed."

Gideon rolled his eyes, but kept working.

"It worked with my Mary," Mike said, joining Gideon at the ore pile and keeping up with him easily. "You go straight to Paddy's after the shift ends today, and you don't turn up at home until you're sure she's good and sorry for treatin' you poorly."

"Sorry," Gideon said, tight-jawed and shoveling faster. "I don't happen to have another twenty-dollar gold piece in my boot, Mike."

"Well, we're not goin' to Paddy's to *drink*, are we?" Mike countered, swelling with pretended indignation.

"Why else would you go there?" Gideon retorted, sweating. He was starting to get used to the hard physical labor, but he still ached all over.

Mike paused in his work, stepped closer, and lowered his voice. "Because there's a meeting," he said. "In the back room."

Gideon stopped, rammed the head of his shovel into the pile of raw copper. "What kind of meeting?" he asked, with suitable impatience. In truth, his heart was beating a little faster, and not because he'd been chucking ore into a mine cart at twice his usual pace.

This might be the chance he'd been waiting for.

"If you want to know," Mike said, every trace of his formerly jovial manner gone, "you'll just have to join the rest of us at Paddy's after the whistle blows, now won't you?"

CHAPTER TWELVE

Lydia met with good news when she entered the Yarbro house that morning, having taken herself firmly in hand on the doorstep and set aside her annoyance with Gideon — for the time being. Rowdy immediately reported that Lark, though still weak, appeared to be out of danger, and baby Miranda, small as she was, thrived. Considerably reassured, the marshal of Stone Creek returned to his duties, though he promptly sent his deputies, one posted at the front and one at the back, in case Mr. Fitch should return.

Lydia's spirits were dampened a little, though, when it occurred to her that the deputies might have been instructed to keep her, her aunts and Helga *inside,* while keeping Fitch or any strangers out.

Helga reinforced that interpretation by declaring that, if she was going to be held captive, she might as well make herself useful, and set about putting the children and the house to rights, since some things had gone by the wayside when Lark took sick.

The aunts seemed snug and content after they settled in the smaller of the two parlors, paging through an album of photographs and chatting quietly, and Lydia, with nothing to do once she'd looked in on Lark and the baby and found them both sleeping peacefully, wandered about, growing increasingly restless. It wasn't that she had imperative errands to run, it was that she knew she wouldn't be *allowed* to, and that chafed her increasingly independent spirit.

She'd changed, since arriving in Stone Creek, and not just because she'd experienced ecstasy with Gideon, either. She was stronger, somehow, more inclined to take chances. More of a *Yarbro.*

She had Lark, and the example she'd set, to thank for that, she supposed.

There was some brief and blessed distraction at midmorning, when Maddie and Sam O'Ballivan arrived, just the two of them, to inquire after Lark and get a look at the new baby.

Sam, a powerfully built man, not classically handsome but ruggedly attractive just the same, kept adjusting his string tie. Clearly, he was more at home on the range than shut up in a house, in his Sunday suit, with no one around but a gaggle of women.

Still, whenever he looked at Maddie, the earth seemed to shift slightly on its axis. Lydia, observing this, longed yet again to be loved in the same quiet, fierce way these Stone Creek men seemed to love their women.

How was it possible to be married, she wondered, and still feel utterly bereft, like some spirit condemned to wander between worlds, having no discernible impact on either?

With Maddie occupied upstairs, visiting a now-wakeful Lark and admiring little Miranda, the walls of that warm, welcoming house seemed to close in on Lydia, the same way she suspected they were closing in on Sam O'Ballivan. She'd tried to engage him in conversation, and while he was friendly enough, he was clearly a man of few words.

Suddenly, though both doors were guarded, she knew she *had* to get out.

She still had no specific destination in mind; she simply wanted fresh air, a brisk walk, a chance to think with no one watching her.

Helga was busy gathering sheets and clothing to be laundered.

The aunts remained occupied with the

album, the fresh pot of tea Lydia had brewed and served to them and their constant exchange of threadbare memories.

Sarah had gone home to the ranch the night before, with Wyatt and Owen, to attend to her own house and children, and was thereby unavailable as a companion.

The books in Rowdy's study were appealing, but Lydia felt too agitated to read — she wouldn't be able to sit still, feeling the way she did, let alone concentrate.

When Maddie and Sam left, keeping their visit short out of consideration for Lark, Lydia felt more like a caged bird than ever.

It would be easy enough to leave without her aunts or Helga noticing — but how could she get past the deputies? Rowdy *had* given them direct orders, Helga reported, that none of the women were to leave the house unescorted until he'd received a telegram from the U.S. Marshal's office confirming that Jacob Fitch was indeed back in Phoenix, where he would not present a threat.

As things turned out, it was little Julia, quietly helping Marietta to dress and undress a doll in a corner of the main parlor, who provided the answer.

"If you wanted to leave the house," Lydia ventured, settling herself on a nearby settee

281

as if to watch the children at play, something she was sure she would have enjoyed on any day but that one, "without going out either the front door or the back, how would you go about it?"

Julia looked up at her thoughtfully. "I'd climb out a window," she said succinctly, as one who spoke from experience.

"Is there another way?" Lydia asked, smoothing her skirts. She needed clothes of her own — as it was, she had nothing but the things Lark, Maddie and Sarah had contributed, and those didn't fit properly.

"Sure there is," Julia said, turning her attention back to her little sister and the doll. "There's the cellar door, and the coal chute. Hank crawled out that way once to go fishing with his friends after Mama told him he couldn't because he hadn't done his chores, but his clothes got all black and Papa caught him and made him copy three whole chapters of the Bible, one from Deuteronomy, one from Leviticus and one from Numbers. Hank said he'd rather take a whipping than do that again."

Lydia suppressed a smile. "I think I would agree with him," she said.

"Me, too," Julia replied sagely. "But Papa and Mama don't believe in spankings, so we have to copy Bible chapters when we're bad. And we don't get to choose something nice, either, like the Sermon on the Mount or the second chapter of Luke or Letters to the Romans. It's most always from the Old Testament."

Lydia leaned forward slightly, distracted from her escape plan. "How old are you, Julia?"

"Eight," Julia replied.

"You are very wise and well-spoken for your age," Lydia remarked, and she was wholly sincere — as well as a little alarmed. She sensed that Julia was a few steps ahead of her, knew Lydia's questions weren't idle ones, though she'd tried to present them that way.

"Mama says that's the beauty of having to copy Bible chapters when you misbehave. It makes you smart. Getting spanked only makes you want to fight back."

Before her aunt Nell and, indirectly, Lark had rescued her from her stepmother, Mabel, as a child Julia's age, Lydia had suffered many kicks, pinches and slaps, though never in her father's presence. "Your mama," Lydia said, "is a very intelligent woman."

"I know," Julia agreed, and then she looked straight at Lydia with those penetrating Yarbro-blue eyes of hers, confirming

Lydia's earlier theory that the child would not be easy to fool, despite her tender years. "If you try to sneak past Papa's deputies," she warned solemnly, "you might have to copy down *all* of the Old Testament."

"Are you going to tattle, Julia?" Lydia asked, thinking how easily she had come to love this spirited, amazingly insightful child, and her brothers and sisters, too.

"No," Julia immediately answered. "Tattling means you have to write out all of Exodus."

"Oh, my," Lydia said.

"So I won't tell," Julia vowed, watching as her little sister stripped the doll of one dress and reached for another, "and neither will Marietta, even though she's still too little to write out Bible chapters."

"Marietta won't tell," the smaller child echoed, "even though she's still too little to write out Bible chappers."

Lydia rose, debating between the coal chute and the cellar. She'd go back home, she decided, and fetch her watercolor set and the small journal she painted in, since Helga had had the presence of mind to tuck those things into her valise before the flight from Phoenix. Painting always soothed her when she was restless.

Since the coal chute might be a tight fit,

and she didn't want to spoil a borrowed dress, she opted for the cellar door. "I'll be back before anyone misses me," she promised. Then, nearly overcome with affection and guilt at drawing a mere child into a plot of deception, she added, "If anyone asks where I've gone, please don't lie."

"I wouldn't lie," Julia said. "That's Revelations, twice over."

Chuckling, Lydia took her leave.

Helga was busy in the backyard, she discovered, when she returned to the kitchen, working the lever to make the washing machine agitate and chatting — almost *flirting*, actually — with the balding deputy manning the back door.

After trying to talk herself out of what was probably an exercise in foolishness, and failing miserably, Lydia drew a deep breath, let it out slowly, and descended the cellar stairs, batting through cobwebs as she went and squinting to see in almost total darkness. She returned to the kitchen, found a stubby candle and matches, and made a second attempt, this time with a flickering light to show her the way.

She soon found the cellar doors, a pair of them, heavy and with daylight showing between their wooden slats, but the latch would not give, even after she'd set the candle aside and used both hands to tug at it. It must, she decided, have been padlocked on the outside, perhaps to prevent the children from rambling in uncommon hours.

That left the coal chute, a prospect she had hoped to avoid.

She gave herself another silent lecture, counseling patience and decorum, but that was as unsuccessful as her previous effort.

The chute was next to the cold furnace, a great iron monstrosity of a contraption, surely equal to the task of heating an enormous house during cold northern Arizona winters. In Phoenix, it rarely snowed, but Lydia knew only too well that wasn't the case in the upper part of the state, where freezing blizzards were not unusual.

Holding the candle, she peered into the chute, using her free hand to test for coal dust. When it came away relatively clean, she began calculating the dimensions of the steep wooden shaft.

Although she was, of course, larger than Hank, the last known individual to attempt passage by this route, she was not a large person. Lydia once again chided herself, but found her desire not only undiminished, but on the increase. She would take a pleasant walk, fetch her watercolor set from the other house, along with her painting tablet, and return.

Where was the harm in that?

If Jacob Fitch had still been in Stone Creek, word would surely have gotten back to Rowdy by now? After all, the town was not large, and the comings and goings of strangers surely didn't go unnoticed.

And it wasn't as if she would have to go through the coal chute *twice,* after all. She could return by way of either the front door or the back, enjoying the chagrin of either deputy. What was the worst thing that could happen? she asked herself. She wasn't a child; Rowdy couldn't force her to copy out Bible chapters.

Extinguishing the candle, and pushing up her sleeves, Lydia crawled into the coal chute. The climb was steep, and the shaft soon narrowed.

And she quickly *discovered* what the worst thing that could happen actually was, because it did.

After making only a few inches of progress, a foot at most, she realized she was *stuck.* She couldn't go forward or back.

Lydia fought down her first inclination, which leaned distinctly toward utter panic, and concentrated on breathing. That inspired her to let out all the air in her lungs and try to scoot in one direction or the other, but that didn't work, either.

Her imagination, overdeveloped by years of reading, ran wild.

In her mind's eye, she pictured a wholesale search, everyone in the Yarbro family, especially Gideon, turning the town of Stone Creek upside down looking for her. All the while, she would be trapped in this shaft, like a bird in a stovepipe, slowly dying of thirst or starvation.

It might take *weeks* to die.

The prospect increased her panic, so she dispensed with it. Surely, if she screamed for help —

As yet, though, her pride would not allow her to do that.

She was far too embarrassed.

So she lay there, considering all possible fates.

None of them were appealing.

When she heard Rowdy's voice from behind her, at the opening of the chute, relief though it was, she very nearly didn't answer.

"Lydia?" he called. "Are you in there?"

"I'm sorry, Aunt Lydia," Julia piped up, "but Papa came home and asked me straight-out where you'd gone, and I had to tell him the truth or write out all of Revelations."

Despite her humiliating and possibly dangerous predicament, Lydia had to smile at the child's remark.

"I'm stuck," she replied. Surely her voice was muffled, but since she'd heard Rowdy and Julia, she assumed they could hear her, as well.

"I can see the bottoms of your shoes," Julia announced.

"Julia," Rowdy told his daughter, "be quiet."

"I don't have to copy Revelations, do I?" Julia asked her papa. "I told you the truth, as soon as you asked me."

Rowdy's chuckle echoed into the coal chute. "No, sweetheart. You don't have to copy Revelations." Then, to Lydia he said, "Hold on. This might take a while."

Lydia felt Rowdy's hands grip her ankles, and sheer mortification blazed through her. A proper lady did not allow a man to *see* her ankles, let alone grasp them. Unless, of course, that man was her husband.

"Hold on," Rowdy repeated. "I'll give you a tug or two, and that ought to suffice, but you might get a few slivers."

Slivers were the least of Lydia's concerns at the moment. Rowdy *would* free her from the coal chute, even if he had to tear out part of the cellar wall to achieve his purpose. But then she'd have to face him.

Lydia's chagrin was complete when she heard a second voice — Gideon's.

"What the he— devil is going on here?" he demanded.

What was *he* doing in Lark and Rowdy's cellar? Wasn't he supposed to be mining for copper?

"Aunt Lydia," Julia answered cheerfully, "is stuck in the coal chute."

Even through the tops of her high-button shoes, Lydia knew Gideon's grip from Rowdy's. She'd felt it before, when he'd arranged her feet wide apart on the edge of their mattress, so he could —

Lydia's blood heated, and it seemed to make her whole body swell, lodging her even more tightly in the narrow chute.

"Do you need any help?" she heard Rowdy ask his brother, over the pounding of blood in her ears.

Gideon's response was wry. "I think I can handle it," he said.

She heard Rowdy and Julia leaving the cellar, mounting the stairs.

And then Gideon pulled.

Lydia felt a splinter pierce the plumpest part of her bottom, and bit her lower lip to keep from crying out.

Gideon tugged at her again. This time, she moved a little, and there were no more slivers.

"Are you all right, Lydia?" he asked, with mingled concern and amusement.

"Just let me smother," Lydia responded wretchedly.

Gideon chuckled. "You're not getting off *that* easy, Mrs. Yarbro."

He gave her another wrench, harder this time, and dislodged her further.

Her skirt and petticoat had ridden up as he pulled, since the space was so tight.

Her legs were free with the next tug, and then her bottom.

"What an opportunity," Gideon drawled. "Fortunately for you, Mrs. Yarbro, I am a gentleman."

He took her by the waist then, and hauled her the rest of the way out.

Stood her unceremoniously on her feet and turned her around to face him.

Her face flamed, even though her skirt and petticoat had righted themselves by the power of gravity.

She must have looked a sight, covered in dust, if not soot, with her hair coming undone from its pins. Operating on pure bravado, she asked, "What are you doing here?"

Gideon chuckled. "I was about to ask you the same question," he said. "Good God, Lydia, what could possibly have possessed you to try to climb out through the coal chute?"

The enterprise *did* seem even more ridiculous in retrospect than it had at its inception, but something in Lydia, pride perhaps, demanded that she brazen this through. She hiked up her chin, glared at Gideon, and refused to answer.

"Are you all right?" Gideon asked again, taking a gentle hold on her shoulders. And although he sounded quite sincere in his concern for her general well-being, even in the near darkness she could see the twinkle of merriment in his eyes.

He was *enjoying* this.

"I have a splinter," Lydia said, quite without intending to.

"Where?" Gideon asked matter-of-factly.

"Never mind where," Lydia retorted. "Get Helga. She can take it out."

Gideon chuckled at that. The candle was still flickering on the nearby crate where Lydia had left it, and he bent to take hold of it. "Let me see," he said.

"No," Lydia replied.

He looked her over, even turning her around once. When she faced him again, she saw a wicked grin on his face.

"I think I know," he told her. "Hold your skirts, and I'll take a look."

"You will *not* 'take a look'!"

But he'd already turned her away from him again. With one hand, he hoisted her skirts up, with the other, he tugged her bloomers down. Seeing the splinter, he let out a low whistle of exclamation.

"That's a dandy," he said.

Lydia closed her eyes, bit her lower lip, resigned to her lot, and yelped a little when Gideon dislodged the splinter in one deft motion.

Having met the emergency, he patted her bare bottom once, pulled her bloomers up again, and let her outer garments fall back into place.

"Go away," Lydia said, keeping her back to him. If she had to look into Gideon's face, and see the laughter she knew would be dancing in his eyes, she would die.

"Not a chance," Gideon answered.

And he turned her about again, cupped a hand under her chin.

"Look at me," he said, when she didn't open her eyes.

"I can't," she answered.

"Why not?"

"Because I know you think this is funny."

"Hell, Lydia, it *is* funny."

She opened her eyes, glared at him. "If you hadn't asked Rowdy to hold me prisoner in this house —"

The light of that single candle, now standing on the crate again, played over the handsome planes of Gideon's face, but the light coming from *inside* him, glowing in his eyes, was brighter still. It was partly amusement, yes, but there was a certain bafflement there, too, and some realization dawning, quite against his will, if his expression was to be believed.

"Oh, for God's sake, Lydia," he said impatiently, "*you're* the one who climbed into a coal chute. Stop trying to make this my fault. You do understand, don't you, that if Julia hadn't told Rowdy where to look for you, you could have died before anyone found you?"

"I would have screamed," Lydia allowed, with indignation. "Eventually."

"That would have done a lot of good," Gideon argued, "with everyone except Lark out roaming the countryside, trying to find you. And since my sister-in-law is two floors above this cellar, she wouldn't have heard a thing."

"I was just fine," Lydia said.

"You would have run out of air sooner or later," Gideon told her grimly. "*Damn* it, Lydia, if I were another kind of man and you didn't have a big gouge in your backside from that splinter, I *swear* I'd turn you across my knee right now, and blister you."

Lydia tried a different tack. After all, men had been known to change from one kind to another in very short order, hadn't they?

"Can't we just forget this?" she asked, forcing a light tone into her voice. "Act as if it never happened and go on from here?"

"No, Lydia," Gideon said, "we *can't*. I'm taking you home. I'm going to clean that puncture wound of yours, and apply some iodine or salve, if there is any, and leave you in the care of Helga and her stove poker."

"I can put salve on myself," Lydia protested, too proud to ask about the leaving part.

Gideon took her firmly by one elbow and steered her toward the cellar stairs. "Yet *another* brilliant idea, Mrs. Yarbro," he said, sounding quite put out now that she was in no danger of screaming herself hoarse and then smothering. "I wish you'd do me a favor and *stop thinking*."

Lydia balked, not wanting to go upstairs and face everyone. By now, Julia, if not

295

Rowdy, would have regaled the whole household with the tale of Aunt Lydia getting stuck in the coal chute.

"They'll laugh," she protested helplessly.

Gideon didn't answer, didn't even slow down. He simply propelled Lydia up the steps and into the dazzle of daylight filling the kitchen.

Lydia blinked, briefly blinded.

Helga came into focus, but she was apparently alone in the room, and she did not seem inclined to laugh.

"Give us an hour," Gideon told Helga, hustling Lydia toward the back door, "and then come home and arm yourself with the poker. I've got a meeting later, and it's one I can't afford to miss."

"A meeting?" Lydia asked, as Gideon jerked open the back door, and Helga, frowning at her and shaking her head, did not make the slightest move to prevent Lydia's forcible removal from the house.

"It has to do with my job," Gideon explained, his tone uncharitable in the extreme. "If I still *have* one, that is."

He made no attempt to avoid the busiest part of town as they headed for home, even though there were surely alternate routes they could have taken. He hustled Lydia up the driveway, around the side of the jailhouse, and right out onto Main Street.

Her clothes were rumpled and dusty.

Her hair was tumbling from its pins.

"What will people think?" Lydia whispered, more to herself than to Gideon.

"I don't give a damn what they think," Gideon growled, and walked faster, his strides gobbling up the ground, dragging her right along with him.

It seemed an eternity before they reached their own house, and by that time, Lydia had been subjected to numerous speculative stares and, from the men they'd passed, a few snickers to boot.

Having thus made a public spectacle of her, Gideon fairly thrust her over the threshold and into the quiet kitchen.

"Why are you acting like this?" Lydia demanded.

"Because," Gideon said, after a private but visible struggle of some kind, "you could have smothered in that chute. Because one of Rowdy's deputies came to the mine to tell me you'd slipped out of the house somehow and nobody could find you and I was sure Fitch had managed to get hold of you, and that scared the hell out of me, Lydia. *Because*, for the second day in a row, I had to leave the mine on your account."

Before he could offer any more *becauses,*

Lydia pulled free of his hold on her arm.

He immediately took it back again. Squired her up the rear staircase, along the hallway, and into the bathroom. Only then did he release her, and she stood there with her figurative feathers ruffled and quite at a loss for words.

"Take off your clothes." Gideon gave the command in an offhand tone, busy pilfering the cabinet as he spoke. He found a dusty bottle of iodine and turned to see Lydia still fully dressed.

Raised his eyebrows.

"I'll attend to my — *wound* myself," she said.

Exasperated, Gideon shook his head, set the iodine aside on the sink, sat down on the lid of the commode, and unceremoniously hauled Lydia stomach-down across his thighs.

Incensed, she struggled mightily, but he held her with ease, with his left arm hooked around her waist. With his free hand, he threw her skirts up, jerked down her bloomers, and examined the splinter puncture again, prodding gently with his fingers.

"Hold still," he said gruffly, when she continued to squirm.

Lydia hoped her bottom wasn't blushing, like the rest of her. "Gideon," she protested miserably, though she'd stopped trying to get away from him, having found that impossible.

"This is going to sting a little," he warned, referring to the iodine, she hoped, and not some instantaneous change in his character that would enable him to "blister" her.

When he applied the medicine, the burning sensation was terrible, and Lydia flinched and gave a howl.

Gideon patted her bare posterior, stood her on her feet, and rose to his full height. Without another word, and whistling under his breath as though determined to make bad matters worse by mocking her, he walked out of the bathroom and left Lydia to recover her dignity as best she could.

She righted her bloomers first.

Then she turned on the cold water tap and splashed her face with water until some of the burning had subsided.

Retreat would have been the better course, but, as with the coal-chute incident, Lydia found herself advancing instead.

CHAPTER THIRTEEN

Gideon was downstairs in the kitchen, when Lydia descended from the second floor. And he wasn't whistling anymore.

No, he was pacing, impatiently waiting for Helga to return, so he could finish his shift at the mine and then attend the mysterious meeting he'd mentioned earlier, when they were still in Lark and Rowdy's cellar.

Having proven to her satisfaction that a display of temper would get her nowhere with this man, Lydia decided to follow her own ill-received suggestion and pretend that nothing had happened.

Knowing that Rowdy and Wyatt consumed copious amounts of coffee, she assumed that Gideon did, too, and set about rinsing out the blue enamel pot, lighting the fire in the wood cookstove, and brewing up a batch.

The action was not conciliatory, but if Gideon wanted to interpret it that way, she would not disabuse him of the notion.

"Will you be out late tonight?" she asked casually. "At this — meeting?"

Out of the corner of her eye, she saw Gideon's face harden slightly. "Yes," he said flatly. "I *will* be out late, Lydia."

She stiffened at his tone, set the coffeepot down on the iron stove top with a little clang. "I see."

"What's keeping Helga?" Gideon fretted.

"You told her to come back in an hour," Lydia replied coolly. "It hasn't been that long."

"So I did," Gideon said, with a note of something new in his voice — new and unsettlingly mischievous. "So I did."

A wicked little thrill, wholly out of keeping with present circumstances, tingled through Lydia's system and then gathered in one particularly private place. "But she could return sooner, of course," she hastened to say.

"I've been neglecting you," Gideon said.

In that moment, the whole kitchen seemed as hot as the inside of the cookstove, at least to Lydia. She couldn't trust herself to speak — as furious with Gideon Yarbro as she was, she might have said something wanton.

He stepped up behind her then, drew her back against him.

She felt his manhood against her lower spine, searing through her clothes like a length of steel pipe, fresh from a blazing furnace. And she trembled with need and hope and pure fury.

He kissed her right shoulder, brought one of his hands around to cup her breast, rousing the nipple to press hard against the bodice of her dress.

"Gideon," she whimpered, hopeless. She knew only too well what would happen next: he would pleasure her into near madness, and then leave her wanting.

He drew her back from the stove, and she felt her skirts and petticoats rising.

"Not here," she gasped, already breathless, already lost. "Gideon, not in the *kitchen*—"

His chuckle vibrated through her as he nibbled at the nape of her neck. "Right here," he murmured. "In the kitchen."

His right hand was inside her bloomers now, resting splay-fingered against her bare abdomen.

Lydia groaned, leaned back against him, the way she might have sagged against a brick wall, even as ordinary horse sense demanded that she make him *stop,* immediately.

She tried, though not very hard. "Let's at

302

least — go upstairs —"

Gideon's fingers eased lower. He tasted her left ear. "We have an hour," he reminded her, his voice low and husky.

He parted her, began the slow, rhythmic circles he knew would drive her insane.

A low cry of rising need escaped her.

Gideon murmured into her ear, between nibbles, soothing her even as he increased the pressure of his fingers.

Unable to help herself, Lydia set her feet apart, arched her hips against Gideon's hand, half hated him when he gave a gruff chuckle at her ready surrender.

"That's it," he said.

Her knees melted, her head went back, pressing into Gideon's shoulder, and her breathing was quick and shallow.

Gideon supported her with his left arm, continued to pluck and ply and caress. His manhood was so big, so hot, and so hard, that Lydia dared to hope that *this time,* he wouldn't be able to contain his desire. This time, he would have her, and damn the consequences.

The inexorable climb began; Lydia flexed against her husband, caught in the first wickedly delicious throes of what promised to be a shattering release of all her pent-up energies and emotions.

When the eruption came, long, frantic minutes later, Lydia shouted at the force of it, and moved wildly against Gideon's hand, and, like the previous times, he did not cease his ministrations until she was totally satiated and yet still convulsing, every few moments, with the inevitable aftershocks.

He might have taken her then — she actually felt the struggle to resist her raging inside him, resting against him as she was — but for the creak of the hinges on the side gate and the sound of Helga's voice, commandeering the aunts up the walk toward the back door.

"*Damn* it," Gideon muttered. Then he withdrew his hand from Lydia's bloomers, letting her skirts fall back into place, and eased her quickly into a chair.

Lydia, dazed and still rocking at her core, did not know whether to be grateful to Helga for coming back before she was expected, or to be furious with her.

"You would have taken me," she said sorrowfully. Had that happened, Gideon wouldn't have been able to leave her — his honor wouldn't have allowed it. The chance was lost — until next time.

"Yes," Gideon said, sounding grim, "I would have taken you, God help me." Moving to stand at the sink, with his back to the room, probably to prevent Helga and the aunts from seeing the bulge at the front of his trousers and guessing what had been going on in the kitchen, he lowered his head and breathed slowly and very deeply.

Lydia closed her eyes, hoped she wasn't too flushed.

The door opened, and Helga herded the aunts inside.

There was a moment's silence.

"Oh, dear," Helga said.

Lydia's face flamed.

Gideon muttered something and dashed out without a word, bent on returning to the mine.

"Are you coming down with a fever, dear?" Mittie asked, laying a cool and papery hand to Lydia's forehead.

"She certainly doesn't look well," Millie agreed fretfully.

"Perhaps," Mittie theorized, "it was delirium that made her try to climb up the Yarbros' coal chute. From the fever, you know."

Helga gave a mild snort. *"Perhaps,"* she said, entirely for Lydia's benefit, surely, though she was addressing the aunts, "we should have stopped by the mercantile for a little while, to look at yard goods, the way you wanted."

"I think Lydia ought to lie down," Mittie persisted.

"Oh," Helga agreed, "she should lie down all right."

Lydia opened her eyes at last, threw the housekeeper a peevish glance. "That," she said, "will be quite enough, Helga."

Helga chuckled, shook her head once, and then clucked her tongue. "What would you like for lunch, *Mrs.* Yarbro?" she asked, every bit as cheeky as before. "You must be hungry, after the morning you've had."

Lydia narrowed her eyes. "I'll thank you," she countered, "never to mention the events of this morning again."

Unruffled, Helga set aside her handbag, and her calico bonnet, and took her apron down off its peg. Her expression, as she began assembling things for the midday meal, was downright saucy.

The aunts, blissfully unaware of the charge still pulsing in the air, decided to freshen up, and vanished into their room.

Helga hummed a little tune as she worked.

Lydia waited, in silence, until her legs felt solid enough to support her.

Then she left the kitchen, with as much dignity as she could summon, to find her watercolors and her painting tablet. Upstairs, after filling a glass with water at the bathroom sink, she settled at the desk by the window overlooking the front yard and the street beyond, and dampened her brush.

By the time Helga called her to the table for lunch, sometime later, Lydia had a rather good likeness of Gideon well under way. It showed just his head and shoulders, since presently she did not wish to consider the rest of his anatomy.

With his face slightly averted, the painted Gideon looked pensive, almost wistful, and he was gazing off into a distance that seemed to call to him.

The man sitting in the chair facing Jacob Fitch's desk at the First Territorial Bank was not of the ilk generally permitted into this most private sanctuary. He bore a long and ragged scar on his lean right cheek, his dark hair hung in stringy, unwashed hanks, and some noxious substance — probably tobacco juice — had hardened in his handlebar mustache. His odd, colorless eyes resembled nothing so much as water, frozen into puddles, and his gaze was level.

"What can you tell me about Gideon Yarbro, Mr. Bailey?" Jacob finally asked, though it galled him to address the fellow as though he were a gentleman. He wanted the interview over, the task undertaken and promptly completed.

Bailey took his time answering. Jacob had engaged him soon after his ignoble return from Stone Creek the day before — without Lydia — to dig up whatever information he could, concerning Yarbro's past.

The man had to have skeletons in his closet — everyone did.

"I haven't had much time," Bailey said, at last. He reminded Jacob of some sharp-beaked scavenger bird, waiting for the last gasp of a dying creature so he could peck and pull at the carrion. "But I do know that his family name has some luster to it. Have you ever heard of Payton Yarbro, Mr. Fitch?"

Jacob frowned, searching his memory. *Payton Yarbro.* It did sound familiar, though only vaguely. "I'm not sure," he said. "Possibly."

For the first time, Bailey smiled, but it did nothing to warm his eyes, and the show of rotten teeth was unsettling. "Payton Yarbro," he explained, slowly and with insulting patience, "was the best hand for robbing a train since Jesse and Frank James. His sons rode with him in the early days, and two of them — a pair of identical twins — were still looting vaults and cash boxes until a few years ago. Rumor is, they're down in Mexico or South America now, spending the proceeds on señoritas."

Jacob waved a dismissive hand. "It's *Gideon* I'm interested in, not the history of the Yarbro clan."

Bailey's gaze instantly chilled; Jacob felt the drop in temperature from across the wide, gleaming expanse of his mahogany desk, a Fitch heirloom, and wished he'd spoken more prudently. His dealings with Thaddeus Bailey had not been extensive as of yet, but he'd gathered enough to know he'd be safer prodding a coiled rattlesnake with a short stick.

"I've sent some telegrams," Bailey said. "No answers yet. Investigations take time, Mr. Fitch. Time and money."

Jacob leaned back in his chair, tented his hands and braced them under his chin, wanting to seem at ease. He could only imagine what his mother would say if she knew he'd deliberately courted *this* sorry specimen of humanity, but of course she never would. Jacob would make damn sure of that.

"Money," he repeated, musingly. "I gave you a fair amount last night, Mr. Bailey, when you agreed to undertake this . . . investigation."

Bailey leaned forward slightly. "It's my understanding, Mr. *Fitch,* that you want

Gideon Yarbro dealt with. What we need to be clear on is whether 'dealt with' means digging up a scandal or two, breaking some of his bones or something . . . more permanent."

Jacob's starched white shirt grew damp between his shoulder blades, and his heart kicked over a beat or two before resuming a steady rate. He began to itch everywhere, as though he'd broken out in hives, but he didn't scratch. He couldn't afford to show any sort of weakness. "That depends," he said, at considerable length.

"On what?" Bailey asked mildly.

"On whether or not the authorities would come knocking on *my* door, should Yarbro meet with some sudden and tragic misfortune. I have a reputation to protect. Everything depends on the confidence the public places in me."

Bailey smiled again, and acid roiled in Jacob's stomach, eating away the lining. His heart bumped painfully over several hard beats.

"Why, you'd have an alibi, wouldn't you, Mr. Fitch?" Bailey said. "If anything happened to Yarbro, I mean. You'd be right here in Phoenix, the whole time, going on about your business for all to see. Looking after that grand new house of yours, and your dear mother."

The sweat on Jacob's back instantly turned clammy. Bailey, a man of obviously low character, was letting him know he'd done some checking — not merely on Gideon Yarbro, but on *him,* as well.

The message, if he wasn't imagining it, was that, if their arrangement were to turn sour for some reason, Bailey had already decided on the most effective way to retaliate.

Jacob considered paying the man off, sending him on his way, and forgetting the whole idea of getting back at Gideon Yarbro, but all the while he knew it was too late for that. He'd confided in Bailey, over numerous rounds of whiskey in one of the seediest saloons in the city last night, told him about the thwarted wedding, Lydia's abduction and how she'd refused to return with him when he'd gone, in the company of two of the U.S. Marshal's best men, to fetch her home from Stone Creek.

They'd briefly discussed what a sad thing it would be if Yarbro happened to die young, and leave Lydia a poor, defenseless widow, but not actually agreed to set a clear plan in motion.

From the question Bailey had just asked, however, he'd registered the underlying implication: Jacob most definitely wanted Gideon Yarbro dead.

Even if Jacob called him off, with generous compensation for his time, Bailey might hang around, figuring he'd found himself a meal ticket, asking for favors, then demanding them. With Yarbro alive and well, after all, Bailey couldn't be blamed for anything, but if he told the wrong person what they'd discussed and word got around, Jacob, a respected man in the community, with a great deal to lose, might be ruined.

Folks could be self-righteous. Hearing the gossip, they might well believe it, and take their money out of his bank, find other lenders to underwrite their loans. Exclude both him and his mother from social circles that were lucrative for Jacob and of critical importance to the august Mrs. Fitch.

With Yarbro laid out in a pine box, on the other hand, Bailey wouldn't dare engage in loose talk, lest he wind up with a hangman's noose around his neck. Moreover, if he had any sense at all, he'd leave Phoenix and never come back.

Realizing he'd left Bailey's remark dangling too long, while he'd mulled the situation over, Jacob cleared his throat. "It would have to look like an accident," he said cautiously. "That is imperative."

"Young men meet with accidents all the time, don't they?" Bailey replied, smiling. "And the widow, well, she might just be grief-stricken enough to come right back here and marry you, mightn't she? After a decent interval, of course."

Jacob allowed himself to imagine that for a moment — Lydia, mourning her dashing young swain of a husband. She'd be pliable in her despair, and most likely poverty-stricken, with those two old ladies hanging around her neck like a pair of albatrosses. And there would be Jacob, waiting to forgive her, reinstall her in the Fairmont mansion, give her position, security and plenty of pin-money for hats and hair ribbons.

Yes, he would forgive her, treat her with the utmost tenderness, despite the fact that she'd given Yarbro — willingly, it would seem — what rightfully belonged to him.

He'd looked forward to deflowering Lydia on their wedding night, and it would gall him until the end of his days that Gideon Yarbro had gotten to her first, but upon reflection, there *were* compensations. Virgin brides tended to weep and whimper a great deal, and bleed. Now that Yarbro had broken her in, there would be none of that non-sense. He, Jacob, would not have to pussy-foot around — he could assuage his lust for

313

Lydia as often and with as much vigor as he chose.

He felt himself harden, just to think of laying Lydia down and rutting into her whenever he wanted.

And that would be often.

"What will it be, Mr. Fitch?" Bailey persisted. "Do I merely 'investigate' Gideon Yarbro, or do I solve the problem for good?"

"How much?" Jacob asked, shifting in his chair.

Bailey might have taken that for fidgeting, an attack of nerves. Or he might have guessed the truth, that Jacob's only real regret about the whole affair would be that he hadn't killed Gideon Yarbro with his own hands and watched as the light faded from those insolent eyes.

"Five thousand dollars," Bailey answered. "Half now, and half when there's been a funeral in Stone Creek."

"How do I know you won't abscond with my money?" Jacob asked, ever practical. He was, after all, a banker, descended from generations of savvy lenders. "I'd have no recourse if you did."

Bailey straightened the cuffs of his filthy shirt. "No," he agreed. "You wouldn't. I guess you'll just have to take a chance, won't you, Mr. Fitch?"

Now that things had gone as far as they had, Jacob had no choice.

"When can I expect results?" he asked, taking a small brass key from his vest pocket, inserting it into the lock on his top desk drawer.

"When the time is right," Bailey answered. "Matters like this can't be handled hastily. Once I have answers to my telegrams, I'll know plenty about Mr. Yarbro over and above his outlaw pedigree — which might be a problem all by itself, if he takes after his old daddy."

Jacob cleared his throat again. What he was about to tell Bailey might dissuade him, since he'd brought up Yarbro's illustrious family more than once, but better if it happened *before* he'd handed over twenty-five hundred dollars to seal the bargain.

"You mentioned Yarbro's brothers," Jacob said evenly, "the identical twins —"

"Handsome as Lucifer himself," Bailey broke in, "and their own guardian angels probably couldn't tell them apart."

This, to Jacob, was neither here nor there. He wanted Thaddeus Bailey out of his office and this nasty business over with. He wanted to console Lydia on her terrible loss, and the sooner, the better. "Yarbro has two other brothers," he said. "One of them,

Rowdy, is the marshal up at Stone Creek. The other one, Wyatt, is a rancher."

"I wondered if you'd trouble yourself to mention them," Bailey said, grinning. "It's a point in your favor that you did, Mr. Fitch. Because Rowdy and Wyatt Yarbro are the main reason I have to have five thousand dollars to do this job. Both of them rode with Payton in their day, like I said, and they're not the sort a prudent man tangles with. If they even suspect that their young brother died anything but an accidental death, hell's back acre won't be far enough to run."

Jacob had only met the elder Yarbro brothers once, the day before, and he'd been in too much of a state over Lydia's steadfast refusal to see reason to pay them much mind. Still, he'd gathered enough to see the truth in Bailey's assertion.

And he was afraid. For a moment, he wished — again — that he'd never scoured the low-life saloons in the rougher section of Phoenix for a man willing to do some dirty work.

But that moment soon passed.

Jacob was used to getting what he wanted, and what he wanted was Lydia. Gideon Yarbro was very much in the way.

He pulled open the desk drawer, took out

a stack of hundred-dollar notes, every one backed by federal gold, and counted out twenty-five of them on the desk top.

Paddy was remarkably receptive that evening, when the crew of dirty, sweating, thirsty and penniless miners trooped into his saloon, Gideon among them. A pair of drifters stood at the bar, nursing whiskey they'd probably paid for with cash money, but Paddy didn't protest when Mike O'Hanlon slapped them both on the back, simultaneously, and boomed, in his usual ebullient way, "Private party, boys. And I know for a fact you wouldn't want to intrude."

"I was sort of hankerin' for more whiskey," one of the drifters replied, looking aggrieved.

The second, clearly the brighter of the pair, took his friend by the back of the shirt and ushered him out.

"Will you stand good for a round or two, Paddy?" Mike asked, in the same spirit of good will. "For the sake of the Auld Sod, if nothin' else?"

The change in Paddy's outlook was, to Gideon, remarkable. "Sure, Mike," he said, smiling and under no apparent duress. "Sure. For the sake of the Old Sod."

After leaving Lydia, Gideon had gone straight back to the mine, and done the work of two men, lest Wilson should rise from the bed where he was mending from a broken nose and broken pride, as well, and tell him to collect his pay and be gone. And partly because he needed to expend a lot of energy, fast.

Wilson hadn't come back, though, and if someone on the crew was serving as his eyes and ears, which was unlikely but definitely not impossible, they had not told the foreman that the new man was unreliable.

Yet.

For all that he'd swung that shovel like a man digging up someone buried alive, Gideon hadn't been able to expel his need for Lydia. Truly, if Helga and the aunts had not returned when they did, he would have relieved his fetching and only too willing wife of her virginity right there in the kitchen, in the broad light of day.

Not the most delicate way, he reflected, resigned, to breach a woman's maidenhead. That required privacy, a lot of tenderness, and a certain amount of patience.

But he'd snapped, with Lydia bucking against him and crying out his name the way she had. He'd lost sight of all the good reasons he had for not carrying things to their natural conclusion. When Helga and the aunts had inadvertently intervened, he'd been both furious and profoundly grateful.

Still, though hours had gone by, he was raw with the want of Lydia.

She'd be in bed when he got home, he thought. She was his wife, and no one on earth would refute his right to enjoy her as such. No one, that is, except himself.

"Chin up, young Yarbro," Mike said, whacking him halfway over the bar again, and nearly causing him to choke on the sip of whiskey he'd just taken.

"Damn it, O'Hanlon," Gideon said, after wheezing for a few seconds, "if you do that again, I'm going to land a haymaker in the middle of your stupid Irish face."

Mike laughed uproariously, not the reaction Gideon would have expected. "That's the spirit, young Yarbro!" he shouted gleefully. "That's the spirit! By God, there's hope for you yet!"

Gideon took another gulp of whiskey, still wondering at the change in Paddy. And still imagining Lydia alone in their bed at home — by God, it *was* their bed, not hers alone — and he'd be damned if he'd sleep away from her another night, even if it meant suffering the tortures of the damned trying to keep from taking her.

"Still havin' troubles at home, I see," Mike crowed, loud enough for everyone in the bar to hear. Then, with a sweep of his arm, he made sure the others took note. "Young Yarbro, here," he announced, "is havin' troubles at home!"

"Mike," Gideon growled, flushing from the base of his throat to the roots of his hair, "*will you* shut up?"

"Get a babe on her," someone suggested. "That will give her somethin' to look after. A woman needs to look after things."

Gideon sighed. He had a part to play, and he'd best play it, for all it was worth. Grinning, he turned to take all the men in. "And you're all authorities on how to treat a woman, I suppose?"

To a man, they all claimed expertise.

"And how," Mike O'Hanlon contributed, when some of the braggadocio had died down, "can you plant a babe in a woman's womb if she won't have you in her bed, young Yarbro?"

"She'll have me," Gideon said, more annoyed than he wanted any of them to know.

Mike raised both eyebrows and leaned into Gideon's face. "When?" he asked. "She's not having you now, is she, or you wouldn't be draggin' your chin on the ground, like you have been ever since you

320

started work at the mine."

"Leave the lad be, Mike," O'Brien said. "We're here for a meetin', now aren't we?"

"We oughtn't to stand for it," another man said. "Damn their eyes, the owners have already cut our pay twice this year. If they do it again, we'll be workin' for nothin'."

"We're *already* workin' for nothin'," someone else said.

"They let the night crew go," O'Brien reminded everyone. "It's down to us, and here's Wilson raisin' hell that we're not sending enough ore out of the hole to suit those greedy bastards. Mark my words, the coolies will come next!"

The remark raised grumbling agreement and this time, Gideon noticed, O'Hanlon didn't try to quell the talk.

"If we walk out," Gideon reasoned, "won't they be *more* likely to hire Chinamen to replace us?" He was well aware that both Mike and Paddy were watching him closely.

"Not if we fight back," O'Hanlon said.

"How do we do that?" Gideon asked. At last, he seemed to be getting somewhere. Come the day after tomorrow, when he met with his contact in Flagstaff, he'd have something to report.

"We get guns," O'Hanlon answered. "We take over the mine, and if they try to send coolies in, we pick them off like ducks in a barrel."

"Jesus, Joseph and Mary, Mike," Paddy put in, setting both hands on the bar to lean forward, his belly spilling past the spatula-like tips of his fingers. "They'll call in the army. And those of you the riflemen don't kill will hang from the rafters of the court-house over in Flagstaff!"

Imagining the kind of shoot-out O'Hanlon had proposed, Gideon suppressed a shud-der. The army wouldn't be the first to arrive at the mine if the crew took it over, Rowdy would.

Rowdy, with his two aging deputies. Rowdy, with a wife and five children at home, one of them barely two days old.

Bile surged into the back of Gideon's throat, scalding it raw, and he swilled more whiskey to wash it down. Wyatt and Owen would stand with Rowdy, and Sam O'Bal-livan, too, among others. But the chances were good that one or more of them would take a bullet.

"Worried about your big brother, the marshal, young Yarbro?" Mike drawled, close to his face again.

"Hell, yes," Gideon retorted, longing to shove the other man back.

No other answer would have satisfied

Mike O'Hanlon, and maybe that one didn't, either. But though the stony suspicion in his eyes didn't change, the Irishman turned merry again. Hail-fellow-well-met.

"It's all just talk, young Yarbro," he said. "Just talk, from desperate men."

Gideon wasn't convinced of that, and assignment or no assignment, he meant to warn Rowdy that the trouble brewing at the mine might be more serious than anyone — including the owners — had ever suspected.

After that, nothing more was said about shooting coolies, but Gideon stayed until Paddy finally drove them all away from the bar, claiming he was out of whiskey and wouldn't have more until after tomorrow's train arrived from Phoenix.

Cold sober, even though he'd never drunk so much at one time in his life, Gideon left with the others. Like before, the men broke off into smaller groups, even though they were all headed to the same place.

All except Gideon, that is. And Mike O'Hanlon.

"I'll just see that young Yarbro gets home in one piece," O'Hanlon announced to the departing company, though no one had asked.

"I'll be fine, O'Hanlon," Gideon protested.

But he couldn't shake the other man.

" 'Tis a fine house," O'Hanlon said, when they reached Gideon's front gate. "More of your rich sister-in-law's doing, I suppose?"

Gideon sighed. "Something like that," he said. O'Hanlon had already known, of course, exactly where Gideon lived. Suspicious as he was, he'd have made a point of finding out. "What are you afraid of, Mike? That I'll slip over to my brother's place, knock on the door, and tell Rowdy what was said tonight, over at Paddy's?"

"Can't stop you from doing that," Mike said. "Tomorrow's Saturday — a half day. I reckon the news will keep until after the whistle blows."

Gideon waited.

O'Hanlon turned to face him, straightened Gideon's collar in a way that was at once fatherly and threatening. It took all Gideon's forbearance not to fling the other man's hands away. "These are hard and perilous times," Mike said. "Have a care, young Yarbro. Have a care."

With that, and a sorrowful expression, the Irishman turned and walked away, whistling softly under his breath as he vanished into the shadows.

CHAPTER FOURTEEN

It must have been after midnight, by Lydia's best guess, when she heard Gideon's footsteps on the rear staircase, then moving slowly along the hallway. She waited, not even breathing, when he paused outside her door. Braced herself for the moment when he would certainly move on to the next room.

But the green-glass doorknob turned, rattling a little, and through her eyelashes, Lydia saw the outline of Gideon's impressive frame, rimmed in the merest hint of light, the source of which she could not determine, since there were no lamps burning in the corridor.

"Are you asleep?" he asked, very quietly, and his words were clearly enunciated, not liquor-slurred as she might have expected. He'd been quite abrupt, telling her he'd be out late, and she'd naturally wondered if the "meeting" he'd planned to attend was being held in a saloon.

To offer any reply at all, Lydia sensed, would upset some precarious and inexplicable balance between them, so she didn't answer.

Gideon sighed audibly — and came into the room.

Lydia's heart shimmied up into her throat and flailed there. She wondered if Gideon had guessed she was awake, perhaps by the too-rapid meter of her breathing or some other sign she'd unwittingly given, but she still did not speak, or move.

He closed the door behind him, with a soft click, and crossed to the rocking chair. Sat down to begin pulling off his boots.

With a smile in his voice, and some gravity she had never heard before and found mildly alarming, he drawled, "I know you're not sleeping, Lydia."

Not willing to admit the game was up, Lydia raised herself sleepily onto her elbows. "What time is it?" she asked, with a feigned yawn.

"Late," Gideon said. The second boot made a thumping sound as he tossed it aside.

"Are you drunk?"

He laughed, low and somewhat raggedly. "I wish I were," he said, rising out of the chair, leaving it rocking a little in his wake.

"Why?" Lydia asked reasonably.

He didn't answer, but crossed the room and leaned down, pressing his hands into the mattress on either side of her, to plant a smacking kiss on her forehead.

Her heart was still fluttering, still struggling in her throat, and she had to force her words around it, causing them to sound as if they'd been scraped from her vocal chords. "Is something wrong?"

Gideon sighed again, thrust himself upright again, pulled his shirttails from under the waistband of his trousers. "*Everything* is wrong," he said wearily. But he continued shedding his clothes, and when he was completely and magnificently naked and turned back the covers to join her in bed, Lydia instinctively moved over to make room for him.

He'd washed up, perhaps downstairs in the kitchen, because he smelled of soap and well water, instead of sweat, like he should have after a day's work at the mine. In fact, his hair and skin were still a little moist.

"Tell me," she said, very softly.

"I can't," he answered, but he took her into his arms, snuggled her close against the hard warmth of his torso, and gave a deep, almost despairing, sigh.

She could not help noticing the length and heat of his manhood pressed against her lower midsection, and the sensation forced a little whimper from some hidden, reluctant place within her. After a moment's hesitation, she grew bold enough to slide her hand down over the stonelike, ridged flesh of his belly and take hold of him.

He groaned, but did not push her away.

By instinct, some fundamental knowledge bearing no relation to experience, Lydia stroked him, pulling her hand gently along his length.

"Woman," he ground out, writhing slightly and uttering another groan, "if you have a shred of mercy in you —"

"Nary a shred," Lydia said lightly; it was heady, she discovered, to be the one in control for once. The one setting the pace, making the rules, deciding what was enough. Who would have guessed it could be so easy to bring a strong, stubborn man so swiftly to heel? "You've shown me no quarter, Gideon Yarbro, and I'll show you none, either."

As she had in the kitchen that morning, she felt the struggle within him, knew he wanted to turn away, put a stop to what she was doing to him, but he couldn't. His need was too great. His breath came in gasps, and his powerful hips rose and fell, causing the bedsprings to creak rhythmically, as she tightened her grip a little, and raised and lowered her hand more swiftly.

He rasped out some half-strangled oath.

"Shall I do to you what you did to me?" Lydia asked, dizzy with the power of *administering* pleasure, instead of yielding to it.

Her words wrung a muffled shout from Gideon, and then, in the space of a heartbeat, everything shifted. In one breathtakingly quick motion, he was on top of her.

The dimmest glow from the streetlamp nearest the house strayed through the windowpanes, caught in his hair and revealed the complex perfection of his features. "Unless you tell me to stop, *right now,* Lydia," he warned, "I'm going to be inside you in about three seconds."

She did not tell him to stop. Drawing on that strange well of wanton audacity that seemed to open and close inside her of its own accord, she reached down and took hold of him again. His flesh pulsed, slick, against her palm and the backs of her fingers.

His mouth fell to hers, exploring at first, then hungry, and then plundering. With one motion of one hand, he dragged her nightgown up to her waist. All the while, Lydia worked him into a greater frenzy, and returned his kiss with all the force of her most primitive, most unspeakable needs.

Their tongues tangled, did battle.

When Gideon tore his mouth from hers, he tried one last time to circumvent the inevitable. "This — is going — to hurt —"

"Shh," Lydia said, still stroking him.

He gave a long, desolate moan then and literally tore her nightgown away, baring her to him. He slid down to her breasts, and thus out of Lydia's grasp, then suckled and tongued her nipples until she was as lost as he was.

She finally closed her hands around the sides of his head, burying her fingers deep in his hair, and, with a strength she hadn't known she possessed, drew him up again, and kissed him.

He used one knee to part her legs, and her eyes widened when she felt him at the moist portal of her femininity.

Resting on his forearms, he looked down at her, and even though his face was mostly in shadow, she saw a terrible quandary in his eyes and the set of his jaw.

"Quickly, Gideon," Lydia whispered. "Do it quickly."

The muscles in the sides of his neck corded visibly, so great was his effort at restraint. But then he drove into her, in one swift thrust that took him to her depths.

The pain was blinding — Lydia could not help crying out — but beneath it flowed an elemental passion, wild as a river at flood tide, a mysterious force born of nature itself, and utterly undeniable.

Gideon waited, far inside her.

And she began to move beneath him, carried, driven, by that unseen river, helpless as a leaf swirling on the surface.

Gideon, too, was lost. He nearly withdrew, drove deep again, and there was more pain, but Lydia's need was stronger, ferocious and demanding, causing her to abandon all but the violent, frantic straining of her body to take more of Gideon inside her and then still more.

He covered her mouth with his again, muffling both their cries, and when at last release consumed Lydia, in a great, cataclysmic shift of Creation itself, Gideon, too, was consumed.

Amid all that, the straining and the gasping and the crying out, Lydia felt his warmth spilling into her, rippling with life, and she gloried in receiving him, cradling him and — please, God — his child, in the sacred shelter of her womanhood.

They were a long time recovering, lying

there, entangled in each other's arms and legs, Gideon's face buried in the curve of Lydia's neck. She soothed him, murmuring and stroking his muscular back, as tremor after tremor moved through him. Finally, again by instinct, she raised herself a little on the pillows, and gave him her breast, smoothing his hair with her hand as he suckled, tentatively at first, and then with a hunger that soon had them both groaning again. Needing again.

Lydia guided him to her that second time, arched her hips to take him in, and now they mated slowly, gently, and with a grace so beautiful that tears of absolute wonderment came to her eyes. But the end was no less strenuous, no less fevered, than the one that had gone before.

The pain, though milder, continued, but it was no more than a distraction to Lydia — she was wholly absorbed in receiving Gideon, and in giving herself to him, holding nothing back. By turns, she surrendered, and she conquered.

When exhaustion finally overtook them, Gideon succumbed first, literally awake one moment and asleep the next, and in the last moments before she tumbled into her dreams, Lydia wept. She wept in silence, but not restraint, without asking herself why, without trying to untangle the nearly overwhelming and utterly contradictory emotions knotted inside her.

And, finally, she slept.

Gideon awakened just before sunrise, and remembered.

Drawing back the covers gently to look at Lydia, sleeping placidly with a slight, faintly angelic smile curving her lips, he saw faint smudges of blood on her thighs, and more staining the sheets, and even though reason reminded him that this was normal, an instant of pure horror seized him.

What in the name of Christ had he *done?*

He'd bedded a lot of women in his time, but never — *never* — a virgin. And this wasn't just any virgin — this was Lydia.

In those moments, Gideon was profoundly glad she was asleep — because tears came to his eyes, tears of shame, tears of awe and wonder. She'd given, and then given more, in the night, and it must have been agony for her; there was the blood, the damning evidence. Had she been *pretending,* clawing at his back, hurling her body upward to collide with his, bucking beneath him like a wild mare, when blessed release finally came?

Gideon saw her stir, dragged a forearm

across his eyes just before she opened hers. When she smiled and slipped her arms loosely around his neck, he was completely confounded, and so overcome with wretched joy that he could not have spoken, even if he'd known what to say.

Sleepily, she kissed the cleft in his chin.

He swallowed hard — so hard that she noticed, and tilted her head back to look directly into his face.

"Gideon? What's the matter?"

He shook his head, tore his gaze loose from hers. Thrust himself away, shifted to the other side of the bed, rose to his feet, sat down again.

He felt Lydia move, knew she was sitting up.

Her hand rested lightly on the middle of his back. "It's the blood, isn't it?" she asked, very gently.

"I'm sorry," he managed hoarsely. "Dear God, Lydia, *I'm sorry*."

There was another shift of the mattress, and then she was kneeling behind him, wrapping her arms around him, drawing her lips across the top of his right shoulder, the kiss leaving a trail of sparks behind as it passed over his bare skin.

"Don't be sorry, Gideon," she said softly, but with something nigh on desolation in her voice. "Please don't be sorry."

He let her know, with a motion of his body, that he was about to stand, waited until he was sure she wouldn't lose her balance when he did.

Then he got to his feet and, with effort, forced himself to turn around and meet her eyes. "*Shouldn't* I be sorry, Lydia?" he asked miserably. He thought of Mike O'Hanlon, and the talk of taking over the mine by force, and holding it with guns. He thought of Rowdy and Wyatt and Owen and Sam O'Ballivan, imagined them under a hail of bullets. He thought of his ride to Flagstaff in the morning, the report he would make to some go-between who didn't give a damn what the miners' wives and children went without, or who got shot, as long as the copper ore kept flowing. "I can't stay," he told her, rounding the bed, picking up his scattered clothes, wrenching them on. "And what happened between us last night is only going to make leaving that much harder."

At the edge of his vision, he saw that Lydia sat in the middle of the bed now, the covers drawn tightly around her. A single tear slipped down her left cheek.

"Go, then," she whispered. "Just *go,* and be done with it."

Furious with himself, not with her, Gideon grabbed up his boots and stormed out of that room, into the corridor. There, he leaned against the wall next to the door for a few moments, fighting to regain his composure.

When he had, he hauled his boots on, ran his fingers through his hair, and with that to suffice for grooming, took the front staircase, in case Helga was in the kitchen, and left the house.

The cool, early-morning air braced him, cleared his head a little.

Still, memories assailed him. He'd taken Lydia in a fury of need the night before, like a whore, not a virgin. God Almighty, the headboard had slammed against the wall fit to crack the plaster, and the racket the bedsprings made would have awakened the dead, let alone a nosy housekeeper sleeping in the tiny nook under the main staircase. And he didn't even want to *consider* what must have gone through the *aunts'* minds.

He tried to shift his thoughts to matters at hand, as was his custom, and was only partially successful. By his calculations, it would be another half hour before the starting whistle sounded up at the mine, and although daylight would soon spill over the hills, it was still fairly dark. On the off-chance that Rowdy might be up and around,

Gideon took the least obvious route he could to his brother's house.

Sure enough, lights glowed at the kitchen windows, though the rest of the great house was dark.

Grateful and at the same time wondering how to phrase what he had to say, Gideon knocked lightly at the back door.

Rowdy opened it, a cup of coffee in one hand, Pardner at his side.

If he was surprised to find Gideon on his doorstep at that ungodly hour, it didn't show in his face or his manner.

"Come on in," Rowdy said, stepping back. He added, as Gideon moved past him, "Do you feel as bad as you look?"

Gideon managed a crooked grin, shoved a hand through his hair. "Worse," he said.

Rowdy arched one eyebrow at that. "Sit down," he said. "I'll get you some coffee. As Pappy used to say, it'll put some hair on your chest."

"Hair on my chest?" Gideon retorted, dropping into a chair. "The stuff you make would strip rust off a mile of railroad tracks." He leaned to stroke Pardner, who'd sidled up beside him to rest against his thigh, offering canine comfort. Hell, he *must* be a pitiful sight, if even the dog felt sorry for him.

Rowdy brought him the coffee and it was every bit as bad as usual, but it did have a quick effect. Gideon very nearly checked his chest for a fresh crop of hair.

"You had breakfast?" Rowdy asked.

"No," Gideon answered. "But it's a half day at the mine. I won't starve before quitting time."

Rowdy grinned. "My eggs are a sight better than my coffee," he said, setting a skillet on the stove. "While I'm cooking, you can tell me what brings you here before the sun's even up, little brother."

Gideon sighed, stroked Pardner's head a few times. The house was quiet, with everyone still asleep except Rowdy and the dog, and there was something nice about being there, inside a circle of warm light, and welcome. "They've cut wages at the mine," he began, "and the men are riled. They're expecting coolies to come in, take over their jobs."

Rowdy, busy cracking eggs into the skillet, turned to look at him. "You know, Gideon," he interjected quietly, "as detached as you sound, like an observer and not somebody who needs his job to make a living, a man would think you weren't one of them. The miners, I mean."

Gideon averted his eyes for a moment, let

the remark pass without comment. "It's probably just talk," he went on, after clearing his throat once, "but one of the men — Mike O'Hanlon — suggested they take over the operation by force, hold it with guns."

The eggs began to sizzle in the pan. The smell made Gideon's mouth water — he'd missed supper the night before and now, despite all the things that were bothering him, he was hungry.

"I know Mike," Rowdy said easily. "He's a big talker, but I can't see him doing a damn fool thing like that. There'd be no way out — the army would come and the whole crew would eventually hang."

Gideon recalled the look in Mike's eyes the night before, when they'd stood outside the gate at the Porter house, after the "meeting" at Paddy's. "Maybe not," he allowed. "But do you want to take that chance?"

Rowdy worked a spatula under the eggs, flipped them over, lobbed them onto a plate. Brought them to the table, along with a fork. Only when he'd done all that did he answer Gideon's question. "No," he said. "I reckon I don't."

Gideon nodded, tucked into his breakfast. He was running out of time; he'd have to hurry if he wanted to reach the mine by the time the whistle blew.

"*Are* the mine owners planning to bring in Chinamen, Gideon?" Rowdy asked evenly. "Cut the other men out?"

"How would I know?" Gideon asked, but he felt color surge up his neck, pound under his jawline. Christ, he *hated* lying to Rowdy; for one thing, it was damn near impossible to carry off, and for another, it made him feel ungrateful. He'd have been up shit creek, after their pa died, if it hadn't been for Rowdy taking him in, letting him pretend to be a deputy.

"Maybe you *don't* know," Rowdy allowed, watching him. "About the Chinamen, anyhow. But I'd bet my last pair of boots that you're working for the owners, and if I've figured that out, O'Hanlon and the others will, too." He paused. "You're playing a dangerous game here, Gideon. If you won't pull out for your own sake, then do it for Lydia."

Gideon had said what he'd come to say, and the subject of Lydia was off-limits until he'd figured things out. He'd finished the eggs — devoured them, more like — and the mine whistle was due to sound any minute now. Tight-jawed, he pushed back his chair and stood, and spoke as if Rowdy hadn't struck bare bone a few seconds before. "I need to borrow a horse on Sunday," he said, carrying his plate to the sink. "Will you lend me one?"

Rowdy frowned. "Sunday? Isn't that when the women planned to throw that wedding reception shindig for you and Lydia?"

Gideon felt a trapdoor open somewhere in his midsection. "It was Lark's idea," he said, "and she's in no condition to put a party together."

"I guess you're right," Rowdy said, though he sounded a little too uncertain for Gideon's comfort. "What do you want with a horse?"

Gideon unclamped his back teeth. "I just need the use of one, Rowdy, for a day. If you don't want to lend a cayuse, just say so."

"Take the damn horse," Rowdy bit out, narrowing his eyes.

Gideon was at the door by then. "Thanks," he said. "For the eggs *and* the horse."

"You be careful," Rowdy said. "You be *real* careful."

Since that was a promise Gideon couldn't make, he didn't reply.

He was halfway to the mine when the whistle blew, three long, shrill blasts that danced down his spine like a spill of cold water.

After Gideon had gone — a long time after Gideon had gone — Lydia got out of bed and stripped the sheets from the mattress, dropped them in a pile on the floor. That done, she took clean undergarments from the scant supply in the top drawer of the bureau, and a pretty blue-and-white print dress, donated by Maddie O'Ballivan, from the wardrobe.

Down the hall, in the bathroom, she filled the tub with very hot water and lowered herself gingerly into it.

She was sore between her legs, sorer still in her heart.

She and Gideon had consummated their marriage — and he still planned to leave.

Slowly, like someone in a trance, Lydia washed, rose out of the water, toweled herself dry and put on her clothes. She brushed her teeth, combed and replaited her hair, pinned it into a matronly chignon at her nape.

When she descended the kitchen stairs, Helga was at the stove, stirring a pot of oatmeal, though the aunts were not yet in evidence. They were not early risers, as a general rule.

Once again, Helga was humming, but when she turned and saw Lydia's face, she stopped instantly. "Oh, child," she murmured. "What is it? What's happened?"

"The sheets," Lydia said, skirting Helga's gaze, "they'll need washing. And I don't want the aunts to see."

"Never mind the sheets," Helga said softly, leaving the spoon in the oatmeal to cross to Lydia and take her by the shoulders. "What's he done to you, that young scoundrel? *Tell me,* Lydia, and I'll give him what for."

Lydia smiled sadly. It wasn't as if giving Gideon "what for" would change anything. "If only I hadn't sent that stupid letter," she muttered with a shake of her head. "We'd still be in Phoenix, in our own home, with our things around us and —"

"And your heart wouldn't be breaking?" Helga prompted, her kind eyes filling with tears. When Lydia started to protest, the other woman cut her off. "Don't try to deny it," she said fiercely. "I've got eyes in my head, and ears, too. I *know* why the sheets need washing, Lydia. And I know a bride with a broken heart when I see one."

Lydia reddened. "Helga —"

"When I catch up to that *husband* of yours —"

Lydia was about to confess that she was as much to blame as Gideon, since she'd practically seduced him, when Mittie poked her head out of the bedroom the aunts shared, smiling.

"Goodness, what a relief to wake up," she piped cheerfully. "I dreamed the house was falling down around our ears. The crash was horrendous."

Millie edged past her, tightening her wrapper around her impossibly small waist as she entered the kitchen. "How strange, sister," she said. "I had the very same dream."

Just then, a giggle, partly hysteria, partly amusement, bubbled up and escaped Lydia.

Helga, stony-faced, laughed, too.

The aunts looked puzzled.

"Was there a thunderstorm?" Mittie asked, turning to Millie. "Perhaps there was a thunderstorm, and we only *thought* we dreamed the house was falling down."

Helga and Lydia exchanged glances.

"Yes," Helga said. "Bless your hearts, there *was* a thunderstorm. That's what you heard."

The aunts brightened, clearly relieved.

"Breakfast is ready," Helga said. "All of you, sit down."

Everyone did, including Lydia, after a

brief hesitation.

"What are you going to do today, dear?" Mittie asked her niece cheerfully.

"I was planning to call on Lark," Lydia answered. She hadn't planned beyond that, so her next statement was a revelation to her, as well as the aunts and Helga. "Then I think I'll pay a visit to the general store, see what kind of merchandise they carry."

The aunts looked eager. "Might we go with you?" Mittie asked. "It would be so nice to browse."

"We haven't any money," Millie reminded her sister.

"Well," Mittie answered sportingly, "it doesn't cost anything to *look*."

"I suppose you'd be safe enough," Helga allowed, spooning dollops of oatmeal into the bowls she'd already set at each place at the table. "There's been no sign of Jacob Fitch, and the general store is right in the middle of town — lots of folks around."

"Don't you want to come with us?" Mittie asked, concerned. The aunts hated for anyone to feel left out.

"I have laundry to do," Helga said, at last joining them at the table. And that was clearly her final word.

Half an hour later, Lydia and the aunts knocked at the Yarbros' front door.

Sarah admitted them, smiling, and Lydia soon found out why her sister-in-law was in such a cheerful state of mind. Lark was not only out of bed, but sitting in the main parlor, clad in a blue silk dress instead of a nightgown and wrapper, with little Miranda in her arms and the other children crowded around her.

She greeted Lydia and the aunts with a beaming smile.

"You look wonderful!" Lydia marveled.

"I can't stay up too long," Lark answered happily, "but I'm definitely on the mend." Studying Lydia's face, though, Lark's smile dimmed a little. "Is something wrong?"

"No," Lydia lied briskly.

"We're going to the mercantile," Mittie announced, as pleased as a child anticipating a splendid outing.

"But we can't buy anything," Millie said.

"Of course you can," Lark countered, smiling again, although when her eyes strayed back to Lydia, there was worry in them. "Just tell Mr. Blanchard — that's the storekeeper — that Gideon will settle up with him later."

"Gideon," Lydia pointed out carefully, troubled by the air of gentle avarice suddenly shimmering around her aunts, "works in a mine."

Lark's smile intensified. "Perhaps he does," she answered smoothly. "But he's not poor. Did he tell you he was?"

Lydia was taken aback. In Phoenix, Gideon had told Lydia he could provide for her and the aunts and Helga, but she'd been too troubled about her impending marriage to Jacob Fitch to pursue the subject.

"I don't think he's ever said he was poor," Mittie mused, turning to Millie. "Has he, sister?"

Millie turned questioningly to Lydia. "Is your husband poor, dear?"

Sarah, hearing all this, gave a little chuckle.

A spirit of rebellion rose within Lydia; she did not own a single dress, other than Aunt Nell's wedding gown. Everything else, except for the undergarments she'd been wearing when Gideon removed her from the mansion in Phoenix, was borrowed. She glanced at Lark, who smiled again, encouragingly, and nodded, before answering Millie's innocent question.

"If he's not," she said resolutely, "he soon will be."

CHAPTER FIFTEEN

"And how was your brother this fine mornin'?" Mike O'Hanlon inquired lightly, the moment Gideon took up his shovel in the belly of that accursed mine.

Overhead, timbers creaked under tons of earth. "Fine," Gideon said, with a smile that was deliberately hard, brief and spare. "Made me breakfast, in fact."

Ignoring Gideon's reply, Mike looked up. "Whole thing could come down on our heads anytime," he observed. "One more thing the owners won't trouble themselves with — shoring up timbers."

"I guess that's a danger in any mine," Gideon observed. "Not just this one."

"And why should they care what happens to us, young Yarbro?" Mike asked, again as if Gideon hadn't spoken. "They don't mind starvin' our children. Don't mind that our wives have to beg storekeepers for grace and another week to pay, just to put a bean on the table. No, sir, as long as the profits are rollin' in, that's all that matters to them."

Gideon rested on his shovel handle for a moment. Thanks to the release Lydia had given him the night before, he felt a lot easier in his skin, and his muscles, though they still ached, didn't throb in protest every time he pitched more ore into the cart. He thought about what Rowdy had said to him at the table that morning — that if he'd guessed Gideon was spying for the owners, O'Hanlon and the others had, too.

"It's clear you took the time to watch my house and follow me to Rowdy's before dawn, and that's a lot of trouble for a man to go to, it seems to me. You've been trying to get under my hide since I signed on. Why don't you just spit out whatever it is you have to say so we can get on with loading ore?"

Something flickered in O'Hanlon's eyes, respect perhaps, but a certain contempt, too. "I've been working in holes like this one since I was nine years old, young Yarbro," he said slowly. "And I know an outsider when I see one. You don't belong here. Your clothes are too good, your house is too fine, and your family is too important in this town. Even without the way you talk, I'd know by your manner that you're educated, used to *thinkin'* for a livin', not sweatin' for one. If it's true that a man carries the measure he's taken of himself in his eyes, you're not one of us."

Wilson strolled by just then, with a bandage covering most of his face. "Back to work," he growled. "We're not paying you men to shoot the breeze."

"Sod off, Wilson," O'Hanlon answered easily, never looking away from Gideon's face. "Well, young Yarbro, you wanted my opinion. What say you to it, now that it's been offered?"

"I say," Gideon answered evenly, "that you're full of sheep-dip. I need this job, just like you do. I'm just as worried about coolies and the timbers supporting the shaft and all the rest. As for my clothes and my family and *the look in my eyes,* you'll hear no explanations from me, and no apologies."

"I guess we understand each other, then," Mike said. "I know you're a Judas, and *you* know I know it. But I'll not harry you again, after what I'll say next. When you speak to the owners, young Yarbro, you tell them we've taken all we're going to take. You tell them we're tired of seein' our children go hungry and our God-fearing wives ashamed." He moved in closer then, tapped hard at Gideon's chest with a forefinger. "*You tell them,* Mr. Yarbro, that we'll *bury* their precious ore, and ourselves with it, before we'll crawl before them like whipped dogs *one more time.*"

Before Gideon could reply to that, the timbers groaned again, a long, ominous whine.

"I'm gettin' out of here!" one of the men shouted. "Before the whole damn town comes down on me!"

Even Wilson looked troubled.

"Everybody out," he said, with grave reluctance. "Now."

Although Lydia had felt like doing some vengeful spending when she and the aunts left Lark's place, when presented with the actual opportunity, she was not so certain. Gideon worked hard down in that mine, and probably for a pittance, though they'd never discussed his wages.

Mr. Blanchard, the storekeeper, greeted the three women warmly and with recognition, addressing Lydia as "Mrs. Yarbro" and immediately making it plain that her husband's credit was good in his establishment.

The aunts busied themselves looking at ribbon and yard goods, enjoying the outing for what it was — a new experience. In

Phoenix, they had never gone out to the shops — the few things they required were delivered — and except for the dresses and hats Gideon had bought for them on the day of the great escape, she'd never seen them in anything but their black mourning dresses or nightgowns and wrappers.

Lydia decided it was safe to give her aunts free rein — despite their earlier, faintly disturbing response to Lark's suggestion that Gideon could well afford the things they needed, she knew they were far more interested in looking at things, and touching them, than purchasing.

She, on the other hand, needed bloomers and camisoles and petticoats, a decent nightgown, too — Gideon had ripped away the one she'd been wearing, after all, and it was past mending. She could use a few dresses, as well.

She made her selections carefully, and with an eye to thrift and true to her expectations, the aunts wanted only a paper of pins, a bottle of violet-scented toilet water, and a dime novel with a depiction of a gunslinger, pistols blazing, on the cover.

As Mr. Blanchard was tallying up the price of these goods, Lydia stood at the counter, waiting patiently and wondering if Helga had gotten the stains out of the bedsheets.

A whimper from behind the counter snagged her attention, and she creased her brow in a frown. "What's that?"

"Oh, it's just this pup," Mr. Blanchard said. "Found him out in the alley last night, poor little critter. The wife brought him in and put him in a basket, hoping he'd rally, but there's not much hope of that, between you and me."

Lydia rounded the counter without permission, and saw an impossibly small black-and-white puppy of indeterminate breed curled up in the bottom of a shallow wicker basket. She crouched, her skirts pooling around her, and laid her hand ever so gently to the dog's thin back, felt the little creature shiver.

"Wife has cats," Mr. Blanchard went on, benignly regretful. "So we can't keep him. He'll probably die, anyhow, but we figured since his life, short as it was, must have been hard, the end ought to be made easy."

The dog whimpered again, a mewling sound more suited to a newborn kitten, and looked up at Lydia with imploring eyes. As a child, her aunt Nell had permitted her to take in strays, but they'd always either died or wandered away again, the way animals do.

"What's his name?" Lydia asked softly,

aware of the aunts crowding up behind her, peering down at the poor little scrap cowering in the bottom of Mrs. Blanchard's basket.

"Never bothered with that," Mr. Blanchard said, but there was something new in his voice. "Would you want to take him home, Mrs. Yarbro?" he asked. "I wouldn't blame you if you didn't — he's not long for this world, as anybody could see —"

"I *will* take him home," Lydia said, resolved, gathering the pup tenderly into her hands, holding him close against her bosom as she rose. "Thank you, Mr. Blanchard."

"What will Helga say?" Mittie asked, at once fretful and fascinated.

"Never mind what Helga will say," Lydia replied, nuzzling the pup.

Millie, evidencing rare practicality, had already fetched a baby's bottle from one of the sundry shelves, set it firmly on the counter. "He'll need milk," she said. "Papa once saved a whole litter of blue-tick hounds with milk — remember, sister?"

"Indeed I do," Mittie answered. "They were born too soon, and their mother had died, and dear Papa brought them into the cooking-house and made the servants feed them cow's milk and they all came around in time. Grew up to be the best hunters in the county."

Lydia stroked the tiny dog, loving the warmth of it, the softness of its fur, the look of beleaguered hope in its eyes. The "servants" Mittie referred to had been slaves, and old Judge Fairmont had probably loved them — in the same way he'd loved those hounds.

If this puppy perished — and there was every chance he would — Lydia knew she would be heartbroken. But, like her ancestor, she had to try to save him. Turning her back now would be simply impossible, whatever the cost to her.

"I could have a gallon of milk sent over, no charge, of course," Mr. Blanchard offered, watching Lydia with kindness in his eyes. "We get it fresh from Mr. Sayer's cow."

"That would be fine, Mr. Blanchard," Lydia said. Now that her arms were full of puppy, she took a second look at the other purchases.

"I'll send the other things around, too," Mr. Blanchard said.

"We can manage the pins and the toilet water," Mittie insisted staunchly.

Lydia smiled, thanked the storekeeper again, and left the store.

The aunts hurried along the sidewalk on either side of her, reminding Lydia of quail chicks trotting behind a hen.

"Such a snippet," Millie commented, a little breathless because Lydia was setting a fast pace. "Whatever shall we call him?"

"I think you've just solved that problem," Lydia said, at once enormously cheered and wary of the sorrow that might lie ahead, compounding the inevitable loss of Gideon. "Snippet is the perfect name, it seems to me."

Soon, they were home again.

The aunts rushed to find a blanket and a basket to make Snippet a bed.

Helga, pinning the freshly washed sheets from Lydia and Gideon's bed to the clothesline, shook her head. "Land sakes," she said. "What do we need with a dog?"

But her eyes softened as she came closer and reached out to touch the quivering puppy.

"The point," Lydia said gently, "is that *he* needs *us.*"

Helga looked worried. "See how he shivers, Lydia? He's not well."

Lydia lifted the little bundle slightly, kissed the top of Snippet's head. "He needs a little tending, that's all."

"And you need something to tend," Helga said wisely.

Barely half an hour later, a boy arrived,

driving a buckboard, and dropped off Lydia's purchases and the promised gallon of milk.

When Gideon arrived home from the mine, looking grim and most reluctant to face her, he found his wife sitting cross-legged on the kitchen floor, holding Snippet and giving him milk from a baby's bottle, a drop at a time.

The sight of Lydia with the puppy did something to Gideon, made him forget Mike O'Hanlon and the trouble at the mine. Even made him forget the sheets he'd seen, drying on the clothesline, and the damning fact that he'd used Lydia, the night before, in a way he might regret for the rest of his life.

Lydia did not immediately look up, though of course she knew he was there, but Helga caught his eye straight off, and there was a warning brewing in her plain face, threatening as storm clouds gathering on the horizon.

"What do we have here?" Gideon asked, crouching next to Lydia to get a closer look at the dog.

Their gazes connected. Lydia smiled, albeit sadly.

"This is Snippet," she said.

Although he was grinning by then, something about the way she held that pup left Gideon feeling stricken, nostalgic for a life he'd never had to begin with, probably never *would* have. "Suits him," Gideon allowed.

The aunts, who had evidently been opening parcels at the table, judging by the debris of brown wrapping paper and string, fell silent.

Did they expect him to banish the pup? Or was it that they'd heard all the racket he and Lydia had made in the night?

Gideon flushed at the thought. "Can I hold him?" he asked Lydia.

She hesitated, then reluctantly handed over the dog. It nearly disappeared between Gideon's palms, it was so small, and when he held it up close to his face, it licked his cheek.

He laughed, surrendered the pup to Lydia again.

"He mustn't die," one of the aunts said, and when Gideon looked over, he saw that both women's lower lips were quivering.

That struck at something deep inside Gideon, too, the way seeing Lydia with the pup had.

He stood up. "He won't die," he said, though where this certainty came from, he didn't know. The critter was scrawny, and probably too young to be weaned.

"Mr. Blanchard said he might," Mittie-or-Millie argued. "Someone left him in the alley behind the mercantile, and Mrs. Blanchard couldn't take him in because she has cats."

"Papa once saved an entire litter," the other sister said.

Glancing down at Lydia again, coddling the pup, Gideon felt that odd, broken wanting again. But this time, he knew it for what it was. She would hold a baby in the same reverent, infinitely tender way.

A baby.

For all his regretting, he hadn't once thought that he might have gotten Lydia pregnant. They'd only made love that once — but once was all it took, wasn't it?

Unnerved, Gideon shoved a hand through his hair.

"You're home early," Lydia remarked, barely distracted from the pup.

Now, Gideon felt a twinge of envy toward that dog, right along with the sympathy. "Half day at the mine," he said. Lydia didn't need to know that Wilson and the others had been afraid the support beams might give way, and bury the men so deep that they wouldn't be seen again until Resurrection Day.

"I reckon you must be hungry," Helga said to him, with guarded courtesy. "Leaving the house before breakfast the way you did, and by the front door, too."

Inwardly, Gideon sighed. Outwardly, he grinned, because he knew if he ever let Helga get the upper hand with him, well-meaning though she might be, he'd never know a moment's peace from then on.

He nodded. "Obliged," he said. He'd stopped by the bank earlier — like most of the businesses in town, it was open six days a week — and cashed a draft. "You'll be needing some things for the house," he added, taking some folding money from his shirt pocket.

Lydia didn't look up from the puppy, so he finally handed the bills to Helga. Her eyes widened at the amount, but she offered no comment — only turned and tucked the funds into a salt box affixed to the wall.

"We did incur a debt at Mr. Blanchard's mercantile," Millie-or-Mittie confessed, nodding toward the garments lying on the table, amid the wrapping paper and coils of twine. "Lydia abandoned most of her clothes, you know, when we left Phoenix."

Gideon nodded again. "I know," he said. Being a man, he hadn't thought much about

Lydia's wardrobe, but things like that were important to women.

All of the sudden, he felt too big for that spacious kitchen, too awkward, like some large farm animal stabled in a pantry. If he moved in any direction, he was sure to break something — or someone.

Helga had commenced making lunch by then, and the old ladies hastily gathered up the dresses and the wrapping paper and the string. Lydia finally laid the puppy in its laundry-basket bed, smiled slightly as it gave a whole-body sigh and drifted off to sleep.

Again, Gideon's throat swelled painfully. He put a hand out to Lydia, to help her up, and for a moment, he thought she'd refuse to take it, get to her feet on her own. In the end, though, she accepted his assistance.

He wanted to pull her into his arms, hold her, tell her he was sorry, swear that even after he'd gone, she and the aunts and Helga and that puny little dog would lack for nothing, because he'd send home most of his pay, but he couldn't, not with so many people around.

Helga made hash for their midday meal, and Gideon ate hungrily, though he couldn't help noticing that Lydia barely touched her food, and her gaze kept wandering to the puppy.

"I believe I'll go over to Mr. Blanchard's mercantile myself," Helga said, when she'd finished eating. "We could use flour and coffee and a few other staples."

When no one commented, she took some of the money from the salt box, donned a calico bonnet and left.

The aunts cleared the table and began washing dishes.

Gideon watched Lydia watching the puppy for a while, then went upstairs, turned up the gas-flame under the bathroom boiler, and shaved while the water heated for a bath. After a stinging splash of bay-rum to his face, he headed for the bedroom, in search of clean clothes. Most every garment he owned was either dirty or still in his room over at Lark and Rowdy's, but he had trousers and shirts in his valise, the things he'd normally worn, before returning to Stone Creek and going to work in a copper mine.

"I know an outsider when I see one," he heard Mike O'Hanlon say. *"Your clothes are too good, your house is too fine, and your family is too important in this town."*

He'd never failed at a single assignment he'd undertaken, since the day he left college and went to work, he thought, but he'd sure made a hell of a mess of this one. And the irony was, he was going to have to leave Lydia anyway.

His shoulders stooped.

"Gideon?"

He hadn't heard Lydia approaching, hadn't heard the door open — but then, he probably hadn't closed it in the first place. He couldn't recall, and that troubled him — he was losing his grip.

"Are you going somewhere?"

Gideon turned, smiled at his wife. "No," he said. "I just thought it would be good to clean up."

Her smile faltered a little; she looked so small, so vulnerable, standing there. Gideon's heart turned over, as he thought of all the things there were in the world to cause her pain.

"Lydia, the puppy —" he began.

"I know, Gideon," she said, very softly. "Snippet might not survive. You don't need to tell me that."

His throat closed up again. He swallowed. "I could borrow Rowdy's horse and buggy," he heard himself say, though he hadn't consciously formulated the idea. "Show you around Stone Creek a little — maybe take you out to see Wyatt and Sarah's ranch."

She brightened. "I'd like that," she said. "But Snippet —"

"The aunts and Helga will be here to look after the pup," Gideon said, because suddenly it seemed vitally important to take Lydia out in the buggy, a perfectly normal outing for a married couple. "And hovering over him won't keep him alive."

Lydia pondered that, then nodded.

"I mean to take a bath," he told her. "I won't be long. When I'm through, I'll go fetch Rowdy's rig and come back for you."

She still looked troubled. "Gideon, when I came in — the way you were standing — something about the angle of your head —"

"I'm all right, Lydia," he said. He wished — God, how he wished — he could tell her about his real job, and Mike O'Hanlon's suspicions, and even what he'd be doing in Flagstaff the next day, but he couldn't. Not, he realized, because he'd given his word to the mine owners, but because he didn't want to lay his private concerns on her shoulders.

He'd done enough to burden her as it was.

"Are you sure we won't be imposing on Wyatt and Sarah?" she asked. "Just — dropping in on them that way?"

"I'm sure," he said, and because he had to lighten the moment or break under it, he added, "But if you'd like, I could have engraved calling cards printed up and drop one off at their door ahead of time, so they'd know they were about to have company."

Lydia smiled at that. "I'll wear one of the new dresses you bought me this morning," she said. "The blue sprigged muslin, I think."

He nodded, thinking he would have been perfectly content to stand there in that bedroom and look at her — just look at her — for the rest of his born days. But life had a way of moving on, grinding things and people beneath its great wheels, and he could feel forces gathering around him, closing in. All of it made a pleasant buggy-ride with his wife a matter of urgency. Depending on how things went in Flagstaff the next day, he might not set eyes on her again for a long time.

So he went back down the hall, and bathed and put on fresh clothes. Then he headed for Rowdy's place.

His brother wasn't around, but Hank and some of his friends were playing baseball in the lot beside the barn.

"Tell your pa I borrowed the buggy and the gray mare," Gideon told his nephew, as he headed for the barn door.

"Take the sorrel," Hank replied, because such requests were common in his experience. "The mare threw a shoe yesterday."

Gideon smiled, nodded and went on about his business. Found the sorrel, hitched the animal to the buggy, and set out to collect Lydia. On any previous visit to Stone Creek, he would have joined in the baseball game, at least for a little while, but not that day.

Hank waved as he drove past, and Gideon nodded in farewell.

He might see Hank again when he returned the buggy, he thought unhappily — or not until his nephew had grown into a man.

Wyatt and Sarah's ranch land reminded Lydia of a rippling green sea as she and Gideon looked out over the expanse from the seat of Rowdy's buggy. Several hundred cattle grazed in the rich grass, drank at the springs and the small creek, two riders — probably Wyatt and Owen, though it was hard to be sure from that distance — moving among them.

The main house stood upon a hill, a two-story white structure, solid and square, with green shutters and gleaming windows and a veranda on three sides. It was flanked by a sturdy barn, a springhouse and several other small outbuildings.

Gideon's grin was weary as he took it all

in. "You should have seen this place," he said, with quiet pride, "when Wyatt took it over from Sarah's father's bank ten years ago." He turned slightly, pointed to a smaller house, on another hill. "That's Owen's house, there," he went on. "He and his wife, Shannie, are expecting their first child in a few months."

"It's lovely," Lydia said, catching the sound of children's laughter on the slight breeze. She had met Rowdy and Lark's little ones, now she would get to know Wyatt and Sarah's, too. Perhaps, like their cousins, they would address her as "Aunt Lydia," a prospect that pleased her.

"For an old train robber and erstwhile rustler, Wyatt did all right for himself," Gideon said, taking up the reins again, urging the horse on.

They descended a rutted, curving dirt road with a grassy hump bulging high in the middle, and when they drew closer to the main house, Gideon gave a long, shrill whistle through his teeth.

Dogs began to bark, and then four children, two boys and two girls, roughly the same ages as Lark and Rowdy's brood, came running barefoot around the side of the house and up the road toward them. Two dogs frolicked after them.

"Uncle Gideon!" one of the girls cried, her face alight, her long, dark hair flying behind her as she ran up that road. *"Uncle Gideon!"*

Grinning, Gideon stopped the rig, set the brake lever, and jumped nimbly to the ground, catching the child when she launched herself into his arms. He spun her around, both of them laughing, and then set her on her feet again.

Lydia watched as the older two, both boys, solemnly shook Gideon's hand, and the baby, a girl no older than three, hung shyly back until her uncle crouched directly in front of her. The gentle way he spoke pierced Lydia's heart. "And here's my Lucy Jane," he said.

Lucy Jane hooked one finger in her mouth and regarded him with huge cornflower-blue eyes.

"She doesn't remember you, Uncle Gideon," the other girl said. "She was really little the last time you were here."

The tallest of the boys, perhaps eight or nine years old, turned to Lydia, still sitting in the buggy, enjoying the scene and, at the same time, wondering why it made her feel sad.

"Are you our aunt Lydia?" he asked.

She nodded, smiling.

"This is Payton," Gideon said, ruffling the boy's hair. He'd hoisted Lucy Jane onto his hip, carried her easily in the curve of his arm. "That other yahoo is Luke. It was Margaret Alice who tried to knock me down, and —" he looked around, frowned "— where's Mark?"

"It's his turn to churn the butter," Margaret Alice replied. "And Mama says he'll have to copy Bible chapters if he doesn't quit whining about it."

Gideon laughed.

By then, Sarah had appeared on the porch of the big house, a younger and noticeably pregnant woman with a glorious head of copper-colored hair beside her, both of them smiling in welcome.

In the distance, Wyatt and Owen approached on horseback.

Suddenly, Lydia felt shy.

"They can be a mite overwhelming," Gideon teased, having read her expression the way he so often did, climbing into the buggy seat again, with Lucy Jane perched solidly on his lap. "All those Yarbros coming at you in a herd, I mean."

"*Cattle* come in herds, Uncle Gideon," Luke said, speaking for the first time. Like the other children, he had dark hair and very blue eyes. "Not *people.*"

"I stand corrected," Gideon replied, with an affable salute, and started the buggy moving again.

The boys and Margaret Alice climbed nimbly onto the back of the rig to ride along, while the two large dogs, yellow like Pardner, ran alongside, adding gleefully to the fuss with yips and barks.

Lydia, in the center of all this dust-raising, noisy activity, had never felt happier — or sadder. Thus, she did not know whether to laugh or cry.

Sarah greeted her on the porch with a beaming smile and a kiss on the cheek, and introduced her to Shannie, correctly assuming Gideon had told her the children's names. Wyatt and Owen reached the house, dismounted, and left the horses standing, reins dangling, at the water trough.

Wyatt smiled at Lydia, bid her a polite welcome, but the look he tossed in Gideon's direction was slightly less cordial.

"Come inside," Sarah urged, taking Lydia's hand. "The coffee's on, and I'm just about to take a blackberry cobbler out of the oven. Shannie and I have been baking all afternoon." She paused. "Oh, Lydia, I'm so glad to see you."

Sincerity shone, beacon-bright in Sarah's eyes, and Lydia was moved by the sight.

She truly *was* a member of the Yarbro family — except to Gideon.

Wyatt lingered, holding his black round-brimmed hat in one hand, and so did Owen.

Glancing back, expecting Gideon to follow, Lydia saw him set Lucy Jane down, so she could scamper into the house with the other children.

"I'll have a word with you, little brother," Wyatt said to Gideon, and though he probably hadn't intended for Lydia to hear, she did. Meeting her gaze, then looking away, Wyatt spoke again. "Owen, you go on inside and have some cobbler before it's all gone."

Gideon stood with his hands on his hips and a stubborn set to his jaw, looking at Wyatt.

Owen stepped onto the porch, smiled affably down into Lydia's worried face, took her by the arm, and escorted her briskly into the house.

CHAPTER SIXTEEN

Wyatt tugged off one leather glove, then the other, the ones he always wore when he rode, and stuffed them both into a hip pocket as he held Gideon's gaze, there in front of the ranch house. "Rowdy tells me," he said very quietly, "that he thinks you're in some sort of trouble. Says you've gotten yourself snarled up someplace between the workers and the men who own the mine. Is that about the size of it, Gideon?"

Gideon felt heat rise in his neck. He *hated* feeling like a little brother, especially since he was as tall as Wyatt and taller than Rowdy, but they were both more than a decade older than he was, and a lot more experienced, and in that moment, like it or not, he *did* feel like a kid.

"That's about the size of it," he finally allowed.

Wyatt propped one foot against the side of the porch, put his hat back on and adjusted it slightly, so the brim shaded his eyes from the Arizona sun. "Did it ever occur to you that, being your kin and all, Rowdy and Owen and I might want to help? Sam O'Ballivan, too?"

Gideon shoved a hand through his hair. "I won't see you putting your lives on the line like that," he said. "You've got wives and kids, Wyatt, and Owen's Shannie is in the family way, too."

Wyatt's gaze slid briefly to the closed door, and one corner of his mouth tilted upward in a spare Yarbro grin. "You've got a wife, too," he pointed out. "But there's something about the way you are with her — something I can't quite work out in my mind, not all the way, anyway — that bothers me, Gideon. I guess the closest I can get to it is to say that you seem like a man who's only passing through, not meaning to stay in Stone Creek — or with Lydia."

"After this — after this assignment is finished," Gideon admitted, to himself as well as to his eldest brother, "I'm not going to be welcome in Stone Creek, Wyatt. If I'm gone, I can send Lydia money. If I stay, I might not live very long. I figure Lydia's better off with an absent husband than a dead one."

"You mean to *run*," Wyatt said flatly.

Gideon colored up for certain then. Went crimson, if the heat in his face was any indication. "I wouldn't put it like that," he said.

"Well, I would," Wyatt countered. "I've lived on the run, Gideon, and so has Rowdy. And you can take it from me — it *isn't* a life. It's an existence, and barely that."

"You have Sarah and the kids, and Rowdy has Lark —"

Wyatt leaned in. "And you have *Lydia,* you thickheaded fool," he growled. "You've got to stake out a claim to a piece of ground, literal and figurative, dig in the heels of your boots and *stand,* Gideon. If there's fighting to be done, Rowdy and I will fight right beside you, but there's not a damn thing we can do if you're hell-bent on turning tail and running."

"This isn't your problem," Gideon ground out. If Wyatt hadn't been right, he'd have taken a swing at him — and he was tempted to, anyway. Trouble was, that would have upset the women and the kids, and on top of that, Gideon wanted to keep all his teeth.

"That's where you and I differ in our opinions, little brother," Wyatt said. "What concerns you concerns me, and Rowdy, too. *Damn* it, Gideon, that woman in there *loves* you. Practically eats you up with her eyes every time she looks at you. Do you have *any* idea how rare that is, and how flat-out, bone *stupid* it would be to throw her away? She might wait for you for a while, might even be content to cash the bank drafts you send her and carry on. But *I'll* wager that one fine day some likely-looking fellow will come moseying along and she'll get herself a divorce — it will be easy, if you abandon her like you're talking about doing — and marry right up with him. Hell of a thing for you, if you come to your senses all of a sudden, turn up back here ready to buckle down and act like a man instead of a kid, and find her gone."

Even though that was pretty much what Gideon had been telling himself he *hoped* would happen — that Lydia would eventually remarry, settle down to a happy life with a man who would be good to her — the thought made him half-sick now. When he'd finally claimed her fully, it had been more than a physical bonding — it had forged him to her in deeper, less definable ways that felt sacred — and permanent.

"It's best if I cut her loose," Gideon insisted, but he couldn't look at Wyatt as he spoke. Instead, he stared out over the dancing green grass, and the cattle and everything Wyatt and Sarah had built by linking their hearts together, as well as their minds and hands.

"All right, then," Wyatt said, sounding beaten. Gideon wasn't deceived by his brother's tone, though — no Yarbro, at least not Wyatt or Rowdy — was *ever* beaten. Like their pa used to say, the only way to keep them down was to kill them. "What about Jacob Fitch?"

Gideon had to release his jaw before he could answer, he'd clamped it down so hard. And he looked straight into Wyatt's eyes now. "You said you'd look out for her. You and Rowdy."

"We will," Wyatt agreed. "But you're missing the point, Gideon. Looking after Lydia is *your* responsibility. We'll be brothers to her, make no mistake about that, but *you* are her husband."

With all his concerns about what was going on at the mine, and all the new feelings making love to Lydia had unleashed in him, Gideon had pushed the problem of Jacob Fitch to the back of his mind. "Don't you think he'd have done something by now, if he was going to?" he asked, but he sounded uncertain, even to himself.

"I think," Wyatt said, "that Fitch is the kind of man who'll wait as long as he has to, for the right opportunity to make his move and pay you back for taking Lydia away from him. Sooner or later, that opportunity *will* come — and you can be damn sure, Gideon, that he won't miss it."

"Looks like I'm caught between a rock and a hard place," Gideon said, with a lightness he didn't feel and a laugh that fell short of humor.

"You sure as hell are," Wyatt agreed. "But you've got brothers, and you've got friends. And you've got a lady who would face down the devil for you. Take it from me, Gideon — I speak from experience — there is *nothing* more important than the love of the right woman."

Gideon thought long, and he thought hard. His throat scalded, as though he'd swallowed acid, and so did the backs of his eyes. "Things might get ugly, Wyatt," he finally said. "*Real* ugly."

Wyatt chuckled, slapped Gideon's shoulder and then let his hand rest there for a few minutes. "I can handle 'ugly,' " he said. "Did I ever tell you about that gal I lived with for a while, before I went to prison down in Texas, all those years ago? She'd have made a fine addition to Pappy's train-robbing gang — she could have derailed the Illinois Central just by standing on the tracks."

Gideon laughed — really laughed — and *Christ*, it felt good.

Hope flickered, somewhere in the general area of his heart, but it was a faltering flame.

"Do you love Lydia, Gideon?" Wyatt asked, his voice quiet and his eyes serious again.

"Yes," Gideon answered. "I'm pretty sure I do."

"You might start by *telling* her that. And while you're at it, tell her you mean to make a life with her, right here in Stone Creek."

"There'll be trouble, Wyatt," Gideon reminded his brother.

"And I'm even better acquainted with trouble," Wyatt retorted easily, "than I am with 'ugly.' " He paused, slapped Gideon's back again, though with less force this time. "Now," he said. "Let's go on into the house and get some of that blackberry cobbler before Owen finishes it off."

It was dark when Gideon and Lydia got back to town, and the sky overhead was spattered with bright stars. From the moment Gideon and Wyatt had entered the house, earlier that day, and claimed their shares of Sarah's delicious cobbler, Lydia had sensed a change in her husband.

But maybe it was only wishful thinking.

She'd found it all too easy, surrounded by
Wyatt and Sarah's happy, boisterous family
and the sturdy walls of that house, to
imagine herself and Gideon a few years in
the future, with children of their own.

"You go on in and see to Snippet," Gideon told her, drawing the horse and buggy
to a stop in front of the Porter house. "I'll
wait till you're inside, then take the rig back
to Rowdy's barn and put the horse up for
the night."

Without waiting for Lydia's reply, he
secured the buggy's brake and the reins.
Jumped to the ground and then helped her
down as carefully as if she were made of the
thinnest glass.

He opened the front gate for her, and as
she passed, he spoke again, gruffly. "Lydia?"

She stopped to look up at him, saw flecks
of starlight in his eyes. "Yes?"

"I'm going to want to make love to you
again when I get back, if you're willing. And
it'll be easier on you this time, I promise."

Lydia's cheeks burned, not with embarrassment, but with sweet anticipation. "I'm
willing, Gideon," she said softly.

She saw wanting in his face and in his eyes
as he looked at her, and sadness, too. He
touched her cheek.

"There's trouble ahead, Lydia," he told

her. "It's of my own making, mostly, but it's trouble just the same."

Lydia supposed she'd known that all along. "Whatever it is," she said quietly, "we can handle it — together."

He nodded, then grinned slightly. "Go on in the house," he said, "so I can get this horse and buggy back where they belong and come home to you."

Lydia's heart swelled with a hope she hardly dared entertain. What had passed between Wyatt and Gideon, she wondered, to bring about this change in her husband? Knowing the disappointment would be too great to bear if she asked Gideon, straight-out, if he meant to stay after all, and he said he didn't, she locked the question away in her heart.

As soon as she'd stepped into the house and closed the door behind her, Lydia hurried to the nearest window. Watched as Gideon stood gazing after her for several long moments, then climbed into the buggy and drove away.

Once he'd disappeared from sight, she went on to the kitchen, found Snippet sitting up in his basket. After turning up one of the gaslights, she took the baby's bottle from the counter, filled it with milk at the icebox, and put it into a pan of water. Set

380

the works on the stove to warm up a little.

"You seem a mite stronger," she said to Snippet, scooping him up for a nuzzle between his pointy little ears and a brief visit to the yard.

Once outside, and set on his wobbly feet, Snippet lifted one tiny leg against the bottom porch step, and his stub of a tail wagged when Lydia praised him for a job well-done.

He'd taken what milk he could manage and gone back to sleep in his basket by the time Gideon returned, entering through the kitchen door, the way he usually did.

Lydia was just washing her hands at the sink, and she smiled curiously at Gideon, over one shoulder. He looked as though he'd *run* all the way from Lark and Rowdy's.

His eyes smoldered as he gazed at her, but there was tenderness in them, too. Having locked the door, he simply held out a hand to Lydia, and waited.

She went to him.

He took her into his arms, and mischief danced in his eyes now. "Are the aunts light sleepers?" he asked.

Lydia laughed and blushed at the same time. "No," she said. "But Helga is."

Gideon sighed philosophically. "Then I guess we'd better use the bed."

"Gideon," Lydia scolded, though not with much conviction. "The things you say."

Without letting go of her hand, and grinning, Gideon turned the gaslight out and strode in the direction of the stairs, pulling her with him.

"The things I say, Mrs. Yarbro," he told her, as they climbed the steps, "are nothing compared to the things I'm about to *do.*"

That time, she was too breathless to scold.

As soon as they'd reached the bedroom, Gideon moved to light the bedside lamp. Probably looking for matches, he opened the desk drawer.

Lydia saw him go still in the dimness.

He took the watercolor portrait she'd tucked away out of the drawer, examined it in the glow from the window, and looked up at her. Because he was facing into the darkness, she couldn't see his expression.

"You painted this?" he asked, after a very long time.

Shyly, Lydia nodded. "It's not very good, but —"

Still holding the picture, he turned away again, found the matches he'd been looking for before, and lit the wick in the lamp. "Not very good?" he countered. "Lydia, it practically *breathes.*"

She knotted her hands together, unsure of

what to say.

"Is this how you see me?" Gideon finally asked.

She bit her lower lip. Nodded.

He grinned. "I had no idea I was such a handsome devil," he said, setting the picture carefully back in the drawer before turning to look at her again — and seeing the tears in her eyes. He whispered her name, all merriment gone from his face.

"Did you look closely at that picture, Gideon?" she asked, wiping away her tears with the back of one hand. "Did you see the leaving in it?"

Very slowly, he opened his arms. "If you'll have me, Lydia Yarbro, I'd just as soon stay," he said gruffly.

And she flew to him, threw her arms around his neck.

He held her very close. "Lydia?" he murmured, close to her ear.

"Yes?"

"I'm pretty sure I'm in love with you."

Lydia leaned back, looked up into Gideon's face. "Did you just say — ?"

"Yes," he answered. "I said I love you."

"You said," Lydia corrected, "that you were *pretty sure* you loved me."

Gideon chuckled. "So I did," he agreed huskily.

She smiled. "I'm not sure I want to settle for 'pretty sure,' Gideon Yarbro."

He began hauling up her skirts and petticoats. "*I'm* not sure you're in any position to argue," he teased. "And isn't there something you're supposed to say back, when a man tells you he loves you?"

Need rushed through her; she felt his thumbs hook deftly under the waistband of her new bloomers.

"Lydia?" he prompted, murmuring the name, tilting his head to nibble at her right earlobe.

"I'm — *pretty sure* — I love you — too," Lydia gasped out.

"Fair enough," Gideon allowed, easing her bloomers down just far enough to reach in and cup her most private place with one hand. With the heel of his palm, he stroked his way to bare skin, already moist with the want of him. "Fair enough."

Somehow, without her knowing, he'd maneuvered her to the wall; she felt it at her back. Her breath came hard, making her breasts rise and fall, the nipples hard against the inside of her camisole. "Shouldn't we — use the — bed?"

"Eventually," Gideon said. "How does this damn dress open?"

All the while, he was making those slow,

easy circles between her legs.

Lydia gasped again, as he began using his fingers. "It — *oh, dear God* — it buttons — up the back —"

He turned her away from him, still plying her, still plucking and teasing. With his free hand, he worked the buttons in question, with his mouth, he tasted her nape.

Lest she lose her balance, Lydia pressed her palms to the wall, tipped her head back, bit deep into her lower lip to keep from shaming herself by begging — *begging* — Gideon not to stop what he was doing to her.

But he did stop — at least long enough to remove the dress and petticoat and untie the ribbons at the front of her camisole, so that her breasts spilled free. The bloomers slid to her ankles — she kicked them away.

Gideon chuckled at that, turned her around. "Standing up," he told her, his voice gravelly, "that's how I was going to have you in the kitchen yesterday — and that's how I'm going to have you right now."

Lydia's eyes widened — oh, but he was caressing her again, *still,* preparing her for taking, and that quelled all thought of propriety.

"But first —" he murmured.

She'd managed to keep her hips still until

then, but now they were moving, surging against his hand. *"Gideon —"*

He knelt.

"Oh, no," she whimpered, even as a thrill of desire flamed through her.

"Oh, yes," he countered, and then he put his mouth where his fingers had been, and this time, there was no pillow to muffle her groans.

Lydia's eyes rolled shut; she gave herself up to the wicked pleasure he wrought with every expert flick of his tongue, every motion of his lips. He nibbled, and then he was greedy, and Lydia pressed her bare back to the wall, and drove her fingers into Gideon's hair, and held him to her.

She tried to be quiet. She tried so hard.

But he drove her relentlessly, and when he finally satisfied her, his hands cupped around her bottom, she shouted his name, and then shouted it again.

Again and again, even after she'd reached the pinnacle, her body bucked and flexed, until she finally sagged into Gideon's arms.

He rose, lifting her with him, carried her to their bed.

Laid her down.

Dazed, she still saw the worry in his eyes. Knew he was remembering the night before, the blood. "Lydia — ?"

She reached for him.

With a groan, he fell to her, still clothed, although his shirt was open to the waist. Had she done that? In her frantic passion, had she somehow opened his shirt, driven by the need to press her palms and fingers to his bare skin?

She didn't know, didn't care. "Now, Gideon," she whispered. *"Now."*

She fumbled for the buttons at the front of his trousers; he moved her hand aside, opened them himself. And then, wonderfully hard, with one thrust of his hips, he was inside her.

She was vaguely sore, but this time, there was no pain.

Lydia crooned, loving the feel of him within her, even though she knew it would soon drive her mad.

"Does — it — hurt?" Gideon rasped, poised over her, his hands pressed deep into the mattress, holding himself still with a visible effort.

Lydia turned her head from side to side on the pillow and crooned again, and that one sound, evidently, was Gideon's undoing. He took her in earnest then, and the bedsprings squeaked gloriously, and the headboard slammed against the wall, and when the friction became too much for both of them, their cries of release mingled in the night air, Gideon's a low, hoarse shout, Lydia's a near howl, keening and primitive.

And when they caught their breath, they both laughed.

They were covered in plaster dust.

He rose early the next morning, while Lydia was still sleeping.

The temptation to burrow between her legs and suckle her awake, and directly into the throes of a violent climax, was over-whelming, but he'd save that for another morning. With luck, there would be hundreds of other mornings.

First, though, he had to go to Flagstaff. Meet with his contact from the head office of the mining company — and resign.

He'd be back before sunset; in the meantime, he had to trust Helga and her stove-poker and, indirectly, his brothers, to keep Lydia safe.

He had so many plans, but they all began with quitting his jobs — as an agent and as a miner. He didn't know how he'd find another, but he'd saved a lot of his earnings over the years since he'd started working. He could take care of Lydia, her aunts, Helga *and* the little dog.

He dressed quickly in the darkness, took

his .45 from the high wardrobe shelf where it had been since he and Lydia had come to this house, strapped it on.

Unlike the morning before, because he wanted to make sure Snippet hadn't taken his last breath in the night, and spare Lydia the shock of discovering him if he had, he took the kitchen stairs.

Helga was up — did the woman ever sleep? — bustling around the kitchen. She had the coffee brewed — the aroma made Gideon's mouth water — and the dog was still among the living.

Eyeing Gideon, Helga said, "You really should move that bed away from the wall."

Gideon chuckled and nodded, crouched to greet Snippet.

"I'll tell the aunts there was another thunderstorm," Helga volunteered, pouring coffee for him and handing it to him as he stood straight again, "but sooner or later, they're going to wonder why the grass isn't wet."

Gideon laughed at that, took a sip of the coffee. It was hot and strong and a damn sight better than Rowdy's.

By then, Helga had spotted the gun on his left hip. Noted, by the look in her eyes, the easy way he wore it, like it was part of him.

She went a little pale. "Gideon — Mr.

Yarbro — what — ?"

"Call me Gideon," he said.

Helga propped her hands on her ample hips. "All right, *Gideon,*" she replied. "Where are you going at this hour — even the mine is closed on a Sunday — wearing an I-mean-business shooting iron like that one?"

"There's something I have to do," he answered, already edging toward the back door. He still had to get a horse from Rowdy's barn, saddle it and make the two-hour ride to Flagstaff, and even though he wasn't supposed to meet his contact until noon, he wanted some time to scout around town a little. And he meant to stop in and see Ruby, his stepmother, at her saloon. Tell her he was married and everything.

That would please Ruby. In her own way, she'd been good to him while he was growing up. Never blamed him for letting four-year-old Rose, her only child, run in front of that wagon that day.

"Don't you want breakfast?" Helga fretted, following him to the door.

Gideon shook his head, stepped off the porch.

"But —" Helga protested.

She went right on talking, but by then, he was too far away to hear.

390

■ ■ ■ ■

Thaddeus Bailey took his work seriously, and when he hadn't gotten a single response to his telegrams of inquiry concerning Gideon Yarbro, he'd gone to the streets instead. That was where the most reliable information was to be found, anyhow.

He'd thrown the man's name around a little, as bait, in this saloon and that one, and, as if by divine providence, not that Thaddeus believed in such things, he'd finally hooked himself a fish.

A small, thin man in a bowler hat had perked up his ears at the mention of Yarbro, and Thaddeus, ever watchful, had noticed. Bought the man a few shots of whiskey to loosen his tongue.

An easterner, by his speech and dress, and plainly feeling out of his element in the Wild West, the fellow had finally gotten drunk enough to admit that he was bound to Flagstaff on the morning train. Wasn't it a coincidence that Thaddeus had mentioned the very man he'd been told to meet up with?

With a little more whiskey and, later, by slamming the little man up against a wall in an alley and putting a knife to his throat,

Thaddeus had learned the rest.

Gideon Yarbro had been an agent with Wells Fargo and Company, fancy that, and he'd worked for Allan Pinkerton and a railroad company, too. Now, he was in the pay of a Chicago mining outfit — a big one, with deep pockets.

The little man — Thaddeus never learned his name — was really just a clerk. It was almost a pity to cut his throat, but since he'd surely go prattling to the law, claiming he'd been assaulted, forced to hand over important paperwork to a tall man with greasy hair and a scar on the right side of his face, Thaddeus was left with no choice.

With something like regret, he used the knife.

Sidestepped the spurt of blood with a skill born of long experience.

He considered reporting his discovery to Jacob Fitch, since the man clearly didn't trust him, then decided against that course of action. Better to wait until he'd completed the job and could collect that other twenty-five hundred dollars.

Soon as he had it, he'd be headed for San Francisco, where he meant to board the first boat for South America.

Maybe, he thought cheerfully, he'd even run into the Yarbro twins again. Ethan and

Levi, their names were. Offer his condolences on the tragic death of their younger brother, Gideon.

Ruby had aged, but she was still a beautiful woman, with copious red hair and a good figure. And though the saloon wasn't open for business, today being a Sunday, Gideon could see that it continued to make a good profit. The sign out front, above the swinging doors, had gold-gilt letters, the bar was of gleaming mahogany, hand-carved in some distant and exotic country no doubt, and there were new paintings on the walls. Not of the languishing naked women one might have expected in such an establishment, though — these were tasteful scenes of Englishmen riding to the hunt.

Ruby had always had class.

"Married," Ruby marveled quietly, smiling a little. Except for that hair, she could have passed for a respectable woman, instead of a former madam and present saloon owner, dressed as she was in a tailored blue skirt and jacket with white silk cording stitched onto it in curlicues.

Society in general might not have respected Ruby, but Gideon did.

"Married," he confirmed. She'd had her cook rustle up a plate of bacon and eggs, along with a pot of coffee, when he'd arrived, and he'd been grateful, since the ride from Stone Creek had left him ravenous.

"I don't suppose you'd consider bringing this bride of yours to meet me sometime?" Ruby asked, almost shyly. "If you ever get back to Flagstaff, I mean."

"I'll bring Lydia around," Gideon said.

"Jack would get such a kick out of you being old enough to get married," she went on, shaking her head a little, letting the loneliness show in her eyes for just a moment. She'd known Gideon's father, Payton Yarbro, as Jack Payton; he'd used an alias, since he'd been wanted in practically every state in the Union until he'd died over near Stone Creek. Her husband's past had been no secret to Ruby — they'd had a child together, Rose, and their grief at her death had driven them closer together, not further apart — but to her, the famous train robber had been and would always be "Jack."

"You ever think of getting married again, Ruby?" Gideon asked.

Ruby gave a snort, took a sip of coffee from her fancy china cup. "Sure," she said. "Maybe I'll just snare me a minister, say. Wouldn't the congregation love that?" She paused, gave a rich, throaty chuckle at the thought. "No, Gideon," she went on presently. "At my time of life, any man I'd rope in would be after the contents of my purse and nothing else. Anyhow, your old daddy sure enough ruined me for any other man. He was something, Jack Payton was."

He'd been "something," all right. Fully sixteen before he made the discovery, Gideon had been surprised as hell when he'd learned who his father was. Even more surprised to meet up with his outlaw brothers, later on.

"You been to Rose's grave yet?" Ruby asked when he didn't say anything.

Gideon shook his head. "Going there next."

"I bought her a new marker," Ruby said, her voice soft and faraway now as she remembered her lost child. "It's a white marble angel. Best to be had. And those good Christians finally ran out of room in their churchyard and had to move the fence out a ways to accommodate their worthy dead, so now she's *inside* that cemetery, my Rose, like she ought to have been all along."

"I'm sorry, Ruby," Gideon ground out. Any mention of Rose always cut deep, even though twenty years had passed since the accident. The scene was still as vivid in his mind as if it had taken place five minutes before.

"Gideon," Ruby said firmly, probably reading his expression. "You were *six years old.* You couldn't have prevented what happened."

Gideon shoved back his chair. Turned away, hoping Ruby wouldn't see that his eyes were wet. "Guess I'd better go," he said, raw-voiced, and he started for the side door, by which he'd entered.

"Gideon," Ruby said, strongly enough to stop him in his tracks.

He didn't turn around.

"You want to do the best thing you could to honor Rose's memory? Be happy with that new bride of yours. *Live,* Gideon. That's what would please your baby sister most."

Gideon swallowed, nodded, and left the saloon that had been his home until he was nearly grown.

He always said, "See you," when he left Ruby after his rare visits.

That time, he couldn't say anything at all.

CHAPTER SEVENTEEN

The murder made the front page of the early edition of the Phoenix newspapers, and Jacob Fitch, more interested in the financial page, might have merely skimmed the piece, if the words *Copper Crown Mine* hadn't jumped out at him as if they'd been set in bold type.

The Copper Crown was in Stone Creek.

And so was Gideon Yarbro.

And Lydia.

Troubled on a visceral level, his good breakfast souring in his stomach, Jacob read the article. The victim had been identified, the piece stated, by means of the hotel room key found in one of his pockets, as one Matthew Hildebrand, of Chicago. An employee of the noted mining company, the reporter stated, Hildebrand would be sorely missed by his friends and employers, and was survived by, etc., etc.

Cold to the marrow of his bones, Jacob

laid the newspaper aside. Looked *through* his mother, seated across the table from him in the august Fairmont dining room, rather than at her.

This, he thought grimly, could not be a coincidence.

"Are you all right, dear?" his mother asked solicitously. She'd coveted this mansion ever since Jacob had issued the first of several mortgages to old Judge Fairmont, and now that she had it, sans Lydia and her aunts, she was content with her lot. Her gaze, always shrewd, dropped to the folded newspaper resting beside Jacob's place, watched as his fingers thumped rhythmically atop it.

The table was Mother's favorite piece, of all the booty in the house. It was a fine antique, one of the many exquisite pieces the Judge had acquired after the fabled flight from Virginia. If Lydia's chattering aunts could be believed, the piece had once belonged to Jefferson Davis.

But Jacob could not think of tables and Confederate presidents, nor was he able to utter a word in reply to his mother's question.

Murder. A man had been murdered, and he'd been indirectly involved. Not only that, he had personally engineered a *second* murder, one that would soon occur, if it hadn't already.

As much as Jacob hated Gideon Yarbro, he suddenly, belatedly, realized he'd made a terrible mistake.

"Dear God," he choked out, at long last. "Dearest *God,* Mother, what have I done?"

Crushing, seizing pain seared him, blazing in the center of his chest and then radiating outward, numbing his limbs, clouding his vision.

"Jacob!" his mother cried, bolting from her chair. *"Jacob!"*

He shoved back his own chair, gasping, blind to everything but this horrendous agony, tearing him apart from the inside. He felt himself fall, registered more pain, mild by comparison to the wild spasms of his heart, as his head struck the edge of the table.

He heard his mother screeching for Maggie, the Irish serving girl she'd hired as soon as the foreclosure was complete.

He had a brief flash of Lydia, swathed in black and weeping.

But not for him.

No, she was not weeping for him.

Jacob Fitch felt his body and soul sunder then, and his last conscious thought flared, brilliantly dazzling, in his mind.

God forgive me.

■ ■ ■ ■

"Where is Gideon?" Lydia asked happily when she came down the kitchen stairs that morning and found Helga at the stove, as usual, and Snippet mewling for his milk.

Helga looked distinctly uncomfortable. "I'm not sure," she said. "He — he went out, first thing."

Lydia bent to scoop Snippet from his bed near Helga's feet. Nuzzled his warm puppy-neck. "That's odd," she remarked, her voice light, since the uneasiness Helga's words roused in her was still only a faint flutter in the pit of her stomach. She was still soaring because of the promises Gideon had made in the night, with his body as well as his words. "The mine is closed today, isn't it?"

"Yes," Helga said, and the look on her face was so glum, so fretful, that Lydia stopped where she was, even though Snippet's need to go outside was probably urgent.

"What is it, Helga?" Lydia asked.

"It's probably nothing," Helga replied, trying to smile.

"Helga," Lydia persisted, keeping her voice low so she wouldn't awaken the aunts.

Still trying to smile, and still failing miserably, Helga shook her head, dried her hands on her apron with anxious grabs at the cloth. "He was wearing a gun," she finally said. "I asked where he was off to, so early on a Sunday morning, but he wouldn't say."

Lydia's heart raced, and the fluttering in her stomach took full flight, like hundreds of butterflies rising at once. "Most likely," she said, "he's gone hunting with Rowdy or Wyatt —"

Helga didn't answer.

"Did Gideon say anything else about what he meant to do, Helga?" Lydia persisted, realizing she was clutching Snippet too tightly and loosening her grasp a little. "Anything at all?"

"Just that there was something he had to get done," Helga said, looking utterly defeated. "I don't like it, Lydia. It's been nagging at me ever since Gideon went out that door. I think we ought to tell Rowdy."

Lydia agreed, but she wasn't sure Gideon would appreciate her going to Rowdy and raising an alarm. After all, Gideon was a grown man, and even though it was rare for anyone but soldiers and officers of the law to carry a gun, now that the twentieth century was well under way, he might simply have decided to engage in some target practice. "But he didn't say where he was headed?"

Again, Helga shook her head.

Lydia took Snippet outside, set him down in the grass, waited distractedly while he sniffed and waddled and finally relieved himself. Then she picked him up again and carried him back into the kitchen.

The aunts were up and around by then, wearing their customary mourning dresses, and even though Lydia had seen them in those same garments countless times, that day, the sight disturbed her. Made her think of funerals.

"I'm going to find Rowdy," Helga said, resolved.

The aunts grew round-eyed.

Lydia gently placed Snippet back in his basket. "No," she said. "I'll find Rowdy. You stay and look after things here."

"Lydia —"

"That," Lydia said, opening the door to leave, "is my final word."

She found her brother-in-law in his office, a letter in his hand, his face almost gray, with lines chiseled into it.

Lydia watched from the threshold as Rowdy slowly folded the one-page missive, laid it aside, and met her gaze.

"Lydia," he said, with an effort at affability, though his voice was hoarse. "What brings you here?"

Lydia's attention was fixed on the letter. "Bad news?" she asked.

"Yes," Rowdy answered. "Came yesterday, I reckon, but I didn't get around to looking at the mail until a little while ago. There's been a death in the family."

Lydia's heart nearly stopped, before reason returned. Gideon had shared her bed the night before, and he'd only left *that morning.* No one would have had time to write and send a letter announcing that he'd died.

"Who?" she asked tentatively.

"No one you know," Rowdy said. "My brother Nick — Wyatt's and Gideon's, too, of course — died a couple of weeks ago, of consumption."

"I'm sorry," Lydia murmured.

"We weren't close," Rowdy answered, but he still looked as though he'd been trampled by the news. "Not recently, anyhow."

Lydia bit her lower lip, not knowing what to say. Turned as if to go, turned back. "Rowdy —"

"You obviously came here meaning to tell me something, Lydia," Rowdy said, with a ghost of his usual easy grin. "What is it?"

"Gideon — he left the house early this morning," Lydia paused, faltering. Feeling like a foolish, interfering wife. "I wouldn't trouble you with it, especially now — but Helga said —"

"Lydia," Rowdy said, crossing the office to stand facing her. "What's bothering you?"

"Helga said — Helga said Gideon was wearing a gun-belt when he left."

Rowdy absorbed that, swore under his breath, confirming Lydia's persistent fear that something was very, very wrong. "Damn it," he said. "I forgot all about it, but he asked to borrow a horse. Said he needed it this morning, and wouldn't tell me why." Although he didn't say it, Rowdy's expression told Lydia he had his suspicions where Gideon's whereabouts were concerned, and that sent a shiver of pure dread through her entire being. "If he felt the need to take along that .45 of his —"

"Rowdy?" Lydia's voice trembled. "What's happening here?"

He took her by the shoulders, gently moved her aside, so he could get through the doorway. "I'll handle it," he said, his tone abrupt now, stepping out onto the quiet, sunny street.

Lydia immediately followed. *"Rowdy,"* she repeated, much more insistently this time. "What — ?"

He called to a boy, who came running, freckled face alight with what must have

been hero worship. Along with Sam O'Bal-
livan, Rowdy was practically a legend in
Stone Creek, and probably far beyond. "Yes,
Marshal?"

"You go and get a horse out of my barn,"
Rowdy said gravely, "and ride like the
Apaches were after you for Wyatt's place.
Tell my brother I can't wait for him — he'll
have to catch up as best he can, and he
ought to bring Sam O'Ballivan along, too.
I'll leave word for them at Ruby's Saloon,
over in Flagstaff. You got all that, Jimmy?"

Jimmy nodded. Repeated the instructions
almost verbatim to prove it.

"Go," Rowdy told him.

Jimmy raced around the corner of the jailhouse, for the lane.

"Flagstaff?" Lydia asked, as Rowdy hurried back inside to strap on his own gun-
belt. His horse, a handsome pinto gelding,
was already saddled and ready in front of
the building.

"It's about a two-hour ride from here, and
it's the only place I can think of where Gideon would go on horseback," Rowdy explained brusquely. "Phoenix or anyplace
farther away, he'd have taken the train or
the stage."

"I want to go with you," Lydia said, as
Rowdy strode past her, resettling his hat as

he went.

"That's out of the question," he answered flatly, untying his horse from the hitching rail, swinging up into the saddle. "But you can do me a favor, if you will. Tell Lark where I've gone and that I'll be back as soon as I find Gideon."

Lydia, rooted on the sidewalk, felt another tremor race from her head to her feet, this one so cold it scorched her through and through. There was no sense in arguing with Rowdy — he'd already made up his mind — and besides, no words would come.

He tugged once at the brim of his hat in farewell, reined the horse around, and rode away, first at a trot, then a gallop.

Lydia watched him until he was out of sight, gathered her composure as best she could, and went to relay his message to Lark.

She found her sister-in-law in the kitchen, seated in a rocking chair, a shawl draped modestly over one shoulder as she nursed baby Miranda. Marietta played on the floor at her feet, with a stack of wooden alphabet blocks, arranging them in perfect order and reciting, *"A — B — C —"*

Seeing the three of them, presenting a happy domestic tableau as they did, Lydia felt her fear for Gideon — for all of them —

intensify. Rowdy had been worried enough, when he'd learned that Gideon was armed, to immediately send a messenger for Wyatt and Sam O'Ballivan and then rush away so quickly that he hadn't even taken the time to stop and tell his wife he was leaving town. Gideon was in real danger — and now Rowdy and Wyatt would be, too.

"Lydia, your *face*," Lark said, moving as if to rise from her chair. "Whatever is the matter?"

"*H — I — J — K —*" Marietta continued.

"Please, don't get up," Lydia told Lark quickly. She stood just inside the back door, as though her feet had turned to stone, wringing her hands, and she knew she must be an alarming sight, since she'd cast aside all decorum, lifted her skirts and *run* along the lane to the Yarbro house. Her hair, neatly plaited and then wound into a bun and pinned at her nape before she left the bedroom that morning, was dangling down her back now, the braid starting to come undone.

Lark used her schoolmarm voice then, the one Lydia hadn't heard since she was a child, and even then it had never been directed at her, but at the bigger boys who'd dared to roughhouse in her classroom. "Lydia, *sit down* before you drop, and tell me what's wrong."

Lydia forced herself farther into the room, pulled out one of the chairs at the table, dropped into it. "Maybe nothing," she said, trying to sound brave. *Maybe everything.*

Carefully, she explained the facts as she knew them — that Gideon had left early, riding a horse he'd borrowed from Rowdy and armed with a pistol. She related that Rowdy had decided to go after him the moment he'd learned that Gideon was carrying a gun, and asked that she come and tell Lark where he'd gone.

Listening, Lark's eyes widened, and some of the color she'd so recently regained after her travail seeped from her cheeks, leaving them mottled.

"He sent a boy for Wyatt, too," Lydia finished. "Wyatt and Sam O'Ballivan." She'd leave the news of Nick Yarbro's death for Rowdy to relate, as it was his place to do.

"Dear God," Lark murmured.

"What shall we do?" Lydia whispered.

"What wives have always done," Lark said, with some irritation. "Wait."

A tear slipped down Lydia's cheek, but she quickly wiped it away, lest Marietta see. The child had already stopped playing with her blocks, and sat gazing worriedly up at her mother.

"Is — is there anything you need?" Lydia asked Lark, afraid that her sister-in-law, her dearest friend, might suffer a setback. She'd nearly died, bearing little Miranda, after all, and a serious shock might compromise her recovery. "I could make tea —"

"Kitty will be coming by to look after the children in a little while," Lark broke in, with a shake of her head. "As soon as church is over." Suddenly her eyes widened, and she put a hand to her mouth. *"As soon as church is over —"*

"What?" Lydia asked anxiously.

"The reception, Lydia," Lark said. "The wedding reception! The whole town and half the countryside will be heading for your place as soon as the services let out —"

Lydia closed her eyes. Sarah and Lark had planned to hold a party for her and Gideon — she'd known that since soon after the hasty ceremony in the Yarbros' parlor — but she'd assumed, because of Lark's recent ordeal, that the event must have been cancelled. And she had never thought of the reception again after that.

Now she recalled the large variety of cakes and pies she'd seen in Wyatt and Sarah's kitchen the night before, when she and Gideon had paid that unexpected visit. More, surely, than even two grown, hardworking men, their women and a brood of active children could eat.

She heard the echo of Sarah's voice. *"Shannie and I have been baking all afternoon."*

Of course, the wide variety of baked goods had been intended for the party.

"Oh, no," Lydia whispered. "No." As frightened and anxious as she was, she simply could not face a party, *especially* one meant to celebrate her and Gideon's marriage. It seemed incredible that, as recently as that morning, the prospect would have delighted her.

"Lydia," Lark said, employing her school-voice again, "I am sorrier than you will ever know that things turned out this way — I should have told you that Sarah and I had decided the reception ought to be held no matter what — but there is nothing to do now but carry on. It's too late to stop people from coming — we'll just have to make the best of this."

Lydia could see that saying "I can't" would get her nowhere with Lark. Finished nursing the baby, she was closing the bodice of her dress, the shawl resting across her lap now, and raising her infant daughter to her shoulder. She rocked gently in the chair, patting the baby's tiny back.

Slowly, Lydia stood. Whatever her own reluctance, she couldn't leave Helga and the aunts to deal with the entire town of Stone Creek and, as Lark had put it, "half the countryside" on their own. Somehow, she must get through the festivities, all the while silently praying for Gideon's safe return, and Rowdy's and Wyatt's and Sam's, as well.

"Sarah will come by for me later," Lark told her quietly. "We'll help you, Lydia — Sarah and Maddie and I."

Lydia nodded, stopped by Lark's chair, bent to kiss her sister-in-law on top of the head before leaving.

Helga had known about the party, of course, Lydia realized. The aunts, too. Either they'd thought she knew it was still being held, or they'd hoped the surprise would lift her spirits.

As for Gideon, well, he'd gone to Flagstaff — if Rowdy's guess was correct — to do something that might require the use of a gun. A wedding reception — even his own — was clearly less important.

When Lydia turned into their street, she was taken aback to see a line of buggies and buckboards already parked in front of the house — tables were being set up in all parts of the yard, under Helga's busy direction, and the aunts stood huddled together on the porch, clad in the bright dresses Gideon had bought for them in Phoenix. People streamed through the front gate, carrying baskets full of food, bouquets of flowers and wedding gifts — these last heaped on one of the tables and in the grass surrounding it.

She saw a butter churn and several brightly colored quilts, pots and teakettles and fine embroidery work.

Entering by the gate, Lydia nearly turned and fled, despite Lark's insistence that the celebration must be gotten through. She might have, if she hadn't been afraid poor Snippet would be terrified by all the ruckus — and if the aunts hadn't spotted her and left the porch to come and meet her.

"Lydia, dear!" Mittie cried, sweetly dismayed. "Your *hair!*"

Lydia rummaged within herself for a smile, found one that might do, though it was flimsy, and shut the gate behind her.

She nodded to well-wishers as she passed, moving one-foot-in-front-of-the-other toward the steps of the kitchen porch, doing her best to ignore their curious glances.

"I put little Snippet in your room," Millie confided in a whisper when they were all in the kitchen. "In his basket."

"What happened to your hair?" Mittie persisted, fluttering like a colorful little bird flapping its wings to rise off a windowsill.

"Don't fret," Lydia said, kissing the old woman's lightly rouged cheek. "I'll make myself presentable in no time at all."

"Oh, good." Millie beamed. She'd always been a stickler for good grooming, especially when there was company to entertain.

Lydia proceeded to the stairs, climbed them, and walked slowly along the hallway to the room she'd awakened so happily in just a few short hours before.

Gideon's absence seemed to pulse there.

She remembered the expression of proud admiration on his face after he'd stumbled across her watercolor portrait of him.

She remembered their lovemaking and, most of all, she remembered his words.

I'm pretty sure I'm in love with you.

If you'll have me, I'd rather stay.

Lydia raised the knuckles of both hands to her eyes and pressed hard, in an effort not to cry. Snippet whimpered piteously in his basket, near the foot of the bed, probably alarmed by all the activity in and around the house, but possibly sensing her grief, too.

Had Gideon been lying when he'd said he loved her?

Had he intended, when he left their bed and their house that morning, to keep on going, to put her and Stone Creek behind him, for good?

He'd left town very early, and Rowdy had said Flagstaff was two hours away on horseback. It was nearly noon now.

Gideon could be far beyond Flagstaff, even on board a train, headed for parts unknown. He'd have taken his gun, surely, if he wasn't planning on coming back.

Lydia almost hoped he had lied about staying, and gone elsewhere, because as terrible as that would be, it was better than what Rowdy must have feared, given his haste in going after his younger brother.

In the near distance, church bells began to peal, signaling the end of that week's services. Lydia hadn't even heard them before, when they must have rung to call worshippers to their pews.

Now, the joyful exuberance of the sound made her cover her ears for a few moments, but when Snippet gave a puny howl of terror, she went to him, lifted him from his basket, soothed him until the bells stopped ringing.

Reassured, he immediately slept when she put him back a few moments later.

Lydia summoned up all the resolve she

possessed then. She straightened her shoulders. She went to the bathroom down the hall, fixed her hair, and smoothed her dress. She even pinched a little color into her cheeks.

That done, she marched herself downstairs and outside and joined the party, accepting congratulations at every turn, and enduring the unspoken question she saw in everyone's eyes.

Where was Gideon?

Lark arrived, as she'd promised, with Sarah and Owen and Shannie, Owen looking glum at the reins of the buckboard. Clearly, he would rather have gone along with Wyatt and Sam to help Rowdy look for Gideon, but someone — most likely Sarah — had prevailed upon him to stay behind.

The Yarbro children, Lydia soon learned, were all to remain at Lark and Rowdy's place, with Kitty Venable watching over them.

Despite her profound agitation, Lydia *was* greatly comforted by Lark and Sarah's arrival and, soon after that, Maddie O'Ballivan's, too, but she would still have preferred to be wherever Gideon was.

In heaven or in hell — or in Flagstaff.

Such grand occasions as this one were rare in Stone Creek, of course, and folks seemed to enjoy themselves. There was a great deal of laughter and happy talk, and no sooner than the tables had been emptied of food more appeared.

Lydia played the part of a welcoming bride, shaking hands, trying to remember names, even choking down part of a piece of cake at one point. Someone brought a chair for Lark, while Sarah and Maddie served food and greeted new arrivals and bid farewell to those who had to leave early because they lived on distant farms and ranches and had livestock to tend. Sarah, Maddie and Lark must have been as worried as Lydia was, but one would not have guessed it to look at them.

And not one person, at least in Lydia's hearing, said a single word about the conspicuous lack of a bridegroom.

After he left Ruby, Gideon whiled away some time walking up and down Flagstaff's main street. The shops were all closed, since it was the Sabbath Day, but he spotted a clerk lurking toward the back of a jewelry store and, suddenly inspired, rapped hard on the display window.

The clerk did his level best to ignore Gideon, but to no avail.

Gideon kept rapping on the window, a

little harder each time, and gesturing for the man to unlock the shop door, until he finally did.

Even then, though, he barely poked his head out. "Sir, I'm afraid we're closed," he said prissily. "It's *Sunday,* after all."

"Well, you're here," Gideon argued affably. "So you might as well work."

"It just so happens I *am* working," the clerk replied indignantly. "I'm taking inventory."

Gideon pointed toward a golden band in the corner of the window, gleaming with tiny stones and displayed to considerable effect in a rose-colored velvet box set atop a miniature replica of a Grecian column. "I want to buy that ring," he said.

The clerk shook his head, tried to shut the door.

Gideon stuck his foot in to prevent it.

"It is the *Sabbath,*" the clerk protested in a hissing whisper.

"Seems to me," Gideon interrupted, his right boot still firmly planted between the door and its frame, "if you're worried about going to hell for working on a Sunday — selling me a ring, I mean — well, that horse is already out of the barn, isn't it? If you're taking inventory, after all —"

"Oh, for heaven's sake," the clerk sputtered. "That wedding band costs *twenty-five dollars.* It has diamonds in it. Garnets, too. And since I don't know you from Adam, I certainly don't plan on extending credit."

Gideon took the necessary funds from his shirt pocket, held it up for the clerk to see. And did not withdraw his foot.

The clerk went beet-red, finding it hard to resist a cash sale, even if it meant spending eternity up to his neck in hellfire. "Wait here," he instructed.

"Oh, believe me," Gideon drawled. "I will."

The inventory-taker left the doorway, took the ring and box from the window, and held them practically under Gideon's nose for inspection. His knuckles were white, though, his grip was so tight in case there was skulduggery afoot.

Gideon handed over the twenty-five dollars with one hand, and grabbed the ringbox with the other.

"Much obliged," he told the flustered clerk.

The fellow slammed the door in his face and made a show, through the glass in its center, of turning the lock and pocketing the key.

Gideon laughed, admired the ring once more, snapped the box shut, and dropped it into his pants pocket.

He found another shop open just down the street — the proprietor must have been a heathen — and bought a piece of rock candy the size of his fist.

Rose had loved rock candy above all earthly pleasures — not that she'd had a chance to know many of those, living only four years the way she had.

The shopkeeper put the chunk of crystallized sugar into a brown paper bag and, a friendly sort, inclined to chat, allowed as how some little girl or boy would be glad to have it. Solemn now, Gideon merely nodded, paid the two-penny price, and left the store.

He made for the churchyard, arriving there some fifteen minutes ahead of schedule — he'd planned it that way.

Church was just letting out as Gideon opened the gate, and folks were visiting out front, the way they might be expected to do after being penned up for an hour or two of somber reflection upon their sins, but he paid them no mind.

It took him a couple of minutes to find his sister's grave, once outside the cemetery proper because Rose had had the temerity to be born to a saloon woman and, though the parishioners couldn't have known it then, an erstwhile train robber, but then he spotted the white marble angel Ruby had told him about.

He looked around, without appearing to do so, as he approached the grave, but he was alone in that part of the churchyard.

Reaching Rose's final resting place, he crouched. Blinked a couple of times. "It's been a while," he said hoarsely.

The breeze whispered in the tops of the cottonwoods and oaks sheltering the graves in that quiet churchyard. It was, for all its sadness, a peaceful place.

"I'm married, Rose," Gideon went on, after a few moments spent dealing with the emotions that always attended these visits. "Her name is Lydia, and I think you'd like her a lot."

He smoothed away the dried petals of a bouquet Ruby had probably left there at the base of Rose's headstone. Ruby would have visited at night, most likely, or very early in the morning, when nobody was around to disapprove of her setting foot on sacred ground.

The brown paper bag crackled a little as Gideon opened it, took the rock candy out, placed it carefully where Ruby's flowers had been before. It was crazy to bring presents to a dead child, he knew that, but he'd always done it anyhow. And as long as he had breath in his body, he always would.

"Gideon Yarbro?"

He turned, squinting a little, and chagrined that he hadn't heard anyone approaching, to see a stranger standing over him. His contact — and right on time.

Gideon stood up. Nodded.

The man had a long scar on his right cheek, and he was in want of a bath and barbering. He'd didn't look much like a messenger for a bunch of rich mine owners but, then, that was the point, wasn't it? The men with the big cigars and the private railroad cars liked to conduct this kind of business in secrecy.

"Matthew Hildebrand," the man said, by way of introduction, putting out his hand but not smiling.

Gideon hesitated. The back of his neck prickled. But he finally shook Hildebrand's hand.

"I don't think we ought to talk here," Hildebrand said, glancing toward the church where folks were still milling around. "Too many people." He frowned. "Seems all the saloons are closed, though."

Gideon gave a spare grin, a Yarbro grin. His gut clenched in warning. "I know of one that will do for our purposes," he said, knowing full well that trouble had just found him, as it so often had before.

CHAPTER EIGHTEEN

Ruby hadn't survived in business for so long — or thrived — because she was slow-witted. The moment Gideon stepped through the side door again, and their gazes met, a clear response to his silent warning registered in her eyes.

She slipped behind the bar, glanced over Gideon's shoulder at the tall man walking behind him.

"Pour you gentlemen a drink?" she asked hospitably, with a smile that said she didn't give two hoots in hell about the Sunday laws or the consequences of breaking them.

"Whiskey for me," Hildebrand said.

"Same," Gideon agreed easily, drawing back a chair at one of the tables. "Some of that special stuff, though. The bourbon you keep locked up in the storeroom."

Ruby nodded, slipped out through the doorway behind the bar. It led into her office, Gideon knew, and from there, to the street. He hoped Ruby would heed what he'd been trying to tell her and get the hell out of there, but with her, there was no telling.

Hildebrand sat down, and so did Gideon.

They might have been acquaintances, meeting up again after a long separation, given the air of reserved cordiality they both assumed. Gideon shifted, on the pretense of settling back in his chair, and used his thumb to unsnap the narrow strip of leather that kept his .45 from riding up in its holster.

Ruby returned with the whiskey Gideon had asked for, ignoring an irritated glance from her stepson, and filled two spotlessly clean shot glasses, brought them and the bottle to the table.

Hildebrand looked up at her, and Gideon glimpsed a predatory glint in the other man's eyes before he reached for his glass.

Gideon left his own untouched, as if to savor the anticipation for a while. "Ruby," he said casually, when she lingered next to the table just a little too long, "this is a private conversation."

"Yes, ma'am," Hildebrand agreed, solemnly reluctant. "It is."

Ruby hesitated for another heartbeat or two, and then turned in a swirl of costly skirts and lace-trimmed petticoats to head back behind the bar again. Maybe she hoped distance would suffice — in any case, she busied herself taking glasses from the shelf under that fancy imported bar and wiping each one until it gleamed.

"Women," Hildebrand said, with an amused shake of his head. "Nowhere around when you want one, and can't blast 'em out of a room when you don't."

Gideon made no comment; out of the corner of his eye, he was watching Ruby, wondering why she hadn't taken the hint, gotten out of the saloon and stayed gone.

She hummed a little ditty as she worked, but Gideon wasn't fooled. Though she was a good twenty yards away, she could hear everything they said. Years in a rough and potentially dangerous business had honed her eyesight and hearing to a sharpness seldom seen, even among railroad detectives and Wells Fargo agents.

So why wasn't she following the dictates of those senses?

The wondering was rhetorical; Gideon knew the answer only too well. Ruby kept a shotgun behind that bar, and sometimes a pistol, in case she needed more range. And she was sticking close to one or both.

"You got anything to prove you're the man

my employers sent?" Gideon asked, still with easy affability, every bit as aware of Hildebrand's every move, as he was of Ruby's.

"You doubt that I am?" Hildebrand countered, sounding unconcerned as he tossed back the contents of his shot glass.

"I guess you could say that," Gideon said.

Hildebrand scowled, handed over a packet of documents, glanced once more at Ruby — earlier, Gideon had seen him scanning the back of the saloon several times, as though looking for a way out — and shook his head.

Gideon did not trouble himself to read the papers; his instincts had already told him what he needed to know.

"I do not fancy," the stranger said sadly, "killing a woman."

The remark was incendiary, like a spark striking a pocket of gas in the depths of a mine.

Things happened fast.

Hildebrand drew a knife, brandishing it a couple of times, perhaps to show his prowess.

Gideon overturned the table to put a momentary barrier between himself and the other man, drawing his .45 and rising in almost the same move.

A shot boomed through the otherwise quiet saloon.

Hildebrand's eyes widened and, the knife falling soundlessly to the sawdust floor, he clasped his bleeding midsection with both hands.

Gideon watched, his finger still on the trigger of his pistol, as the man dropped to his knees and pitched face-first into the sawdust.

"Christ, Ruby," Gideon gasped, after letting out the breath he'd been holding. "You just *shot* a man."

Ruby laid a rifle down on the bar with a heavy thump, smoke still wafting from its barrel. "Well, hell," she said, "I couldn't wait all day for *you* to get around to it."

"Better get a doctor," Gideon said, reholstering the .45 he hadn't fired. His shirt, he realized numbly, was soaked with the other man's blood, still warm and sticky. It made him queasy. "Just in case."

"No 'just in case' about it," Ruby answered, approaching but keeping her skirts clear of the pooling blood while Gideon crouched to check Hildebrand for a pulse. She glanced up at Gideon's drenched shirt, frowned. "If I go to all the trouble of putting a bullet in somebody, I shoot to kill."

Ruby's philosophy held true; the man

who'd called himself Matthew Hildebrand was definitely dead.

Gideon drew several deep breaths. The gun-blast had stirred up a ruckus out on the street; the law would be there any minute now. But there'd be no need for a doctor.

"Better open the front doors, Ruby," Gideon said.

She nodded, got her keys, unlocked and drew back the heavy inside doors, leaving the swinging ones open to the daylight.

And the first one through them was Rowdy. Seeing the dead man sprawled on the saloon floor and noting that Ruby and Gideon were the only other people in sight, he shoved his pistol back into his holster and crouched beside the body, just the way Ruby had done.

"What are you doing here?" Gideon asked his brother. It was a stupid question, he knew, but after all, he'd just witnessed a shooting. The smell of blood was coppery in the heavy air, his shirt clung to his flesh in a way that made him half-sick, and tiny specks of sawdust were still settling.

Maybe he was a little addled.

"I'll ask the questions, Gideon," Rowdy said, straightening. "If you don't mind." He paused and a muscle bunched in his right cheek, unbunched again. "Matter of fact, I don't give a damn if you *do* mind." As Ruby had, Rowdy frowned at the mess on Gideon's shirt.

Flagstaff's marshal, badge gleaming on his Sunday coat, banged through the swinging doors before Gideon could think of an answer that would set Rowdy back a pace or two. A thin-faced man, sparely built, the lawman wore a shoulder holster, with the pistol resting square in the middle of his solar plexus.

"Rowdy?" he said, in a tone of surprised recognition. "Rowdy Yarbro?"

"Chester," Rowdy greeted the other man, with a nod. "It would seem we've had an incident here."

Chester approached, looking down at the corpse. Townspeople crowded in through the doorway behind him, like a flock of chickens set on pecking breadcrumbs off the floor of a farmhouse kitchen, but Ruby shooed them all right out again.

"Don't you damn fools know it's against the law to set foot in here on a Sunday?" she scolded.

"Our brother, Wyatt, and Sam O'Ballivan will be along soon, Ruby," Rowdy said quietly, though his gaze was still boring right into Gideon's hide. "I'd appreciate it if you'd let them in."

"Somebody want to tell me why there's a dead man layin' on the floor of a saloon that ought to be closed for business?" Chester inquired mildly, and after a long sigh, deftly turned the body over for a better look. "I got up from the Sunday dinner table to come here, and my Lucille's roast beef is gettin' colder by the minute on my plate."

"There's a dead man on my floor, Chester Perkins," Ruby said, "because I shot the sorry son of a bitch with that rifle over there on the bar. Barrel's probably still hot."

Chester stood, looked Gideon over thoughtfully, then wandered to the bar, tested the barrel of Ruby's rifle with a touch of his fingers, and drew them away quickly, wincing a little.

That was when Wyatt and Sam shouldered their way through the curious crowd outside and strode into the saloon, Wyatt in the lead.

"Are the wives and kids along, too?" Gideon asked dryly, shoving a hand through his hair, resting the other across his middle.

"Shut up, Gideon," Rowdy said grimly. "You may or may not be in trouble with Marshal Perkins here, but you are *sure as hell* up to your neck in shit with *me*."

"You want to whup him, Rowdy?" Wyatt drawled easily, wincing with distaste when he caught a look at poor, gut-shot Hilde-brand lying there on the floor with his eyes wide-open, staring upward into eternity now that Perkins had rolled him onto his back. "Or shall I?"

Gideon took a threatening step forward. After all he'd been through that morning, his temper was frayed, and he was in no mood to put up with any "big brother" crap. "You're welcome to try — either one — or both — of you."

Sam O'Ballivan stepped between the two men. "Rowdy," he said, "stand down until you can get a grip on your good sense. Gid-eon, you'd do well to take your brother's advice and shut up."

Gideon colored up, bit back a response.

Sam's gaze dropped to Gideon's shirt-front, and his eyebrows drew together.

"We got to sort this out," Chester said. "Might be, Lucille's keeping my plate warm and I can get back to that fine dinner before it all dries out."

"I *told* you what happened, Chester," Ruby said impatiently. "I shot him."

"The events leading up to that," Chester answered, "are of some interest to me." His gaze shifted back to Gideon, and for all the folksy talk and the lamentations over his Sunday dinner, Gideon saw a formidable intelligence in the marshal's eyes. "What was your part in this, young fella?"

Drawing a deep breath and letting it out slowly, Gideon recounted meeting Hildebrand in the graveyard, coming to Ruby's to talk in private, and how the other man had suddenly pulled a knife. He'd turned the table onto its side and drawn his .45, fully intending to fire it, but — and he flushed at this part — Ruby had been faster.

Chester listened to all that, the tip of his tongue making a bulge in his right cheek. When Gideon had finished, he sighed and shook his head.

"You say he called himself Hildebrand?" Chester asked.

"Matthew Hildebrand," Gideon confirmed.

Chester bent, gingerly folded back the sides of the dead man's gore-splattered coat, felt the pockets, probably looking for some kind of identification. He didn't find anything, and for some reason, Gideon didn't tell him about the documents, which must have been lying there in the sawdust someplace close by.

The lawman didn't speak until he'd straightened up again. "There was a man by the name of Matthew Hildebrand murdered down in Phoenix last night," he said. "I got a wire about it before Lucille and I went to church this morning — said I ought to be on the lookout for a fella matchin' this man's description. I guess I can wire the federal marshal back and tell him we got his suspect right here in Flagstaff."

Sam put a hand on Rowdy's shoulder, and a hand on Gideon's, and pressed them into chairs at the next table. Wyatt joined them, and Ruby got out the good whiskey and poured a round for everybody.

Chester Perkins made no arrests owing to the blatant violation of the Sunday liquor law.

The undertaker arrived, word of the killing having spread on its own, with two helpers and an old wooden door. "Chester," the mortician said, patting at his sweating forehead with a wadded handkerchief, "you'd better disperse that crowd out there. This fella ain't a fit sight for the ladies, and we didn't bring a blanket."

Chester nodded, went over to the swinging doors, and ordered the gathering to move on.

Ruby, meanwhile, disappeared into the back of the saloon, where the living quarters were, and returned with an old quilt.

"I just had this sawdust put down fresh," she said, shaking her head at the mess as she offered up the covering.

The mortician and his youthful assistants hoisted the corpse onto the door and draped it with the quilt.

"Much obliged, Ruby," the mortician said. "You won't be wanting this coverlet back, I reckon?"

Ruby wrinkled her nose, shook her head.

Chester appeared to be ready to go back to his roast beef dinner, but he paused by Gideon's chair, laid a hand on his shoulder. Squeezed with vice-strong fingers. "I'll have no trouble keeping track of Ruby," he said quietly, "but where would I find *you,* young fella, if I should happen to get a yen to jaw a while?"

Gideon sighed. "Stone Creek," he said. A sudden chill overtook him, rattled his bones.

"Chester," Rowdy said wearily, "he's my brother — Gideon Yarbro. Wyatt and I will see that he's available if you have any more questions — but we surely do mean to take him home."

Gideon's mind flashed on another saloon, down in Phoenix, when two big men had come in to take their pa home, so their ma could attend a pie social, and he sighed again. He didn't have it in him, at the moment, to fight being taken away like old Horace had, but the way Rowdy was talking made his back molars grind together just the same.

He might have been sixteen again, to hear Rowdy tell it.

"Are you finally ready to admit you've been working for the greedy sons of bitches who own that copper mine?" Rowdy demanded of Gideon, when Chester had gone and the undertaker and his helpers had hauled the dead man out on the door they'd brought along for the purpose.

Gideon leaned forward in his chair, thinking maybe he had some fight left in him after all, but Wyatt put a hand on his chest and prevented further bloodshed.

"I meant to resign," Gideon allowed grudgingly, but only after letting Rowdy's question dangle in the dust-flecked air for a while. "Would have, too, if that rounder had really been who he said he was."

Rowdy let out a sigh, and Gideon heard relief in it. And something else, too. Tensed as Rowdy's gaze shifted from Gideon's face to Wyatt's, and then back again.

"Gideon, since you didn't know our brother Nick, I don't expect you'll do any grieving," Rowdy said, very quietly. Then his eyes connected with their elder brother's. "Wyatt, Nick died a couple of weeks ago. Consumption. I found out this morning."

Nick was, just as Rowdy had said, little more than a name to Gideon. Same with Ethan and Levi, the twins, though all three men were as much his brothers as Rowdy and Wyatt. It seemed a damn strange thing, not to know such close kin.

Wyatt's broad shoulders lowered a little, and he resettled his hat. "Reckon he's been prayed over and buried by now," he said in a voice Gideon had never heard him use before. "No sense heading back there to pay our respects."

"No," Rowdy said, low and quiet. "No sense in that."

Gideon looked from Rowdy to Wyatt and back again. Nick was a real person to them, not just a name. A brother. And for a moment, he hated being so much younger, and not having the same memories they did. Even when those memories could only spawn sorrow.

"What kind of man was he?" Gideon asked. "Nick, I mean?"

"Never got the hang of outlawing," Wyatt recalled, as if Gideon hadn't spoken, wasn't even there at all. "Pappy used to say Nick was so bad at it, he'd rather he stayed back to keep the campfire burning."

"Nick didn't have the knack," Rowdy agreed fondly, but he was talking to Wyatt, leaving Gideon on the outside. "You suppose he ever got married? Had kids and the like?"

"I doubt Nick could have stayed sober long enough to walk down the aisle," Wyatt said.

"He was my brother, too," Gideon put in. And after blurting that out, he *did* feel like a kid — again. One that had spoken out of turn, in a situation where silence was golden. *His* silence, at least.

Rowdy turned to him then, with a combination of sadness and amusement in his face and in his voice. "Yes, he was. Nick was blood kin to you, Gideon. Same as Ethan and Levi are. But families are strange sometimes and, all in all, I'd say you were better off not to have made Nick's acquaintance, nor Ethan's and Levi's, either."

"Amen," Wyatt said quietly.

Rowdy leaned a little closer to Gideon. "Where's my horse?" he asked. "The one you borrowed to come here and damn near get yourself killed?"

Evidently, the brotherly talk, which had spanned all of a sentence or two, was at an end. "At the livery stable," Gideon said, after releasing his jaw. "I'll get him and we'll start for home."

"Sam's and my horses need to rest a

while," Wyatt put in. "We rode 'em pretty hard, trying to get here and save your skin."

Ruby had beaten them to it, that was the implication, though neither Wyatt nor Rowdy said so outright.

Which was a damn good thing, from Gideon's point of view.

"Guess I'll just ride back on my own, then," Gideon said stiffly, pushing back his chair to stand.

"Not looking like that, you won't," Rowdy said. "You'll scare the women into next week if you do."

Gideon glanced down at himself, realized his clothes were stained with the stranger's blood. Or was it his own?

Ruby, who had been holding court out on the sidewalk, probably explaining to all and sundry how Gideon Yarbro would surely have been in a grave next to his sister, Rose, as soon as the arrangements had been made if it hadn't been for her, reentered the saloon.

Wyatt frowned, leaning to get a closer look at Gideon's shirtfront. "I thought that dead fella must have spurted on you when Ruby blasted a hole in him, but now, I'm not so sure."

Gideon stood there, thinking he couldn't have been cut. He'd seen the flash of the other man's knife, but he'd been on his feet with his gun drawn in practically the next moment. There was no pain, either — he was just numb.

Everywhere.

"I'm all right," he said, without his usual certainty.

Rowdy and Wyatt and Sam were all on their feet by then.

"Open your shirt," Wyatt told him.

Gideon pulled his shirttails out — if they wanted proof that he hadn't sprung a leak, he'd give it — and worked the buttons. Felt a draft through the fabric of the garment where there shouldn't have been one.

His shirt was ripped on the right side, and the skin beneath was laid open, too, the gash so deep his ribs showed. Reminded him of a deer, dressed out after a hunt.

He swayed a little on his feet, but there was still no pain.

"Sweet Jesus," Rowdy rasped, pressing him back down into his chair. "Ruby!"

"I'll fetch a doctor," Gideon heard Sam say.

The daylight seemed to solidify into a ball of fire, rushed at him, receded, and rushed at him again.

"Get him to the back," Ruby ordered, from somewhere nearby.

Wyatt and Rowdy must have propped him between them and walked him back to Ruby's rooms; Gideon was too far gone by then to know for sure. Or to care.

All he could think about was Lydia.

He had to get back to Lydia before dark.

She'd be worried if he didn't, and he had so much to tell her, and a ring to put on her finger —

A violent shudder overtook him then. In the next moment, a black void swallowed him whole.

The party had finally wound down in the late afternoon, and Lydia was helping to gather up the usual debris of celebration, when Owen, who had left shortly before to drive Lark home in the buckboard so she could rest and feed Miranda, came racing up the street again, driving that team as hard as if the flames of hell itself were leaping at the spokes of the back wheels.

White-faced, he reined in the horses and jumped to the street, and Lydia felt the ground shift under her feet as he came toward her.

She knew, before he said a word.

"Gideon?"

"There's been a telegram — we've got to get to Flagstaff —"

Helga hurried over, along with Maddie and Sarah. The aunts, mercifully, were already inside, trying to fit leftovers into the icebox.

Sarah addressed her son firmly. "Owen, what did this telegram *say*?"

"Gideon's been hurt," Owen said breathlessly. "Pa wired me from Flagstaff, said to bring Lydia right away."

Helga slid a supportive arm around Lydia's waist. "How bad is it?" the older woman asked, because Lydia couldn't.

"I don't know," Owen answered, beginning to sound panicked. "All Pa said was, Gideon's been hurt and I ought to fetch Lydia there —"

"I'll look after the aunts and Snippet," Helga said, turning to look into Lydia's pale face. "Soon as you're able, you send word back, though."

Lydia would have scrambled into that wagon on her own, getting tangled in her skirts and probably tearing out the hem, if Owen hadn't taken her unceremoniously by the waist and hoisted her into the box.

In a trice, he was beside her, taking up the reins, turning the team and wagon around. Sarah rushed out into the street and handed up her shawl, saying Lydia might need it. High-country nights could be chilly, even in summer.

Owen bent, snatched the wrap from his mother's hands, and gave it to Lydia. And then they were moving again.

The road to Flagstaff was long, winding and bumpy. A horse could cover the distance in two hours — in a wagon, it took nearly four.

Lydia barely noticed the jostling discomfort — her heart had fought its way out of her chest and flown ahead to Gideon, and all she wanted to do was catch up with it.

It was dark when they reached the outskirts of Flagstaff and Owen finally slowed the lathered team. They'd stopped twice along the lonely roadside to rest the horses, in the still-ample light of a waning moon, and during those necessary delays, it had been all Lydia could manage not to race ahead on foot.

She and Owen had barely spoken during the trip, both of them lost in their own thoughts. When they did, they'd had to shout over the pounding of hooves and the creaking of axles.

Wyatt's telegram must have instructed Owen to bring Lydia to Ruby's Saloon, because that was where he stopped the wagon. Or maybe he simply recognized Sam's and Rowdy's and Wyatt's horses at the hitching rail out front. In any case, he set the brake lever with a hard motion of one foot and leaped to the ground, rounding the tired horses at a sprint.

Lydia didn't wait for Owen to help her down; she was already on the plank sidewalk, pushing through the swinging doors of that saloon as though she'd frequented establishments of that sort all her life.

Rowdy, Wyatt and Sam O'Ballivan had been seated around a table over near the bar, playing cards and sipping whiskey when Lydia burst in. Seeing her, though, they all got to their feet so fast they nearly overturned their chairs.

"Where is Gideon?" she demanded, advancing on them, looking wildly around the otherwise empty room.

Rowdy reached out, took her arm. "This way," he said, nodding to Owen.

Lydia found Gideon lying in a small room under the eaves, his chest bandaged. His eyes were closed and he was pale as death and there was dried blood in his hair.

Lydia barely noticed the woman seated at his bedside, holding a basin of water in her lap and bathing Gideon's face.

"Ruby," Rowdy said, "this is Lydia, Gideon's bride."

Ruby stood and set the basin and cloth

aside. Lydia noticed nothing about her, beyond her glorious cloud of red hair and the kindly expression in her eyes. "He looks worse than he is, darlin'," Ruby said quietly. She put an arm around Lydia's shoulders, guided her to the chair she'd been sitting in herself until moments before.

Lydia sat down, reached out tentatively to touch Gideon's arm.

He didn't stir, and his flesh felt warm.

She turned to look at Ruby, all her questions in her eyes.

"Doc Robinson came right away, Lydia," Ruby explained, gesturing for Rowdy to leave them, probably because the room was so small. "Doc cleaned the wound and stitched Gideon up — and that hurt him some, you might as well know. He's got a fever, but it's low, and Doc said it'll most likely be gone by morning."

"Wh-what *happened?*" Lydia whispered, taking the cloth from the basin as she spoke, wringing it out, gently dabbing at Gideon's unmoving face.

"A man took a knife to him," Ruby replied, after a brief hesitation. "Here, let me take that basin. I'll get you some fresh water."

Lydia nodded, grateful but distracted. *A man took a knife to him.* Those words, and the images they brought to mind, made the little room swirl around her, right itself again with a violent jolt.

Ruby carried the basin out and soon returned, as she'd promised, with cool, clean water. She brought a cup of coffee, too, and Lydia never took a single sip. She'd meant to, but she kept forgetting.

It must have been around midnight — and that was only a guess because there were no clocks in the room — when Wyatt came in, quietly told her that he and Owen and Sam had to get back to Stone Creek so they could see to things at home, though Rowdy would be staying behind.

Lydia merely nodded, never looking away from Gideon's still face.

She thought his fever might have dropped a little, but she couldn't be sure.

Ruby reappeared, sometime after that, with a second cup of coffee, steaming hot and fragrantly fresh. "You ought to have this and then lie down a while, Lydia," she said softly. "I'll sit with Gideon, and call you if need be."

But Lydia refused to leave. She was tired clean through, but she knew she wouldn't sleep, or even rest.

"Won't you take some supper, then?" Ruby persisted.

Lydia vaguely remembered supper being offered earlier. She must have refused, though she couldn't be certain.

Either way, food was beyond her, but she did take a few swallows of coffee, in hopes of bracing herself up for the long vigil still ahead.

Dawn was breaking when finally, *finally,* Gideon opened his eyes. Turning his head, he saw Lydia sitting there, with her hair long-since free of its pins and hanging down over her right shoulder in a single heavy braid.

With that slight, wicked grin she knew so well, he extended one hand, caught hold of the braid, and tugged at it lightly. Then he gave a hoarse chuckle and said, "For a moment there, I thought it was the laudanum the doctor gave me last night, making me see things — but you're really here."

Lydia laughed softly, even as tears of utter relief and bone-melting exhaustion scalded her eyes. "I'm really here," she said. "How do you feel?"

"Would you believe me if I said I was fine?"

"No," Lydia answered.

He chuckled again, and then winced. "I've — been better," he allowed. "A lot worse, too."

Lydia let her gaze rest on the old scar marking his right shoulder. He'd never told her how he'd gotten it, and she'd never asked, but things were different between them now. He hadn't left Stone Creek — left *her* — meaning to keep on going.

"I was shot once," he said, shifting slightly and then wincing again. "Around the time your aunt came and took you to Phoenix, after your father was killed. I'll tell you about it sometime, when it doesn't hurt to talk."

Lydia smiled, stroked his hair back from his forehead. "Rest," she said.

"I'd rest better if you'd lie here beside me," he replied. And the look in his eyes was so earnest, and so hopeful, that Lydia did as he asked. Carefully, so she wouldn't cause him added pain, she lay down on that narrow bed beside her husband, and he slept.

And, after a while, so did she.

CHAPTER NINETEEN

A full week had passed before Dr. Robinson declared Gideon well enough to travel, even by train, and during that time, Lydia learned a great deal about her husband. It wasn't that Gideon was suddenly forthcoming — she'd realized by then that intimate confidences simply weren't in his nature — no, it was Ruby who shed light on the things he'd never troubled himself to mention.

Ruby told Lydia about Gideon's little half sister, Rose, how she'd been run down by a wagon one day, chasing a kitten into the street. Only four years old at the time, Rose had been killed instantly. Gideon, then six, had been inconsolable, blaming himself. Winter, spring, summer and fall, Ruby said, he'd gone to Rose's grave every day, before and after school, and sometimes during.

One bitterly cold night, with a blizzard coming on, Ruby said, a full two years after Rose's death, Gideon's father had gone to look in on the boy and found his bed empty. Jack, as Ruby referred to her late husband, went straight to the cemetery, and sure enough he found Gideon right where he'd known he'd be. Gideon had built a little fire near Rose's resting place, and he was having the devil's own time keeping it going in that weather, and when Jack questioned him, he said Rose hadn't liked the dark, and it was so cold, and he didn't want his little sister to be scared.

Remembering, there in the saloon that had been closed for business since Sunday, Ruby's eyes had filled with tears. "Jack kicked some snow over that fire and hauled Gideon home by the scruff of his neck," she'd told Lydia. "Once the boy was safe in bed, Jack came and told me what happened, and he broke right down and cried. I'd only seen Jack Payton shed tears once before, and that was when we buried our little Rose."

Ruby had said other things, too — things Lydia would always hold gently in the safest part of her heart. How Gideon used to gather wildflowers for her sometimes, when he'd been up to mischief or because Ruby had "the melancholies." How smart he'd been in school, and how hard he'd tried to keep his marks a secret from the other kids.

How he'd eaten a whole bowl of cake batter once when Ruby's cook left it unattended to go off on some sudden errand, and been so sick afterward that he'd literally turned green.

Over the course of that week, Rowdy having gone back to Stone Creek as soon as he knew for sure Gideon was out of danger, Lydia and Ruby had taken turns sitting with their increasingly *im*patient patient, but long about Tuesday afternoon, he'd begun to get downright cranky, so they'd left him to grumble alone, at least for short intervals, and gone off to drink coffee and visit, just the two of them.

Under any other circumstances, Lydia reflected, watching her husband struggle to put on his new shirt — Ruby had bought it for him, along with a pair of trousers, since his own clothes had been ruined — because he wouldn't let anybody help him, she might never have gotten to know Ruby — or Gideon — in quite the same way. And she certainly wouldn't have had the singular experience of living in a saloon for a week, either, keeping company with a former madam.

Wouldn't *that* give the aunts a wicked thrill when she related the tale.

The thought of their reaction made her

smile. "We're going to be late for the train, if you don't hurry up," Lydia told Gideon.

He sighed in frustration and dropped his hands to his sides. Allowed Lydia to straighten the sleeves, guide his arms into them, and fasten the buttons. When she tilted her head to look up into his face, though, she saw that his eyes were smoldering and that damnable Yarbro grin had found its way back to his mouth.

It was obvious what Gideon wanted, but the train was leaving in forty-five minutes and they still had to get to the station and buy their tickets.

"Ruby still in back, tallying up how many cases of whiskey she has on hand?" Gideon asked, his voice a throaty rumble.

Lydia frowned at him. They *had* made love, though awkwardly, twice since Gideon had begun to recover — it would have been hard not to, since the bed he'd slept in as a boy was barely wide enough to hold both of them and that made scooting out of his reach impossible — but she'd been embarrassed. Sure that Ruby would hear, and *that* had been late at night. Now, it was broad daylight, for pity's sake.

"Gideon Yarbro," she said, "you will have to wait until we get home."

He ran the backs of his fingers down the

side of her cheek. "That long?"

"That long," Lydia insisted. But she was wavering.

Gideon gave a long-suffering sigh.

Right on time, Ruby appeared in the doorway.

"I had my buggy hitched up and brought around," she said, and she must have sensed the crackle in the air because she smiled a wistful, knowing little smile. "I'll drive you to the station whenever you're ready."

"Have we worn out our welcome, Ruby?" Gideon joked.

A brief but obvious sadness moved in Ruby's face. "It's going to be mighty lonesome around here without the two of you," she conceded, with some resignation. "But you need to get back home where you belong, and I've got a saloon to run, so I'll thank you to get a move on, Gideon Yarbro. There won't be another train to Stone Creek until tomorrow, and I don't think I can put up with you that long."

Gideon chuckled, crossed to Ruby, placed his hands on her shoulders, and kissed her forehead.

"Remember," he told his stepmother, "you promised to spend Christmas in Stone Creek with us. And I don't want to hear any excuses when the time comes, either."

"I'll be there," Ruby said softly. "Though I can just imagine what folks will say when *I* show up. It's not as if people don't know all about me, far and wide."

"The only 'folks' you need to worry about, Ruby," Gideon said, "are the Yarbros, and we'll make you welcome. All of us. That's a promise."

Ruby sniffled once, looked away, looked back at Gideon. "You be careful, now," she said. "No more damn fool stunts like the last one."

"That 'damn fool stunt,' " Gideon replied, "was part of *my job.*"

"Well, you need a different one," Ruby said, jutting out her chin.

"I surely do," Gideon agreed. He'd dictated a letter of resignation as soon as he was able, Lydia taking it down, and Ruby had mailed it off to the owners of the Copper Crown Mine.

Ruby colored up. "I've got a little money put by —"

"Keep your money," Gideon told her gently. "I'm not broke yet, Ruby, and if I was, I could always hit Lark up for a loan."

That last part, Lydia knew, was just talk. Gideon had a lot of pride, and he probably wouldn't have accepted Lark's wedding gift — their house — if he hadn't needed a place to put her and the aunts and Helga. She couldn't imagine him asking Lark, or anyone else, for money.

"We'll get by," Lydia assured Ruby. She'd been going over possibilities in her mind ever since Gideon had decided to give up detective work. There were plenty of rooms in the Porter house, even with the aunts and Helga taking up two of them. If necessary, Lydia had decided, though she had yet to broach the delicate subject with Gideon, they would take in boarders.

"I'm sure you will," Ruby said, moving past Gideon to embrace Lydia. "I'll miss you something fierce." She choked up a little, and her eyes watered, but she rallied at once. Turning to look at Gideon, she added, "*You,* on the other hand, laying around wanting somebody to read to you, or bring you soup, or listen to you bellyaching about being stuck in bed —"

Gideon laughed. "I'll miss you, too, Ruby," he said.

In the distance, the train whistle shrilled. It was time to leave.

Ruby insisted on driving the buggy and, because the seat was so short from side to side, Lydia had to ride through the middle of Flagstaff sitting on Gideon's lap. She blushed the whole time; folks kept looking at them, but she could have ignored that. No, it was the rock-hard imprint of Gideon's manhood burning into her bottom that made Lydia dizzy with achy heat.

Since they had no baggage to speak of — Lydia had been wearing Ruby's clothes all week and Gideon, confined to his bed, hadn't required any until today — all they had to do was purchase tickets, board the train, and find their seats.

All that came after bidding Ruby farewell, though, and that was the difficult part. Lydia cried, thanking her friend repeatedly, and Ruby finally shushed her and told her to 'get on that train and go home.'

"I'll see you both at Christmas," Ruby said, in parting.

The train ride back to Stone Creek seemed endless to Gideon; he wanted to get home, make sound and thorough love to Lydia in a bed wide enough to hold the both of them without their being stacked like cordwood, and sleep. He'd stopped taking laudanum as soon as he could stand to, and the slash in his right side hurt like hell, since he wasn't used to sitting up. The stitches itched, too — he'd been tempted, in fact, to take them out himself, and the doctor's order be damned, but Lydia and Ruby wouldn't have it.

The two hours the trip took up — counting stops in Indian Rock and a wide spot in the road where a mail-rider was waiting to exchange pouches with the conductor — finally passed, and the engineer blew the steam whistle, announcing the train's imminent arrival in Stone Creek.

They'd barely stepped onto the small platform, with the few other passengers stopping there, when an earsplitting boom literally shook the wooden planks under their feet.

Smoke and dust billowed skyward and then descended like an early twilight.

Rowdy, who'd come to meet them, reacted immediately. "The mine!" he yelled unnecessarily. Like everybody else — including Gideon — he ran in that direction.

"Gideon!" Lydia screamed. "Wait! You're hurt — you can't —"

He looked back over one shoulder. "Go home, Lydia," he told her. *"Now."*

Instead, she caught up with him. She might love and honor and cherish, his spirited bride, but she clearly came up short in the "obey" department. "Everybody's always telling me to go home," she sputtered, waving a hand in front of her face because the dust was even thicker now, "and

I'm sick of it!"

Gideon shook his head and moved faster. *Hardheaded woman,* he thought, loving her more than he'd ever thought he could — and that was plenty. *Let her keep up if she can.*

He and Rowdy were among the first to reach the mine entrance, which was criss-crossed with fallen timbers and still belching puffs of dirt and smoke.

Wilson, the foreman, his nose bruised and a little crooked but no longer bandaged, since Mike O'Hanlon had broken it with his fist, hurried over to Rowdy and then just fidgeted, evidently unable to talk.

"Is anybody in there?" Rowdy demanded. It was Sunday, after all, and the mine was closed, but the question had to be asked.

Gideon could have answered it. Breathless and grasping his side, he saw Mike O'Hanlon rise up in his mind's eye as clearly as if the Irishman had been standing right in front of him. Heard O'Hanlon's warning, verbatim, in his head.

"When you speak to the owners, young Yarbro, you tell them we've taken all we're goin' to take. You tell them we're tired of seein' our children go hungry and our God-fearin' wives ashamed. You tell them, Mr. Yarbro, that we'll bury their precious ore, and ourselves

with it, before we'll crawl before them like whipped dogs one more time. . . ."

"Christ," Gideon groaned. And then he headed for the opening of the shaft, knowing he oughtn't to do what he was going to do, but bound to anyway.

Rowdy, left behind, yelled his name.

He didn't stop. He *couldn't* stop.

He climbed down into that pit, making his way from fallen beam to fallen beam, pain searing his side, probably tearing the stitches loose, only too aware that other collapses were inevitable, now that the support structure had been compromised.

Still, something drove him on. Mike O'Hanlon hadn't been his friend, hadn't trusted him. With good reason. Gideon had been squarely on the wrong side of the trouble between the workers and the owners, and just then, he'd have given just about anything to go back and do things differently.

"Gideon!" Rowdy called, from high above, his voice echoing through the dusty gloom.

"Shut up," Gideon called back, once he had the breath. There was blood seeping through his brand-new shirt; his wound was open again. "You want to bring the rest of this goddammed hole down on top of me?"

What Rowdy did next didn't surprise Gideon in the least, because he'd have done the same boneheaded thing. He felt a rain of pebbles, knew his brother was following the same treacherous path he'd taken.

The belly of that mine was as dark as a back closet in hell when Gideon reached it, but there was a faint, flickering glimmer of light down one of the side shafts, and he followed it, drawn like a moth to a candle.

He found O'Hanlon half-buried in timbers and rubble, with a kerosene lantern burning on the ground nearby.

"Young Yarbro," O'Hanlon said, after gathering his inner forces, "fancy meetin' you here."

"O'Hanlon," Gideon retorted, digging frantically to free the other man and knowing it was impossible, "what the *hell* are you doing here?"

"Leave off the diggin', young Yarbro," O'Hanlon said, his voice dreamy. "It's useless, you know. But if you happened to have a drop of whiskey on you, it would be God's own mercy."

Gideon dug harder, tried in vain to move the timber O'Hanlon was trapped under. "Hold on," he muttered.

"No whiskey, then?" O'Hanlon asked, as if Gideon had spoken.

"No whiskey," Gideon replied grimly.

Every bone in O'Hanlon's body was probably crushed, and now a little trickle of blood ran down the man's filthy chin from one corner of his mouth.

"And here's the marshal," O'Hanlon said, his gaze drifting past Gideon's right shoulder. "My Mary's a good woman," he summoned the strength to say. "She knows how to look after wee ones and keep a house like it ought to be kept and cook a tasty meal, when there's food in the larder."

"She'll have a job at our place if she wants one," Rowdy said gruffly.

"Your word on that, marshal?"

Rowdy laid a hand on Gideon's shoulder. Overhead, the remaining timbers groaned and more rubble fell.

"You have my word, Mike," Rowdy said.

At that, Mike sighed and closed his eyes.

Rowdy bent, caught hold of O'Hanlon's wrist. "He's gone, Gideon," he said. "And we'd better get the hell out of here, or we'll be right behind him."

"The mine owners," Gideon muttered numbly. He'd been away from Stone Creek, hadn't known what was going on at the Copper Crown during that time. "They were going to bring in Chinamen?"

"Yes," Rowdy said, taking Gideon by the arm and dragging him back toward the network of beams they'd made their way down only minutes before.

Gideon never had any recollection of climbing back up; he only remembered Lydia waiting for him in the daylight, and Wyatt standing with her.

Nobody in Stone Creek *ever* forgot what happened next.

At the first loud crack of timber, Rowdy took hold of Gideon again, and Wyatt lifted Lydia clean off her feet, and they ran, part of a stream of other people, all of them running, too.

With the second deafening snap, half the hillside fell in, sealing Mike O'Hanlon in his grave forever, and the copper ore right along with him.

Once they were a safe distance away, Gideon pulled free of Rowdy's grasp, gasping for breath, and sank to his knees. Thrust his hands forward onto the ground.

Neither Rowdy nor Wyatt touched him, and Gideon was grateful.

"Gideon?" Lydia whispered.

"Let him be for a minute, honey," Gideon heard Wyatt say to her. "Just let him be for a minute."

"But he's bleeding!"

When he could, Gideon got to his feet.

"God damn those sons of bitches," he

gasped out, dragging an arm across his face, sucking in air. *"God damn them to hell."*

"Time you went home, Gideon," Wyatt said.

They supported Gideon between them, Wyatt and Rowdy did, just as they'd probably done after he was hurt a week before in Ruby's Saloon. And when they reached the Porter house, Helga and the aunts were waiting in the side yard, gazing toward the billow of dust still looming above the collapsed mine, Helga holding Snippet against her shoulder, like a baby.

No one asked for an explanation.

The aunts stepped aside, to let the men pass into the kitchen, but each of them took one of Lydia's hands as she followed.

While the three brothers made their way slowly up the inside staircase, Lydia watched in stunned silence. When she'd seen Gideon disappear into that mine shaft, she'd tried to follow him, but Wyatt had stopped her, held her fast with both arms.

She'd fought like a wildcat to get free, all to no avail, of course, and she'd heard tears in that strong man's voice when he whispered, "No, Lydia. I can't let you go after him. I can't."

Now the aunts pressed Lydia into a chair

at the kitchen table.

Helga bent to kiss the top of her head, and laid Snippet gently in her lap.

Lydia stroked him, and wept — with confusion, with relief, with fear of all the things that might still lie ahead.

Helga moved briskly to put on her bonnet. "I'm going to fetch Dr. Venable," she said, and then she was gone.

Lydia sat numbly in her chair, holding Snippet, grateful for his silky warmth.

The aunts brewed tea, because they *always* brewed tea, believing it to be the antidote for any extremity. And God knew, they'd seen every kind of extremity in their long and eventful lives — war and fire, the loss of the men they'd loved. They'd been torn from their home in Virginia, a place where generations of Fairmonts had lived and died, and then from the mansion in Phoenix, too.

For the first time, even in her distracted state, Lydia fully grasped the depth of courage they'd shown, how adaptable they'd been. Two elderly spinsters, able to confront any calamity as long as they could serve tea.

"Do you think we ought to tell her, sister?" Mittie asked, sounding fretful.

"Hush," Millie said.

Lydia blinked, focused on the two women

she'd loved since she was a little girl. Like Nell, they'd made room for her in their orderly world, never seemed to resent the changes she must have brought about, just by being there. "Tell me what?" she asked, stroking Snippet's back.

The aunts looked at each other.

Then Mittie said, "Jacob Fitch is dead."

Lydia frowned. "Jacob Fitch?" she echoed dully.

"The man you were going to marry," Millie reminded her.

"Sister," Mittie fussed, "Lydia *knows* who she almost married."

A giggle of pure hysteria escaped Lydia.

"It's really not very funny, dear," Millie pointed out. "A man is dead, after all."

"He had a heart attack," Mittie elaborated. "Jacob Fitch, I mean. Right at Mr. Davis's table."

"My word, yes," Millie agreed, putting one delicate hand to her bosom in belated horror. "Dead as a coffin nail."

Lydia stared at her aunts, the news finally sinking in. "Jacob Fitch is dead?"

"That's what we've been telling you right along, dear," Mittie said patiently.

"She's in shock, sister," Millie put in. "You can't expect her to take everything in at once."

"I suppose not," Millie agreed.

"How did you — are you sure?" Lydia asked. She wanted to go upstairs to Gideon, but the starch had gone out of her, as Helga would say. She couldn't have risen out of that chair just then for anything.

"Of course we're sure," Mittie said. "It was in the newspapers, and Rowdy got a wire about it from the United States Marshal in Phoenix, too."

"Tell her about the lawyer," Millie urged.

"The lawyer?" Lydia echoed.

"First I've got to explain that Mrs. Fitch — Mr. Fitch's mother, dear — died, too."

"Tragic," Millie said sincerely, shaking her head.

Lydia closed her eyes.

One of the aunts patted her hand.

Lydia opened her eyes again, saw that it had been Mittie. "Mrs. Fitch?" Lydia prompted.

"She was so upset, what with her son having a heart attack before her very eyes," Millie rushed on, "that *her* heart gave out, too. On the very spot. They seem to have died simultaneously. By the time the serving girl got back with the police, the newspaper said, both of the Fitches were gone to Glory."

"Dear God," Lydia whispered.

"And then a lawyer came," Mittie said. "Right here, to this house. He was looking for you, but we told him you were in Flagstaff because poor Gideon had been attacked by some maniac with a knife —"

Millie's withering glance rendered Mittie mute. "Sister, how you do ramble on," Millie scolded. "Will you *never* get to the point?"

Lydia braced herself up. "And that point would be — ?"

"Of course Mr. Fitch left his estate to his mother," Millie explained. "But since she's gone, too, poor creature, and Mr. Fitch thought he was going to marry you —"

"We're rich again, dear," Mittie said. "Mr. Fitch hadn't changed his will."

The room tilted sideways, as surely as if there had been another blast, somewhere deep in the earth, this one silent but just as forceful. *"What?"* Lydia asked.

"Papa would be so pleased," Millie remarked. "That we haven't lost everything he worked so hard to build, I mean. He wouldn't be pleased that the Fitches are dead, of course. Never that —"

Mittie broke in again then. "According to the lawyer — his card is here somewhere — we've inherited our own house," Mittie informed Lydia, brightening. "And three or four banks, in the bargain."

Lydia put a hand to her mouth. Scrambled to set Snippet safely on the floor before she dropped him.

"We can go home now," Millie said softly. "But of course we must bring Gideon with us. And dear Snippet."

"*This* is home," Lydia said, still reeling.

"But the mine fell in," Mittie reasoned. "Didn't it?"

"What does that have to do with anything?" Lydia wanted to know. She was strong enough to stand now, to climb the stairs and go to Gideon.

"Isn't Gideon — unemployed?" Millie asked. "In Phoenix, he could be a banker."

Shaking her head, Lydia started for the staircase.

Rowdy and Wyatt were just leaving the bedroom when she reached the upper corridor.

Lydia nodded to them, as though they were acquaintances encountered on the street, and swept right on by, into her and Gideon's bedroom.

He was lying crosswise on the bed, staring up at the ceiling. "He had a wife, kids," he said, without looking at her.

Lydia pulled the rocking chair closer and sat down. "Who?" she asked quietly.

"Mike O'Hanlon," Gideon replied.

"Oh," Lydia said, and that seemed to be all that was necessary, because Gideon fell silent again.

Dr. Venable came, with Kitty. Together, in their strange, cooperative way, they examined Gideon. No new stitches would be required, they decided; the scar would be a little worse, that was all. Deftly, Kitty removed the remaining bits of thread from Gideon's flesh, applied salve and a clean bandage, and offered him laudanum, so he could sleep.

Gideon refused, and the doctor and his wife took their leave.

Twilight seeped into the room, but neither Gideon nor Lydia moved.

Helga brought a supper tray and left again.

Gideon didn't eat, and neither did Lydia.

The streetlamp at the corner came on, and the house quieted.

"Lydia," Gideon said.

"I'm here," Lydia replied. She rose out of the chair, at last, like a woman moving in a dream. Stripped off her clothes, donned a nightgown — one of the new ones she'd charged to Gideon at Mr. Blanchard's mercantile that day.

Since Gideon was lying on top of the covers, she couldn't pull them back to get into bed. So she curled up beside him, as she had that first night at Ruby's, after he'd been hurt.

He rolled onto his side. "Everything's going to be all right," he said.

"Yes, Gideon," Lydia responded, touching his face. "Everything's going to be all right."

"I need —"

Lydia kissed him, traced the outside of his mouth with the tip of one index finger, lightly. "I know."

Gideon drew her nightgown up then, with urgency, but with gentleness, too. The garment seemed to dissolve into the ether. Then he somehow got out of his own clothes without leaving the bed, a painful process in its own right. "Do you want — ?"

"I want *you*," Lydia told him.

He eased her legs apart with a motion of one knee, kissed her hungrily.

Lydia arched her back, gave a small, involuntary moan.

And Gideon entered her, in a slow, deep thrust, made of sweet fire.

They moved together, rhythmically, but not frantically, the way they might have done on any other night of their lives. At first, the joining of their two bodies was leisurely, almost like a dance. It was, in its essence, a celebration.

They were alive.

They loved each other.

And they belonged together.

But as the friction increased, so did their need.

Gideon drove harder, deeper.

Lydia received him eagerly, then desperately.

The bedsprings creaked. The headboard clattered against the wall.

And when satisfaction consumed them, they shouted each other's names.

A long time had passed before either of them spoke.

"I love you, Lydia," Gideon said.

She nestled against him, her face buried in his neck, and she answered in kind.

They lay in silence for a while, arms and legs entwined, content.

The darkness deepened, and the old house settled on its foundation, with comfortable, familiar sounds.

Gideon caressed Lydia's breast, and her breathing quickened a little, turned to a gasp when he bent his head and took her nipple into his mouth, suckled.

Lydia crooned, ready for him all over again, and deliciously certain that he would make her wait until her desire had reached a fever pitch.

When at last he was on top of her again, inside her again, he made a sound that was part chuckle, part groan. "Lydia?" he rasped.

"What?" she moaned, nearly lost.

"Remind me —" he paused, with a hoarse gasp, as she raised herself to take him deeper "— to move this — damn bed — away from the wall —"

Lydia laughed.

And then, in the very next moment, she climaxed in a series of violent spasms, and this time, though the bedsprings still creaked, and the headboard still banged against the wall, Gideon covered her mouth with his and absorbed her cries, meeting them with his own.

There were challenges ahead, both of them knew that.

Together, they would beat them all.

EPILOGUE

December 24, 1915

The house — referred to as *Yarbro* house now — was ready.

Proudly, Lydia surveyed the fragrant pine tree standing in front of the parlor window, glittering with ornaments and pretty ribbons, and arched her back to stretch the muscles there. She was in the family way, six months along now and already showing, and both Lark and Sarah insisted she was carrying twins.

Gideon was exhaustively attentive, treated her as though she were made of spun sugar, and that was why he'd gone to the train station alone to meet Ruby and Helga and the aunts, all arriving to spend Christmas. With a heavy snowfall drifting down, and the streets sheeted in ice, he'd insisted that Lydia stay home.

Snippet nuzzled her hand, as if to say he approved of the decorating she'd done, and the baking and the package-wrapping. His name was something of a family joke now; he was huge — the size of a burro, Gideon claimed, exaggerating only slightly — and still growing.

He was also the most faithful of companions. After Helga and the aunts had gone back to Phoenix in the early fall to take up residence in the Fairmont mansion, and with Gideon busy learning to be a banker, Snippet had filled a number of lonely hours for Lydia.

Sarah, a banker's daughter with considerable business experience of her own, had been invaluable to Gideon, helping him to consolidate several banks into one, set up an office in Stone Creek, sort through all the complicated paperwork, and choose reliable employees.

Standing close to the tree, Lydia looked out the window, watching the fat flakes of snow wafting through the wintry darkness, gleaming in the light of the nearby streetlamp.

She'd been surprised when Gideon, after some resistance and considerable strong-arm tactics by his brothers, swallowed his stubborn Yarbro pride and agreed to manage her holdings, all inadvertently left to her by Jacob Fitch. Gideon had said, with a crooked grin, that he supposed it was better than working for Wyatt as a ranch hand, or serving as Rowdy's deputy, and he might as well take hold.

He'd hired one or two of the miners, though most of them had moved on with their families, when the owners of the Copper Crown didn't seem to be in any hurry to reopen the enterprise, and Mary O'Hanlon worked for Lark and Rowdy now, as their housekeeper. Though she clearly mourned her husband, Mary was a cheerful sort, grateful to have a home for herself and her children, and to earn steady wages.

Lark, taking an immediate liking to the woman, and of course relieved to have the help, had had a small but cozy cottage built for Mary and her family, behind the main house.

The baby — or babies — kicked inside Lydia, and she smiled, purely happy. In time, she would probably help Gideon run the bank and oversee their other interests, but for now, she was more than content to keep their home and bear and raise children. Since Mary O'Hanlon's eldest daughter, Colleen, did the heavy cleaning after school and on Saturdays, Lydia had time to read, to paint, to dream.

And since she and Gideon were still

newlyweds — sometimes, she thought they always would be, because their passion for each other never lessened but only increased — they almost invariably made love as soon as he got home from the bank in the evenings. It was a gentle, careful communion now, Gideon being so protective, but nonetheless soul-satisfying for that.

Seeing a closed carriage pull up out front, Lydia smiled and patted Snippet's massive head. "They're here," she told the giant dog, and made her way to the front door, caught the heady scent of the evergreen wreath hanging there as she moved past it onto the porch.

Two buckboards drew in behind the carriage right away, one carrying Rowdy and Lark and their children, the second practically spilling over with Wyatt and Sarah and their brood. Owen and Shannie and the new baby, *little* Wyatt, would be along later, Lydia knew, after the chores were done at the ranch. She'd hold supper for them.

Gideon climbed down from the box of the carriage — officially, it belonged to the bank, and the driver was one of his former mining colleagues — and lowered the hinged metal step so the passengers could alight.

Ruby alighted first, resplendent in red

velvet, with a white fur muff to warm her hands, and a hat to match.

Stalwart Helga came next. She'd gone back to Phoenix, albeit with some reluctance, when the aunts moved home, saying she couldn't trust a stranger to look after them properly. Besides, she'd finally admitted, she'd miss them beyond bearing if she didn't go along, maddening as they were.

Gideon took special care with Mittie — he still couldn't tell the aunts apart, to Lydia's amusement — and finally, Millie was out of the carriage, too.

Busy unloading children, food and gaily wrapped packages, Wyatt and Sarah and Rowdy and Lark remained with the buckboards.

Gideon steered the ladies to the front gate, opened it for them, and waited while they all passed through, but he caught Lydia's gaze right away, and she thought she saw a grin quirk up the corner of his mouth.

Only that morning, he'd finally gotten around to pulling their bed away from the wall, and given the springs a generous oiling, as well. The knowledge was a deliciously private secret and Lydia felt a little frisson of anticipation. Later, when she and Gideon were alone —

But for now, it was Christmas Eve, the

house was redolent of pine and a crackling fire on the hearth and the enormous goose roasting in the oven, and she had a family to welcome. That in itself was something to celebrate — being part of the Yarbro clan.

Ruby reached the porch first, taking Lydia by the shoulders and beaming. "Look at you," she said. "That's a girl you're carrying, or I'll eat this hat, fur and all."

Lydia laughed, and her eyes stung with happy tears. "If this baby is a girl, we're going to call her Rose," she said.

Ruby's face softened with a brief look of nostalgia. "So Gideon tells me," she said, spotting Snippet, standing on the porch beside Lydia. "Is that a dog or a *horse?*" she teased.

Helga, clad in a sturdy, no-nonsense traveling suit of blue woolen, took Ruby's place as the other woman went inside. "Good heavens," she whispered, with a shake of her head, "those old women must still believe in St. Nicholas. They brought *stockings* to hang from the mantle."

Lydia beamed. "They *always* hang up their stockings on Christmas Eve," she reminded Helga. "And we always fill them."

Helga chuckled and entered the house.

Gideon brought the aunts carefully up the walk, one clinging to each of his arms. Snow settled in his wonderful taffy-colored hair and caught on his eyelashes.

Mittie and Millie wore matching green dresses and cloaks of the same hue, hooded and trimmed in black velvet.

"We brought our stockings," Mittie called.

"Aren't you cold, standing there with no coat on?" Millie fretted.

Gideon arched one eyebrow at this, and grinned.

Mittie looked back. "There are a great many parcels in the boot of the carriage," she chirped to Gideon. "Can the driver be trusted?"

"He can be trusted," Gideon assured the old woman.

There was another flurry of happy greetings, once everyone, including Wyatt's and Rowdy's families, had entered the house. Packages were placed beneath the tree, and tucked among its branches, and Snippet reveled in the presence of so many excited children eager to ruffle his ears.

Looking at all of them, taking off their coats and cloaks, settling in for a lively Christmas Eve together, Lydia felt rich beyond her wildest dreams — and it had nothing to do with owning a bank, or the mansion in Phoenix.

She'd have willingly given up all the

money and the property for the sake of any one of these people, let alone the whole "crazy outfit," as Gideon called them.

The driver brought in load after load of gifts, trunks and valises, and beamed from ear to ear when Gideon paid him and wished him a Happy Christmas. As he closed the door behind the man, he turned and met Lydia's gaze again.

"Later," he mouthed and chuckled when she blushed.

Owen and Shannie and the baby arrived soon after that, and the gathering was complete.

The meal was well received — secretly, Lydia fretted that the goose was a little dry — and when it was over, the women crowded the large kitchen, washing and drying dishes and putting leftovers away. The men had gathered in the study, closing the double doors behind them, and the children fought merrily over whose turn it was to pet Snippet.

"I thought Mary O'Hanlon and her brood were coming, too," Lydia said, as she and Lark put clean china plates back into the kitchen cabinets.

Lark smiled. "They're at church," she explained. "Mary thought this first Christmas without her husband ought to be a quiet one. She's put up a tree, though, and as soon as she shooed her chicks off to the services, Rowdy sneaked in with at least three armloads of presents and a ham almost as big as Snippet."

Lydia studied her generous friend. Once or twice, over the course of that rollicking evening, she'd caught Lark gazing wistfully at her ever-expanding midsection. There was no envy in Lark, Lydia knew that — her smart, capable sister-in-law didn't give such things "heart-room," as she would have said. But she and Rowdy couldn't have any more children, and Lydia wondered if that weighed on Lark. If ever a woman had been born to be a mother, it was Lark.

"What?" Lark asked, catching Lydia's fleeting expression of worry.

Lydia swallowed. "Do you ever wish — does it bother you that Gideon and I — ?"

Lark smiled, kissed Lydia smartly on the cheek. *"No,"* she said. "I couldn't be happier for you, or for Gideon, either." Then, dropping her voice to a mischievous whisper, she confided, "There's a certain very exciting freedom in knowing Rowdy and I can make love without worrying that I'll be fat as a cow for the next nine months."

Lydia laughed. "Lark Yarbro!"

Lark's eyes sparkled. Clearly, she was

anticipating things that would happen later on in the evening. "There's only one thing better than Rowdy Yarbro out of bed," Lark said, still whispering, "and that's Rowdy Yarbro *in* bed."

Lydia's eyes widened.

"Have you seen the glances passing between Sarah and Wyatt?" Lark went on. "As soon as that flock of theirs is tucked in for the night —"

"Oh, my," Lydia said. Her sisters-in-law spoke frankly, and she was still getting used to that.

Lark chuckled. "And don't pretend you and Gideon aren't planning exactly the same thing," she finished saucily. "Because I've got eyes in my head, Lydia Yarbro, and that man can't wait to get you upstairs."

Heat surged into Lydia's face, but she couldn't help smiling.

Sarah edged between them then, looked from one to the other. "What are you two whispering about over here?" she demanded good-naturedly.

"We're the Yarbro women," Lark answered. "What else would we be talking about besides the Yarbro *men?*"

Sarah looked back over one shoulder, probably making sure the aunts, Helga, Ruby and any stray children were out of earshot. "Wyatt's been teasing me all night," she said. "A look and a whisper here, a pat there. That man is going to get his comeuppance when we get home."

Lark gave Lydia an I-told-you-so glance.

And they all laughed then.

There was, as it happened, a great deal more laughter that night, inside that sturdy, well-lit house, with snow swirling past the windows.

Stories were told.

The tree sparkled, though there were no candles on it, due to the risk of fire.

The children opened their gifts from Lydia and Gideon.

Snippet received a soup bone.

And, when the visitors had started for home, church bells ringing in Christmas all over town, the aunts hung their stockings from the hooks Lydia had made Gideon put in the mantel days earlier.

Ruby, flushed with the bustle of a noisy Christmas Eve, a new experience for her, pleaded fatigue and went upstairs to bed. Helga and the aunts were soon gone, as well.

Gideon, handsome in his black woolen trousers, shirtsleeves and brocade vest, banked the fire on the hearth. When he turned around, Lydia was standing right behind him, shyly holding a package.

"I thought we were waiting until morning," Gideon said, looking puzzled.

"This is special," Lydia said softly, placing the gift in his hands.

Slowly, Gideon untied the ribbon, laid back the wrapping paper. Saw the watercolor painting she'd taken weeks to get just right.

It was a second portrait of him, but this time, unlike in the earlier likeness she'd done, he was facing forward, with a little smile crooking up one corner of his mouth and peace in his eyes.

"I look like a man who means to stay put for good," he said, his voice hoarse and his eyes suspiciously bright. Then he bent his head and kissed her, lightly, but with a promise of more fevered kisses to follow. "And that's exactly what I am."

The employees of Thorndike Press hope you have enjoyed this Large Print book. All our Thorndike, Wheeler, and Kennebec Large Print titles are designed for easy reading, and all our books are made to last. Other Thorndike Press Large Print books are available at your library, through selected bookstores, or directly from us.

For information about titles, please call:
(800) 223-1244

or visit our Web site at:
http://gale.cengage.com/thorndike

To share your comments, please write:
Publisher
Thorndike Press
295 Kennedy Memorial Drive
Waterville, ME 04901